WIND

FROM A
FOREIGN SKY

WIND
FROM A
FOREIGN SKY

▼

Katya Reimann

A Tom Doherty Associates Book
New York

WIND FROM A FOREIGN SKY

Copyright © 1996 by Katherine A. Reimann

Edited by James Frenkel

A Tor Book
Published by Tom Doherty Associates, Inc.
175 Fifth Avenue
New York, NY 10010

Tor Books on the World Wide Web:
http://www.tor.com

Tor® is a registered trademark of Tom Doherty
Associates, Inc.

Library of Congress Cataloging-in-Publication
Data

Reimann, Katya.
    Wind from a foreign sky / Katya Reimann.—
1st ed.
        p. cm.
    "A Tom Doherty Associates book."
    ISBN 0-312-86007-2
    PS3568.E4858W56 1996
    813'.54—dc20   95-53131
                                        CIP
First Edition: July 1996

Printed in the United States of America

0 9 8 7 6 5 4 3 2 1

In memory of Hobart Reimann and John Sadowy

Acknowledgments

I am grateful to my friends who helped me with this book while it was in manuscript: Wendy Carter, Yoshi Fujishima, Tony Seddon, and Elizabeth Stone. David Cohen, a good friend and sensitive historian, deserves particular thanks for his help.

I got lucky with my editor, James Frenkel, and lucky with my agent, Shawna McCarthy. Their helpfulness and patience have made this a better book, for which I owe great thanks.

Lastly, I want to thank Lenore Cowen and Nathan Bucklin, for giving me a shove and getting me moving when I most needed it.

—K. A. R.

North

BISSANTY EMPIRE

Basson

High Plateau

Lanai Valley

Clarin's Seat

Arciers

Llara's Kettle

Haute Tielmark

BISSANTY FINGERLAND

High Road

TIELMAR

Pontoeil

Sacre Isle

Border Lake

CHANGING LANDS

BOOK ONE

▼

Prologue

All through the night, and much of the day after, they fought about the baby. "You must tell them," Mervion argued. "Tell them and there is the chance that they will have mercy and let you go."

"I won't." Anisia refused. She was proud of her refusal. It was hard to withstand her marriage-sister under the best of circumstances — which these, most definitely, were not. But it was her unborn child, not Mervion's, and it was not for Mervion to decide what Anisia should do. "They are not to know," Anisia said. "Imagine how I feel. We already know they took me only to guarantee your good behavior. If I tell them about the baby, it will merely be another way to get at you. How contemptible do you think that will make me feel, gifting them with another lever to use against you? You won't change my mind on this."

Holding out against Mervion's arguments felt good. Anisia even felt she had bought back a bit of self-respect with her display of obstinacy. Refusing to tell them about the child was a noble gesture, was it not?

But these happy thoughts were now long past and gone. Now Anisia was weeping, blinded with pain and tears. She would have done anything to stop the pain. If the spell that held her had left her any whisper of a voice, she would have been crying to be spared—for her baby's sake, for her own sake—for anything.

Shouts echoed around her, anxious shouts and the unfamiliar roar of broken magic. Men running, doors slamming. Edan Heiratikus, the Chancellor of all Tielmark, was calling a new spell to bind the disaster, his voice a mingling of surprise and rage.

Anisia was not awake to hear it.

Anisia opened her eyes and stared, dazed, around the dark room. The spell had abated. Though movement was painful, she found she could sit up. Her voice was still blocked in her throat, but the pain had gone. How much time had passed?

Anisia Blas was seventeen years old, the sheltered daughter of a gentleman soldier and his gently born wife. Tielmark was a small country, and she had grown to womanhood holding a small but comfortable place within it. In all her young life, she had never knowingly been exposed to danger.

It was a bare four months since her husband had come into his father's estate. Only two months since she had offered Mervion, her husband's half-sister, a place in their new household. Two days short of a week since she and Mervion together had been torn from that life, with no explanations given, save for a paper order authorizing her marriage-sister's seizure and transport to Princeport.

Anisia closed her eyes, wishing that they had other news to give her. She was still in the Keyhole Chamber, still in the Prince of Tielmark's palace, still in mad Chancellor Heiratikus's power. Still in the nightmare.

"Put her down." Chancellor Heiratikus was a tall, rail-thin man with a cascade of silver hair and a commanding manner—a man whose public face gave every assurance of composure and deliberation. When Anisia had first been brought before him, she had been certain that everything would be made right. He would see the mistake; he would let her and Mervion return home to Arleon Forest. Looking into Heiratikus's noble face, the young country-wife had thought that her world was returning to sanity, that the ordeal of their forced travel north from her husband's holding was finally at its end.

That had been before she had seen Heiratikus lose his temper, or heard his voice raised in anger.

Anisia coughed. Her mouth was bitter with bile. She was groggy from the spell, from the unfamiliar clutch of magic in her throat. The Chancellor drifted out of shadows into her field of vision. Happily, his attention was not directed at her. "You look a fool standing there," he said, his voice at once rough and mocking. "Put her down."

Thank the gods he wasn't talking to her.

The object of his hard words, Lord Issachar Dan, stood, stiffly poised, on the massive stone altar at the center of the room. The Chancellor's military officer was a giant of a man: a shadowy, sweat-glistening monster with ritual scars cicatrized on his cheeks. With his blue-black hair and pale skin, Lord Dan was clearly not Tielmaran-born. He was pure-blood Bissanty, a native of the ancient empire to Tielmark's north.

Three hundred years past, Tielmark had been a slave state to the Bissanty Empire. Relations between the two countries had never been anything other than strained. What was the terrifying dark warrior doing in service to the High Chancellor of all Tielmark? Even a provincial woman like Anisia could see that was wrong.

Anisia and Mervion had suffered under a series of hard keepers since they had been presented with the letter of confinement, but Lord Issachar Dan, with his strange looks and overt, almost careless air of brutality, was the keeper Anisia found most threatening. For the casting of the great spell, he had forced Mervion onto the altar. Anisia hadn't been conscious long enough to follow much of what had passed. It was a small mercy.

When Anisia had invited Mervion to join her household, her husband had cautioned her that his half-sister was a spell-caster, a witch who called her power from Elianté and Emiera, the patron goddesses of Tielmark. Mervion had made a display for Anisia of some of her prettier magic — vividly colored weavings and gentle charm-songs. This was magic that could brighten a long winter evening, and Anisia, disarmed and pleased, had welcomed Mervion for it. She hadn't imagined that her marriage-sister could turn these frivolous castings to her own protection.

Indeed, Mervion's small arsenal of womanly spells should have been pitifully small against the Chancellor's high sorceries. The Keyhole Chamber was a sacral place: an altar-chamber where the gods could be ritually invoked to bring gifts of magic and power. The Chancellor had prepared the altar with seven bonds of sorcery to enhance his spell-casting—he'd boasted of it himself.

But the Keyhole Chamber was *Tielmark's* sacral place, and although the frieze that ran atop the twelve walls of the chamber depicted the symbols of all twelve of the high pantheon, it was the Great Twin Goddesses, Huntress Elianté and Lady Emiera, who held the place of honor.

Mervion called to them both for strength, and they answered her.

Her spells of charming, of weaving, of tying and untying—fragile woman's spells that Heiratikus should have rended like rotten cloth—spiraled out like scarlet threads, filled with startling force. The quartet of guards accompanying the women cowered back, horrified, stricken with images of impious trespass. Mervion's bonds slipped from her like silk ribbons unbinding. An eldritch-fire web from Heiratikus was tangled in a silver maze of misdirection—turned aside as though it were of no account.

That was when Anisia understood that the Chancellor, however powerful his sorceries, was not calling his magic from the Tielmaran goddesses.

"Issachar!" the Chancellor called, his voice high and agitated, "get her up on the altar before the scrying starts!"

The dark Bissantyman, his face grayed almost to silver by the light of the magic fire, brushed the other guards aside to grab her. In retaliation, Mervion turned her spells onto him. Her charms slipped past him ineffectually, and Issachar seized her by her wrists. She dropped the magic then and fought him, woman to man, as the guards she had witched to her grabbed at his coats and tried to prevent him from touching her.

Issachar shrugged them off and grappled Mervion up onto the altar, too powerful and brutal to be effectually resisted.

At that moment, Heiratikus caught Anisia in a basket of magic flame, tying her tongue and body. She had been conscious of little after that.

But whatever had followed must have been disaster for Heiratikus. For if the ambiance of the Keyhole Chamber amplified the casting of a spell, it also amplified a spell's failure should it be broken.

Above her, Issachar Dan's dark figure dominated the altar, muscles straining like tight cords. Mervion was still up on the great block with him, her slack body sheathed in sweat, her down-turned face dull and tired. His massive body dwarfed hers, his long fingers had pressed deep purple bruises into the flesh of her bare upper arms. The chapel walls were black with soot. They were both covered in dark ash, and the cicatrized ritual scars on Issachar's cheeks had opened and begun to seep fresh blood.

Heiratikus was cold with fury. Whatever he had intended with the spell he had bound on the altar, it had obviously not succeeded.

"Drop her, curse you, let her go!" the Chancellor shouted.

His dark servant scowled. Like a great bird of prey rejecting its quarry, he released Mervion's arms. Without his support, she dropped off the altar like a limp doll. The gag-spell blocked Anisia's reflexive sympathetic cry.

"Now get down yourself," the Chancellor said. "You look like a fool. Get down. Unless standing there in the gods' eyes has seized your fancy, get down."

"A fool indeed," Issachar said, wiping blood from his face. "You should be grateful that my strength did not fail me as your spells have failed you." For all his heavy muscle, he was a lithe panther of a man, and he took the long step down from the altar lightly, with the menacing balance of a predatory cat. "Seven bonds of sorcery and you did not even bother to name the spell against her. I warned you."

"The others broke so easily—" The Chancellor saw that Mervion had raised her head to follow his words, and cut himself short. "If she has held out—this one time—against me, that is more, Lord Dan, than many better have accomplished." The Chancellor held his dark servant's eyes with his own and smiled, as though at the memory of a past victory that had been very sweet.

Issachar looked away. "I'll relight the lamp," he said.

One of the pair of oil lamps that lit the room had burned dry. The Chancellor smirked at Issachar's back as the dark warrior took up the oil jar to refill it. He shook out his silver hair and turned to address Mervion, his tone jocular, almost amused, as if he hadn't been screaming like a man possessed not moments past.

"Mervion Blas," he said. "I believe you had no idea you could turn a spell of that power from you."

"Before the Great Twins, anything is possible," Mervion answered. Though her voice sounded a little wobbly, she was still defiant. "No one in Tielmark rewards treachery, least of all her gods."

The Chancellor tossed his silver hair and laughed. "What a perceptive child you are."

Anisia caught her breath, praying that her marriage-sister would resist the taunt.

Mervion's bright feline eyes were sharp and angry under the lank tangle of her hair. Even now, her hands clasped to cover the bruises Issachar's fingers had imprinted on her arms, she projected a powerful confidence. She gave her tormentor a level, scrutinizing stare. "I will fight you while I can."

The Chancellor smirked again. "A good answer, Tielmark's daughter. A new weapon made of the old metal. Your sire would have been proud."

"Excellency—"

"Don't interrupt, Issachar. I know what I'm saying." The Chancellor bent his head to Mervion's and spoke, his sharp face looming in hers. He took a lock of her bright hair and wound it round his spider-thin fingers, drawing her head closer to his still. "You're a hard girl, Mervion Blas. But we will break you. Because now we know the truth."

"What truth?"

"Why do you think you are here?"

"You made a mistake," Mervion said. Her voice was still very low, but it was clear from the way she sat, her legs braced underneath her, that she was already regaining strength, recovering. "Your spells challenged the Great Twins in their own country, and my suffering is the price of your mistake—even a modest hedge-witch like myself can best you. The blood is rotting in your veins. Anyone should be able to smell that."

Heiratikus hissed, and dropped her hair. Anisia sensed that if Heiratikus had been alone with Mervion, he would have hit her.

"A bloody destiny brought you here—you and me both. I've made no mistake. I'm going to break Tielmark's throne," he said, eyes icy, voice deathly cold. "And you are going to be the tool by which I do it. I'm going to topple Tielmark's foolish goddess sisters, and return their sacred mother, Llara Thunderbringer, to her rightful place of rule. I'll own Tielmark. I'll own you.

"You flatter yourself that you have bested me tonight—but there was no way that you could have done so, Mervion Blas. I've broken two women on this very altar, searching for the key to destroy Tielmark's Prince—two women and it might as well have been ten. If I had truly made a mistake in bringing you here, you would have followed them into madness.

"But you did not break. You could not break. You think your flighty Goddess Twins saved you? They didn't need to. Pure gold does not tarnish, pure steel does not shatter. Prophecy's players do not descend to madness before their true hour of testing."

"What are you saying?"

"Twice Fair." The words hung in the air like long notes, heavy with magic. "This broken spell has proved you are the woman of prophecy who is *Twice Fair*. Did you ever hear of this particular prophecy, Mervion Blas? Did you ever hear the secret, and know it would spell Tielmark's doom?"

"I don't even know why you have brought me here." Mervion's whisper was underlain with a new note of fear. "What could I know of your precious prophecy?"

"You knew the prophecy's keeper," the Chancellor said, his voice deceptively mild. "And now I know why he fought so hard to protect his secret!"

"Excellency," Issachar interrupted. As he filled and lit the lamp, his temper had cooled. Now his voice had the silky purr of a cat, and something in it quelled even the Chancellor's eagerness. "Tell the girl the whole of the prophecy if you like—indeed the whole of Tielmark's history if you like. But the prophecy's keeper? Leave that unspoken."

Anisia shivered. Leave it all unspoken, she thought, and let us go home.

The Chancellor gave his dark servant a disdainful look. "You did not even think that this girl would be the one," he said. "Too common to be uncommon, you said."

Lord Dan shrugged. He prodded Mervion with his foot, forcing her to look into his eyes.

"Tielmark's Prince is due to be married in three weeks' time," the dark lord told her, "on Prince's Night, the holiest festival of Tielmark's calendar. The night when Empire's traitor, the Fifth Imperial Prince, Clarin, consorted with the gods to make his land a free principality. He made three vows to the gods that night. Two of those vows he kept himself. The third his heirs must renew with their own flesh, for Clarin pledged that his line would perpetually renew itself in a mystic marriage to Tielmark's common blood.

"Twice Fair, on the sixth run's closing night may bear,
A Bloody Fruit, to bride the Prince to ruin."

Issachar paused. The blood was still seeping from the opened scars on his cheeks. He brushed at it impatiently. "This Prince's Night marks three hundred years of Tielmark's freedom, and the closing of the Great Twins' sixth cycle of rule. *Twice Fair—*" He touched a small circle of blood onto Mervion's ash-covered forehead. "You will be the vessel that breaks your own goddesses' power in this land.

He touched his throat, a prayer sign. There was a flare of magic, blinding bright. When Anisia could look again, Issachar had stood back from her marriage-sister. His jagged facial scars had stopped bleeding. The spot of blood on Mervion's forehead had vanished.

"You were right about this one, Excellency," the dark lord said. "And I was wrong. This girl must be the one *Twice Fair*. But it is only half the riddle solved. Now we must discover why you were right."

For the first time since the sorcery had commenced, Mervion

looked across to Anisia and met her eyes. The look on Mervion's face was agony and fear combined.

The Chancellor may not have known the answer to this riddle.

But, if Mervion was indeed half the answer, both Mervion and Anisia certainly did.

chapter 1

▼

Gaultry never carried her knife on market days. No one carried weapons on market days, and everyone agreed it made for fewer fights—or at least fewer serious fights.

But for Gaultry, shedding her knife was only the first part of a day-long trial. Market day in Paddleways village meant changing her hunting hose for long skirts, her knife belt for her Aunt Tamsanne's good red sash. Worse, market day meant trying to cut a convincing figure as she haggled with the village crowds.

It felt unnatural. When the villagers looked at her, it seemed they always saw her aunt, who was commanding and wise, or her sister, who was charming and wise, before they saw Gaultry, who suspected she didn't impress anyone as either of these things. Somehow, dealing with Gaultry, the village people always knew that they could hold to their price, and get it.

But today, much to her surprise, it had been different. Today, with the breaking of the new spring, she had begun to find her feet as a trader. Mother Liese, the baker, let her have a third loaf of bread without arguing, and Coln, the village blacksmith, gave her a score of nails for half the price she'd been expecting. So what if Coln teased her that the look of surprise on her face was worth what he lost on the price. "Let a wild rabbit out of a trap, you get the same expression!" He laughed. But so what? She'd got her price. Her clever older sister could scarcely have done better with an hour of hard bargaining.

Tamsanne would be pleased when she got home. Tamsanne had assured her niece numerous times she'd find her place in the world of tongues and trading. Gaultry had always found it hard to believe her.

But not today. Gaultry was finished with her business by early afternoon. She declined a surprising offer from Coln and his wife to stop in for an early tea.

"Tamsanne's expecting me," she had told the friendly blacksmith.

"Then plan to stay for tea next time," Coln pressed her. "That's Prince's Night. Annie can ready a cot for you if you'd like to see the fireworks."

"Next time won't be until after the Maying Moon. Tamsanne wants me at the cottage for Prince's Night."

"Making you miss the Prince's marriage celebrations here in the village? That's not kind."

Gaultry shrugged. "Paddleways will be too crowded for the likes of me. I won't want to come."

Coln, who was stocky, not at all shy, and loved to drink a holy day through, did not believe her. "Tell Tamsanne there's places for you both if she changes her mind."

"I will," Gaultry said, hoping he didn't think her rude. "It's a kind offer."

Afterwards she packed up to head home with bundles that were far heavier than she had hoped for.

It was a long three miles from Paddleways village to Aunt Tamsanne's cottage. Gaultry's satisfaction with the day's good trading lightened her step for the journey and it was a pleasantly sun-filled day for the walk.

The first mile was fields, empty today save for the wild birds. Then came a shallow ford with ancient stepping stones, washed a little too far apart by years of winter flooding to be usable. Beyond came the great woods, Arleon Forest. Past the ford, the track dwindled to a narrow path, hemmed in on either side with tender spring shoots. Gaultry folded the hem of her skirts into her sash and quickened her pace. She was eager to reach home and put aside her market clothes.

The path wound deep into the woods, first across a broad marshy bowl, and then up through a heavily forested boulder slope. Gaultry concentrated on the rising ground, her pace steady as she picked her way among the rocks, her big pannier basket balanced on one hip, a clutch of string bags on the other. The young huntress was a strongly built woman, with long legs and the efficient grace earned of her many years spent roaming the woods. She had come this way to market since she was a very young child, and Tamsanne had held her hand to support her. In those days, even empty-handed, the climb had not been so easy. Remembering, a smile crossed her lips.

Settling into her pace, she began to whistle.

She turned a corner, passed between a pair of ancient, moss-covered oaks, and stepped into the grassy clearing that marked the start of the pine plateau. Intent on the ground under her feet, the warmth of the early afternoon sun as it slanted down through the trees and touched her back, she was not at first aware that she had company.

Eight men were waiting for her in the clearing. Mounted men, with lean soldier's horses, dun and gray. But these men wore dirty leathers and dark cloaks instead of soldier's gear and armor, and insignia or heraldic badges were conspicuously missing from their shoulders. Behind them, spread loosely among the spindle-trunked pines, were half a dozen hunting dogs, coarse runners with ragged gray fur and orange-brown predator's eyes. They had waited so quietly for her, men and dogs both, that Gaultry was deep in among them before she even realized that they were there.

The dogs gave her the first warning: ears folded, tails low, and eyes suspicious; she could tell at once that they were set against her. Two men shifted, closing a loose wall across the path behind her.

Her hand went reflexively to her belt, but, of course, it was market day. No knife.

"Good afternoon, Gaultry Blas." That was the leader, a heavy man with lank yellow hair and three days of beard on his chin, a makeshift captain's sash of red buckram looped over one shoulder.

He took his horse a few paces towards her, close enough that Gaultry could smell the sweet grain on its breath. "We've been to some trouble to find you."

Gaultry didn't know him, or any of the others. She could think of no reason for the men to want to assault her, and was for a mad moment more puzzled than alarmed. Surely her successful day's shopping from the village could not be the lure?

"What do you want?" she asked. Even to her own ears, her voice sounded high and unconvincing. This was the worst thing she could have said, and the worst way she could have said it, both confirming her identity and admitting fright. "Who are you? What do you want?" More foolish questions. She bit her lip to stop herself from asking the same wrong questions a third time, and moved her basket from her hip to her front, where she could hold it shut with both hands.

The men were enjoying her fear. Looking from one face to the next, she tried to guess what it meant that they were here, set to attack her in Arleon Forest. This was a planned attack. A random attack she could perhaps understand, but this?

The leader, grinning at her obvious confusion, dismounted, and stepped forward. He was taller than Gaultry, and heavily muscled. His frame seemed very broad and strong as he came towards her. "Who are we? Why, we've been sent as saviors, Gaultry Blas. We've come all this way to make you safe." He grinned again, suddenly nasty. "Did you ever guess such a shy, pure girl as you could be so threatening?"

Gaultry retreated one step, then another. She wished that she had her knife, that she wasn't encumbered with a day's worth of shopping, that she knew what in the great gods' majesty the man was going on about. They could not be forest outlaws—Tamsanne, her aunt, had a pact with the local outriders. Indeed, anyone local, even a renegade, would have known better than to attack one of Tamsanne's nieces. Any other day Gaultry would have been armed, able to protect herself. But today, loaded with market goods, encumbered by cursedly billowing skirts—

The leader made a signal with his hand. His men closed off the path. One man chirruped to the dogs, and the whole pack of them were on their feet, whining, nervous, and eager.

Their leader was very close now. Beneath pale, straw-colored brows, he had guarded, orange-brown eyes—a predator, like his dogs. He held her eyes with his, the smile beneath them brutal, and gave his men another signal. The circle of horses tightened, the riders readying to dismount.

"Who sent you?"

"You're nicer looking than we were told to expect," the leader drawled, ignoring her question. He let his orange-brown eyes flicker down her body, taking in her blue market dress, her bundles and basket, the spring posy someone at market had tucked into her sleeve, the bright cloud of her fox-colored hair, worn loose for the day in the village. He dropped one hand to the strap of her basket. "That's good," he said. A cat stalking a sparrow, with her as the sparrow. Gaultry jerked away.

"Don't touch me."

Two of the men behind him laughed openly at that. Her mouth was bitter with bile; panic rose in her. Everything she said only whet their will to attack. She could see their taste for her helplessness and her fear sharpened, even as she watched them.

She stared around the circle, searching for a friendly face. Whoever had picked these hunters had chosen well. One man, maybe two, wore the cold face of duty. The rest were flushed, leering, expecting violence and gladdened by the expectation. She quavered, indecisive, knowing she should stall them, or at the very least deny she was the woman they'd named, but her mind was an awful blank. She could only focus on the unanswerable questions. Someone had decided that she, the daughter of a soldier and a hedge-witch, a woman with no business to speak of outside the bounds of Arleon Forest, was a threat.

With one hand still holding her basket's strap, the leader dipped into the leather bag at his hip, and pulled out a pair of manacles— roughly forged iron with teeth on the inner circles of the bracelets. He looked into Gaultry's eyes, hypnotically intense, and reached for her wrist. Touching you is the least we'll do, his eyes told her.

Gaultry dropped her basket, her net bags, everything, and stumbled back, thrashing with elbows and hands against the encroaching

circle. The leader grabbed her sash and pulled. She tore away, slipping as the sash untied abruptly from her waist. Reeling as she tried
to find her balance, she bounced off the barrel ribs of a horse, cursed,
and ducked under the brown curve of its belly.

Astonishingly, she was clear of the circle.

She fumbled, finding her feet as the hunters laughed and clumsily rounded their horses to the pursuit. Stumbling past the dogs, she
sprinted for the cover of the trees, her mind empty save for the
spasm of flight. She barely noticed the lash of branches and leaves
against her arms and body as she ran, headlong, into the green embrace of the forest.

Running blind, she tumbled almost at once into the middle of a
bramble bush, the black briar's thorns catching her skirts in a thousand places. The common pricking pain of the coarse, wine-red
canes on her hands brought her back a little from her terror. The
belling sound of a hunting horn rang sweet and clear through the
woods behind her. Gaultry swore, and ripped herself free. These men
were hunters, and she had just gifted them with a running quarry to
hone the edge of their aggression. Starting to run was probably the
worst thing she could have done. Not that she could have borne the
indignity of passively allowing herself to be captured!

Behind her, the hunters laughed and shouted, rallying the dogs,
whipping up their horses. She tucked up her skirts, cursing as the
cloth slipped and flapped against her legs, and ran on.

She was a fool. Her heart was near to bursting in her chest and
her lungs were heaving and her head was spinning with the wish
that she was running faster. She was a fool.

Mervion would never have panicked like this. Her clever older
sister wouldn't have lost her nerve and bolted. Mervion would have
charmed the men—or their horses, or the dogs—and turned the
entire pack in on itself with confusion, making her escape under the
cover of that confusion. Or she would have bluffed and diverted their
attention while she prepared a spell or warding to cover her flight.

At the very least she would have tied up her skirts properly
before beginning to run.

But not Gaultry. For Gaultry, the thinking usually happened
after she'd already made the big mistake.

Another clamor of the hunting horn broke her futile self-castigations. For now, a declining head start in a race she seemed destined to lose was her only advantage. She was free in the woods and she had always prided herself that the woods were her element. Now she was going to have to live up to that pride.

Loud baying howls sounded through the trees. Too close. The dogs could move faster through the thickening brush than the men on their horses. She was going to lose her lead to the dogs before she lost it to the men.

Gaultry sucked in a ragged breath. Her legs were failing her. She needed more speed.

She would have to try a spell. A taking-spell, to spirit the strength she needed—perhaps even from one of the beasts that pursued her—into her own body. Then, if she was lucky, she would be able to maintain a lead on her pursuers until she reached Tamsanne's boundaries. Then—perhaps—Tamsanne would sense her distress and help her.

Her taking-spell was her strongest magic. A deer would have been best for it, but with hunting sounds echoing through the forest, there wouldn't be a deer for miles around.

It was going to have to be a dog, the first dog that caught her. She'd have to catch it with the spell and pull the strength from it before the rest of the pack reached her and dragged her down.

Gaultry cut through a clump of saplings, trying to seize a moment's cover to prepare her spell. She took a long breath.

Huntress Elianté, she prayed. She tried to focus her mind, to tap an inner reservoir of calm. *Hear my cry.*

The sharp crackle of breaking brush was all the warning that she had that the race was over. She whirled, meeting the tawny-gray wolfhound as it rose to seize her. There was another dog at its side—

The dog's full weight bashed against her and knocked the breath clean out of her lungs. They crashed together into the bracken, the second dog snapping for room to join them. Gaultry found herself pressed down in the loose pine-mold of the forest floor, gasping for air. The dog clawed and snapped for her neck. If it caught her throat in its jaws, it would pin her in the bracken and hold her until the huntsmen closed in for a live kill.

If it closed its teeth on an artery when it seized her throat, she wouldn't get a chance to wait for the huntsmen.

White fangs thrashed at her face as she scrabbled frantically to impose her taking-spell onto the animal's aggressive will. Fetid breath blasted her face; she recoiled, sickened. Next to them, the second dog bit her ankle and howled at the triumph of having caught her.

"She's down! Hold her, Butcher, hold her!"

Gods, Gaultry thought, despairing. They were close enough to hear the dog's howl. Soon there would be four more dogs—

There was dog slobber on her face. Her lip had split, and she had the warm metal taste of blood in her mouth, but finally she got hold of one of the animal's small ears and gave it a vicious twist. The terrifying beast yelped—a sharp contrast to its deep-throated bark— and Gaultry had a clear moment in which she had its full attention. She locked her gaze into its yellow hunt-wild eyes, and let it look deep inside her.

It yammered in terror, and tried to escape, but the spell had already crested and lashed out to take it. The yelp subsided into a whimper. Gaultry tried to block her fear of the second dog as she held her mind open for the strength the spell had opened. Her mind and body sucked in the turbulent mist of the animal's spirit, briefly closing her vision. The dog's hot hairy body, knocked into a near coma, slumped against her.

When her sight cleared, her vision was the high-contrast green and purple of dog-sight. The casting was clumsy—she'd taken more from the animal than she'd intended. She had its will to hunt along with its will to race, a dangerous mixture of animal urges.

The second dog, hair bristling on its spine as it sensed the casting, bared its teeth and stood away, stiff-legged. Gaultry struggled to her feet, giddy with power, and tried to ignore it. The first dog's keen nose had come to her with its speed, and her senses were flooded by rich forest smells. She was ready to fight, to prove her pack dominance—

She was ready to get herself murdered, she told herself wryly, drawing herself back from a snarl. She'd taken the dog so she could run, not so she could brawl with a dog-pack. Forcing herself to turn away, she pushed her legs out into a fresh sprint.

As she compelled it to leave the fight, the dog's maddened spirit turned its will to speeding her run. A pure animal thrill in the chase, and something of its madness, shot through her body. Fighting or running, she was in a poor state to keep the stolen strength under tight leash. With rangy dog-spirit coursing through her legs, she moved faster than any horse through the tight maze of trees. Suddenly the grim hunt had turned into a race, and it was a race that Gaultry was winning. Now that the dogs that trailed her knew Gaultry commanded a witch's powers, their pursuit was no longer eager. There was a subtle change in the tenor of their barking. They were pulling their pace short, letting Gaultry extend her lead.

There was a correspondingly angry timbre in the men's hunting calls as she started to slip away. A wave of elation seized her. For Gaultry, running as a hunting-dog was almost as effortless as running as a deer, and she'd done that often enough. She sprinted full out now, exhilarated, risking braining herself against a tree, but it seemed she could feel the Huntress in her, encouraging her to run. Was this how a dog always felt as it ran and hunted?

The ground under her feet began to slope down. Already she was coming off the high pinewood plateau where the hunters had accosted her. The dry river gully was not far. Once past that, she'd be less than a mile from Aunt Tamsanne's cottage. With the slight incline in her favor, her pace was faster than ever. She pushed herself faster still down the hill, her stride crazily long. There was a rough doggy joy in her. She would win her race. She would tell Mervion about it: about how she had turned blind flight into a successful bid for escape. She could see her sister's face now, she could—

A rabbit-hole opened under her foot. Gaultry was wrenched off balance. The ankle that the second dog had bitten crumpled. Lunging forward, she slid, throwing her arms helplessly wide in a frantic effort to brake. Then there was an unexpected lurching drop as a woody hollow opened in front of her, and down she went, tumbling, turning, smashing herself past a rocky ledge as she made a final roll and hit the hollow's mossy bottom.

Half-dazed, she fought to regain her feet, to reorient. Blood bubbled down her left leg, sickening and warm. Fresh panic gripped her as she felt the first stab of pain. She tried to stand. Her knee buckled beneath her weight.

A dog barked, closing in. She cursed her own foolishness, prayed to Elianté—to any of the gods—that the lead dog would miss the hollow and draw the hunt past her, and hunkered down, hoping to make herself less conspicuous. Frustrated tears sprang to her eyes, as she tried not to beg the Huntress Elianté for favor. It was said that the Huntress was deaf to beggars' pleas.

The lead dog crashed noisily through the undergrowth nearby, then slowed, puzzled. Gaultry heard it overshoot the hollow and run, barking with frustration, somewhere into the woods near the dry gully. The next dog, unfortunately, had a better nose. It broke through the bracken above the hollow, spotted Gaultry, and let out a trilling howl. Another shaggy gray wolfhound. The running game was up.

Gaultry brushed away tears, fighting despair, and tried to ready herself for whatever was to come. She would try a last casting to protect herself, a better prepared, more cunning casting, and if that failed—well, she would fight on while she had the breath for it.

Above her, the dog barked nervously and stood back. It could sense the gathering of magic down at the bottom of the hollow, and wanted no part of it.

The same was true of the first rider who reached her. Though he shouted and jumped down from his horse with evident keenness, he took only a single step towards the edge of the hollow. Gaultry made a warding gesture with her hand, and threw out a weak cord of power. The man flinched, put his hand to the side of his face, and backed away. The thin crackle of magic that had curled past his ear had nothing potent in it to hurt him, but the threat of magic was sufficient to make him hesitate.

If only she had tried to bluff when they'd first stopped her! Perhaps they would have feared her then. Now, having whipped up their anger with her flight—she didn't want to think what a fool she had been.

"View-halloo! She's here!"

Gaultry glared at the first rider with what she hoped was a threatening look. He contented himself with waiting on the lip of the hollow.

The rest of the pack, dogs and horsemen alike, crashed noisily through the trees towards them, shouting and calling. Gaultry released the dog-spirit. Despite her physical distress, it was still snapping and eager. Its mood wouldn't help her if she had to parley. Or beg.

How would Tamsanne have advised her, or Mervion? Gaultry pushed the thought away. Neither Tamsanne nor Mervion would have let them start the running game. Neither would they have ripped the strength from a hunt-crazed dog and presumed it would help them escape. And if either of them had, they would have kept their attention fixed on the ground beneath their feet and resisted the call of the spell to cede control to the dog's unruly animal will.

Gaultry hunched up, hoping to look threatening and strong, a hope that rapidly drained as one rider after another joined the first man, until all but the leader were ranged on the hollow's lip above her.

She could hear them breathing: hard, heavy breaths as they stared down at her with dark, unfriendly faces. Their silence was more unnerving than threats.

It was an uncomfortably long time before the leader caught up with them. When he finally broke into view, his horse was strained-looking, and covered with foam. He himself was soaked with sweat. Back in the first clearing he had been steady and controlled. When she fought to escape he had laughed, sure that he and his men could take her. Now he'd lost face and he was angry.

There was a long pause while he stared down at the fallen huntress. Her fine, sharp-boned face was white with pain, but, though rumpled from her fall, she was hardly winded. Her attempt to comport herself bravely was not so futile as she imagined. Looking down at her proud face, the leader knew that the only reason he'd caught her had been the fall she had taken. The knowledge that his men could see this as well as he could did not please him.

"We have orders to take you." His orange-brown eyes bore into hers, but his words, spoken loud and clear, were mostly for his men. "You're wanted alive, which is fortunate for you, by my present thoughts."

Gaultry could see in his face, in the wet curl of his lips, in the motion of his hand on his belt, what he meant to attempt. She could stop that with a spell, but he would probably kill her if she publicly humiliated him a second time. What could she do to divert him into a beating or simple assault?

"You say that you know who I am," she said. "Do you, truly? Do you know why I walk in the woods alone?" She kept her voice low, trying to hide its tremor. "Why would I walk alone, unprotected? Can taking me be so easy?"

She crossed her hands over her torn knee, and called a fresh casting.

Her blood foamed on her leg. The red spatters fizzled, turned green, and bubbled to a viscous greenish-black.

"Touch me now and you'll curse yourselves forever. I'll turn the blood in your veins to lead."

Three of the hunters glanced anxiously at their leader. Save for the first rider who had reached the hollow on the dogs' heels, they were all in their saddles. For a moment, Gaultry's heart leapt, thinking she might win the standoff. Then an unhappy whine from one of the dogs broke the silence—and with it the short moment of stalemate.

The leader forced out a hard laugh, and swung down from his horse. "Try your curse on our master, and see if it sticks there. Or not. I don't fear you, girl." He handed his reins to the dismounted man, and started down into the hollow.

The drop was slick, wet, and steep. Halfway down he missed his footing, his heels gouging a long brown scar in the moss. Catching himself, he took another cautious step.

"Careful, Reido," one of his men called. "His lordship didn't warn us she was a witch."

"Which lord?" Gaultry asked, grasping at straws. "Did Arleon send you?" The Duke of Arleon was the forest's overlord.

With a curt nod, Reido shut his man up. "She's not a witch," he told his men. "She's barely even a woman grown, making threats she can't back up." Unbuckling his belt, he took another step towards her.

"I have a brother—he'll ransom me—"

For some reason that made them all laugh. Some of the tension left Reido's body, as if she had said something so dim-witted that she'd inadvertently proved her threat had no teeth.

"Why are you laughing?" she demanded, angry despite her fear.

Reido grinned, and shook his head. "It's not for you to know."

His predator's eyes raked her body. "You're a fast bitch, you know." His voice was a cold whisper, for her, not for the men. "I'm going to break you for testing me." The iron manacles were once again in his hand, the chain that linked the bracelets chinking menacingly.

"My curse will follow you past my death."

"Maybe. If you have a curse to lay on me." The men behind him roared with fresh laughter. Gaultry clawed out, hoping to draw blood. The big huntsman knocked her blow aside, and grabbed one of her wrists. Exploiting her weakened knee, he rolled onto her body, pushing his weight against her bad leg. One of his knees pinned the folds of her dress as he wrestled her wrist into the first of the manacle's bracelets.

Horrified that he had trapped one hand so easily, Gaultry snatched her other hand clear, and wound it in the folds of her dress, as far out of his reach as she could manage. Once he locked both her wrists in cold iron, she wouldn't have a chance against him. One hand at least had to be free to invoke her last desperate casting.

Misinterpreting her retreat for fear, Reido relaxed. He pushed her manacled wrist above her head. "You really don't know why we're here, do you?"

She stared her hatred at him, refusing to give him the satisfaction of an answer.

His eyes steady on hers, he hiked her skirts up over her knees. The man's orange-brown eyes taunted her, dared her to fight. She stared stonily back, trying not to show either fear or pain.

Then he reached down and gouged his fingers into the open

wound on her knee. She screamed, and fought to escape. He used her spasm of pain to pry her legs apart.

"Hear her cry," one of the hunters called. "Make her scream again, and she'll promise you her blessing, not her curse."

Gaultry shook her head, trying to clear the haze of pain. The hunter's words maddened her—as if her suffering was a joke, as if she wanted his captain grunting in rut atop her. She would call the spell. A last humiliation for Reido, if nothing else. The calculation in the way he hurt her had earned him that.

Reido was looking for the encouragement of her pain—he could have it! She let herself cry out again. The men on the hollow's rim hooted and catcalled. Reido, excited by their applause, thrust his hips against hers and reared up to smirk his triumph at his followers. Rucking up his long tunic, he let his gut slap against Gaultry's stomach. More catcalls.

She pulled the hand that was buried in her skirts clear. Her fingers sizzling with heat and power, she released the spell.

The big hunter roared with horror. Gaultry tried to wriggle away, not sure whether to feel gladness or fear. She'd hit him with a witch's bane, a protection spell that had frozen and withered his man's flesh against her leg. He'd never take her against her will with that hex on him.

Whether he beat her to death or not in payment for it was another question entirely.

Horror, shock, and blossoming rage passed across Reido's face. Despite the spell he'd seen her cast on her own blood, despite his own men's willingness to believe her, Reido himself hadn't believed she was a witch. Gaultry, struggling to free herself from between the big hunter's legs, was newly surprised. What little reputation she possessed was as a huntress and spell-caster, yet her attackers seemed unaware of either skill.

A split-second whistle interrupted the buzz of her thoughts. She ducked instinctively into the moss. Reido, more exposed than she, did not get a chance to duck. Cut off in midcry, he sprouted a black-feathered arrow high on the left side of his rib cage, an arrow that pierced him through to the heart. It happened so fast: the whistle, then the bright red ribbon of blood jetting down from the point of entry. Reido gave a throaty gurgle, a last pawing struggle, and collapsed, his face fixed in a shocked grimace.

Gaultry, gawking with surprise, clawed out from under the corpse, and stumbled shakily up onto her good leg. With seven men left on the hollow's edge, this was no time to question her deliverance.

"Who's next?" She flung her hands wide, and called green fire to her eyes.

One horseman turned to flee, and the horses of the other men, the scent of blood in their nostrils, were eager to follow. The dogs, already anxious about the magic used against them, added to the confusion, racing underfoot with the horses as they disappeared among the trees.

Unlocking her injured knee, Gaultry sank onto the grass and stretched both her legs out. The color spell was spent and her blood was back to running crimson, but the early mix of green and red spatters remained, a nauseating sight. On her right wrist, the iron manacle cut painfully into her arm's circulation. Hand and wrist both throbbed, well on their way to turning an unpleasant color of purple-under-white.

Reido lay facedown, not a yard in front of her, the fatal arrow's long shaft protruding from his rib cage. His leather tunic was soaked with blood. His pale dead legs were an obscenity against the fresh green of the moss. Gaultry focused on the arrow, trying to avoid seeing the gore. Black feathers with an iridescent green and purple sheen. Pretty—and like the hunters who had now fled, not local.

What had she got herself into, to have men hunting and dying for her on a warm spring day?

"I've hurt my knee," she called. "I can't walk." Silence, and perhaps a whisper of bracken moving. Around her the forest seemed to sigh and grow quiet, save for the rasping of her own breath.

On another day the little hollow would have been a pleasant place: leafy-green, surrounded by pale, moss-covered oaks. Even now, the bright spring foliage, dappled gold by the rich afternoon light, was lovely and fresh. Soft wind ruffled the branches overhead.

The sounds of the horsemen as they fled among the trees faded as they ran.

Young branches across the hollow rustled, and parted to reveal a new form. Gaultry found herself staring up into the face of a tall, powerfully built man. His gray cloak was touched with a sheen of forest green—colors that blended with the forest trees.

His dark, cropped hair was soldier-short, emphasizing hard, wolf-ish features. Cold gray eyes like winter ice. He had a fresh arrow nocked in his stubby, sturdy-looking bow. As she watched, he drew the bowstring to critical tautness, raised the arrowhead.

In Reido's eyes there had been cruelty and the hot promise of pain. In this man's eyes there was only the bitter shadow of death, a dark shadow that held her, stupefied, with fright. He was a bleak predator, battle-hardened and lethal. There was nothing Gaultry could do to stop him as he sighted the arrow at her heart. She opened her mouth, but no words came out.

Then something in him shuddered, and his black anger loosened. He shook his head, un-nocked the arrow, and deftly unstrung his bow. He had the effrontery to smile, as though the moment of terror had never been.

"Beauty in distress. With more distress to come, I daresay, if we don't get you moved." A door had closed—or opened—and the violence had been put away. "Lucky for you I was here."

He came down into the gully and gave Reido's corpse an inquiring shunt with his boot.

"That's the end of his troublemaking," he said.

"Thank you for that," Gaultry managed. Her mouth was dry as sandpaper.

Above high, flat cheekbones and an arrogantly tilted nose, his deep-set wolf's eyes turned, severe, to measure her.

She forced herself to smile and plucked at her skirts, covering up her legs. His expression softened, and he smiled again, as if to reassure her.

"I am indeed lucky that you were passing." She tried to choose her words carefully, to join him in pretending that he hadn't threatened her. Light-headed with worry and confusion, she bowed over her torn knee, tried to pull her wits together. It could no more be chance that he was passing than it had been chance that Reido and his men had attacked her. She could only hope that he did not mean to hurt her, that the violence she had seen in him was truly put away. "I'm beholden to you, Master Archer. They were sent to waylay me. They didn't like it that I tried to escape."

He nodded. "They'll be back once they've had a chance to re-group. Let me strap that knee and see about getting that iron off your arm. Then we'll get you moved before they can come back." He kneeled by Reido's body and commenced stripping the corpse of its tunic and shirt. "I'll make some bandages."

He was quick, efficient, and a little callous, moving the dead man's heavy body as though it was no weight at all, and ripping the bloody shirt into even strips. Watching him, Gaultry half-wondered that she had found the hapless Reido and his men so frightening. Compared to this man, her earlier attackers had been bumblers.

If this man had been sent to abduct her, he wouldn't have wasted time scaring her and letting her run.

He found the key for the manacles on a blood-soaked string around the dead man's neck and tossed it over. "More luck for us that one of his lackeys didn't take off with it," he said, hands busy in Reido's hip bag. "Nothing here to say who sent them."

"Don't you know who they were?" she asked.

"I knew that they were attacking you," he said.

He bound her knee in a tight military wrap, using the least bloodied part of Reido's shirt. Close to, he was less stark than he had first appeared, up on the hollow's edge. She could see now that the wolfish features were handsome, that the winter gray eyes could soften and charm.

Despite his efficiency, something in his manner suggested that he was tired to near exhaustion. A deep tension ran through his body—a tension that the lowering of his bow to her had not en-tirely dismissed. As he wrapped her knee, his hands were strong and firm, but there was an uneasy pressure in his fingers as he pulled the bandage ends tight and made her wince. Her involuntary recoil brought an odd hint of emotion to his eyes—fear?

"You're not hurting me, you know."

"I know," he said shortly, tapping her bandaged knee as he tied the last knot. "Thank the gods for that," he added, so softly she almost missed hearing.

"There," he said, taking her hand. "Beauty in somewhat less distress." A bitter light filled his eyes, and his tone was mocking. Was he laughing at her, or himself?

She jerked her hand free. "I don't see what's funny," she told him. "A man is dead for me, and I don't even know why. Are you trying to tease?"

His eyes cooled. "I'm trying to rescue you. Or so I thought."

"I don't understand," Gaultry said. His quicksilver changes of temper made it hard for her to know if he was friend or foe. "And I wish you would explain. I don't even know who you are — let alone what you're doing here in Arleon Forest."

"Put bluntly, I'd say your choices are me, or this man's band of worthies." He shrugged in Reido's general direction. "Which would you prefer?"

"That's not an honest question," Gaultry said, trying to keep her voice calm as angry color rose in her cheeks. "I'm sure you know who I am. And I'm grateful to you, whoever you are, for what you've spared me. So why toy with me? I don't know who you are — why shouldn't I be a little chary of you, a little frightened?"

"Why shouldn't you be frightened?" His broad wolf's face loomed over her. "I couldn't hurt you if I wanted."

She answered him with silent disbelief, and somehow, more than words, that broke his temper.

"You want to know why I'm here? I am— I am— I'll show you!"

He grabbed at her, abrupt and terrifying, seizing her head between his hands, palms covering her eyes, blinding her. She squealed in fear, realizing, too late, that the strange tension that held him was a spell — a powerful geas, and he meant to share its impress with her. Ignoring the pain in her knee, she fought to free herself, but he was too strong, his hands wound too tightly into her hair. A shock of power passed between them, and Gaultry, through the darkness, saw a flicker of light — a flicker of light that coalesced, in a ripple of blood-dark geas-magic, into a clear image.

Like a forced dream, like a hot explosion of fire, the image blos-

somed and opened. Herself. Her past. Herself as a tangled woods-
child, dirty and wild, green eyes blazing in temper, slim child's body
coiled with rage. A desperate emotion seeping from her—*don't go,
don't leave me! Traitor! Traitor!* Tears were mixed with the anger, the
fury. Behind this dominant image, a confused mix: images of herself
and Mervion, exchangeable childish figures, running beneath broad,
green-leafed trees, happy; Mervion in her old summer dress; Mervion dancing, graceful; herself carrying her old winter hat—the hat
filled with fish.

Trembling, she put her hands over her rescuer's, nervously trying
to pull them away. "I don't understand," she said. "Those are a dead
man's memories."

He loosed her and stepped back. "A dead man who put a geas on
me to protect you before he died. And very pleased your father was
with himself when he did it." Her rescuer's voice was embittered.
"Believe me, it wasn't a gift that I asked for. Now, shall we sit here
and talk, or will you let me help you? I have a horse. I'll share my
saddle with you until we're someplace safe. That's my first priority."

"And your second is the undoing of the geas?" Her voice shook.
Beneath the magic of the geas, the magic that forced him to protect
her, she could sense little of the man's own feelings, beyond a certain coldness and resentment.

He thought he had been sent to protect a spoiled child. A
spoiled child who was unjustly angry at a man who had loved her.

As if he could know anything of the reasons for which her father
had abandoned her and her sister.

"That's right." He met her eyes, equally level. "I want to fulfill
this geas and get myself free of it. Can you blame me?"

Gaultry shook her head. The geas was obviously a strong one—
it had to be, if it pressed on him so heavily that even tightening a
bandage over a wound distressed him. What was he to her father,
that he should be thrown into bondage as her protector? The old
man had much to answer for. Such a geas was tantamount to enslavement. "But the memories—we're children. My father didn't
tell you—"

"Talk later. Move you first." He offered her his hand, waiting
this time for her to take it.

"I'm not sure I can walk."

"I'll help if you can't."

She couldn't. He had to half-carry her out of the hollow, her bad leg dragging. On level ground she was a little more stable, though he had to hold her shoulder to keep her upright as they went the few paces through the trees to where he'd left his horse.

"Here we are." He propped Gaultry against the animal's glossy side and turned to adjust his equipage.

"I don't know how to ride," she said. He shot her a surprised look, then shrugged. "We'll manage."

His horse was a muscular dapple-gray mare, with slender legs and a spirited curve to her neck. Gaultry, balancing one-legged as her rescuer padded the front of the saddle, gave him a sharp look. In Arleon Forest, only soldiers and the gentry rode horses. Gaultry, judging by the worn condition of the man's gray and green leathers, had guessed him to be the former. Now, looking at the quality of his horse's lines, obvious even beneath the filth of what must have been several days' travel, she wasn't so sure. The worn scabbard of the longsword that he untied from the saddle and slung across his shoulders further muddied her guess. It was a knight's weapon, but the scabbard was so decrepit—

"Ready?" Barely waiting for her response, he slung Gaultry across the bow of the saddle. With her leg dragging, she was as graceless as a sack of potatoes, and she had an awkward time getting her good leg over the pommel. Finding her seat at last, she patted the mare's shoulder, and was startled to find her body was cool and dry.

"It didn't take you much running to intercept us."

"Luckily for you, right?" Her rescuer settled behind her in the saddle. "Let's move. Just relax and try to keep your balance. I'll do the rest."

Under different circumstances, Gaultry would have rebelled against his tone. It had been more than five years since she'd been up on a horse. The last time she'd ridden had been before her father had been made into a gentleman, before he had made his decision not to bring Gaultry and Mervion, the children of his first marriage, into his new life with him. He had owned a horse as a soldier and horses as a gentleman—but it had been seldom indeed that he had ever put either of his daughters up in the saddle. Looking back, Gaultry could only wonder if that meant he'd always planned to abandon his daughters when he'd attained rank.

Thinking on her father, how could she relax and settle into the front of the saddle as her rescuer had directed her? What would he have thought to see her mounted now?

Then the horse lunged forward, and concentrating on staying in the saddle took over. Her knee was stiff, and the tight binding turned her leg awkwardly outwards, forcing her to lean tightly against her rescuer for support and balance. His head was just above hers as they rode. She felt uncomfortably small and helpless, particularly as she could see that her rescuer was comfortable in the saddle, relaxed in a familiar element even as he sent the horse careening forward at an almost recklessly fast pace.

He caught her expression and grinned, sardonic. Don't imagine I'm happy about this either, his eyes seemed to tell her. But all he said aloud was, "Where am I taking you?"

There was nothing for it but for Gaultry to direct him to her aunt's.

chapter **2**

▼

Tamsanne's cottage was hidden in the ruins of an ancient forested-over ring castle. She seldom had visitors. This was
not at all surprising, given the cottage's isolation and its proximity
to the Great River Rush — and to the Changing Lands, the mysterious domain beyond the river border to the south.

The Changing Lands were wild and lawless, dominated by an
ungoverned magic that had brought its trees to waking life, a magic
that trapped its animals — and any human foolish enough to cross its
borders — in lifelong servitude. The border river was little safer,
floating vast rafts of darkly scented mauve and white lilies — a dangerous, swift-acting opiate that could leave a boat without its crew
awake to steer it. Most everyone who walked by the river had seen
the strange dryads that danced beneath the trees on the far bank on
the gods' holy nights. The dryads were the souls and spirit forces of
bonded men and animals. There was no doubt that the Changing
Lands were poison to anything human.

Tamsanne was one of a very few who had chosen to settle in
Arleon Forest — and one of the fewer still who had formed a true tie
to the land there. She had been careful to ensure that both her
nieces understood from an early age that the warnings of the entrap-

ments and sorceries spawned by the Changing Lands were no fantasy. She rejected as nonsense, however, the notion that the forests on the Tielmaran side of the river were similarly unstable. "They say I've condemned the pair of you to dryads' lives, raising you among these trees, but life here is a choice. The land won't take you — unless you ask it to, and you've earned the privilege of its acceptance.

"Here in Arleon Forest, the goddesses' imprint is particularly strong. Witches who pray to the Great Twins for magic, women like myself, prosper in settling here. Here, where their magic is most potent, the goddesses are generous with it."

Gaultry sometimes wondered that her aunt thought things were so simple. The Great Twins were indeed generous in sharing their strength with Tamsanne: Gaultry's aunt was a powerful healer and herbs woman, strong and elemental enough that she could call seed to vital, sprouting life, or send a full-grown oak crashing to the forest floor. But that was Tamsanne. The broad scope of forest magic never seemed to come so easily to anyone else — not least of all to her own nieces.

Gaultry's rescuer guided his mare among the trees at a deceptively smooth canter. His tight grip on her shoulders belied the smoothness of the ride, as did the branches that slashed by their faces, alarmingly close and fast. The outcome of her earlier race would have been different if Reido's men had been equally competent at running a horse through thick brush.

"You were expecting me to be younger, weren't you?" Gaultry asked as her rescuer slowed the mare to a bone-jarring trot.

"I was expecting you to be a child." The dark soldier shifted on the saddle, brushing lightly against her back. "How much further to your aunt's now?"

"We'll reach her outposts soon. You'll see. The forest is greener there. Tamsanne is famous for the early flowers in her garden." She drew a little away — not that there was much room to do so in the crowded saddle. "How is it that you've heard of me and not of Tamsanne?"

"I wouldn't have known of you but for your father. How should I know of your aunt?"

"By asking in Paddleways—or in any village in Arleon Forest, on your way to find me."

"For the past two days, I've let Reido and his men lead me to you. I came up behind them after they had made inquiries after you in High Hill."

"I see," said Gaultry, though she didn't see at all. High Hill was far to the north, almost at the edge of Arleon Forest. Why would anyone have come so far to threaten her? "But my father sending you with a geas to protect me—I don't understand that. Father died at the New Year, and here it is, almost Prince's Night and the first of May. The magic he laid on you seems very strong. How did it let you wait almost five months before coming after me?"

"It didn't," he answered curtly. "You saw the transference. That was all he gave me. I didn't even know your name. Your father lumbered me with the images, and the compulsion to protect you. He was dead before he could tell me who you were. Having so many unanswered questions—it was like I had a wasp trapped in my skull: an angry wasp. Your father hadn't considered that I had other business to attend before I could find the time to discover who you were—let alone where I could find you."

"What my father did had very little to do with what I wanted either," said Gaultry, smarting at his tone.

"So I would have guessed, from what he did give me. Have you always been so angry with him?" He asked the question lightly, but she could see in his eyes that he remembered the dominant image—herself as an angry young girl, furious and disappointed with her father all at once—and that he found it hard to respect her for it.

"That's none of your business," she told him. "As if you could have any idea who was at fault for my behavior." Ahead, one of her aunt's black boundary markers hove into view. "That's Tamsanne's first post. I'll be safe now. Let me down. I'll make my way from here." She tugged blindly at the mare's reins, not caring when she made the horse startle and threaten to spill her riders. She simply wanted to be down, to be away from him. If her father had laid a geas on him, it was no fault of hers! She had asked her father for nothing since that day long past. *Nothing.* Least of all for his protection.

"Don't be silly," he said, his voice rough and angry. "That knee can't take your weight, and if I have to watch you hobble it will probably be the straw that breaks me." His arms tightened around her, forcibly preventing her from jumping off the saddle. His heart hammered against his ribs, hard enough that she could feel it. She stilled for a moment, baffled by the force of his distress. Then, suddenly, she understood. It was the geas magic: pressing him, pounding on his senses, demanding he attend her needs. Even changes in her voice affected him.

Small wonder that the dark soldier was so furious!

It made no sense that her father had managed to cast a geas so strong. She hadn't seen her father in more than five years—not since the horrible day Thomas Blas had come to Tamsanne's and told them all that he had been knighted, that Gaultry and Mervion, forest-raised as they were, would no longer be welcome in his house. Worst of all had been the news that he would not come to Arleon Forest to share the end-of-summer month with them, not ever again.

"It's not the knee that's so bad," she said, trying to compose herself, to put past betrayals from her mind. "Though it does hurt. But you have upset me—you coming here with this geas has upset me. I don't know what my father was thinking, forcing such a pledge on you."

"Judging by what that bastard and his men were about to do back there in the hollow, I suppose we have to call it premonition," he said. He pulled the reins out of her fingers, and gently pressed his hand against the back of her neck, as if trying to ground the geas-magic to her pulse.

Or guilt, she thought to herself. It could be called guilt. Court-life, running after the hounds in the Prince's hunt—that had been Thomas Blas's death. He should never have abandoned his daughters to join that life.

After a moment, the geas-magic calmed. The soldier took his hand away from her neck, and clucked to the mare, urging her back into a walk. "Since the New Year, your image has been plaguing me. I thought I had an idea of what you were going to be like—you're not what I expected."

"You were expecting an angry child," Gaultry said, sullen.

"That's what I was when my father last saw me. It doesn't mean that it's what I still am." Her father's death had come as a great shock, not least because of her recollections of their last meeting, and what she saw as the ironic circumstances of his death. Her father had been killed in a needless hunting accident while wintering at the Prince's court. "Why did Father choose you for the geas? Were you friends?"

"Friends?" He frowned. "I was there when he died."

"His death was an accident? That's the news that came to us." It was too easy to picture the stupidity of her father's death: the old man still thrusting himself to the fore, into the thick of the danger, trying even as death reached for him to win his overlord's eye and praise. An accident during the Prince of Tielmark's New Year's Day hunt. So commonplace, yet so unnecessary. At the south border, in the midst of a hard winter, they had not heard the news until nearly a month after the event.

"It was an accident." He stopped the horse, suddenly abrupt, and shifted her around in the saddle. "Why question that?"

"He was my father," Gaultry said, "and you've just admitted to witnessing his death."

His face was pale beneath his soldier's tan. "I owe you a proper introduction," he said. "I'm punishing you for your father's presumptions—but perhaps he presumed much of you as well."

"By the Great Twins' grace, I swear to you by my life that my name is Martin Stalker. A powerful geas has been laid on me to protect you. I hereby submit to the gods and acknowledge the geas." He crossed his right hand over his heart, and stared into her eyes, as if searching for a new truth to replace the initial impress that her father had set upon him.

To formally acknowledge a geas was to start to limit its terms. But something was wrong here. Gaultry knew something was wrong even as she felt the geas-magic in him quicken, lighting his winter gray eyes to sparking silver, pulling the breath deep into his chest, tightening the grip of his thighs against her own in the saddle. Her father had never intended that the geas should protect only her. Her father had impressed her rescuer's mind with images of Gaultry and her sister both. He hadn't meant the geas just to protect Gaultry. And yet here was Martin Stalker, the protector her dying father had chosen for them both, formally accepting the geas as if it applied only to her, molding the spell with his acceptance, changing it—

"Wait!" she called, trying to stall the magic as it surged and bent itself to a new pattern. "Stop! I know why the geas has been so unnatural, so strong! It's a mistake!"

She reached for his hand, trying to stop the transformation, but it was too late. Her rescuer had chosen the wrong moment—and the wrong place—to invoke his acceptance. As the silver geasmagic in his eyes brightened, a second, vernal green power crackled to life, surrounding the horse with its riders in a flashing cloud of cold fire. Gaultry swore, and jerked round, trying to spot the source of the green magic—her aunt's signature—as it meshed with the silver geas-magic, assessing, groping like a tendril of spectral vine.

Then it recoiled. Her rescuer jolted in the saddle, forced violently back against the crupper. The mare shied and whinnied, newly startled. A second lash of the green fire whipped across them both. Martin, cursing, was slammed over the back of the saddle and off over the horse's rump.

Gaultry, alone in the saddle, lurched sideways, and fought for balance. There was an awkward moment when she thought she would keep her seat; then the horse bucked, and she was in the air.

Gaultry cried out, trying to writhe round so she would miss landing on her bad knee.

She came down on top of Martin. The big soldier had twisted himself almost under his own horse's legs to cushion her fall. Barely pausing to draw breath, he shunted her off onto the turf, and reached for his sword, which, along with his cloak and quiver, had come free of his shoulders.

"It's all right." She caught at his jacket as he struggled to free his weapon from the folds of the heavy cloak. "It's not for us. The geas triggered it. Tamsanne doesn't like unexpected visitors, especially visitors who come with magic. She's arranged things so she doesn't get any. Look—" Gaultry pointed to the bole of the tree that they had just passed. There was a hex symbol carved into the hoary bark, half-hidden by tangled grass. As they watched, it trembled faintly, the cut marks realigning themselves. "She knows we're coming now. That's all."

"Your aunt is a witch." A statement, not a question, but a statement of a fact that was new to him. He was on his feet, scowling, as frightening as he'd been at that first moment when she'd seen him, when he'd tested the geas by aiming his arrow at her heart.

"And what do you think I am?" she snapped back, furious that even though she knew he had the geas on him, she still found herself intimidated. "So what do you want me to tell you? That I think you're a fool to be traveling in this forest without the knowledge of it?"

"Fool enough to risk my neck offering you help." He turned to calm his mare—and perhaps to calm himself as well.

Gaultry sat on the soft turf, waiting to be helped up. They were in Tamsanne's grounds proper now. The leaves were greener, the ground softer. A sweet wind seemed to stir the trees. The attack by Reido's men seemed very far away. She wondered why Martin was so upset—this was something other than his geas-induced sensitivity to her feelings.

"Weren't you watching when I spelled the blood on my leg?" He must not have noticed when she cast the witch's bane on Reido's vitals. But the color-changing of her blood had been so obviously a spell, and he'd cleaned her wound with his own hands. "Didn't you think anything was odd when you mopped green blood off me?"

"There are a number of things I should have better considered in coming here to meet you," said Martin, giving her an odd look. "Who is this aunt of yours? What's her blood?"

"Tamsanne?" Gauntry grinned. "She wouldn't praise you for asking a question like that. She thinks that deeds, not blood, make a person important."

"Let's go," Martin said, suddenly abrupt. "Anything I might need to say will be better said off the trail." He bent to pick up his sword, and dragged the scabbard clear of the cloak.

Gaultry, who had reached out her hand to him, expecting to be helped up, gasped and drew back.

The worn leather of the scabbard had gone clear as glass, and the mighty sword that lay beneath the battered casing could be clearly seen. Some element of Tamsanne's hex revealed magic. Six runes of power winked out along its blade, embossed into the metal like evil, shifting eyes.

For such power, the blade itself would have to have been forged in magic fire.

"What are you doing here?" Gaultry asked, newly bewildered. No common soldier would carry such a weapon. "How could my father have had the power to compel you?"

"This shouldn't be happening," he said angrily, rubbing furiously at the scabbard with his hands, as though he could dispel the magic by dint of sheer physical force. "This shouldn't be happening."

There was something comedic in the intensity of his efforts. As if Tamsanne's magic could be rubbed off so easily! But the comedy hardly undercut the seriousness of what her father had done. The power Martin Stalker carried in that blade—his own will would have to be strong indeed, to enable him to control it. Yet her father had imposed a geas on him, a geas of such potency that the dark soldier had been forced to the far end of Tielmark to find her.

She looked the man over, carefully searching for more clues to his character and strength, as he fussed with his weapon. The oak-leaf brooch at his collar was also lighted with eldritch-fire, as well as the feathers of two of the arrows that protruded from his quiver. The brooch had the twin goddess double-spiral on it—probably a protection piece.

"Tamsanne's had fifty-odd years to get things in order here, you know."

"I didn't. Fifty years." He abandoned his attempt to clean his weapon and slung the scabbard bad-temperedly back over his shoulders, fingers busy with the straps. "She's old to be your aunt."

"Great-aunt, actually." Gaultry let him heave her up into the saddle, wondering if she should warn him about the geas now, tell him her guess that he had misunderstood about herself and her sister from the beginning; that he himself had helped shape it wrongly from the day it had been cast on him, investing it with more power and intensity than even her father had intended. Somehow the moment didn't seem right. Probably Tamsanne would be able to explain it better—that Martin had taken a geas meant to protect two sisters, and molded it into potent protection for just one.

No, now was not the time to confuse him. Tamsanne's hex had shaken him. Instead of returning to the saddle, he walked warily by his mare's side as they crossed the last rise towards the cottage grounds. His air was vigilant, his movements swift and light, his eyes alert and restless, searching for every detail. Spotting another tree hex before Gaultry had remembered it was there, he led the horse around behind it.

"What's that one do? Put a halo over my head?"

What would Tamsanne make of him?

They soon came to the first remnant of the old ring castle's walls, mellow silvery stone with once finely dressed edges, now largely crumbled. Martin gave Gaultry an inquiring look. "More surprises. I thought you said your aunt lived in a cottage."

"She does. We have to go through the ruins to get to the cottage. You'll see."

"This is one of the old Bissanty border castles, isn't it?"

"What's left of it."

The ancient masonry was tangled over with climbing honeysuckle and roses. The path rambled between fallen piers of stone, an occasional carved block with weather-worn figures peeping out from under the greenery. It was a pleasant haven, even without the flowers in full bloom. Martin's mare nickered with pleasure at the fresh plant smells. They rounded the ruinous shell of the most complete of the remaining towers. It was a bare twenty feet high, with almost half of the round entirely crumbled.

Gaultry looked anxiously at her visitor, wondering what he made of it. It was here that she and Mervion had played at knights and ladies when they were children, before the last of the inner stairs had fallen, and it was one of her favorite spots. To an outsider's eye the riot of unseasonable blossoms might contrast uncomfortably with the stark darks and delicate spring greens of the pine plateau forest.

They turned onto the last corridor—a narrow stone passageway now grassy underfoot and open to the sky—towards the remains of the great hall. On the walls here wisteria was growing in unnatural profusion, its stems coiled into looping signs and symbols, entwined thickly into itself and almost strangled by its own burgeoning life. Its pale flowers had blood-colored centers, like tiny red pupils. The blossoms seemed to turn and follow them as they went past.

"I wouldn't want to be in here if your aunt decided that she didn't want company," Martin said, watching the wisteria watch them.

"She likes it to be pretty," Gaultry said. "But she wants it to be useful too." Going past the big loop of vines that had once garroted an intruder, Gaultry made Martin quicken the horse's pace. That had been a night intrusion. The man had advanced with his knife in his hand. Helping Tamsanne free his engorged purple body the next morning had not been pleasant.

It wasn't a story she cared to repeat to Martin.

After the shadows and cover of the forest, the broken rectangle of the great hall was a startling expanse of open turf. Tamsanne's half-dozen ewes, who kept the grass cropped short, grazed lazily in one corner. At the west end, the cottage had been built into the old piece of wall that contained what had once been the hall's main fireplace — now incorporated into the cottage to serve as its kitchen hearth. The cottage itself was modest: a snug building with low eaves, a thatched roof, and narrow windows.

The very snugness of the cottage emphasized the wild view over the old hall's foundations to the south. There the broken masonry of the wall overlooked a wide oxbow of the great border river. Standing on the grassy sward that had once been the floor of the great hall, they had a panoramic view of the broad blue river, and, across it, of the Changing Lands.

On the Tielmaran bank, there was little to see: a rocky expanse of hill, studded with stunted trees, dropped sharply to the mass of reeds at the water's edge. The great bow of the river seemed normal enough. The water was a glossier, more purple blue than was natural, but that was all. Across the water, however . . .

Across the water the land sparkled with fantastic color. The tops of the trees shivered and tossed. The foliage was ever-changing colors, shifting swiftly from the palest spring green through to the darkest, muddiest forest black. Among the bright branches, silver lights seemed to glisten and twinkle. Occasionally there would be a pause, as in a conversation; then the motion would start and build again.

It was a lovely but profoundly intimidating sight.

Martin looked up at Gaultry, shock evident on his face.

"It does stay on its own side of the river," Gaultry assured him, shifting awkwardly in the saddle, a little embarrassed by the intensity of his expression. "You get used to it."

He smiled, what suddenly seemed like the first true smile that he had given her. "It's beautiful."

Gaultry could not help but feel pleased. Most of Tamsanne's infrequent visitors were more cowed than appreciative. "It's like that day and night," she said, a little shy. "Tamsanne says the trees are awake there, asleep here. Sometimes you see the dryads—the captured souls—dancing beneath the branches. That's a little sad—though I don't think they look too unhappy.

"I wouldn't guess that you would." He smiled again, this time a facile smile that didn't reach his eyes. Gaultry, puzzled by his sudden mood-changes and tongue-tied as always when trying to talk seriously with people who were teasing her, looked away, wishing she hadn't mentioned the dryads.

"What have you been up to, Gaultry?" Her aunt bustled towards them out of the cottage, saving Gaultry from having to fumble a response.

Tamsanne had a linen towel over one shoulder, on which she was wiping her hands. She was a short and slightly built woman, with a deeply wrinkled face and out-sized hands which had been thickened by time and work. Bellows, the black dog who was her familiar spirit, followed at her heels. Tamsanne had been busy with some cookery, as the smoke from the cottage's chimney attested, and they'd interrupted her.

Or so she would have it appear.

"Where's your basket?" she asked Gaultry. "Who is this?" She gave Martin a jaundiced look, taking in the worn gear, fine horse, and the glint of her own magic on his weapons.

"Martin Stalker, ma'am." Martin answered for himself. "Your niece has hurt her knee. Some men attacked her in the woods—"

"And you rescued her." Tamsanne finished his sentence for him. "Very convenient." She fluttered the towel at the big soldier, feigning an old woman's gestures. Gaultry smothered a grin. She didn't think her aunt was fooling Martin, and couldn't help but wonder that she even tried. Tamsanne had sharp black eyes, their intensity undiminished by age, and few people could stand up to one of her looks. Linen towel and frail body aside, it was easy, looking into those sharp eyes, to credit Tamsanne as a woman of power. "Not, of course, that we're ungrateful to you for saving her."

"Of course," Martin said. His face was all politeness and courtesy, masking his deeper thoughts.

Tamsanne gave him another hard look. "Well, I can see it's a near thing that she's in one piece. Come down from that animal, Gaultry. I'll take you inside and fix you up. And you—" She turned on Martin. "Follow Bellows here and he'll show you where to stable your animal. Presuming that you're staying the night."

Bellows, at Martin's knee, stuck his snout in the man's hand and sighed. He was a large, somewhat elderly dog with a resigned expression—long used to Tamsanne's preemptive outbursts.

Martin bent and gave him a light pat. "Generous of you, ma'am. I don't see myself making it back to Paddleways tonight."

"Nor tomorrow either if you'll be wanting a spell laid before you go." Tamsanne could be frighteningly prescient—or ruthlessly sly. Gaultry guessed she'd been spying on them since they'd first entered her grounds near the tree hex. "But I think we'll be waiting for your other news before we help you with that one."

Martin gave Tamsanne his own sharp look.

"So I'm right?" Tamsanne said. "Follow Bellows, then, and put up your horse."

"I'll stay," he said. "Perhaps you can answer some questions for me."

"Perhaps," Tamsanne answered, making no promises. She slapped Bellows on the rump to get him moving.

Gaultry stared at Martin's back as he led the mare away. Outside of her father's geas, he hadn't suggested there were other reasons for his trip to Arleon Forest.

"Come get yourself cleaned up." Tamsanne took her firmly by the elbow. "And don't be looking so startled. It's perfectly obvious that something besides the geas has brought him all the way out here to the border. If he held the geas off four months, he wouldn't be here now if he didn't have another reason bringing him."

"You *were* listening!" Gaultry hissed. "Why didn't you send Bellows to meet us?"

"To what purpose?" Tamsanne helped her hobble towards the cottage. "You got here fast enough without my interference."

"You let him trigger the hex with his geas!" Gaultry accused her. "You let him change the geas! You could have stopped him!"

"Stop babbling, Gaultry. You have no idea what you're talking about. As if I had the power to stop him."

Inside the cottage, out of Martin's sight, Tamsanne was gentler. She sat her niece in the padded chair in the nook of the massive stone fireplace — today's cooking fire took up only a small part of the great stone slab — and bustled about the room collecting herbs to dress Gaultry's knee. "Green blood!" Tamsanne let herself smile as she opened Martin's bandages. "That's a new one for you. Did it frighten them?"

Gaultry said she thought it might have done.

Now that she was in a safe place and able to relax, the young huntress was beginning to feel the full force of her injury. Having the wound probed and cleaned was exquisitely painful. Martin, in his haste to get her moved, had left some dirt in the wound. Gaultry distracted herself from Tamsanne's ministrations by describing how Reido had forced his fingers into the gash on her knee after he'd pinned her.

Tamsanne, who had not seen that part of Gaultry's afternoon, frowned. "It's deep, my careless child. What that hunter did made it worse. The kneecap is damaged."

She had been grinding a healer's paste in her small mortar, intending to salve the cut. Now, sighing, she looked to the door. Martin was not yet in sight.

"You can't spend the next fortnight walking around with a stiff knee. I have to fix it now. Stay still."

She made the sign of the double goddesses, a circle traced with her right hand's fingers on her left palm, and touched her fingers to Gaultry's skin. As fresh pain seared her flesh, Gaultry cried out, taken by surprise.

"We'll keep appearances up for the company." Tamsanne

slapped a handful of herbal paste onto Gaultry's knee and strapped it up with a fresh bandage—but not before Gaultry had seen that the skin was smooth, not even a scar to show for her scrape. "Now, let's get you something to eat."

By the time Martin knocked at the cottage door, Gaultry was ensconced by the fire with a plate of stew on her lap, her leg elevated on a short stool. She waved as he entered, wondering how much pain Tamsanne expected her to pretend she was feeling.

"Come in, come in, close the door." Tamsanne ladled some stew onto a plate. "Have some supper with Gaultry—by the fire, if you will."

"Thank you." The tall soldier piled his saddlebags and weapons against the wall near the fire and settled himself into what was ordinarily Gaultry's chair, stretching his legs to meet the heat. He'd washed. Bellows had shown him the rain barrel and he'd cleaned the remains of the afternoon's gore from his hands.

"Have you been admiring our view?" Tamsanne handed him a plate of stew and their company spoon—metal with a cluster of leaves on the handle.

"It's awe inspiring. Though why you put yourself so close to the border I don't quite comprehend."

"Don't you?" Tamsanne flashed him a severe look. "The answer is plain enough to my eyes. Drawing strength from the earth itself for fifty years is as good a way as any to build strength."

"Fifty years?" Martin said, taking his first mouthful of stew. "An entire cycle of the Great Twins' calendar."

Tamsanne shot him an unfriendly look. "That's right," she said.

The soldier tapped his spoon against his plate, lost in thought. "I didn't come here knowing that your niece was born to a witch's blood," he said. "Or that she was kin to a witch tuned to Tielmark's Prince's cycles." He reached back to where he'd leaned his sword against the wall with the rest of his things, and touched the scabbard. The leather looked almost normal now, but the outlines of the six power runes could still be seen, glowing faintly green through the thin leather. "Fifty years is a long time to power-build. Six fifties is as long as Tielmark has been a principality free of Bissanty." He drew his hand away from the sword and took another mouthful of stew.

"That's so," Tamsanne said. "And this year will close another cycle."

Gaultry was astonished to see her aunt smile, if a little grimly, and move the pot of stew where he could take more if he wanted it.

Setting down the ladle, the old woman seated herself away from the fire, half in shadows, and took a handful of her skirts, twisting the cloth thoughtfully in her hands. "Why don't you tell us why you have come here?"

Martin stared around the cottage at the dried herbs, the heavily carved beams, the strange oddments of Tamsanne's craft, seemingly considering his answer. He looked at Tamsanne, sitting poised between shadow and light, something intangibly aggressive in her pose. Lastly, he looked at Gaultry where she sat, her bright hair shining in the firelight, her down-turned face slightly flushed as she stared at her bandaged knee.

When he finally spoke, it was to ask his own question. "Mistress Tamsanne, do both of your nieces follow your craft?"

Gaultry snapped her head up, startled. Earlier this afternoon he hadn't mentioned—or indeed even seemed to know about—Mervion.

"What would you imagine?" Tamsanne said dryly. "Both girls grew to womanhood under this roof."

"What about Mervion?" Gaultry asked. "Mervion is at Blas Lodge. What do you want with her?" Blas Lodge was her half-brother's—formerly her father's—hunting lodge.

"She's neither at your brother's house, nor is she safe," Martin said.

"Where is she?"

"She's in Princeport, held prisoner at the Prince's court."

"Princeport?" Gaultry stuttered. "What is she doing there?" Princeport, on Tielmark's coast, was a week's journey north from Blas Lodge—an even greater journey if one counted finding a reason to have business in the Prince's capital.

"Tell us," Tamsanne said, suddenly intent. "Gaultry, be quiet and let Martin speak."

"You've heard that the Prince is to be married this year on Prince's Night?"

"In three weeks' time," Tamsanne replied. "All Tielmark knows."

"We heard the wedding announcement on the heels of the news of my father's death," said Gaultry. "It was important enough that a second rider came south through the snow with it." More important than the news of a local knight's death. The mood in Paddleways village had swiftly turned from mourning to celebration when the announcement of the Prince's marriage plans was made known. Gaultry, still struggling with her reaction to her father's death, had not known whether to feel grateful or dismayed to see the response to his demise superseded by joy at the Prince's announcement.

Martin nodded. "Nobody knows who the new Princess will be—"

"Nobody's supposed to know," Gaultry interrupted, her memories making her voice gruff. "Tielmark is closing the Great Twins' cycle this year. The Prince isn't supposed to announce his choice until he presents her to the gods on Prince's Night."

"That's the tradition," Tamsanne added dryly. "Outside of the fact that Benet has held the throne for seven years now, and it's high time he was married."

Gaultry smiled at their guest, struggling to regain her composure. "Aunt Tamsanne will never admit that Tielmark's cycles are important, all evidence from the Great Twins to the contrary."

"Not so!" Tamsanne retorted. "I've seen enough life that I won't deny any such thing. Tielmark's greatest Prince, after Clarin-founder, was Briern-bold. Briern married on the centenary, and ruled for almost a full cycle after, so the goddesses must have been pleased by his marriage." It had been Prince Briern who had inflicted a shattering defeat against the Bissanty armies, destroying forever Bissanty pretensions to retake Tielmaran lands by force.

"What about the Princess Corinne?" Martin asked, a curious edge in his voice. "She was married on Tielmark's two hundred fiftieth. Every planting her reign saw through to harvest was plentiful and rich."

"Exactly." Gaultry nodded. "Aunt Tamsanne's just being difficult. She knows our Princes owe it to the Great Twins to sanctify their marriages to the goddesses' cycle."

Tamsanne, eyes intent on the hearth-fire's flames, shrugged.

"Tielmark has been blessed with some strong leaders," she said. "Starting a new fifty-year cycle with a princely marriage has never hurt us."

"Not yet," Martin said softly. "And this in the face of the ever-present plotting by our former imperial sovereign to crush our independence."

"The Bissanties can plot all they like." Gaultry snorted. "They're too weak to carry a real campaign against us."

"That's true," Tamsanne said. "And a fighting man like you must know it."

"I've fought my share of summer campaigns against the Lanai," Martin admitted. "I don't guess Bissanty troops will ever follow them across our borders." Since Briern's day, the Bissanty had limited their attacks against Tielmark to sporadic campaigns against the Lanai, the tribal nation who lived high in the rugged mountains on Tielmark's easternmost border. The Lanai's summer fields lay in the alpine valleys near the Bissanty borders, and were vulnerable to Bissanty attack. In years when the Bissanty felt strong, they would send their soldiers to burn the Lanai fields, driving the tribes west into Tielmark in search of sustenance. "But Bissanty offers Tielmark threats other than physical invasion."

"Princess Corinne banished the last Bissanty provocateurs when she came into power after her wedding," Gaultry said. "Which is the main reason she ranks among Tielmark's greatest leaders."

"Did she?" Martin asked. "Then how is it that Tielmark has a half-Bissanty Chancellor now?"

Gaultry wasn't sure how to answer. She glanced at her aunt, but Tamsanne's attention was fixed deep in the hearth-flames. "Tielmark's Chancellor," she said slowly, "must be approved by the ducal council before taking office. We don't get all the news here at the border, and perhaps we hear even less out here in the woods, but my understanding is that Chancellor Heiratikus's Tielmaran connections far outweigh the burden of his foreign blood. His mother was Melaney Sevenage, one of the seven witches who helped old Princess Corinne consolidate power after her marriage — what's funny?"

Tamsanne had snorted, but she wouldn't answer when her niece pressed her.

"In any case, what has this got to do with Mervion?" Gaultry turned back to the dark soldier.

"Chancellor Heiratikus has taken complete control over the arrangements for the Prince's wedding. Publicly, this might seem innocuous enough. But privately, a great evil has started to move through the Prince's court. Heiratikus had the Prince sign warrants of arrest for three young women, one for each moon of this new year. The first two of these women are dead. The third woman is Mervion Blas."

He paused. Silence filled the room. Finally, a piece of wood, burning in the fire, dropped down in the grate: the small noise broke the moment.

"Are you suggesting that Benet, through his Chancellor, plans treason against Tielmark's gods?" Tamsanne said, her voice sharp as the crackling of fire. "That's treason in itself."

"I'm no traitor," Martin said proudly, his face filling with a pulse of anger, black and strong. "Above my liege lord, Prince Benet is my master, before the gods' eyes. But the Prince is no longer master of himself. If his Chancellor is not stopped, there will be more deaths, more madness."

"If you have proof—" Tamsanne began.

"Proof!" Martin exploded, throwing down his plate. "What proof could I hope to carry out here into these hinterlands that might convince you? Sorcery has taken our Prince; Chancellor Heiratikus's black sorcery. The process of our law has already been corrupted. The Duchess of Melaudiere, my own liege lord, tried to intervene to save the women the Chancellor seized. By law, she owns access to her sovereign. But the Chancellor barred her from even a public meeting where she might have argued her case.

"Louisette D'Arbey, the second to die, was like a daughter to Melaudiere. The Duchess, fighting back with her own magic, broke through a shield of sorcery and managed to see her once before her death. Louisette was raving mad, a broken shell. But even in her madness, a spell was left behind to guard her tongue, lest the least clue of the sorcerous trials she had endured at the Chancellor's hands should come to light.

"The day after the Duchess gleaned that vision, Louisette's broken body was discovered on Prince's Path, the terrace beneath the battlements of the Chancellor's winter offices. She died slowly: her death agony was so great it broke the gag-spell on her speech. She gibbered to the man who found her that Heiratikus intended to make all Tielmark his slave; that, son to father, Heiratikus had pledged to return Tielmark to the enslavement of his father's land."

"It is a strong trust indeed that values a madwoman's ranting over the pledges of loyalty made by the Prince's closest advisor," Tamsanne said.

"Louisette wasn't mad until the Chancellor broke her! To toy like that with a woman's life and soul is the highest treason!" Martin was out of his chair, fury raising his voice. "Tielmark revolted against Bissanty rule three hundred years past to free itself from just such arbitrary abuse of power. To this day, the Bissanty Emperor sanctifies his every edict in his subjects' blood; cruel offerings and depravities are his due. That's not the law our Prince is pledged to uphold here in Tielmark!"

The old woman drew back into herself before the barrage of Martin's words and angry gestures, wrinkles deepening, her very flesh shrinking into itself along her bones. Gaultry, seeing her aunt's change, put aside the empty plate she'd clutched throughout the debate, and edged into the fireplace nook.

"Martin —" she said warningly. His indignation was so great he didn't notice.

"My life, my blood, are pledged to protect my Prince, just as the Prince's life and blood are pledged to protect Tielmark. I don't sit quiet and safe in a deep forest, ignoring rising threats to my homeland! If you doubt my motives in coming to you —"

He advanced a step too near. Tamsanne tired of his bluster. She made a small, impatient gesture with one hand.

The big soldier was back in his chair, the palms of his hands locked to his knees. There was no tingle to betray the working of magic, no hint of force or violence — but there Martin was, back in his seat.

It was to his credit that he did not try to fight the spell, and more to his credit that he recovered his composure instead of continuing to lose it. "I'm wrong to raise my voice to you." He had regained

Thomas had turned forty, Arleon had granted him the living at Blas Lodge, a mellow old hunting house at the edge of the forest, north of Paddleways.

It was there that he had met his first wife, Severine. A wild forest-witch with no court connections, Severine had been an un-suitable match for a man who should have consolidated his social advancement through a marriage into the hedge-gentry, and, in-deed, the marriage had proved ill-fated. Severine had died less than a year later, as she birthed their daughters. Thomas's second mar-riage, contracted bare months after Severine's death, had been a more conventional arrangement with the daughter of one of the Duke of Arleon's knights. Gilles, Thomas's son by his second wife, was less than a year and a half younger than the daughters of his first marriage.

Following his remarriage, Thomas Blas had fully entrusted Mer-vion and Gaultry to Tamsanne's care. They'd shared one month with their father at the end of every summer, until they reached their woman's year, at fourteen. That was the year the Duke of Arleon had made him a knight and Thomas had told Tamsanne that he couldn't have the girls to Blas Lodge again.

Gaultry's face went hot, thinking back to that dreadful morn-ing—the memory of which her father had given Martin, prime among all his memories of his daughters. That day, she had tried to demand an explanation from her father, desperate to know why he was shutting them out of his life. He had refused to answer. She closed her eyes, seeing again the image her father had re-tained of her. So angry. So wild. Every mannerless word she had said must have been more proof to him that his woods-raised daughters had no place in his new life as a titled gentleman.

"So it was only when you found out that the Chancellor's new prisoner was Mervion Blas, Thomas's daughter, that you realized you had to follow the geas and find his other daughter?" Tamsanne asked. "You haven't met Mervion yourself, that's clear."

"Why do you say that?"

"Gaultry and Mervion are twins," Tamsanne said. "I think you've blinded yourself to that fact long enough."

"Twins? The impress Thomas Blas laid on me showed only one girl—"

"Two girls. One face. Didn't you wonder at the geas's strength? Coming from a dying man—a dying man who was not a practitioner of magic—didn't you and those who sent you here wonder at its power?"

"Twins?"

"We're not so alike now," Gaultry said. "But as children—"

"Put bluntly, you've taken a geas for the protection of two daughters and compressed it into a vow of protection centered on one only. Small wonder it sits so heavily on you!"

"Aunt Tamsanne—" Gaultry began, distressed.

"Be quiet, Gaultry. This young man speaks too loosely of vows and blood. Bring me the Rhasan cards. I find I want to ask the gods a question. Or two."

Gaultry scrambled to her feet, increasingly worried. The Rhasan cards were part of her aunt's most powerful, and most carefully used, magic, a magic that dated back past the first Prince of Tielmark's rule, back past even the rule of the Bissanty Empire, to the days when wandering tribes had moved freely through all the lands that bordered the Great Sea. Tamsanne's deck was very old, and had been in her maternal line for generations.

The deck was stored in a bone coffer in Tamsanne's private cabinet. The cabinet had four shelves, each carved of a different wood. The Rhasan deck coffer always sat on the top shelf, the shelf that was built of a blood-red piece of oak. It was wood that had washed across the Great Rush from the Changing Lands, Tamsanne said. Gaultry hastily retrieved the deck, still in its coffer, and carried it, unopened, to her aunt. Drawing up a short stool, Tamsanne sat down opposite their guest.

"I'm going to show you some cards," the old woman told him, carefully opening the coffer and drawing forth the cards. "Because I can't decide if you are a rogue or a fool. The geas on you suggests that my nieces' father, together with the Great Twins, thought you the appropriate protector of my nieces. You have already twisted the geas so that you are bonded to protect only one niece. Despite what you will find to be the unpleasantness of this casting, I need to see how your futures lie together. Make yourself ready."

Martin twisted in the chair. "This isn't necessary," he said. "I'll swear on all the Great Twelve if you like—"

"Stand behind him, Gaultry," Tamsanne said.

Gaultry did as she was told, her heart thumping. Tamsanne meant to have her share Martin's card. That act in itself could strengthen the geas-bond.

Tamsanne opened her hands, showing the cards, and solemnly shuffled the deck.

The cards were not exceptional in themselves. Martin shuddered with relief, as though he had expected something more impressive. Crudely printed with black and red ink, the brittle rectangles of paper were hardly a sight to inspire awe. They looked like something carters would play with after an evening's drinking.

Tamsanne turned the top card over.

"Martin Stalker," she said.

It was the Black Wolf. For one moment the card was a pale yellow rectangle, the wolf a coarse woodcut drawing: big teeth, ears and paws, a long stave grasped between toothy jaws—then, like a cresting wave, the image swamped Martin and Gaultry both. The cottage disappeared. Gaultry flinched, and found herself trapped in a vision-world of flat yellow edges, pierced by cold blacks. Martin was the massive black wolf that stood before her, dull blond glints in his fur, an expression of haunted despair in the long, slanted eyes. As she watched, the wolf snarled, dropped the stave, and seized his own tail, saber teeth mercilessly gnawing the flesh to the bone, self-annihilating and wild. The young huntress recoiled, and threw up an arm, as if to protect herself.

Tamsanne replaced the card at the bottom of the deck, and the yellow landscape was gone.

Martin was bolt-upright in his chair, his face deathly white. He covered his eyes with his hands—seeming not to realize that Tamsanne had released the spell that held him in his seat.

"So we see you have not come to harm Gaultry—which we already knew.

"Now here is Gaultry, because it is fair that you should know her soul as she now knows yours.

"Gaultry Blas," she said, invoking her niece's full name.

Another card. Gaultry had girded herself for the Huntress—the goddess Elianté's card. The only other time Gaultry had seen Tamsanne read cards from the Rhasan deck, the old woman had pulled cards for both her nieces—the same troubled year that Thomas had abandoned them, for once and for all, to her care. Gaultry had come up as the Huntress Elianté, Mervion as the Lady-Queen Emiera. That had seemed right to them both, as young twins who worshiped the Great Twins.

But instead it was an unfamiliar card. A flower. An exotic flower, printed on blue paper. Gaultry puzzled through the archaic script at the card's bottom: the Orchid.

The image unfurled and seized her. Martin's card had burst across her in plain colors: yellow, black, and red. But with this card, her own, the vision-world exploded upon her like a flaming firework. The flower was not a grown orchid: it was a seed. She was the seed. A seed slipped secretly into the hollow of a black oak's roots; a seed planted and nurtured in the heart of the forest, rooting, settling, sending up a single pale stalk. A first leaf unfurled, then a second, and then a single gorgeous bud had dimpled and puckered into shape. A blush of purple darkened the pale green. The lip of the blossom creased gently, slit open: the golden anthers within quivered, straining to reach the light—

The card was back at the bottom of the deck and the image was gone. Tamsanne was trembling, her fingers awkward, her body more like an old woman's than Gaultry had ever seen. Something in Gaultry's card had shaken her so badly that she almost dropped the deck.

"And here," Tamsanne said, her voice brittle with worry, "is the one who is set against you."

Martin and Gaultry cringed. But this time, the stiff rectangle of paper remained just that. A card. The Holy Bird. The card of the mother goddess, Llara. Patroness of the Bissanty Empire, in days

long past Tielmark's highest god. Clean white bird with a black out-
line on clean white card.

Tamsanne looked into their surprised faces and barked a short,
unhappy laugh. The cards were back in the coffer, the coffer was
shut. "Did you truly think to see your enemy?

"Put the cards away, Gaultry. I've seen well beyond enough for
one night."

"Tell us what you saw," Martin said to Tamsanne. "Did you see
what we saw, or more?" Tamsanne, rising stiffly to return to her seat
in the half-shadows, paused.

"You, Martin Stalker, came here hoping for freedom from a
geas—and to discover why Mervion Blas survived a test where
others failed. If you have found more here than you expected it is
not for me to tell you why. Today I pulled a dangerous card for
Gaultry—or perhaps for all of us here in Tielmark. I also pulled a
dangerous card for you.

"You're a strong man, Martin Stalker. It would be well for you to
relearn the role of protector. Whatever the secrets be that turned
you from protector to self-devourer—they are safe, if you can call
them that, in your own heart. What more would you ask of me?"

"Give me your blessing to bring Gaultry back with me to Melaudiere," Martin said. "If she is Mervion's twin, the Duchess may be
able to scry her, and determine what the Chancellor intends."

"She'd be safer remaining here."

"If Mervion is in danger, I won't hide here like a coward,"
Gaultry broke in hotly. "I'll do what needs to be done to help her."

"I didn't say I'd discourage you," Tamsanne said, extending her
gnarled hands to the fire as though she felt a sudden chill. "Not that
throwing yourself into unnecessary danger is the same as helping
Mervion. Nevertheless, visiting Melaudiere under Martin's protection could be the wisest course of action. Gabrielle of Melaudiere—"
Tamsanne shot Martin an ambiguous look that might have had a
little mischief in it. "Gabrielle of Melaudiere has had fifty years to
build her reputation as a seer and enchantress. Martin may be correct in saying she may be able to see the role the Chancellor has writ
for Mervion in his plots."

"Then I'll go," Gaultry said.

"Quickly decided," Tamsanne said dampeningly. "I'm sure Mervion would be happy to know she has such a ready champion. Doesn't it concern you, not knowing how Mervion was delivered from your brother's house into this Bissanty Chancellor's power?" Tamsanne turned to Martin. "Indeed, how was it that Mervion came into the Chancellor's power?"

"One of the Chancellor's underlings brought her to Princeport."

"Alone?"

"Anisia Blas, her marriage-sister, was with her." He paused. A half-angry look flitted across his face, as though he resented having to make any explanation. "It was through Anisia Blas that the Duchess came to know that Mervion had survived the Chancellor's testing."

Gaultry had met her young marriage-sister only once. Gaultry and Mervion had gone to Blas Lodge after the news of their father's death had reached them, and attended the grim winter burial. By then Gilles and his young wife had already been in possession of her father's holdings. Anisia was gentle but, to Gaultry's mind, a slightly silly girl, too young to be married, too young to be playing chatelaine to a substantial rural household. It was annoying to Gaultry to have to acknowledge that such feelings were colored by envy. When Anisia, with Gilles backing her, had invited her newfound marriage-sisters to join her household, Mervion had been disappointingly eager to accept. "They'll need my help," she had told Gaultry, trying to allay her younger twin's jealousy. "And you won't need me at Tamsanne's until the midsummer harvest."

Anisia, all unwittingly, had fed Mervion's growing hunger for new sights and challenges, a hunger that life at Tamsanne's could not satisfy. For that, Gaultry had found it hard to like the girl.

"Where is Anisia now?" Gaultry asked.

Martin shrugged. "Still in Princeport, for all I know. Unless the Duchess has managed to free her."

"Gaultry must not go to Princeport," Tamsanne said firmly. "Princeport would be too risky. Bringing the twins together where the Chancellor might bind them in his power — it's too dangerous, particularly given that we don't know what is at stake."

"At stake?" Martin said. "Tielmark's freedom from Bissanty is the stake, and the gods' support of our Prince. We can't survive as a free nation without the Great Twins' support."

Tamsanne stood, looking deep into the embers of the cooking fire, as though the dying flames could give her an answer. "Melaudiere may be able to say why Gaultry pulled the Orchid card."

"Why do you think I pulled it, Aunt Tamsanne? Does it mean the Huntress has turned her face from me?"

"I don't know what it means. I know only that it portends a great threat to Tielmark. Whatever pledges—" Tamsanne looked sharply at Martin—"any of us have made to our Prince or our gods."

chapter **3**

▼

Long after Martin had been put to sleep in the attic over the chimney, Tamsanne woke Gaultry from her pallet of blankets by the fire.

"You're going out?" Tamsanne was dressed in a dark shawl and long skirts.

"He's asleep. I'm going down to the fen to pray."

Gaultry pushed her covers aside and put her bare feet on the cold stone of the floor. The fire had burned down to banked embers. It was past midnight. "Let me come with you."

"I want to go alone." Tamsanne brushed her niece's tumbled hair back from her worried face. "Stay. Rest yourself for tomorrow."

Gaultry reluctantly settled back into her bed. "He talks a lot about pledges and vows. And blood."

"He's a young fool. All Tielmarans owe it to themselves to support their Prince. Even before they owe it to the Great Twins."

"In the woods, the first question he asked about you was to know your blood. I said you thought deeds, not blood, were what gave a person importance."

Tamsanne sighed. "In Tielmark, blood itself can be a deed. Vows can pass from parent to child."

"That's not the worst way to pass on a promise."

"Isn't it?" Tamsanne stared up at the little wooden door that led to the attic. "You think the geas your father laid on that young man is worse?"

"Martin hates it! I hate it too! To be forced to wear an unasked-for magic harness—"

"It saved you in the forest. I doubt either of you regret that. And it may save you again before this business finds a closure."

Gaultry stared stubbornly at her aunt. She would not play the child and say she preferred violation to owing her father a debt of gratitude for having sent Martin to be a protector, but that was very near what she felt. "Father abandoned Mervion and me when we most needed him," she said. "I won't forgive him for that."

Getting to sleep again after Tamsanne left her was not easy.

"**H**ere," Tamsanne said. "Put it on."

It was a little after sunrise. Martin was out in the stable, readying his horse. Tamsanne had been out all night, with only Bellows for company.

Gaultry touched the delicate ring of mottled-gray stone that her aunt offered to her, then took it in her hand. It was a traveler's amulet. The stone ring was warm on one face, cool on the other. The young huntress looked round for her aunt's familiar. The old dog, returning with Tamsanne, had retired to a corner by the fire and curled into a tight ball. His dark fur seemed thin, touches of blue skin showing on his ears and tail. His doggy eyes, sensing Gaultry's gaze and cracking open to return her stare, were bloodshot and weary.

"It is strong," Tamsanne admitted, seeing where Gaultry was looking. "Don't take it off until after you find Mervion. Or until after you've burnt it to a cinder using it to protect yourself."

Gaultry tied the ring onto a leather thong and pulled the thong over her head.

"Don't go beyond Melaudiere's seat if you can help it." Tamsanne made the spiral of the goddess-sign and took her niece's hand. The image of the Orchid card, the pale plant growing shyly, deep in the crevice of the black oak, flared briefly between them. "Why you pulled that card is the question that most needs answering. Concentrate on that above all."

"I'll make it my first concern after finding out why Gilles sent Mervion to Princeport in the first place," Gaultry promised. It had been agreed, the night before, that Martin and Gaultry would stop past Blas Lodge on their way to Melaudiere, to discover if Gilles, Gaultry's half-brother, was unharmed.

After a quick breakfast, Gaultry swiftly completed her own travel preparations. There was little for her to do. Dressing in her sturdiest tunic and hose, she tied her bright hair under a cloth cap, and made a satchel of her short hunting bow, some underclothes, and her second-best dress—her blue market dress needed repairs after the previous day's escapades. She threw the long butter-nut brown cloak that Mervion had spun for her over the lot, and was ready.

This was her usual hunting costume. She cut a striking figure wearing it. When Martin brought his horse to the cottage door, he gave her an appreciative look. "You're quite the young woods-queen this morning. How's the knee?"

Tamsanne and Gaultry, thinking over the journey ahead, had decided to dispense with pretense. "Recovered," Gaultry said primly, ignoring the compliment as she helped him tie her bag onto the crupper of his saddle. "I won't have to ride with you today."

He raised his eyebrows, teasing her a little. "Don't you want to share a saddle with me?"

Her cheeks went hot, and she turned nervously to Tamsanne. No, she didn't want to share his saddle. The pulse of her father's geas-magic waxing and waning in him, responding to her every mood, was too disturbing. She didn't want to think on her father, on how or why he had trapped this man into service. That was a cycle that could only make her more upset—and Martin more upset as his feelings tuned to hers.

"Start today with Gaultry running," Tamsanne said, coming to her niece's rescue. "You'll make better speed with her running than by fatiguing your animal all day with the weight of two riders."

"Fine," Martin said. "So long as her knee can take the pace."

"Give my regards to Gilles," Tamsanne said, as Martin made a last adjustment to his saddle and swung up. "I'll be thinking of you both."

"And of Mervion too, I hope," said Gaultry, giving her aunt a clumsy hug. Martin turned his horse for the forest, making a final salute.

Tamsanne stood at the cottage door, not moving until they were hidden from her line of sight by the trees.

They started with a gentle jog, Gaultry leading the way through the maze of narrow forest paths that led down towards the main track. It was a warm day, and the gentle jogging was easy and pleasant as the sun slowly rose in the sky, filtering long slanting rays down through the forest branches.

Gaultry, her eyes on the rubbly surface of the track, soon found her thoughts drifting to the leg of the journey that lay ahead. She had been to and through Paddleways village many times, and ranged beyond it often enough, the times she'd served as a tracker for the villagers during their seasonal hunts. But she could count on the fingers of one hand the number of times she'd been past Paddleways to Blas Lodge.

Her strongest memory of Blas Lodge was from her last visit as a child, when her father had still been alive, and a loving, if distant, presence in the twins' lives. That had been the summer after Prince Benet's coronation. It had been an unusual summer. Benet's father, Ginvers, was dead of a poisoned wound he'd taken in battle during the summer campaign against the Lanai. Prince Ginvers's death had caused disruptions that had echoed out to the farthest reaches of Tielmark. Instead of spending his usual month at Tamsanne's, Thomas Blas had brought his young daughters to summer at his own house. He'd shared his table with them, and even encouraged them to befriend their younger half-brother. The wonderful time they had spent together that summer had only intensified the surprise and pain their father had brought them the next year. Gaultry and Mervion had cried many nights, remembering that long summer month at Blas Lodge and wondering what they had done that had convinced their father that they could have no place there.

Of course Gaultry's most recent trip to Blas Lodge had been for her father's burial, barely two months past. The traveling, through the worst of the winter snow, had not been easy, and the news of Thomas Blas's untimely death had rested heavily on both sisters.

But for Gaultry, the return journey had been far worse. She'd known then that Mervion was coming home to Tamsanne's only to pack, eager to return to Blas Lodge to take up her place with Gilles and Anisia. Despite Mervion's assurances that the "visit," as she called it, would be only for the spring months, Gaultry had known that Mervion was unlikely to return to Tamsanne's on a permanent basis.

For Gaultry, the two days at Blas Lodge had been peculiarly wretched. Thomas Blas was put hastily in the ground on the first day. The second was preoccupied by arrangements for Mervion to join the lodge household. Gilles and Anisia, married less than two months, had seemed young and frightened, full of childish trepidations, their mourning for Thomas Blas more a matter of alarm that they had been plunged into the charge of an isolated rural estate than of grief at his untimely death. Gaultry, already a little jealous at the depth of their grief—they had been close to Thomas Blas in a way that she and Mervion had been denied—had been hurt by Mervion's eagerness to leave Tamsanne's to help them settle into Blas Lodge and life at the edge of Arleon Forest.

The young huntress had spent most of her time at the lodge yearning for home, and yearning uselessly for Mervion to want to be going home too. Unlike Mervion, whose magic had always taken a social bent, Gaultry drew strength from the cover of the deep-woods forest, and away from the heart of that source, she felt vulnerable. Mervion had always been the talker for the pair of them on market days—indeed, up until the past spring, when Gaultry had gone by herself to help with the villagers' seasonal hunt, without Mervion to help her, she had always felt shy and awkward, despite the villagers' friendliness.

On that return journey, through the depths of the winter snow, a selfish part of Gaultry had been forced to acknowledge privately that with Mervion gone, she herself was going to have to make more of an effort: in the village, with Tamsanne, and with any newcomers who came through Arleon Forest. She and Mervion had come close

to quarreling over it. Adjusting to life without Mervion's support
had been a real challenge. To an outside observer, it might have
seemed that Gaultry had taken over Mervion's business in Paddleways village easily enough, but, behind her facade of calm, the tran-
sition had been painful. Compared with Mervion's charming ease of
manners, Gaultry felt that her own efforts at sociability were painfully awkward.

Just as she found it painfully awkward to exchange pleasantries
with the man at whose horse's side she now trotted.

"Do you think Tamsanne's right, sending us to my brother's
before we go to Melaudiere?" she asked.

Martin, intent on gauging Gaultry's stamina, had been moving
his mare at short trot-and-walk stints, leaving the young woman to
her thoughts. Her question broke his concentration, startling him.

"Blas Lodge is on our route north," he said. "According to my
liege Melaudiere, your marriage-sister risked her neck in passing on
what she knew concerning your sister's torture—and Heiratikus's
hunt for you. Without Anisia Blas, I would not have arrived in
Arleon Forest in time to save you from Reido's men. Visiting your
brother will be risky—but your aunt is right. We—you—owe it to
your kin to stop there."

They reached the outskirts of the village well before noon,
agreeing together to take the track around the village rather than
pass through it. Lunch was a thin meal, cheese and bread, eaten
under a tree as they watched a farmer and his two sons working their
field. Martin ate without speaking. Gaultry suspected he was bored
with their slow progress—or picking up on her own boredom.

"We could go faster," she told him, when they finished eating
and he got up to pack the remains away.

"Oh?" He looked pointedly at her still-bandaged knee.

Gaultry flushed, wishing her aunt had let her unbind it. "It's
stiff, yes, but we should press on."

"We should," he agreed. "We don't know where the men who
attacked you yesterday have regrouped—or even if they've regrouped. The sooner we're past your brother's house and on the road
to Melaudiere, the happier I'll feel."

"Then let's run a-ways," Gaultry said. "Let's run now." Guessing that he would agree, she leapt up and began to run, stealing a lead as he fumbled to buckle the last saddlebag.

Once in the saddle, he caught her easily, pushing the horse a few paces past her on the track. The look he shot over his shoulder as he crowded past was somewhere between a smile and a challenge—she smiled back, and ran faster, bringing herself level with his stirrup.

They raced on together past the last outlying fields north of Paddleways, past hay fields that didn't need spring plowing, past the village's northern screen of orchards, and back into wooded country. It was not very long before Gaultry began to regret the demanding pace she had teased Martin into setting for them. His pretty mare seemed tireless. She trotted briskly, her head held proud and high, her slender legs keeping a relentlessly even rhythm that it became increasingly difficult for Gaultry to match.

Having provoked the game to start, Gaultry's vein of stubbornness forced her to continue long after she began to want a rest. Shooting a quick glimpse at Martin's calm profile, Gaultry wished with increasing fervor that he'd think to spare her, and suggest a rest. The dust from the road permeated her clothes, then her nose, then her throat. She met his eye again and saw that he was half-hiding a smile.

"We aren't going to get there in one day, are we?" she called up, her voice choppy despite her effort to be casual. "Can we have a rest?" They'd reached a crossing, a small wooden bridge over a stream with a rocky bed. The water looked deliciously cool and welcoming, the grass by the side of the road particularly soft and inviting.

"If you like." He grinned.

"Yes!" Gaultry threw herself down next to the bridge. There was a wide V of dampness down her back. Taking a covert look at the mare, she was relieved to see that she too was grateful for the stop. Martin, to her slight annoyance, was relaxed and cool.

"Quite a test." He slid out of his saddle, rewarded the mare with a brief pat, and came to sit above Gaultry on the wooden rail of the bridge. "I begin to see how you managed to make headway against Reido and his men."

"I wasn't racing just now," Gaultry said, not wanting to explain about the dog she'd taken strength and speed from the day before. Despite the geas, the Rhasan card of the night before had shown her there was much he was keeping hidden. It wouldn't do to be fully open to him.

"The gods help me if you had been."

Gaultry smiled. "I've run wounded deer to their finish, and foxes to their dens. But I can't outlast a horse like yours." Not without a spell to help me, she added privately.

"Does Mervion run with you when she's home?"

Gaultry shook her head and grinned. "She's more subtle than I am. She makes things come running to her. I wish I had more of her spirit in me—I'd find myself getting into a lot less trouble. Except—" She frowned, bending to rub her legs so they wouldn't cramp. "Except in this last matter."

She looked up at him. "Mervion and I follow Elianté and Emiera, the holy twins. Mervion's always been for Emiera, the Lady-Queen—and I for Elianté, the Huntress. If there wasn't such a strong division of ways between us . . . maybe Mervion wouldn't have left Arleon Forest, and been taken by the Chancellor's men."

"That's a question you can ask Melaudiere when you meet her," said Martin. "If you think past choices are worth revisiting."

"Tamsanne knew the Duchess," Gaultry said, changing the subject. "I guess she's old enough that even out in Arleon Forest she's heard of all the court players. But I haven't. Who is she?"

"Melaudiere? She's the third highest of the ducal council, behind Basse Demaine and Haute-Tielmark—but if you count years, she's held rank longer than any of them."

"What does that mean?"

"She's the same generation as Melaney Sevenage, the Chancellor's mother. She was one of the Common Brood—the seven witches who served at old Princess Corinne's wedding. That means she should have her Prince's ear," Martin said seriously. "As she felt that she did, until just before the new year, when things changed very quickly and Heiratikus seized control."

"Tamsanne must have known that," Gaultry said, wishing that her aunt wasn't so fond of keeping secrets. "And how did you come to serve the Duchess?"

"I took a pledge of fealty."

Gaultry sat up, annoyed. "That's no answer. Was it Melaudiere who tried to remove your geas?"

"Leave that, Gaultry. We've established that my trying to get the geas removed was misguided."

Tamsanne, Gaultry thought, had been right to warn her to keep her distance from this man. His mouth was a hard line, and she could see his temper was rising. It seemed they couldn't help striking sparks off each other, even as they exchanged the simplest of questions.

"Don't be angry."

The responsive switch of emotion in the winter gray eyes, from ice to a quickening warmth, made her curse him and her father both. Looking into his handsome wolf's eyes, she too quickly lost any sense of what was geas-magic and what was Martin.

"Elianté's blood," she snapped, and turned away. "I'm already tired of looking at you and seeing that damn geas-magic staring back!"

Seeking escape, she went down to the little stream's edge and shucked off her shoes. Wading in up to her knees, she let the water cool her, wishing her temper could be as easily soothed as a pair of travel-worn feet.

When she returned to the bridge Martin had cut up some fresh bread and cheese.

"You should stop worrying about what your father did to me, or what I did to the geas." He handed her a slab of bread. "Having met you, knowing there are real reasons you need my protection, the geas already fits more comfortably. Knowing that Mervion should have been a part of it helps. It's nobody's fault that I compressed a geas meant for twins onto you alone. It just happened."

"I stole Mervion's protection," Gaultry said, bitter. "If you could just meet Mervion, you'd understand. If she was in my place, you'd *still* probably find the geas had tailored itself onto me. She'd convince you it was all meant for my protection, and give up the part that was meant for her."

He smiled. "She sounds like someone worth knowing."

Would she have wanted to share this man's protection with

Mervion? Gaultry cast a shy look at him as she ate her sandwich.
Her father had chosen a fine man to champion them—or was she
merely prejudiced in his favor because, despite his pangs of temper,
he was so responsive to her moods?

She went back down to the stream to wash her hands knowing
he watched her closely as she did so. Beneath the geas, which exposed his emotions to her so constantly, he was a very private
man—a quality that made the geas rest all the more heavily on
him. He resisted sharing even the simplest of information.

Why, for example, wouldn't he tell her how he had come to
serve Melaudiere?

She could use the geas to force him to confide in her. The idea
repelled her even as it came to her. Why he was affecting her like
this, making her think such pettiness?

He stood on the track by his horse and rubbed the strong line of
muscle that ran up her neck under her mane, encouraging her with
soft words for the next leg of the journey. The sun shone on his dark
hair, his strong hands cupped the mare's head as he whispered into
her pricking ears. He was a well-made man: tall, strong, and handsome, and perhaps a little like her memories of her father, before he
had turned on his daughters and abandoned them.

A lump rose in her throat. Martin would not have been there to
help her if he had not had the geas bond on him. How ironic that
her father, who had not honored the bond of blood between them,
had been the one to put such a powerful bond of magic on this man.

"Would you mind if we walked the next piece?" She climbed
back up onto the track and gave the mare a brief pat, trying to draw
a little comfort from its calm animal body. "I don't want to run
now."

"You could ride while I run, if it's change you're looking for."

"I'd fall off. I don't know the first thing about riding."

"Then sit on her at a walk. I'll teach you while I stretch my legs."

He was more soldier than gentleman, she thought, pleased by
the offer. A gentleman wouldn't presume to teach a forest-girl to
ride. At least there was that difference between Martin and her father! Something in her feeling oddly relieved, Gaultry grinned and
let him help her clamber into the saddle.

The remainder of the afternoon flew by. Despite his sometimes forbidding manners, the big soldier was a patient teacher, with a good sense of detail. He showed her how to sit properly, tuck her knees in, and keep her hands low and firm on the reins. He was amused by the concentration she brought to the lesson, not understanding that her will to learn everything at once overlay a desire to familiarize herself with a new animal, a new animal over which she could practice her magic, borrowing speed, strength, and stamina when she had need of them.

Gaultry had little knowledge of horses. In her rejection of the things her father had loved—Thomas Blas had been born to a family of ostlers and grooms, and he had worked with horses from his childhood—she had dismissed the animal as fast and flashy, better for little more than the superficial enhancement of a man's prestige. But Martin's mare had impressed her with its spirited show of endurance. During the morning's run, the mare had known that Gaultry was racing her, and she had shaken her dark mane, and stomped her neatly clipped hooves, proud, and let Gaultry know with every quiver of muscle that she wouldn't submit to coming second in a race against a paltry human. This was an animal that Gaultry could respect.

By the time evening came, Gaultry had learned enough that she could feel the mare's spirit floating in the lithe body beneath her, and she could have channeled it into her body if she had so desired. Triumphant, the young huntress lay her palms flat on the animal's shoulders, reaching into the flesh to touch it delicately with her own mind, laughing as the mare rolled a suspicious eye at her.

—*Not today, my beauty*—she assured the mare silently, drawing gently back.

"You've got a good rapport," Martin called up, startling her. "Now relax, and concentrate on your seat."

"What about going faster, or jumping?" she asked.

"I won't let you learn to jump on this horse."

When it was almost dark, they made camp in a pine copse not far from the road. Martin both selected the site and insisted on doing the work to set up the camp. He knew how to get a fire going without fussing, and how to cook camp food so that it tasted of something other than cinders. It was a pleasant, well-sheltered refuge.

"I'll take the first watch."

Gaultry was just tired enough not to argue. He settled himself with his back against a tall hemlock. Gaultry kicked together a pile of pine needles to make herself a soft place to sleep, and unbound her hair.

"Don't stare," she said, lying down and curling into her cloak.

"I'm not staring," he said softly. "I'm wondering."

"Wonder while you're looking somewhere else."

It seemed her eyes had barely closed, her body scarcely relaxed, when Martin's mare started and gave an anxious snort, jerking on her tether. Gaultry, shaken into wakefulness, stumbled to her feet, grabbing reflexively for her bow. A dark shape loomed over the fire, scattering sparks.

"Martin!" A horrible flurry of horses and men filled the clearing.

"Save yourself! Get back under the trees!" There was a terrible building fury in his voice, cut through with geas-magic. Gaultry whirled away, trying to follow the order. A man on a tall horse blocked her. As he came down off the horse, she darted back a pace and nocked an arrow in her bow.

He didn't have a weapon, and he was fool enough not to expect her to use hers.

Her arrow took him in the chest, with a horrible splash of gore. He fell, shrieking, and did not get up.

Behind him, another. Gaultry recognized this one from the previous day's attack. She glanced around. Three other men, all mounted. That left two of Reido's band of seven unaccounted for.

Martin slipped in behind her, protecting her back, and the onslaught was suddenly checked. His sword flashed out, clearing a space in front of him. Gaultry nocked another arrow, trying to ignore the muffled crying of the man she'd shot.

Their attackers had lost the element of surprise.

"They haven't got armor on," she whispered. "Or at least the one I shot didn't."

"More fools they," he said. "Not that I do either."

Their attackers hung back, wary, and waited for an opening. The man Gaultry had shot was on his knees, trying to crawl away.

Finally one man stepped forward, breaking the stalemate.

"Leave her to us, Stalker-man, and we'll let you live."

"They know who you are!"

Martin ignored Gaultry and menaced the man with his sword. "I'll kill any one of you who dares so much as to touch her."

They attacked, lightning-fast. One man charged with his horse, forcing Gaultry and Martin to choose between losing the protection of each other's backs or being trampled. Gaultry's arrow skittered harmlessly into the trees. She caught a quick glimpse of Martin's sword flashing out to disembowel the rider. She reached for a fresh arrow, but her quiver, hastily thrown on her shoulders, skewed out of reach, and she wasted precious seconds fumbling. There was time only to grab a single arrow before she took a blow in her ribs that made her gasp and drop the bow.

"Take her!"

There were two of them. She got one in the groin with a knee, bucking like a deer as the other grabbed her shoulder. This one got his face too close. She struck out with the arrow. The point ripped his cheek. He hit her in the face and she had to let go of that as well.

"Bitch-Queen!" The man couldn't hold her alone. "Stop wetting yourself and give me a hand" — this to the comrade she'd kneed in the groin. That worthy clutched at her legs. She kicked out again and caught him in the stomach.

"Gods, she's strong!"

"Take her arms. I'll get her legs." With their combined strength, they wrestled her to the ground. Her hair flew wild in the struggle, and tangled painfully in the melee. The man she'd kicked seized a thick handful and snapped her head back. It felt as if he'd broken her neck, but she went on struggling, scrabbling at the ground for a stick, a stone — anything she could use to protect herself.

"They're not holding him!" There was panic in the man's voice as he glanced across to where Martin was wreaking havoc on the rest of the party.

"Knife to her throat. It'll keep him off." The words were like a splash of cold water. Gaultry stopped her panicked struggling. She clenched one fist into her stomach and began to pray, calling a spell, a bane so fierce it would make both men regret they'd dared raise a hand against her. Her fear and her anger would fire the spell—

The man who held her legs let go suddenly and threw up an arm, trying to shield himself, only to have his guard shattered by Martin's sword. The remaining man let out a cry—cut short, as Martin scrambled across Gaultry's fallen body to finish him. The little copse of pines went deathly quiet.

Gaultry climbed dizzily to her feet, appalled by the slaughter. In the red light of the fading embers of the now-scattered fire, Martin was a demon, his dark hair sleek against his skull, his blade black with blood, his eyes pools of violence. Gaultry had seen plenty of forest savagery in her day—chases and pack fights and animal squabbles for territory, and even merciless hunts for outlaws and murderers—but nothing compared to this, one man cutting down others as if they were wheat before a scythe. An uncontrollable fit of trembling seized her. The witch's bane that she'd called in anger and left uncast pulsed threateningly in her hand, wouldn't fade. Feeding from her fear, it took on an uncomfortable, pulsing life, burning, uncontrollable, in her palms, waiting to be cast—

Martin did not, could not, understand. "Gaultry, calm down."

"You killed them. All of them." She stared wildly at the shattered bodies, the spreading damp of blood.

"What would you have had me do?"

"They weren't trying to kill me."

"They were trying to kill *me*. They would have killed *me* and taken *you*." His eyes were hot, dangerous. He took her by the shoulders and shook her, trying to stem her rising hysteria, lest she whip them both into panic. "Are you saying that you wanted that to happen?"

"Don't touch me! You should have offered them quarter—" Gaultry wrung her hands, trying to stand free. If she touched him, the spell would take him.

"They wouldn't have honored it." He loosed her abruptly, his battle-flushed face hurt and angry, and looked away, around the darkened clearing, the wreck and bloody carnage grimly lit by the dying embers. "Believe me, they wouldn't have honored it."

Gaultry wrung her hands, trying to turn the bane aside, fighting now to turn the power she'd called back into herself.

"This has become a foul place," he said, sensing her upset, but at a loss to understand. "If we must argue, let's do it somewhere where we don't have an audience of the dead."

The spell dimmed, and seemed to quiet. Gaultry almost burst into tears with relief. She didn't want to argue with Martin about the attack. Not now. She recovered her bow and the arrow she'd dropped when the man had hit her. As for her killing arrow, she snapped off the vane with its distinctive red feathers and left the rest of the shaft in the dead man's chest.

"Maybe I should take one of their horses," she said, looking dubiously at the skittish shapes that lingered just outside the fire's light.

"That's the most sensible suggestion you've made yet."

Gaultry was too shaken to make a decision. Martin picked for her: a big sorrel mare with a black nose. They cut the saddles from the remaining horses and sent them running into the woods. Martin would have searched the bodies, but the suggestion nauseated Gaultry, so they left them where they lay, unmolested. Neither had words for the other as they picked their way carefully along the dark track, and left the death-site behind them.

Half a mile down the road, they found another sheltered spot. Still without speaking, they gathered a fresh pile of kindling. Martin built a new fire.

As the flames leapt up, Gaultry saw, for the first time, the spreading stain of blood on Martin's shirt.

"You're hurt."

"I took a cut on my ribs. It's fine."

His face was white with pain. "Martin," she said, her revulsion against the violence in him shading to concern. "Sit down. I'll bind it." She opened her satchel, and pulled out the bandage Tamsanne had prepared the night before. "I don't need this anymore, but it can do you some good. Get out of your shirt."

"Don't try to tell me your aunt didn't cure you last night," Martin said. He scowled and pushed the bandage away. "You weren't doing today's running on yesterday's knee."

"She decided to cure it after she had the poultice made." She showed him the salve that Tamsanne had spread on the inside of the cloth. "Look, it's clean. I wouldn't offer it if I thought it wouldn't do you good."

Giving the bandage a suspicious look, he grunted assent. "All right. You'll have to help me with my shirt."

The blood on his body had begun to clot, and the range of motion he had left in the arm on the same side as the body cut was feeble.

"I'll help you." Gaultry touched his good shoulder, trying to distract him from the pain. "I'll help you."

His body was flushed with the heat of battle. Underneath his sturdy gray and green jacket, his shirt was white, finer linen than Gaultry expected. The sword cut that ran across it had ruined it. Martin smelled sweaty and bloody but not unpleasant. As she pulled his shirt off his shoulders she was a little embarrassed to find herself covertly admiring his body and arms, the strong column of his throat, so close to her own. Around his neck, he wore a glass amulet—a green fish biting its own tail. She pulled his left arm free of its sleeve, revealing a long, recently healed scar that ran almost the length of his arm. As if any of this mattered while the blood spread like an unstoppable stain down his chest.

The new sword stroke cut from his right collarbone around to the left of his rib cage. At first she was relieved, seeing the mostly shallow wound, a bruise breaking the clean line of the cut where the shoulder strap of his scabbard had crossed his body and protected him. Then she realized that it was the strap alone that had prevented the sword stroke from opening him up like a filleted fish. Had the blow landed with any greater force, the scabbard strap would almost certainly have snapped, and he would not have survived the blow.

Appalled by the risk he had taken, fighting without armor, and still a little intimidated by the brutality with which he'd ended the lives of so many men, Gaultry concentrated on cleaning the wound so that she could bind it.

"It's better than it looks," she said encouragingly, wishing she didn't have to hold her head so close to his as she worked.

"It feels better, now that I can see it." He rotated his arm, trying to bring back the full range of movement. "What happened to you?" He touched the place on her cheek where the man had hit her.

"Nothing—compared to what I did to him." Pushing his hand away, she told him about gouging the man's face with the arrow. "He called me a bitch-queen."

"Appropriately enough."

"Hardly." She finished the binding, and rocked back on her heels, nervous and more than a little light-headed. Something had shifted between them, and her fright for him, and of him, was gone. She wasn't sure about the emotion that replaced it.

"That should do you," she said, and fumbled for his shirt.

"Should it?" He took the cloth she'd used to clean the wound, and began to wipe at the slick of blood that had run down his body below the cut—the blood Gaultry had been too shy to do more than dab at. There was blood everywhere: on his stomach, on the top of his hip, across the belt of his trousers. Gaultry stared, fascinated, watching his hands.

He glanced up. Seeing where her eyes had come to rest, something deep in him brought out a harsh laugh. The gray wolf's eyes, meeting hers, went dark and intense. She stood hastily, tucking in her shirttails. He stood too, fluid as water.

"Why are you laughing?" she demanded, trying to step away. He was frightening her anew. She didn't like the brooding look on his face, the hard, flat cheekbones that caught the firelight, the arrogant curl of his mouth.

"Why are you asking?" He reached out and twisted a handful of her hair into a thick rope, drawing her to him. "I can feel every damn thought that goes through you."

His lips were on hers, he was kissing her, and she was doing nothing to stop him. A shocking heat lanced through her spine, and she stared at him, bewildered. He was a dark wolf with dangerous eyes, a wolf that had been sent to protect her. She shouldn't want him. For a moment she relaxed against him, luxuriating in the feel of his body beneath her hands.

Then she looked into his dark eyes and saw the now-familiar slash of silver geas-magic cutting through him. She cried out, disillusioned, and tried to push him away, convinced that the spiral of feeling between them was a twisted thing fed by magic, by a bond that had nothing to do with real desire. "Don't touch me!" Her voice was a hoarse whisper. "I don't want this!"

Dark fought with silver in his eyes, neither dominating. "I'm here to protect you, Gaultry." He was still kissing her. "I can't hurt you."

He didn't understand her fear: he could feel the pleasure running through her body like fire, and he didn't want to know her fear. "Gaultry—" He took her hands in his, his gray wolf's eyes flickering to dark, to passion.

Something blind and angry in her leapt out, and the spell she'd called earlier, for the hunters, coursed from her hands, more powerful than she had intended. He gasped with pain, and doubled over.

She stared down at his pain-filled body, horrified.

Then his face turned up to her, and she found herself transfixed by the murderous eyes of the black wolf, sharp and clear as when she'd first seen them on the Rhasan card.

Fear overtook her; any hope of reason departed. She scrambled away and tripped against his mare, where he'd tied her close by them. Before she could even think what she was doing, she burrowed her hands deep in its mane and threw her mind open like a shuddering funnel. The mare shrieked and stamped in alarm, feeling her animal-spirits siphoning from her. Gaultry's body shuddered with burgeoning strength.

The horse slipped to the ground, legs thrashing.

Gaultry tossed her head, flooded with the animal's power, and learned faster than she wanted that a horse was not just strength and stamina: it was also nervous emotion, emotion that was bundled over a hidden mass of animal-panic. Combined with her own overexcited condition, taking from the horse was a foolish, foolish folly. Its will swamped hers, magnifying and expanding her fright, her desire to flee—and then Gaultry was off, running breakneck down the road.

In the shrunken corner of her mind that was still capable of rational thought, she could only bitterly reflect that this had been happening to her far too frequently these past days.

chapter 4

▼

A considerable time later, the unfrenzied corner of Gaultry's mind grew strong enough to overcome the mare-spirit's panic. With a painful spasm of mental focus, she coiled the amorphous beast-energy into a tight knot, soothing it with gentle whispers as she had seen Martin attempt back at the bridge. Relief flooded through her as the nebulous spirit responded, relinquishing control of her legs. With the magic gone, her legs went from numb to cramped agony, the muscles rigid beneath her skin like frozen bands of iron. She flung the mare's champing spirit free, squatted down at the side of the road, and burst into relieved tears.

The road stretched away, before her and back, dark and featureless, the trees jagged silhouettes against the night sky. Gaultry wiped lank tangles of hair from her face, quaking with exhaustion and tears. How far had she come? The sliver of the newly waxing moon, low on the horizon, did not cast enough light for her to make an accurate guess.

Her feet were cold, wet, and the sole of one of her shoes was gone. Her clothes were mud-smeared, ragged from countless clashes with roadside bushes. She had no idea how far she'd traveled from their second camp. Had Martin stayed with the body of his fallen horse, or had he tried to keep pace with her in the dark?

The thought that he might be waiting with the body of his horse, confused and angry, brought Gaultry a fresh wave of self-pity. The fiasco of terror and flight was her fault. She had known he was reading her feelings—known, and yet she had let curiosity rule her, allowed herself to desire him, allowed herself to be excited by the desire he had returned to her—even as she had known that it was geas-inspired. Then she had punished him for having let the geas make him respond to her.

The bout of tears slowly dried, the crying venting some of her wearied tension. Dimly at first, she became aware of the cold of the night, the loneliness of the empty road. The woods were quiet around her, quiet with the caution of the wild things that had heard her distress.

Standing tiredly in the cold dark of the wheel-rutted road, she could acknowledge to herself that she owed the geas-bound soldier an apology, but her mind rebelled against the prospect of exposing herself, and all her new confusions, to him—him and his damned geas-sharpened perceptions of her innermost emotions. She was exhausted, cold, and in a ragged condition. He would read those feelings right off of her, and that would only make things worse.

She didn't want to retrace her path on the road and meet him. Not just yet. She would forge on to Blas Lodge, and hope to get there and have a little time to recover before having to face him.

Hugging her arms against her body for warmth, she turned northwards, and started walking.

A little after sunrise, she came to an old mile marker, ancient moss stubbling the slate column almost up to the lettering. It was older than her father's tenure at the lodge, reading "Hanting, 4"—Arleon's old name for the lodge before he had bequeathed it to Thomas Blas.

Another hour of walking and she would reach the lodge itself.

Stepping near, Gaultry ran her fingers across the chiseled number, shivering with an internal ice that had little to do with the chill of the brightening spring morning.

She had come preternaturally far running with Martin's horse in her legs. Farther even than a panicked horse should have been able to run in half a short spring night.

Her spell had accomplished more than she had asked of it.

Despite the relative ease with which Gaultry performed her taking-spells and color castings, she was the first to admit that her magical skills, with Mervion's, were seldom as intense as either sister yearned for. Certainly their capacity to wield the goddesses' magic could not compete with the stories that Tamsanne had shared with them of their mother Severine's powers. Severine had been a healer and huntress both—indeed, she had met Thomas Blas on the day she had succored a great black boar, turning the entire hunting party of the Duke of Arleon past her—save for the single man, her future husband, who had crossed through the shining labyrinth of her castings to find her. Gaultry and Mervion had always envied the complex tapestries of spell that had underlain such tales—a complexity neither of them had come near reaching with their own spellcasting.

Tamsanne had counseled patience and application.

But even Tamsanne had not been able to fathom the heights of concentration necessary for her nieces to learn even the most superficial level of control. As Mervion and Gaultry had reached maturity, they shared a private understanding that the scope of the magic at their call had stark limitations. There was a seemingly insurmountable blockage to the power they could call from the Great Twins. It was as if each of the sisters had inherited the ability to work only an incomplete half of Severine's powers. Channeling their efforts together, they sometimes sensed the swift stream of complex magics, and, fewer times still, they were able to wield that power to form a new spell, but neither relished the prospect of dependence on the other to fulfill a casting's promise. Worse, on the infrequent occasions when the twins did work together to perform a new casting, both came away with a frustrated sense of the latent power that lay unused in the other, further fueling their dissatisfactions.

This was one area in which Mervion had outstripped Gaultry's more typical lack of patience. For Mervion, Tamsanne's assurances that power would come with time had long since worn thin. "I'm tired of being told I *should* be able to command more power; that I *will* be able to call more power," she had confided to Gaultry, months before the news had come of their father's death. "I'm not *learning* anything here." At the time Gaultry, focused on the forest and its numberless secrets, had failed to appreciate the depth of her sister's discontent with their secluded life.

The stone of the mile marker was cold under her fingers. Four— she was four miles from Blas Lodge.

Something had broken free inside her, allowing her spells a dimension of power dangerously beyond her comprehension or control. What she had done to Martin, and then what she had done with the horse, were magics beyond what she knew she could control with any confidence. She left the stone and walked on, quickly despite her tiredness, as though the stone itself frightened her.

If she could not predict their effect, she could not go on casting spells. That way was a clear-marked road to madness and self-destruction. A dreadful loneliness stabbed her. The injustice that her power should begin to blossom now, on the road, away from Tamsanne, who might have advised her, pierced her like a spectral knife.

After a long and cheerless hour, the turn for Blas Lodge was a welcome sight. The lane was a winding, pleasant track, shaded on both sides by silver beeches. Bluebells and striped foxgloves dotted the banks of the lane and the long grass beneath the trees. Beyond, her brother's narrow fields were tidy and well tended. A feeling of homecoming warmed her.

The lodge was set well back from the road, sheltered in a gentle fold of the land. It was a mellow building, with stone foundations and a rough wattle-and-beam construction. The new wing, built by her father, had a stone-faced endwall and a slate roof. Gaultry had an early memory, from one of her infrequent visits, of the stonecutters laying the new wing's foundations, and of climbing, against her father's orders, on tall stacks of masonry as the workmen started on the endwall. Her father had insisted that Mervion and Gaultry in turn lay the endwall's cornerstones, telling them that he wanted the foundation to have both the Great Twins' and the little twins' blessings. She smiled at the memory, simultaneously proud and sad. However brutal he'd been in his later abandonment of his daughters, at least something of them had always remained at his house.

Rounding the last bend of the beech-lined lane, the rambling U-shape of the lodge's main building came into view. A single horse stood in the house's cobbled forecourt, three men in attendance. The quiet of the court, the yard, and the fields closest to the house was a little unsettling.

Before Gaultry could reconsider her approach, she was sighted.

"It's Gaultry! It's my sister Gaultry!" Gilles. He was one of the men by the horse. He put down a tool and darted out to meet her. "Gaultry! What's happened?"

Gilles had lost weight since their father's funeral. The bones in his face had taken a prominent, even delicate, look. Although he had exchanged his drab mourning clothes for the bright clothing of a landed gentleman, he looked younger than ever, less settled in his new role as master of Blas Lodge instead of more so. A single green jewel dangled from one ear, sparkling in the light, and his long chevalier's locks shone, beautifully dressed, in the morning sun. In a blue velvet surcoat and slashed linen shirt, he did not look at all like a man with a wife and a half-sister imprisoned miles from him in the nation's capital. He looked like a nervous new-made squire, a boy eager to run at his master's stirrup, currying favor.

"What's wrong?" he asked, reaching her. His face furrowed with concern. "Who's done this to you? Whose blood is this?" He touched the front of her tunic, his eyes wide and shocked.

"Gilles." Gaultry took his hand, reassured by his obvious concern. "I'm so relieved to be here."

"You look awful," he said. "Come inside, sit down, tell me. Is something wrong with Tamsanne?" He signaled one of the men who waited by the horse to come and help him escort her to the lodge door.

"Tamsanne's fine," she said. "And I am too, or will be after I rest. But I'm not here for myself, Gilles. We had word at Tamsanne's that Mervion and Anisia have met trouble."

They were on the front steps. Gilles turned jumpily to face her, his slanting green eyes—eyes that he, with Gaultry and Mervion, had inherited from their father—narrowing. "What are you saying?"

Beneath her exhaustion, Gaultry berated herself for not having planned better how to greet him. Gilles was so young—too young for the responsibilities her father's death had hung on him.

"A messenger from one of the dukes came to Tamsanne's. He brought the news that Mervion and Anisia had been arrested on Prince Benet's warrant and hied up to Princeport."

"It's not true!" Gilles said, surprise spreading across his young face. "Who was the messenger?"

"A soldier from Melaudiere. His name is Martin Stalker."

At Martin's name, Gilles went stiff. "I'm sure he didn't tell you anything more than that," he said grimly. "Other than lies to make you believe him. How did he get Tamsanne to trust you to him?"

"Do you know him then?" she asked, startled in her own turn. "He's a good man," she said, trying to think how to tell Gilles about the geas. "He protected me on the road—"

"He's responsible for this?" Gilles touched the dry blood on her tunic.

"It's his blood," she said. "He had hold of me for a time, before—before I made him let go." The scene between Martin and herself was not something she wanted to share with a young brother.

"Is he still following you?"

"I imagine so."

"Take my sister upstairs," Gilles bid his yardman. "Bed her down in the new wing. Have the women bring her water and fresh clothes."

"Gilles—"

"Gaultry, please. You're tired. Go rest and get yourself cleaned up. I'm sending a party out to meet this escort of yours. You have nothing to worry about."

The yardman plucked at her elbow. Gaultry, quite sure that she didn't like being pushed into anything, particularly by a younger brother, held her ground. "I have plenty to worry about. Where are Mervion and Anisia?"

"They're in Princeport, of course. But they're certainly not there on an arrest warrant." Gilles's face lightened, and a proud grin flick-ered on his mouth. "It's costing me a fortune to rent them quarters in town, but Anisia wanted to see the Prince's wedding, and I couldn't refuse her. I'll be joining them in a week's time. I'm already shutting up the house so I can join them."

"Martin said—" Gaultry began.

"I don't know what lies he told you. Right now I don't care. The short of it is, you're safe. You need sleep, and I'm going to send out my men to bring him in. We can discuss the details later.

"Go upstairs, sister-mine, and get some rest. We'll talk every-thing else out later." Gilles nodded curtly to his man, gave Gaultry a quick peck of a kiss on the cheek, and darted away across the fore-court, the tails of the new surcoat flying like a flag at his back.

"Do you want to go after him, Lady Gaultry?"

Lady Gaultry? Gilles's servitors had learned new manners since she had last visited. It was, however, reassuring to hear the man of-fering her the choice.

Gilles's plan to close the house and go up to Princeport for the Prince's wedding sounded innocent enough. It was his fraught reac-tion to the news that Martin was following her that was troubling.

"Do I want to go after him? Of course I do!" Gaultry sighed, and watched her brother turn the corner of the house. It would be long hours before her brother could hope to meet up with Martin, even with both sides on horseback. Her bespelled trek through the night would be the guarantee of that. "I should be there when they meet, lest there be some misunderstanding, but Gilles is right. I've got to have some sleep first."

The yardman took her to a small, paneled bedroom, high on the second floor. When she saw the clean bed that awaited her, dizzying exhaustion finally overwhelmed her. She held onto the bedpost to keep herself upright as a succession of women came to light a fire and bring up a hip-basin and ewers of warm water. Two young housemaids helped her with her filthy clothes, and then sponged her down in the tub. The warmth of the water sent her spiraling towards sleep. There was a clean shift for her to sleep in—someone said it was Mervion's.

And then there was the bliss of the bed. Gaultry crawled between the soft sheets and immediately fell asleep, with not even a whisper of a dream to haunt her.

When she awoke, late afternoon light filled the sky outside her small window. She lay on the bed, absolutely still, listening, wondering what had brought her up to wakefulness. The noise came again. The harsh clash of metal on metal. Beneath that clatter, a cry of distress, a curse.

The window, irritatingly, gave her a fine view of the mews at the back of the lodge. Whatever the noise was, it had come from the front of the house.

Her bedroom door was locked, an unpleasant surprise. When she hammered on it, a high, girlish voice answered, at once hesitant and polite.

"Lady Gaultry?"

"Let me out!"

"Lady—"

"Let me out! I'm going to be sick and there's no basin in here. Let me out!"

There was a pause, and then the sound of someone fumbling with metal keys came to her through the door's thick panels. Gaultry listened intently as her guardian fitted a key into the lock, and cautiously turned back the bolt. The second she heard the latch click, she shoved the door open.

"Lady Gaultry!" Her guardian was a tiny girl with ginger-colored hair and an apologetic expression. "Lady Gaultry!"—this last to Gaultry's back as she dashed past the girl down the hall, hunting for a window that opened onto the useful side of the house.

At the head of the stairs, she found what she wanted.

The view the window gave her was degrees less desirable.

Gilles stood in the forecourt below her, surrounded by a cluster of his men. Beyond this grouping, there was a round half dozen of mounted men in hunting gear—soldierly men, wearing unfamiliar green livery with a black star on the breast. These obviously had only just made their arrival. They were still in their saddles, or close by horses that were burdened by heavy bundles and traveling bags.

And Martin was there. Martin whom she had told them was following her on the road.

He'd been brutally mistreated, perhaps even dragged on a line from a horse's saddle. His clothes were in rags. They'd put an iron collar on his neck and fettered it to his ankles with a short chain. He was on his knees, his hands locked behind his back. His pose should have suggested vulnerability, but instead, more than ever, Martin was a coiled predator, intimidating despite his bonds. His expression was focused, unemotive, his eyes bright.

There was blood on his throat. The iron collar gleamed, scarred at its front where it had taken the force of at least two blows.

Gaultry's brother stood in front of the bound man, gripping the sheared hilt of the sword he had shattered against the collar on Martin's neck. For the second time in as many days, a strap of metal had saved Martin Stalker's life.

"Bastard," her brother snarled, and dashed the broken hilt down to the cobbles.

"At least I can handle a sword." Martin's voice was faint and drained, but still mocking. "Care to waste your next-best blade against me?"

There was an unpleasant crunch as Gilles's foot took the big soldier in the ribs. His fierce boyish face, white with rage and humiliation at having failed in his attempt to lop off the head of a chained man—in front of both his men and the green-liveried strangers. "You should be dead," he screamed in the bound man's face, his young voice cracking with fury. "Dead!"

If Martin had an answer to that, Gaultry couldn't hear it beneath the sound of her brother's blows.

No one stepped forward to stop him. It was excruciating long moments before Gilles regained control of himself. Then, rage spent, he turned away, tears tracking his cheeks. His shoulders sagged. His voice, when he finally spoke, was barely loud enough for Gaultry to catch the words.

"I'm not going to make it so easy for you. You're going to the Prince's court. They'll deal with you there. Far better than I. I'm too young, and you—you are too evil and too strong for me." Self-pity, mingled with self-loathing, filled his words. "Aquilles Beriot is coming tonight. He'll take care of you for me."

"Beriot?" Martin rasped. "So you're a fool as well as a coward. If Beriot's coming here, he's coming for your sister. Can't you see that?" Gaultry was surprised Martin had the energy left to answer. He was back on his knees, wolf's eyes blazing—the last defiant feature in a body bowed with pain.

"What do you mean?" Gilles demanded.

"It wasn't enough for you to sell one sister to the Prince, was it? What have they offered you for the second twin? A baron's laurels? A place at court? Was it easy, selling your father's blood for a traitor's favor?"

Gilles interrupted him with another brutal kick. "How dare you speak so of my father! You! A murderer! You're the traitorous one!"

"Don't betray Gaultry too," Martin choked. "Honor your common blood—"

Gilles signaled two of his men. "That's enough," he said. "Take this man to the lock-house. He can cool his heels there until Beriot arrives."

The men he called exchanged an uneasy glance. It was obvious, from the way they raised Martin up by the shoulders and gently lifted him off the cobbles, that they were unsettled by their young master's behavior. All the same, they obeyed him.

It was over. The company began to disperse, some going to stable their horses, some coming inside.

Gaultry, breaking the paralysis that had gripped her from the moment that she'd looked down and seen Martin, stepped back from the window, her heart pounding so loudly she was sure that the little ginger girl, standing next to her, could hear it.

She wanted to run down to the court and beg Gilles to explain his seemingly senseless attack, but the awful lack of self-control, of honor, in her brother's murderous attack warned her against this. Her mind reeled, remembering the clash of metal on metal. Even if Martin was all the things her brother had called him, Gilles had no right to usurp the role of public executioner. What could have pushed Gilles—a kindly soul, growing from an extended boyhood

in her father's shadow to a warm and impetuously generous man—
to such lengths? He'd called Martin evil, but it was his own attack
on Martin that was evil.

Voices at the bottom of the staircase interrupted her thoughts.
She was going to have to move, or they would discover that she had
witnessed the beating.

She had made a grave mistake in coming here, in letting herself
be lulled by the superficial appearance of normality. Now, with Martin in her brother's power, she too was trapped.

Gilles may have been convinced that Martin was a murderer and
that this Aquilles Beriot was to be trusted, but Gilles did not know
about the geas, or about the Rhasan magic Tamsanne had invoked.
Tamsanne could not have been wrong about allowing Gaultry to
travel with Martin. Of that much she was absolutely certain.

If Gilles was truly ignorant of the danger that threatened herself
and Mervion, she was going to have to try to use that ignorance to
her advantage, to free Martin and herself from the trap that had
been set for them.

The ginger-haired girl who had let her out of the room was shivering, watching Gaultry from big, frightened eyes. "We shouldn't
have seen Master do that," she said, nervously looking up into the
taller woman's face.

"What's your name?" Gaultry asked her.

"Alys." The girl's voice was less than a whisper.

"Well, Alys, do you know who I am?"

"The master's sister, Lady."

"That's right." Was it Gaultry's imagination, or were the downstairs voices coming closer? Would the girl cover for her if she went
back into her room? Her best appeal, she decided, would be to the
girl's own guilty conscience. "You weren't supposed to let me out,
were you?"

Alys flushed, and shook her head. Gaultry, who felt that she herself had spent too large a part of the past two days getting things
wrong and having to apologize, could not help smiling a little to see
her guilty expression.

"Good. Well, you haven't let me out of my room, have you?"
Gaultry fumbled for the knob, holding the young girl's eyes with her

own. "I was exhausted, you see. I slept the day through. Never even rose to check the locked door." Alys goggled. Gaultry narrowed her eyes and smiled. "You've met my sister, haven't you?"

"Yes, Lady."

"You know she's a witch?" The girl nodded, mute. "Just remember, *I'm* the evil twin." Gaultry stepped into the room and snapped the door shut, leaving the girl to wrestle with her own conscience, and, perhaps, her fear of witches.

She stood and waited just inside the door, breath inheld. There was a long pause, and then, finally, the bolt turned in the lock. Was it her imagination, or was there a furtive sound to its movement? Grinning, Gaultry crossed to the bed, picturing poor Alys as she cowered in the corridor, trying to get the room locked again before anyone caught her doing it. It was a reassuring picture.

Once you'd shared guilt with someone, Gaultry knew, it was a hard thing to turn back and betray them.

chapter **5**

▼

Gaultry lay on her bed as the small room darkened, her hand crossed to her throat, her fingers touching her aunt's amulet. The fear of discovery that had spurred her to bully Alys, that had got her back into the room undetected, had faded. She had returned to numbed detachment — as numb as she had been when she'd watched her brother's boot, over and over, connect with Martin's ribs.

She had always thought of Gilles as a shy but generous boy. When Mervion and Gaultry had come to the lodge for their father's burial, there had been nothing in her brother's demeanor that had challenged this early impression. The five years that had elapsed since they'd last seen him had been enough to change the twins from girls to women, and Gilles from a boy into a man — or at least a man in society's standing, if not quite yet in his own boyish person. He'd retained his youthful warmth: "I want us to be close again," he had told his sisters, holding his pretty wife's hand as she had nodded her approval. "I never understood why he distanced you from us. It wasn't what I wanted." He and Anisia hadn't been honor-bound to share the lodge with Gilles's half-sisters — it had simply been what they had both wanted.

Now, his coward's attack on Martin overshadowed everything. She pushed away the image of Martin, still in chains, his throat slashed open to the bone as Gilles stood above him, sword sullied with blood. Elianté give blessing that, even chained, Martin had been agile and strong enough to prevent her brother's attack from succeeding.

Gilles could not have committed such an ugly act without either malign magic or lies having grossly twisted his natural sweet nature. She had to believe that his faith that Mervion and Anisia were safe was equally unnatural.

She thought back to the welcome he had given her this morning, when she'd arrived at the lodge. There had been nothing in his manner to suggest she was foolish to trust him. Even his man had felt free to defer to her, offering her the choice of going along with him to meet Martin on the road. There had been nothing to warn her that her brother's house was in any way unsafe.

Except this.

Gaultry rolled over and buried her face in the pillow.

Until she and Martin were once more free, she would have to pretend that she trusted her brother, that she believed that he was capable of telling her the truth. That was probably all the advantage she and Martin had left now, with him in her brother's lock-house and her in her brother's power.

She reached into her shift to touch her aunt's amulet, and prayed.

She was alone and awake in the room for hours longer, half-mesmerizing herself with a witch's meditation. Just after dark there was a muffled rattle of hooves and wheels on cobblestones—a coach entering the forecourt. The arrival of the man Gilles had threatened Martin with? Not long after, there was a soft knock at the door.

"Lady Gaultry? Are you awake?" Another of Gilles's overpolite servants. As if anything other than common blood had ever run in her veins, Gaultry groused.

"I'm awake," she replied ungraciously.

The door was unlocked and opened. A thin girl, not Alys, entered, carrying a candle. "Have you rested? The master begs your company at his table tonight." Nothing in her words or manner suggested that Gaultry was constrained to answer one way or another.

"I'm rested," Gaultry said. "Will I need to dress?"

"I've brought you some of your sister's things."

The dress was Mervion's handiwork, a deep burnt-orange material that would have been several shades darker than her hair. There were tippets of embroidery on the sleeves—a simple pattern of flowers that Tamsanne had taught them, but beautifully worked. Mervion had worked magic on the threads as she had sewn, binding a color spell round them to give the flowers a subtle, glowing luster. It was beautiful, and it was so like Mervion to have fretted, and troubled, and got each detail right, that Gaultry felt a lump rise in her throat.

The girl helped the young huntress dress, combing and braiding her hair, and dusting her face and arms with fine white powder.

The powder made her cough. Gaultry was more than a little uncomfortable stepping into her sister's finery. She couldn't help but ask herself what this beautiful gown was doing here if Mervion had indeed gone to Princeport simply to see the Prince's wedding. Gaultry was someone who could pack for an extended journey and neglect to include either brush or comb, but Mervion would remember every detail, as careful with her packing as she was with her sewing.

It didn't make sense. The dress was beautiful. It fit like a glove, each dart cunningly cut against her body, even before the girl had tightened the dress's laces. If Mervion had traveled to Princeport intending to make a debut at the Prince's court, she certainly wouldn't have left it behind.

"When did my brother start to primp for dinner?"

An uneasy look shifted on the girl's face.

Gaultry tried to make light of the remark. "Not that I didn't need primping, mind, after the state that I arrived in."

The girl seemed to think that was funny, but she was too shy to laugh. Tying off Gaultry's braid with an orange ribbon, she slipped a mirror from her pocket.

Gaultry was not prepared to see Mervion's face looked back at her from the circle of glass. It was something of a shock. The quirk of the mouth, the smooth waves of hair, glinting red-gold in the candlelight, the slant of the green eyes. The only thing left of Gaultry was Tamsanne's stone amulet on the leather thong around her neck—that and the deep circles under her eyes, attesting to the night she'd lost to running.

She pushed the mirror away, disturbed. The differences between herself and Mervion were more than the clothes they wore, or the way they dressed their hair. She removed the amulet and held it in her hand. The girl watched, her dark eyes curious.

"Have you heard of my aunt Tamsanne?" Gaultry asked. "She witched this to protect me. But I don't think it goes with the dress."

"Tamsanne is a good lady," the girl said, her voice very low. "You should wear it for her."

Was it Gaultry's imagination, or had the girl's fingers tightened on the candlestick?

"I'll wear it under my sleeve." Gaultry looped the thong over her wrist, pushing the amulet up out of sight. "How's that?"

"It looks good." Something in the girl had relaxed. She had forgotten to call Gaultry "Lady" for the umpteenth time.

Gaultry smiled, and thanked her. That made the girl nervous again. "I'll take you downstairs to the Master now, if you're ready." It was clear she was eager to finish with Gaultry and make her escape back to the kitchen.

Since January, there'd been extensive carpentry in the old hall, the core of the original building. New walls had been put up to divide the old long space into smaller rooms. Gilles, it would seem, no longer dined with his servants.

Gaultry's young dresser ushered her into an intimate, low-ceilinged room with blond-wood wainscoting. The two men seated at the table rose. Her brother and a stumpy, powerfully built man with cropped iron-colored hair.

"Lady Gaultry," the girl announced, and shut the door behind her.

Gilles looked well. The only clue to reveal his earlier tantrum was a hint of red in the corners of his eyes. "Gaultry," he welcomed her. "Meet Aquilles Beriot, the Baron Blamire. We've been discussing your visit to Blas Lodge."

The Baron reached for her hand. "Lady Gaultry."

"Sir," Gaultry said, uneasy. She guessed she had gotten his formal address wrong—but hadn't he?

He bent and kissed her hand, his mouth curled in something like a laugh. Aquilles Beriot was missing half an ear, probably lost in battle. It lent his face an ominous asymmetric look. His dark eyes were ruthless and hard; the lines around his mouth and eyes suggested internal determination. Something in him made the hair rise at the back of Gaultry's neck.

"Your brother has been telling me about your troubles," the Baron said, holding her gaze with his. "But the story is muddled. We've been hoping you could clarify some issues."

"You have business in Arleon Forest?" Gaultry asked, sitting down as Gilles held her chair. The stocky Baron had sat without waiting for her brother.

"There are some matters of your father's estate that your brother and I need to discuss."

Gaultry looked at her brother. Gilles, still wearing the blue surcoat he'd had on this morning, now wore a fresh shirt in pale yellow silk underneath. The green earring was gone, but there were new flashy rings encrusting his fingers. Yet as he sat down across from her, next to the Baron, he seemed younger and more vulnerable than ever, too young even to be playing dress up before a titled guest.

The gorge rose in her throat. How could she think of him as vulnerable, after what he'd almost done to Martin?

She fumbled with her napkin, fighting to hide her revulsion.

"Before you ask, Gaultry, let me tell you what happened while you slept. I sent my men out after Martin Stalker. They took him on the road just a few miles south of here. Do you remember old Redreul? Stalker killed him before he had a chance even to draw his sword from his scabbard."

Gaultry knew Redreul, a grizzled forester, from visits dating back to her childhood. Despite many differences, the two of them had shared a love of the forest, and they'd spent some pleasant hours in each other's company. If Gaultry had any friend in the old hunting lodge, it was Redreul. Gilles could hardly have given her news that would have been more likely to upset her.

Her stomach churned as she searched her brother's face, not sure

whether she could or should believe him. At least upset was the reaction they were expecting.

"Only Redreul?" she managed to ask.

Gilles flushed. "You know something of the man's prowess."

"I saw him fight." *For me,* she added to herself. *I saw him fight
for me.* "What does he have to say for himself?"

"He admits duping Tamsanne, to get you to come away with
him. He said you got wind of his true nature when he attacked you."

As if Tamsanne was so easy to dupe. Gaultry thought back to her
panic when Martin had taken her in his arms, and her ears burned.
The first part of her brother's news was clearly nonsense — but there
was a sardonic tone to the latter words that sounded like the Martin
she knew. "Got wind of his true nature." As if she hadn't learned his
deepest nature during Tamsanne's Rhasan reading, as if the geas
hadn't been there in his eyes, shining silver for Gaultry to see, as
he'd held her body against his, in the firelit clearing of the second
campsite.

"That's what he said?"

"The very words."

"I suppose it must be truth, then."

Beriot put his hand on Gilles's shoulder, silencing him. Two
women entered at the servants' door, bearing covered plates.
Gaultry didn't like that it was Beriot who curbed the talk before the
servants, subverting her brother's perogative as Master. Gilles
seemed neither to notice nor to care. There was silence as the
women served the meal and brought wine to the table.

At least it was Gilles who dismissed them back to the kitchen.

"Your brother tells me that Martin Stalker threatened your sister
Mervion."

Gaultry stared at Beriot, trying to take his measure. Though he
was a short, stocky bear of a man, she sensed within a mind whose
quickness belied his heavy body. Growing up largely isolated in the
forest, the huntress often compensated for her inexperience with
people by looking in them, and imagining what animal they most
resembled. That was easy with someone like Martin — who even
without a Rhasan card claiming him had a dark wolf in all his features. Or like her brother, who reminded her of an untried young

stag, beautiful and tense, uncertain if he was truly ready for the clashes of manhood. With someone like Aquilles Beriot, where the body gave few clues to the mind within, the animal was harder to see. She suspected it would be something nasty, like a deep-forest wolverine.

"What was your aunt thinking, allowing a girl of good birth to travel with a soldier?" The women were gone now, and Beriot was permitting conversation.

Good birth? What could the man mean? Neither her mother nor her father had even been born with a second name, and it had been her father's vainglorious aspirations to gentle rank that had got him killed! The question rankled. "I can take care of myself," Gaultry said. "In any case, Tamsanne was the one who insisted we stop through here before we went off anywhere else. If it wasn't for her, I wouldn't be here."

"Did he say where he was taking you after?"

"Princeport, of course," Gaultry answered without hesitation. It was only half a lie. She had sensed from the beginning that her travels would not end in Melaudiere.

"The capital?"

Gaultry gave the Baron a level look. "He said Mervion and Anisia were in Princeport. Where else would I be going with him?"

"And your aunt wasn't worried to send you?"

He was probing for something. She could feel that in the way his dark eyes touched her, in the way he glanced from her to her brother—assessing, not nervous. Had he been here when Mervion and Anisia had been taken to the capital? Had he sat in this room before, with Mervion the one he had asked the probing questions?

Quite suddenly, a cold touch of fear clenched her stomach. She could not imagine that Mervion had let herself be taken without a fight, yet there was Gilles, calmly eating his plate of beef, as if Mervion and Anisia really had traveled north at his expense, pretty forest gentlewomen, going to witness the marriage of their Prince like any other loyal Tielmaran citizens. Gaultry did not believe it had happened that way.

"I don't know why Tamsanne trusted me to him," Gaultry finally answered, aware that the Baron waited her answer. "I think she thought he could protect me. He was a frightening man, but he protected me. It can be hard to judge which fears need overcoming. And which fears," she moved her fork on her plate, avoiding his gaze, "are nature, or from the gods, and should be respected." Braid your words with the truth, she thought, or they'll know at once that you're lying.

"Your brother says your aunt follows the goddesses' art."

"They call us witches hereabouts, unless we've shriven ourselves before the Great Twins to become their clergy."

"Your aunt used magic to foresee whether or not you would be safe with the stalking-man?"

"Tamsanne has lots of strong magic," Gaultry said. "That doesn't mean she tells me how it all works."

"Fifty years of practicing?" He said the words so lightly, she would not have known this was the key question, if she hadn't seen Martin jump the night before, when Tamsanne had told him of her life in Arleon Forest. Aquilles Beriot had the same light in his eye now, the same curious light.

"Tamsanne's an old woman. She's been in Arleon Forest a long time." She looked at Gilles. "What have you been telling your guest?"

"Only all your family's secrets." The Baron raised his wineglass to her. "Such closed lives you live, down here at the edge of the forest." He diverted the conversation from Tamsanne, describing his interest in Arleon Forest. How different it was, he said, from his land in the northwest of Tielmark, how broadening was the nature of travel. Gaultry, her mood darkening, finished her plate, wondering how, in the few words they'd exchanged, she'd managed to let the information that he'd wanted slip.

"What I don't understand," she said, as her brother refilled her glass, "is why Martin Stalker came all the way out to Tamsanne's to lure me away. What was he trying to accomplish?"

Her brother went stiff, and a shadow of this afternoon's purple rage entered his expression. Beriot clamped a heavy hand on the younger man's slim wrist, giving Gilles a warning look. "You don't want to know the why of it," the Baron said. "It can only upset you."

"That's all the more reason I should know now, rather than later."

"Now that he's been secured, perhaps she should know." That was Gilles. Gaultry could hardly believe how overtly he was deferring to the stocky Baron—as if it was the Baron's right to decide what she should know, and what her brother could tell her.

"Martin Stalker was in the hunting party the day your father died. It was his sword that pierced your father's chest and killed him."

"Our father's death was an accident—"

"If you can call it an accident to half cut a man's heart out of his chest, yes, it was an accident."

Gaultry hardly knew how to react—Gilles did it all for her. He clapped his hand over the Baron's for comfort, and rocked a little in his seat. His eyes were bright with grief and hate combined. Like this afternoon's attack on Martin, it was not a response he should have allowed himself in public. It was too strong, too unthinking. Her grief and shock were great too, but they could not compare with what her young brother was showing—and this was fresh news to her, not something she was already familiar with.

"Gilles—" she said, taken aback by the force of his reaction. "Gilles, is it true? Why would he kill our father, and then come after me?"

"He's a cold-blooded murderer," Gilles moaned. "Father's heart was almost completely destroyed—I saw it, when the body came here, and the priest put it into the coffin. Stalker cut him down with a magic blade. How could it have been an accident?"

Gaultry bowed her head, fighting to control her emotions, determined not to show what she was feeling before the horrible Baron. She pictured Martin's sword, his magic sword with its six runes of power, her imagination coloring it dark with her father's blood.

She didn't want to believe them.

Yet why else would Martin have turned her aside when she'd asked him how her father had chosen him to carry the geas? The dark confusion of images that Thomas Blas had passed to Martin, suggested the death agony of emotionally unfinished business. On this point at least, she knew with a sudden clear certainty, her brother was not lying to her.

Martin should have told her. He must have known that she would find out the truth. He should have known that waiting with the truth would only make it hurt more—

"Gaultry, the Baron wants you to go to Princeport tomorrow."

"Whatever for?" Gaultry stared at him wildly, her eyes bright with unshed tears.

Gilles rubbed his hands, fiddling with his rings, nervous. The Baron shot him an impatient look. Gilles gave a little shudder, and tried to complete an answer.

"You could see Mervion, and confirm that she really is as happy as I've told you."

"Gilles, you've given me a terrible shock. I can't think about Mervion just yet."

"I think you should go," he pressed. "After what you've suffered these past days, the last thing you need now is to go back to Tamsanne's, pretending it didn't happen."

He was going to press her until she agreed to go. That much was clear. She wasn't sure whether this was frightening or ridiculous. As if she was already under whatever bonds had been put on her brother, and couldn't see the leap of illogic in all this!

"Gilles, you've said yourself Princeport is a huge expense. I don't have the funds to go." She snuffled, wiping her cheeks with the back of her hand.

"I'll pay," Gilles said, eager.

"You could travel with the guard that takes Stalker north. It would save your brother's horses," the Baron interjected smoothly. "As my guest, I'd be honored to guarantee your safety—if your brother agrees, of course."

As if Gilles had ever held that kind of authority over her.

"Gilles?" It wasn't hard to infuse her voice with doubt. "I'm not so sure I'd want to travel with Martin Stalker. He's a frightening man—and now that I know all that you've told me, about father—"

"If the Baron says he'll guarantee your safety, your safety is guaranteed, Gaultry."

"But this is our father's killer. You want me to travel with father's killer?"

Gilles turned to Beriot, his face openly begging the man to answer for him.

"If you insist," Beriot said. "I'm sure your brother can arrange an
independent trip north for you. You could even wait a week and
travel up with your brother when he closes the house here. But think
of all you could see if you get there early. Princeport is already starting to celebrate, and it may take you some time to accoutre yourself
for all the festivities. Go north in my carriage, take the extra week,
and spend it with a dressmaker."

Gaultry smoothed the dress that Mervion had so lovingly sewn
and embroidered, wondering what the Baron saw when he looked at
her. In affecting Mervion's dress, it seemed the men also thought
that she had affected her elder sister's likes and desires.

"I've already told Mervion I'd cover her costs—you could share
with her," Gilles told her.

She stared at her brother, a little despairing, and fought to conceal her emotions from the Baron's keen eyes. Gilles was so far under
the Baron's influence he seemed to have lost his awareness of his
sisters as women with distinct personalities. If the situation wasn't
rapidly becoming desperate, his offer would have been simply comi-
cal. But what could she do now, other than continue the charade,
and pretend she had no suspicions that anything was wrong. If she
could just get them to lower their guard, to trust her, there was a
chance they'd expose some weakness, and she'd see a way to break
free of the trap that was closing in on her from all sides now.

"If you're sure it will be safe, Gilles, of course I'll agree to go."
That was the woman that the Baron hoped her to be. A nervous
woman, deferential to her male protector.

She didn't enjoy the look of eager relief on Gilles's face as he
raised his glass to toast her decision.

chapter 6

Despite many worries, two days of near constant tension took their toll on her body and Gaultry slept deeply. She
woke only when a serving woman set a tray on the bed table with a
hard thump.

"Lady Gaultry. I've brought you traveling clothes. And your
breakfast."

Another new face, this time full cheeked and pleasant, though
grave in the streaming morning light as she laid out the food. Chest-
nut hair shot through with gold framed her fine face. A different
mold entirely from the nervous rabbits who had served her thus far.
Gaultry hastily threw back her blankets.

"I can do that," she said, claiming the tray.

While Gaultry ate, the new woman showed her the traveling
dress: rich gray velvet with a crushed pattern of roses and vines.
There was white lace at the sleeves and throat. "It was finished after
Mervion left," the woman said, answering the unspoken question in
Gaultry's eyes.

"I'm sure I'll ruin it before she ever sees it," Gaultry said, a little
rueful. "Isn't there something sturdier I could borrow?"

It seemed there wasn't. As Gaultry dressed, the woman insisted on putting a few things into a bag for her: a comb, a clothes-brush, the night-shift, sundry ribbons and pins. She called a girl to fetch things as Gaultry admitting lacking one item on the list after another. "It's not a trouble," the woman told Gaultry, when she feebly protested. "And you'll be grateful enough that you didn't win your no when you're on the road."

Gaultry found her slightly bossy manner soothing.

"Do you know Mervion well?" she asked, when the woman was pressing the bulging carpetbag into her hands. "I think you must do. Mervion looks after me just as you have done."

"You're her twin. You're very like her."

"In all but manners and charm," Gaultry quipped.

The woman smiled, briefly showing dimples. "You shouldn't tease yourself. You're her image." She hesitated, as if intending to say more, but a step in the hall intervened and the moment was past. "I'm needed back downstairs," she said, her steady gaze dropping from Gaultry's to the floor, her carriage suddenly overtly deferential. "Unless there's anything else your ladyship would be wanting."

"Nothing," Gaultry stumbled out, unprepared for the woman's abrupt switch of manners. "Thank you for helping me."

The door opened, framing a soldier in Blamire's green livery. "They're ready below. Are you?"

"Just about," Gaultry answered, annoyed. The questions she could ask this woman, if only they had a second or two longer. "Why don't you take my bag down?"

He took the bag, but stood and waited for her.

The chestnut-haired woman bent to retrieve the breakfast tray, moving so quickly that the bread knife clattered to the floor. Gaultry leant reflexively, almost knocking her head against the woman's as she too ducked to grab it.

"Mervion did not go willingly to Princeport." The woman's voice was less than a whisper against Gaultry's ear. She plucked the knife from Gaultry's fingers, gave a half-curtsy, and spun away. She had timed her words so that Gaultry could not hold her to ask more.

"Well?" The soldier's tone was an unpleasant foretaste of the manners she could expect on the road. He moved to let the serving woman pass him with the tray.

"I'm ready." Gaultry sourly told him.

In the downstairs entry hall, Gaultry had an awkward moment. She found she couldn't look Gilles in the face. The serving woman's brief warning was a leaden echo in her brain: Mervion did not go willingly to Princeport.

"You're looking better for the night's sleep," her brother said, holding out his hands.

Avoiding his eyes, she gave him a hasty embrace.

"I still feel like a shadow," she said, trying to justify her poor composure.

"My men took some things off Martin Stalker when they found him. Do you want to see if they retrieved anything of yours?"

She nodded.

Everything was piled on top of a scarred wooden chest by the side of the stairs. Martin's sword in its sheath—dull brown now, giving no hint of the great blade that lay beneath the worn leather—lay across the top of the pile. His pack, his bow. Her bow was missing, but the feathers of their arrows combined jutted from his quiver. Four gold sovereigns, some silver. "The silver's mine," she said, and pocketed it. Martin's double-spiral pin was nowhere to be seen. Probably one of her brother's men had stolen it. She lifted her cloak. Underneath, embarrassingly, was her satchel of clothes and underthings, pawed open for anyone to see. She hastily balled up the clothing to shove it out of sight.

Aquilles Beriot came in just then and caught her at it.

"Ah. You've found your property."

She ducked her head, and kept on stuffing.

"So pretty to see a young woman blush," he said, reaching to take the carpetbag. "I trust you had a quiet night." He kissed her hand, his dark eyes on her face. He somehow seemed to understand that the courtly gesture, to him so familiar, such simple custom, totally unnerved her.

Once she'd taken what she wanted, Beriot called another of his men to collect the remainder of Martin's things and stow them in a sturdy leather chest with stout copper strapping. "We're sending the effects along with you," he told Gaultry, locking the chest and pocketing the key. "But no one will need anything from this box until my return to Princeport."

The effects. That made it sound as though Martin was already dead.

The Baron folded Gaultry's arm into his, and gave her a close smile. "My men will ensure your safety," he told her. "Never doubt that." His hand, when it touched her arm, was hard and sensual, and she was suddenly aware that Beriot had been careful to make sure she was entirely ready for the journey before letting her into the forecourt. His thumb was pressed to the pulse of her wrist, and his body seemed tense, as if he was braced to counter her if she jumped.

The lodge doors opened. She stared up into the deep blue of the outdoors sky, willing the rhythm of her heart to remain calm. It's a simple exercise, she reminded herself. Almost the first trick Tamsanne had taught her. If she just steadied her heartbeat, the Baron would not know her fear.

Stepping outside onto the cobbles, Gaultry caught her first sight of the conveyance that would be taking her to Princeport. It was a grim black carriage, harnessed up with four strong horses in iron-tracings. As two menacing-looking men strapped the chest with Martin's belongings to the fender at the rear, she took in the heavily reinforced bars that framed the door, the tiny mullions on the undersized windows.

"Gilles." She reached out to him with her free hand. "Surely you don't expect me to travel all the way to Princeport in that box? It's four days, maybe five." Gods, if she had seen the damned thing before this morning, duty to Martin aside, they'd have been hard put to get her to agree to go.

"You'll be fine." His objective in sight, the Baron let some steel surface. "There'll be two guards riding with you to make sure he minds his manners. Conner here—" He gestured to a tall fox-faced man with a sergeant's braid on his shoulders—"Conner here has instructions to see to your comfort. And I myself," he said, his hand on hers suddenly warm, "I'll be only two days behind you, once I've finished my business with your brother. I'll check on you in Princeport. You've nothing to worry about."

He was marching her towards the carriage as he spoke. Already she was at the folding steps, the hideous prison on wheels looming above her. Already he'd pushed her so one foot was on the steps.

Martin was inside, seated facing the carriage's rear. Squeezed in beside him on either side was a pair of unhappy soldiers. The cramped interior already smelled rank with heat and sour sweat, despite the outside cool of the morning air.

Gaultry didn't need to feign her surprise.

"You've cleaned her up nicely, Beriot," Martin said, his voice rough and tired. "Lamb to the slaughter." He strained abruptly against the grasp of his guards. "What did they tell you to get you to agree to come?"

Gaultry took her foot off the first step and turned to the Baron. "Couldn't you gag him or something? How can you expect me to travel with him if he's going to be working at me like this?"

"It's a good idea."

"Don't be stupid, Gaultry. You can still escape—"

The carriage-guard on his right elbowed him in the face. Martin, snarling, turned on him. The other guard drove a punch into Martin's back. Gaultry wrenched free of the Baron's hand and backed away, cringing from the ghastly sound of fists striking the bound man's flesh. The sight of her with Beriot's hand on her had infused Martin with a burst of angry strength. Howling like a mad animal, he fought his way half out of the carriage, using his manacled wrists as a club. Men rushed from all corners of the forecourt to push him back inside. Gaultry, left to herself for a few precious moments by the melee at the carriage door, stumbled against the carriage-tracings, and suddenly knew what she was going to do.

At her first tentative touch, the nearest of the four coach horses champed its bit, and turned its head towards her. Mild equine eyes met green.

Eyes rolling, it laid back its ears. Gaultry cupped her hand over the bottom of its spine, above the base of its cropped and ribboned tail.

The horse shied and thrashed its tail, trying to shake her hand.

"Gaultry, what's wrong?" Gilles grabbed her elbow, almost upsetting everything. She looked at him vaguely.

"The horse is scared."

"They've got him quieted now. It's time for you to go. Gaultry?"

She pictured the dark track of the horse's spine, the cloudy labyrinth of emotion between the flattened ears—

"Gaultry!"

"I'm ready." The horse gave its tail a last thrash.

"I'll miss you, Gilles." She offered him her hand. Even knowing that it would be both impossible and foolish to try to say something to him, the temptation was there.

His servants had called her Lady Gaultry since her arrival. Did that mean that her brother had been rewarded for some service with a rank that went higher than mere knight?

"Gaultry—" He pulled away.

She brought his hand to her cheek, forestalling words. His hand was cold and nervous, yet a tingle of heat seemed to strike her. Two images. Day and night; dream and nightmare. Anisia and Mervion, smiling as they walked hand in hand. Martin. Martin with blood sheeting his body, laughing as he cut the heart from her father's still struggling form.

She was jostled from behind. Her brother's hand, and with it the images, was gone.

"My pardon." It was Beriot. His fingers pressed her flesh. "They're ready for you."

Gilles stood, hands hiding his mouth, his eyes, above the hand, a confused blank. Then she saw what she should have seen earlier, in all his jerky movements, his fidgeting hands.

His wedding ring was gone. In its place was an austere black signet, decorated with a green cross. She didn't need one of Tamsanne's hexes to see that the ring was a magic bridle, keeping Gilles in his place, turning his honor to ashes. The power in the rune was so strong it fairly sang out.

Her last thought as the Baron bundled her into the carriage was that Mervion would have noticed the ring at once, without having to have Gilles's hand stuffed clumsily against her face.

*   *   *

It was nasty sharing the carriage with a bound, beaten, and gagged Martin and the two bad-tempered soldiers. The cushions smelled of mildew, an odor that started bad and increased in unpleasantness as the day and the carriage slowly heated. By craning out the carriage's two small windows, Gaultry established that her escort was a force full ten strong, excluding the coachman. Martin and his guards, sitting opposite here, looked progressively uncomfortable as the morning wore by, the three of them wedged tightly into a space designed for two. The sun beat on the tarred roof of the carriage with increasing intensity, making the carriage's interior even more disagreeable.

"One of you should share my seat," Gaultry finally offered, when she had enough of watching the trio twist in their discomfort. Without a moment's hesitation, the man on Martin's left shifted to her side. He didn't thank her.

At noon, they reached the first wayside inn. A fresh pair of horses grazed in the paddock nearest the yard, the same dark bay color as those harnessed to the carriage. Beriot had come south expecting for someone to make the return trip north in his carriage in a hurry.

"Change of horses?" She tried to ask the question casually, as Beriot's sergeant opened the carriage door.

"The lead pair only. The others will have to wait until evening." Conner looked approvingly at the seating arrangement, and offered her his hand. "Stuffy in here, hey?"

Lunch was fleeting—cold chicken and bread eaten outside on the inn's yard tables. The day had turned hot—almost summerlike. The closeness of the carriage had left Gaultry dirty and sweaty. Her hair sweltered on her neck where it had fallen from her braids. The woman with the breakfast tray, despite her helpfulness on other counts, had proven herself a poor hairdresser. When Conner asked Gaultry if she was ready to go, she requested a moment to hang back and attend to it.

"Don't go far," he warned her.

"Just to where the men won't watch me."

He granted the sense of that.

Back by the inn's pump, she rummaged in the bag for the comb the woman had packed her. She felt a fool, fumbling, tidying her hair as the entire entourage waited.

The first thing her fingers touched after pushing aside the balled clothing from her satchel and the neatly folded clothes from the lodge was the smooth cold handle of a knife.

There was something else. A slip of paper, folded over the blade.

She combed and braided her hair with trembling fingers, acutely aware that by now she had the attention of most of Beriot's soldiers. It was good that she hadn't known what she had in the bag when she first got into the carriage. Returning the comb to the bag, she palmed the paper.

The woman in her room this morning must have been a very good friend of Mervion's.

"Where are the privies?" There must have been something funny in her voice. Conner sent a man with her to stand outside while she did her business.

The inn's privy was a ramshackle shed over a pit. Inside, there was limited light. Gaultry put her back against the fragile door and unfolded the paper.

It was a list of laundry. But the writing was Mervion's, and, after a moment of panic, Gaultry recognized the calligraphic letters of a spell. "Huntress hear me," she whispered, praying that the guard was out of carshot, was insensitive to the gathering of magic. She spoke the word to undo the warding. Her sister's neat script writhed like rain dancing on a window's glass, and reformed as her sister's true message. It was addressed to her younger sister:

Gaultry,
Gilles has received news from Princeport. He won't say what it is, other than that he knows now that our father's accident was no accident—it was murder. Something is dangerously wrong. This news is bait for our poor brother.

The messenger who brought it is not a good man. His name is Aquilles Beriot. Death fills his mind, the deaths of G and Anisia—but not mine, and I don't understand that—if A and I do not agree to return to Princeport with him. If we do not go, at best, there will be a fight; at worst, cold killing. Anisia has no spells, but she too guesses something is wrong. Something is wrong with Gilles. He is eager for us to go, and senses no evil. I fear Beriot has put him under a spell.

I don't know if I'm right to go north. I am frightened, but how can I not go, knowing I hold the lives of our dear ones in my hands?

If Anisia returns to Blas Lodge alone, this message will be sent to you.

Elianté and Emiera protect us all.

—M

Gaultry wiped her hand across the writing. It was a laundry list once more. She crumpled the paper and threw it into the privy-pit. Her body shook; her mind was a haze of anger. It was quite one thing to be told that one's sister was in peril. It was another entirely to read it in her own words.

Mervion would have been rigid with fear before even considering writing her younger sister such a letter. Gaultry was the younger twin by only a matter of minutes, but Mervion had always tried to shelter her from fears and dangers—whether her own or anyone else's. Even now, she asked nothing of her younger sibling. Her letter told all that was needed for action, but it neither begged help nor cried for vengeance.

If it had been Gaultry's letter, she would have asked at least for vengeance.

She closed her eyes, and prayed fervently to the Great Twins to help her seize the revenge that Mervion would never have asked for.

When she finally opened the door, there was nothing in her manner to alarm the privy-guard. She moved coldly across to the pump, retrieved the carpetbag, and returned to the carriage.

The inside guards had already resettled in their seats, one next to Martin, one next to her. They hadn't waited for her to renew the invitation. She bowed her head and stared at her hands, trying to visualize what it would mean to her, killing these men in cold blood so she and Martin could escape. A bare two days past, Martin's slaughter of Reido's men had made the bile rise in her throat.

Today she was going to have to do her own dirty work.

The carriage lurched into motion.

"Where will we be stopping tonight? Will there be a town?"

"An inn."

After another hour, the interior of the carriage had heated to the point of real discomfort. Gaultry's velvet dress prickled against her body. Martin, who was still gagged, looked distinctly ill.

"Perhaps it's time to take his gag off," Gaultry said. "He must be miserable enough by now that he'll agree not to bother me."

"What do you say, Stalker-man?"

Martin rolled his eyes in assent, and they ungagged him.

"Stupid bi—"

"Another word and I'll have them put it back on you!"

Giving her a dirty look, he satisfied himself with fixing her with a resentful stare, his handsome mouth set in a disapproving scowl. His eyes were dark and angry, no glimmer of the silver geas-magic lightening them.

She studied Martin's shackles, ignoring the display of temper. A short chain ran from his wrists to his collar—the iron collar with the bright gouges on its front, testament to her brother's murderous attack. The chain that secured his ankles had slack in it so it could be looped over his wrists. Fortune was smiling on them: the locks that secured the separate elements did not look oversturdy. With the serving-woman's knife to aid her, Gaultry guessed she would be able to free him.

The carriage turned a steep corner. Gaultry craned to see out the small window. They had emerged from the forest, and were entering the mouth of a narrow valley. On one side of the road, the ground dropped sharply away to a swift-running river, white water boiling across jagged stones. Across the water was a densely wooded hill, with knife-edged towers of white limestone lancing steeply up through the trees. Ahead, the road crossed the river on a narrow wooden bridge, then recrossed it, time and time again, to avoid the craggy valley walls. With the river below the road swollen with spring snowmelt, the outriders were not going to be bunched around the carriage as they passed along the next mile or so.

She stared at Martin's collar, at the bright gouges on the metal.

How near a thing it had been, that her brother had not reduced him to a headless corpse.

"Martin," she said, "look at me."

"What is it?" He met her eyes, and she reached out to him with her magic, as though he were an animal, as though she had the power to take the strength or the will from him. She formed an image of him as he had been at the slaughter of Reido's men; she pictured him as her brother had been shown him, merciless and bloody over their father's body. She opened a channel in herself, as she would have done if he had been an animal. Martin's eyes sharpened to silver as the geas sensed what she wanted, but all the geasmagic in the world could not help dislodge a man's soul as an animal's spirit could be dislodged. The terrible emptiness of failure, the failure of her spell, rushed towards her. Reason, not animal passion, drove this man's fighting spirit, there was nothing material she could take from him in this way, only dark emptiness. . . .

She began to cough, at first softly, then as though the beginnings of an asthmatic fit had seized her. Martin stared at her, sensing the void, feeling the surge of magic but failing to understand what she intended by it.

Gaultry wheezed and doubled over, sliding the carpetbag between her knees. She pulled out a handkerchief and blotted her face. "Gods, it's warm!" She twisted restlessly, her shoulder pressing the soldier at her side. "Don't you feel the heat closing in?" She clutched at his leg, and began to take big, shuddering breaths, her other hand over her stomach.

The carriage-guards shuffled warily.

"I can't breathe," she gasped. "I'm suffocating."

"You could unlace her," the soldier next to Martin suggested. "Lean forward, Lady. Thierry will loosen your laces."

"Leave her alone," Martin barked. "Don't touch her."

Gaultry, one hand groping for the knife, could have kicked him.

"She needs to breathe, Stalker-man. Let her be the one to say no—"

"I don't care," Gaultry interrupted, injecting a note of panic into her voice. "Stop the carriage, untie me—I'm suffocating."

The soldier's hands were on her back, catching at her laces. The carriage lurched as it went up a little rise, and spilled him against her. They were approaching the first of the wooden bridges, they'd hit it any second now, the wheels would roar as they crossed over—

"Just the laces," Martin was saying, openly angry. "Now get away from her."

The lead horse's hooves clattered like small thunder as they hit the wood of the bridge.

Gaultry unbent her body like a sprung bow, jamming herself and the soldier at her back against the side of the carriage, pinning him against the tall seat-cushions. The blade was out and through his throat before he knew she had a weapon. The second soldier cried out, and reached for her, too surprised to grab for his weapon first. She slashed out at him, slicing one of his palms. He shouted, but no one could hear him over the thunder of the carriage and its four horses and its metal-rimmed wheels, all clashing against the wooden bridge.

The soldier went for his weapon with his uninjured hand. Gaultry threw herself on top of him. If he got his sword out of his scabbard, she would be dead. For a moment they swayed on the seat, three hands scrabbling at the pommel of the sword. Then, hardly thinking as she did it, she blasted him with a witch's bane. In his shock at the sudden ice in his vitals, he left an opening for his ribs.

Leaving the knife in his body, Gaultry fell back on the seat opposite, panting, sickened by the gore now spread throughout the carriage.

The man with the cut throat was still alive, and feebly struggling. Cursing and crying together, Gaultry freed his sword, and tried to complete what she'd started.

"Stop." Martin clumsily imposed his body, and almost got his own throat cut as she flailed with the blade. "That's not the way to do it." He took the sword from her with his still-manacled hands and finished the man with a single clean stroke.

The carriage bumped off the bridge, the clatter of hooves and metal wheels dropping away to a steady rumble. Gaultry doubled over and vomited on the carriage floor. Martin sat by her, waiting for her to finish. His calmness amid all the carnage was infuriating.

"You were going to ruin it." She spat, wiping her mouth. "What were you going to do next? Warn them to get ready to fight you off?"

"After your performance the other night? What was I supposed to think? You've got a seriously impaired idea of who and what you need to be protected against."

"That's right." Gaultry lurched forward, her new anger helping her regain her composure. She jerked the knife from the second guard's rib cage. "I'm just a stupid lambkin, headed innocently to the slaughter." She grabbed the chain that led to Martin's neck, jerking his head down so she could wedge the knife into the collar's lock.

"Hey!" he protested, as she furiously ground the blade back and forth in the link. "Be careful!"

"Oh, shut up!" The carriage clattered onto the second bridge as the lock unexpectedly broke, and she almost stabbed him in the chest. The near mistake hardly helped her mood. She wrenched the collar from his neck and got to work on his hands.

"What did you expect me to do with that bastard leering at you?" he groused. He hadn't seen her mistake with the knife. "You might have given me some clue that you weren't fading off in a faint—or a trance. What was that spell?"

"The one I failed to cast on you?"

He nodded. She thought of the void she'd opened in herself, trying to build her resolve to kill, and decided he wouldn't want to know the answer.

"Why would you want to know anything about my castings?" she said, roughly turning his hands to insert the blade in the bracelets' locks. "Shouldn't you be more concerned about our outriders? There's a full ten of them." The manacles clattered onto the floor.

"Ten?" He massaged his wrists. She stooped to free his ankles, slipping in the mess on the floor.

"The good news is that your weapons are traveling with us." She told him about the Baron's chest. "Though we won't be able to get to them until after. Also—I looked—your magic pin is missing."

"It is?" His hand went to the shoulder of his coat, and he turned the lining inside out, revealing a hidden pocket. "I was expecting trouble before your brother's men caught up with me. Luckily for us." Along with the silver double-spiral brooch, he pulled out the glass fish amulet.

She touched the edge of the fish amulet, not wanting to meet his eyes. "I didn't mean to set them on you."

"I know. That night was my fault too. I guess I was congratulating myself too warmly that I hadn't been sent to rescue Thomas Blas's sulky child after all." He grinned, and drew his amulet back on over his head. "Take a look out the window and tell me what's ahead."

"We're in a long valley. The road cuts across the river on these wooden bridges at least twice more."

"That's good."

"I've got a spell waiting on the hind horse at the left. If you'd like, I can make it go to sleep."

"That's better." He gave her a sharp look. "One day soon you're going to tell me a little more about these spells you're casting. You could start with the trouser-shitter you laid on me the other night."

Gaultry, having no desire at all to explain that spell, hastily went to look out the window.

Martin picked up the carriage-guards' swords. Rejecting the first, he made a practice pass with the second. "It'll do. Where are our guards riding?"

This took some awkward craning at the window to determine. "Three in front—maybe four. Conner, Beriot's sergeant, is in the rear with the big grouping."

"Good. Are you going to use that knife again, or the other sword?"

"I don't know how to use a sword."

"Try. The reach might save you." He showed her the proper grip. "It cuts with the sharp edge, you know." She flushed, but there was nothing to say. She'd been hacking at the wounded soldier with the dull edge.

He didn't need a geas on him to know why she was embarrassed. "Don't worry," he said. "You were brave even to try it."

"Martin," she said, faltering. "I felt like a butcher."

"It's even money to bet that you'll have to do worse, before this Prince's Night is come and gone. Do you know, this is the same carriage that your marriage-sister and Mervion took to Princeport?"

The reminder of Mervion dulled her regrets. She nodded her

head. "I'd guessed. Mervion left me a letter. She said Beriot had come for her and Anisia. She had no idea why."

"So you knew all along what a bastard Beriot was?" He laughed. "You had me a little worried, coming up to the carriage arm in arm."

"I saw what Gilles tried to do." She toed the collar with her foot, wishing that she were bold enough to take his hand in hers, to press his warm fingers to her face. "And we are Rhasan-bound to know the truth of each other's souls. You'll never hurt me."

"Well," he said, his gray eyes darkening. "I wish I'd known that all through the wretched night I just spent in your brother's lock-house."

"You should have known I'd side with you," Gaultry said, smiling. "Which is a little different than trusting you blindly."

"That's the truth."

There was something hard and jubilant in his face as he turned his attention to the attack. "Stop the horse immediately after we get over the next bridge." He rubbed the brooch on his shoulder, and the silver pin flared golden, as though it had caught a reflection of flame. "I'll stop the seven behind us from coming after us."

She started to ask him what he meant, but the clatter of the horses onto the wood of the next bridge cut the question short.

chapter 7

There were straps sewn into the sides of the carriage for just such an eventuality as its turning over. A good thing. When Gaultry seized the horse's strength, the heavy animal stopped dead in its tracks, dragging the rest of the horses with it. The carriage shuddered, then rolled. For Martin and Gaultry, the roll felt like a spinning somersault. The carriage-guards' bodies crashed past them onto what had been the ceiling, limbs flailing like grotesque rag-dolls. Martin recovered from the macabre tangle quickly; Gaultry, taking the strength of the horse into her body like an additional blow, was at first stunned.

"Come on!" Martin kicked at the stout, metal-bound door. It was stuck, or locked, or both. "Help me with this!"

Unwinding her wrist from the strap, Gaultry shakily came to help him. She slammed the door open with two well-placed kicks, the strength of the meaty carriage-horse powering her blows. The expression on Martin's face as he watched the door fly open and twist on its hinges almost set her laughing madly.

"Go on, Martin!" she told him.

The tall soldier snapped out of his surprise and scrambled out the door. Gaultry, following him, slipped on a smear of blood and missed seeing him invoke the spell from his brooch. By the time she was free from the carriage's wreckage, the bridge was burning hot as a bonfire and already half-collapsed. Conner, on the far bank, shouted orders at his men, calling for them to regroup.

On this side were four riders and the overturned coach. Three of the four horses, tangled pitifully in the tracings, were neighing and plunging in terror. The fourth—her horse—lay, oblivious, on its side. It was about to be kicked into a bloody slab of meat by the frantic struggles of its harness-mates.

She picked up her skirts and raced to its side to save it.

Mercy for the horse had nothing to do with it. Gaultry had only had an injured animal's strength in her once, and it was not an experience she cared to repeat.

"Stay with me!" Martin called. "Leave the horses!"

She had no choice but to ignore him, tremulously moving in on the thrashing animals. If she had known a spell to make an animal calm, she would have cast it then. Having the power of a horse's animal-spirit in her body didn't do anything for the real strength of her bones. If one hoof connected, bone would crush, and she'd be down for days, if not worse.

Out of one eye she could see the riders on their side of the river circling in on Martin—the coachman was out of sight, probably in the ditch beyond the coach.

"Leave the damn horses and help me!" Martin shouted.

As he spoke, the torpid horse took a hoof in the hind leg. The sympathetic pain that Gaultry felt was shattering. The impulse to double over, clutch her knee, and howl, was almost overwhelming. In desperation, she lashed out with the sword—the front pair of horses bolted away, tripping over trailing straps. She whirled and cut the last active horse's bulging jugular before it could deliver her any more damage, sympathetic or otherwise.

"Gaultry!"

"Coming!" She ran clumsily to him, one leg dragging.

One man was already dead, a second wounded, knocked from his horse. He limped away from the melee, clutching his thigh, trying to stem the bleeding. The pair of riders who were still in the fight circled, wary. Gaultry stained the horse-blood that coated her sword vivid green, and brandished it at the horseman who had come round to her side. "Get back! One scratch from, ah, from the Ichor of Wree and the goddess will take you!"

Whether or not the ploy succeeded, the man avoided her and kept on circling.

Behind her, there was a cut-off scream. Martin, seizing his moment, had struck. He whirled to face the remaining soldier. "Which will it be?" Martin asked him. "My sword or her magic?"

"Don't waste yourself, Lexi!" That was Conner, shouting across the bridge. "Run! Take the horse and run!"

The man needed no second warning. He reined his horse round and urged it into a frantic gallop. Martin took a few steps after him, then stopped, let him go.

"We'll retake you soon enough!" Conner shouted. His foxlike face was red with anger. He threatened them with a last sword flourish, then wheeled his horse round back the way they had come, followed by the remaining outriders.

"They'll go back to the last bridge to find their way to us through the trees." Martin looked up the valley at the jagged ridges of limestone that loomed up through the rough growth. "Considering the ground, it should take them some time. But we should leave now, to keep our head start."

Gaultry nodded.

"What's that on your sword?" Martin asked. "Would it have killed him?"

"It's dyed horse-blood. Remember the green blood on my knee when we first met?"

"You're telling me you don't always ooze green?"

"How can you joke?" she asked, her gaze sliding to the man he'd wounded in the leg. The downed outrider had made it to the side of the road, where he now sat, a dull look of pain on his narrow face, his shoulders hunched in misery.

The laughter dropped from Martin's eyes. "The coachman, wherever he is, can help him. It's not our concern."

Feeling rebuked, Gaultry looked away. The phantom bruise on her knee throbbed mercilessly. "I guess we should try to get your weapons then."

Beriot's leather chest squatted in the road, knocked clear when the coach had overturned. Martin prodded it pessimistically with his foot.

"We'll just have to hope we can open it quickly. Lend me your knife?" Gaultry handed it over. He bashed at the chest's lock with it, but this lock, unlike those that had fastened his chains, was built to survive a beating.

"It's my knife. Let me try." Gaultry pushed him out of the way, reclaiming the blade. She stabbed the point into the lock, the blow so forceful that the knife stuck into the metal. Then she gave it two driving blows with her healthy foot. Her first kick accomplished little, but the second, connecting at just the right angle, drove the blade four inches into the casing. It ruined the knife, but it also shattered the lock.

"Take what you want," she told him. "I'm going to see about cutting that last horse free." She limped away, pretending not to be aware of his stare on her back.

The fighting completed, Gaultry wanted to get the injured horse-spirit with its bruised knee out of her body as quickly as possible. Her entire leg, though physically uninjured, throbbed like one great bruise, concentrated at the knee. Unhitching the insensible animal from the carriage's wreckage, she pressed her hands flat to its skull. The spell had worked—far better than she could even have hoped, given her recent disaster with Martin's mare. Now it was time to let it go.

The strength and the pain coursed from her, like the passing of a fever. She felt the horse's spirit spreading back through its limbs and body, and held the animal's head steady until it was ready to scramble up on its three firm legs. It gave her a reproachful look, tossed its head rebelliously, and trotted away, moving with only the slightest of limps. This amazed Gaultry, considering the pain she'd been feeling.

Afterwards, Martin helped her coax the downed outriders' horses in. That went quickly enough, though Gaultry ended up making a short sprint for the reins of the last animal, who smelled the blood on their clothes and decided at the last moment that it didn't like them. They released the third horse when it proved lame.

"Speaking of which, I thought you'd hurt your knee again," Martin said.

"No, it's fine."

"Then let's get moving." He swung easily into the saddle of the heaviest-chested horse, bent to adjust the stirrups from the saddle. "Will you be all right to ride by yourself?"

She wasn't. She tried, but she didn't have skill enough to keep the horse moving at a trot. Martin, more steady in his saddle, kept pulling away, then having to rein in and drop back, as her horse refused to keep pace with him.

"It keeps breaking off and walking," she said feebly, the umpteenth time Martin came back for her.

"If you don't have the knack to keep it moving, you'll have to ride pillion with me. We can't waste time mucking about."

Gaultry almost suggested that they go along with her running, as they had done back in Arleon Forest, but she decided that to voice this would simply annoy Martin. So instead she mounted up shyly behind him, and put her arms tentatively around his waist.

"Just don't let go and fall off," Martin said, moving jerkily in the saddle as though she had annoyed him in any case.

Riding together, the spare horse on a lead trailing behind, they made a better pace. The mount Martin had chosen to ride was sturdy and willing to keep going at a good clip, even with two crowding the saddle. Gaultry, lulled by the rhythm, gradually let her arms fall into a more relaxed grip around Martin's waist.

"Do you think the Baron's soldiers will make it across the river?"

"Even if they have to swim, they'll do it."

An hour passed, then another. Still there was no sign of Conner or his men. The road crossed the river three more times, then descended past a lonely country inn into a wider valley. The inn's doors were tightly closed, but the rambling stone building had a hospitable look and there were fires going in two of its chimneys. Gaultry suggested they stop for food, but Martin shook his head.

"These are Duke Ranault's lands. That inn's a border post, though it's not much kept up these days. If we stop, there'll be awkward questions." He stared thoughtfully at the inn's tightly closed doors as they rode past. "Besides which, we should ask ourselves where the outrider who escaped has taken himself."

Gaultry, whose stomach was starting to grumble, said nothing. She hadn't realized that they had already passed out of Arleon's lands.

They rode on in silence after that. Gaultry was taking a slow hammering from the unfamiliar pitching of the horse's body, but she managed not to complain. Martin concentrated on pushing the horses.

A little before twilight, they came to a fork in the road. "The east road leads to Princeport," Martin said. "The west to Melaudiere. Unfortunately, to get to Melaudiere from here we'll have to run across a piece of the Chancellor's lands."

"Why does he have such a big holding?" Gaultry asked. "Isn't the Chancellor just one of the Prince's advisors?"

"He is. But he's all the blood that remains of a lapsed Dukedom. The old Prince—Benet's father—ceded the land to him. There was even some surprise that the old Prince didn't reinvest the title for him."

"He's half-Bissanty," Gaultry said. "It doesn't surprise me."

"Half-Bissanty or not, his mother gave her life so that the throne of Tielmark could survive into its sixth cycle. Despite being born of the enemy, his mother's virtues have meant that Edan Heiratikus has always found it easy to make his way in our court."

"Didn't anyone suspect his loyalties could be divided?"

"There was a convocation of the ducal council to contest his election. But Heiratikus as Chancellor was clearly what Prince Benet wanted, so they confirmed him."

Soon after, they changed horses. The new mount, the lighter horse, was skittish. "She's got a mouth like a pig." Martin grunted, sawing at the reins. "No wonder you were having trouble with her."

Gaultry, happy at having her lack of horsemanship justified, smiled into his back. "Where will stop we tonight?"

"We'll camp."

"Is that such a good idea?" she said. "After what happened the last time?"

"I'm not going to touch you," he said stiffly.

"I meant getting ambushed by armed riders," she said, matching his hauteur.

She couldn't see his face, but she guessed that he was smiling.

The light faded from the tops of the trees. The area was a little more settled than the rocky valley where they'd passed the afternoon. Scattered farms, set well back from the road, dotted the gently folding hills. The land had a feel to it of being long settled and tended. Gaultry, accustomed to the scrubby rotating fields of Arleon Forest, found it a little strange. Even the briars and scrub near the road seemed to bear a farmer's touch. Increasingly, there were thick copses of pollarded trees set close to the road. Gaultry, in her current nervous frame of mind, found herself imagining every one was a potential ambush point.

"Why has Ranault let the woods come so close in on his road? Isn't that asking for trouble?"

"It makes for convenient fuel gathering," Martin said. "Are you worried about the rider who escaped at the bridge? He won't come this way. Wherever he is now, he'll be behind us."

"Why? They know you're Melaudicrc's man. Wouldn't coming this way have made more sense?"

"Ranault has a fortified post about ten miles down the fork we didn't take. If you must know, Ranault is Aquilles Beriot's cousin. If the rider had any sense, and he *did* run, so it's just possible that he does, that's where he'll have gone."

"You said that road went to Princeport."

"It does. It just goes to Ranault's stronghold first."

"You should have told me."

"I'm telling you now."

"So we might have outriders on fresh horses come riding up on the road behind us at any moment."

"Yes, but we're hardly likely to run into an ambush, and that's what you seem to be worrying about," he answered impatiently.

"What's hardly likely?" A new, hard voice echoed out from the trees. Martin, Gaultry, and both the horses started. The skittish horse reared. In her surprise and nervousness, Gaultry lost hold of Martin's waist, and slipped back over the animal's haunches.

Stumbling back from the horse's stamping legs, she made a dash to the other horse, where Martin's bow was tied to the top of the saddle.

Two men, half-hidden by the trees, watched as she fumbled to untie it.

"They're expecting an ambush," one of them commented.

"Or at least she is," said the taller of the pair. "He's not down off his horse yet."

Martin swung down from his saddle and put a restraining hand on Gaultry's shoulder. "We might be getting some dinner tonight after all," he told her.

"Dinner?" the tall man said. "First an ambush, and now you expect dinner?"

The tall man stepped out into the road. He was putting up a long bow, his hands practiced and graceful as he sprung the powerful curve. His partner, a lightly built man wearing gray so dark that Gaultry could make out little more than his silhouette, darted further into the brush to lead out a pair of horses. A scrawny dun-colored dog brought up the rear.

"Do you know these people?" Gaultry asked, disbelieving.

Martin grinned. "Arnolfo and Hassan, meet Gaultry Blas, the woman I am geas-bound to protect. And where have you sprung from?"

"Where have we sprung from?" Arnolfo was the tall archer. His coat was green and gray, the same colors as Martin's. "Other than this cunning trap you've just bumbled into? Melaudiere, of course, and the Duchess. She had some disturbing news about your ward here."

"Did she know about Beriot being sent down again?" Martin demanded.

The archer nodded. "And some other things. Old Thomas Blas had two wives, did you know?"

Martin nodded.

"His puppy, Gilles, is their half-brother. So this is Mervion Blas's full-blood sister. It doesn't look like you've been overconcerned about your role as protector." He looked Gaultry up and down, taking in the disheveled velvet gown, the dirt, the gore, the tangled red flag of her hair. "Llara's grace! Did you find yourself a little war?"

"Something like." Martin grinned.

"Does she have a tongue?"

"I do," Gaultry said, trying to guess from Martin whether the man was being intentionally offensive.

"Pleased to meet you." The archer bowed in an elaborate genuflection. "Particularly pleased that Beriot hasn't slipped his noose over your head. Martin, what in Llara's name are you doing riding hell-for-leather back to Melaudiere's in this neck of the woods? The Duchess said you'd be lucky if you had reached the girl's home by now and got her grandmother to agree for her to come."

"I live with my great-aunt," Gaultry interrupted. "Not my grandmother."

"I got very lucky," Martin said, ignoring her interruption. "Starting from the moment that I got to the edge of Arleon Forest and found I was on the heels of what must have been Beriot's advance party—Reido and his crew," he told Gaultry in an aside.

It was strange hearing the story of the past three days from Martin's standpoint. He mentioned little of the fighting that he had done for her, and said almost nothing about her brother and his behavior. Tamsanne he described well and accurately. Beriot, Gaultry was surprised to learn, had come out to the lock-house during the night and questioned Martin closely about Tamsanne.

"Do you think that was before he had dinner with me, or after?" Gaultry asked.

"After," Martin said. "He wanted any news about your mother's family that he could get. Not that I had any to give him."

"There's nothing to tell. Our lives are very simple."

"Simple can imply many things, Gaultry." For some reason the geas-silver was bright in Martin's eyes.

"What do you imagine you're protecting me from now," she snapped.

He wouldn't answer her. "Let me tell Arnolfo the rest of the story," was all he'd say.

When he got to the story of their escape from Beriot's prison carriage his version of events became more straightforward. He offered an accurate count of the force and number of men set against them—making it clear as he did so that these were the men who might be catching them on the road if they lingered.

"I'm glad I had Gaultry with me," he concluded. "I can't think of anyone I know who has a cooler head for battle. I owe her my life." His eyes were warm on hers, dark and intense.

She couldn't quite convince herself that it was the geas that was coercing him to say that just so she could feel good.

chapter **8**

▼

Arnolfo loosed a long whistle as Martin finished his
story. "So, between burning bridges and wrecking carriages, the
two of you blasted them with one casting after the next, and they
couldn't meet you spell for spell. Poor sods. Well, that should convince the man at court that he's after the right rabbit, if nothing else
does."

Martin nodded. "That sergeant of Beriot's—Conner—can
think on his feet. If he gets to Ranault for reinforcements, he won't
be running up on our tail with just a brace of mangy soldiers armed
with tin swords."

"So what do we do?" Gaultry asked.

"We run." Martin turned to the tall archer. "Gaultry's a poor
rider, and our horses are spent. Can you take her with you on that
monster of yours?"

"If your horses could carry her and you both, she shouldn't be too
heavy for mine," Arnolfo said. "Roddy will hack it." He turned to
his partner. "Hassan, if I take the girl, will you carry my pack?"

So far Arnolfo's partner had let Arnolfo do the talking. Gaultry
might have taken him for Arnolfo's squire, but the lines of experience that marked his dark face suggested he was too old to fill that

role. With his slight body and fine-boned face, he looked more like a devout or a priest than a soldier. "I'll take your pack," he told Arnolfo. His voice was thickly accented, a strangeness consonant with the foreign cast of his face. "But I'm the lightest of all of us. Let me ride one of Martin's horses, and Martin can borrow my mount."

"And give respite to a tired beast who's had to haul my bulk all afternoon?" Martin smiled. "A good idea. Gaultry, how do you feel about riding with Arnolfo?"

"I'll do my best." Gaultry squinted doubtfully towards the horses through the dusk, not wanting to admit her exhaustion. The hours she'd spent balanced on the back of Martin's saddle had taken their toll. For all her doubts about the wisdom of stopping to camp, she was sorely in need of both food and rest.

"We can give you something to eat if you're flagging," Martin said, sensitive as always to her uncertainty. "Arnolfo, what have you got that we can feed Gaultry now in that pack of yours?"

The geas was still at work. Not knowing whether to feel grateful or annoyed, Gaultry simply let Martin bring her food while Hassan and Arnolfo readied the horses.

"You'll be fine with Arnolfo," Martin reassured her, as he watched her tiredly chewing and swallowing the hard rations Arnolfo gave her. "Have a look at his horse."

Gaultry wanted to tell him she didn't need the words of comfort. Then she did as he said and the complaint seemed suddenly unimportant.

Arnolfo's stallion was magnificent.

He was tall and shining, colored like a lustrous pearl, with black legs and nose, mane and tail silver-blond. Arnolfo, catching Martin's eye, led him over. The horse inspected Gaultry, its eye dark as a sloe berry, liquid, intelligent. Gaultry reached to gently stroke his nose, then snatched her hand away, startled, as a shock of magic touched her. The great animal was bursting his skin with magical force. The archer took in her expression and gave a wry smile.

"Meet Rodderstand." He brushed the horse's side lightly. "Not everyone can tell he has it bred in him. Not many, in fact. So I suppose the Duchess had it right in sending us out to you."

Gaultry, intensely curious, touched the horse a second time, prepared this time for what lay within. Tense swirls of magic pressed against her, like banked fire smouldering in dark coals. The strange life force of it warmed her palms, familiar, yet estranged. It was like touching raw earth made living and animate. "He comes from the Changing Lands, doesn't he?"

"Got it in one. Not that I went to the Changing Lands to get him." The archer swung up into the saddle. "And he's not properly mine either—not that that's what he seems to think of the matter, thank Llara." It was a tantalizing mystery, but the archer wouldn't say more.

"Will you help Gaultry up, Martin?" The big soldier did as Arnolfo asked, giving her a last reassuring look. She'd barely settled on the saddle's crupper before the archer tapped his heels against the horse's sides. "We'll wait for you if you can't pace us!" he called, urging Rodderstand into a brisk trot. Martin and Hassan were left to scramble for their mounts.

The scruffy dog, who had emerged from the brush with Arnolfo and Hassan, had sat, unnoticed, a few yards up the road all the time they'd been readying the horses. Now it rose, shook itself, and wriggled its tail, bright eyes intent on the archer. Arnolfo, eyes fixed on the road, didn't acknowledge it. The little animal let Rodderstand pass, then fell into a run behind him, scrawny legs working furiously to keep up.

"Is it yours?" Gaultry asked.

"He's as much mine as Rodderstand is." The archer's tone suggested the dog was a familiar nuisance. "I've decided it would be unfair to lose him by outrunning him. But if he's going to stay with me he has to work for his sup."

He chirruped. Rodderstand swept into a graceful, even canter. Martin, Hassan, and the dog were left in their dust. Riding pillion on Rodderstand was nothing like jolting along on the iron-spined horse, clutching at Martin for balance. Gaultry found herself lulled. The wind in her hair, the strong curve of the horse's body beneath her own, the roadside trees: all became a dark blur under the falling light. As Rodderstand warmed to his pace, the wild magic in his great body seeped upwards, reinvigorating her. After three days of being depleted by spells quickly cast and insufficiently prepared, it was like a swim in warm water—immensely soothing.

"Almost better than taking a nap, hmm?" Arnolfo said, as they waited for the others at a bend in the road. "He can't go all night, but he makes me feel that I can."

Gaultry nodded, shy. "Back there you said you thought the Duchess was right in sending you out to find me. What makes you so sure? It can't just have been that Beriot was coming out to Arleon."

"No, that's true enough. What has Martin told you?"

"He said that the Chancellor was a Bissanty loyalist who had imprisoned Mervion, and driven two women mad with spells. He talked a lot with my aunt. They decided that Melaudiere might be able to determine, through scrying me, what the Chancellor's plans are to destroy the Prince's wedding."

Arnolfo nodded, his eyes on the approaching horses. "Nobody had a clear picture of what Heiratikus meant to accomplish by seizing your sister when Melaudiere sent Martin south. The Duchess wanted to find out who Mervion's mother was. And Martin was the man to send, because Mervion Blas had a little sister, and Mervion's father had put a geas on him to protect the younger girl."

"Who wasn't really that much younger."

Arnolfo let out a quiet laugh. "You should have heard Martin complaining about being sent south from the thick of things to baby-sit. No one knew you were twins."

"Why was Martin coming to ask about our mother?"

"It had to do with an old prophecy," Arnolfo said. "The Duchess guessed from the start that Chancellor Heiratikus was trying to fulfill the terms of a prophecy that dates back to Prince Benet's great-grandmother's time."

Martin hadn't mentioned any prophecies. "Tell me."

Arnolfo twisted in the saddle to give her a curious look. "You don't know it? It's simple enough. Benet's great-grandmother was weak, in thrall to a faction of disaffected nobles who advocated return to the Imperial fold. But Lousielle was loyal to the Tielmaran goddesses, and to the maintenance of Tielmark as a free Principality.

Gaultry nodded. "I know Lousielle. She created the Common Brood so that even if she died there would be a power in place to help her daughter, Corinne, hold her power. She gambled her life rather than yield to Bissanty dominion."

"That's right," Arnolfo said. "Lousielle induced seven of the strongest spell-casters in Tielmark join her cause, founding a secret coven, a coven that she meant to be the guardians of her heir and of the crown of Tielmark after her own death. Elianté and Emiera rewarded the old Princess's faith with a prophecy that bound her witches to the fate of the Prince of Tielmark: *The path of the Prince of Tielmark will run red with the blood of the Common Brood.*"

"I don't see what that has to do with myself or Mervion," Gaultry said.

"Neither did anyone at court. Which was lucky, because it explains why Aquilles Beriot didn't reach you before Martin. Since the Duchess sent Martin to you, a new prophecy has come to light, fueling speculation that the connection must be there to be made."

"A new prophecy?"

"Twice fair, on the sixth run's closing night may bear,
A Bloody Fruit, to bride the Prince to ruin.

Who do you think 'Twice Fair' might refer to, twin who worships the twins?"

"I don't know," Gaultry said, shivering. "Where did the prophecy come from? Why should anyone believe it?"

"The Duchess plucked it from among the nightmares that haunted your marriage-sister's mind. But it's true prophecy. Tielmark's High Priestess, who is in exile now from the Prince's court, confirmed it before the Great Twins' altar."

"I don't see what that has to do with myself and Mervion," Gaultry said, her sudden fear making her stubborn.

"Well, the Chancellor has decided that it means you and your sister. The Duchess, among others, agrees, so Hassan and I are here."

"Roddy tired already?" Martin called, riding up to them through the dark.

"Not a chance!" Arnolfo pushed the great horse back into motion.

The midnight star was almost at its zenith when Martin and Arnolfo finally decided to stop and make camp. They ate a cold dinner of dried rations from Arnolfo and Hassan's stores, not risking a fire. They were fast approaching the border of the Chancellor's holdings. The riders from the Duchess warned Gaultry and Martin that they would have to be ready for an unfriendly crossing at the post stationed there. "They won't like it that Hassan and I are back so soon," Arnolfo explained. "They didn't like our faces—or our passes—when they saw us this afternoon."

What little was left of the night was divided into four watches. Gaultry, the most tired of the four, was assigned the dawn watch. Arnolfo, seeing her exhaustion, insisted that she sleep in his bedroll, saying that he'd rotate into Martin's when Martin rose to take his watch. It was kind of the archer, considering that Martin's bedroll was just two cloaks he'd taken from the outriders he'd slain back at the carriage. Grateful for three watches under snug blankets, and conscious that it would be false to protest that she didn't need the favor, Gaultry bedded down, falling asleep as soon as her head touched the pillow she'd made of her own cloak.

The next thing she knew, Hassan was shaking her awake.

The chilly pre-dawn hours passed with a turgid, mysterious stillness. The young huntress sat with her back against a big oak and grew a little cold as she listened to the birds wake and start to chatter. Already, just three days north of Tamsanne's cottage, unfamiliar birdsongs mixed in with the familiar trills. Oaks with strange, light-colored leaves sheltered the camp clearing. Even the moss that climbed the tree trunks had a subtly different texture. Gaultry thought about her aunt. Tamsanne held that the magic of the Great Twins was most potent under the morning star; she was often up before dawn, and out among the trees, working her magic. Was she awake and moving now?

As the cold of the morning touched her, Gaultry found her thoughts turning to all that Arnolfo had told her. He'd seemed surprised that she hadn't known about the old prophecy, the one connected to Princess Lousielle and the Common Brood. Tamsanne must have known about the old prophecy. Though the story of the Common Brood was popular in Paddleways village, Tamsanne herself had seldom spoken of it at home in the border cottage. The seven witches had married Princess Corinne to her truelove, on

Tielmark's 250th Night of the Princes, having foiled a Bissanty plot to marry Corinne to a scion of the Imperial blood. After her marriage to Valery-the-fair, a common-born shepherd boy, Corinne had enough favor in the Great Twins' eyes that she'd disbanded the Common Brood, and chosen her own counselors.

Tamsanne would have been a young woman then, just starting her tenure at the border cottage. Just as Melaney Sevenage and the Duchess of Melaudiere would have been young women.

Gaultry watched the dawn star until the sun tipped over the horizon and turned the graying sky briefly golden. For a brief moment, she thought she could see the fiery steeds that pulled the great chariot of the sun — then the first brilliant light faded, and left the sky bright morning blue, with nothing godly to see.

The dawn star was gone.

Gaultry knelt next to Martin and touched his shoulder. His gray eyes slitted open, fast as an animal's. Somewhere down under the covers, she sensed his hand already on his sword. Then he saw it was her, and relaxed.

"Good morning." He rolled onto one elbow, and made room for her on the corner of his cloak. "Are you cold?" He wouldn't need a geas to guess that.

"You think Tamsanne was one of the Common Brood, don't you?"

He rubbed his face. "It's early to speak of such things, but yes, I do."

"Even if she was, how could Mervion and I fit the old Princess's prophecy? We're Tamsanne's kin, not her blood."

"I don't know. Louisette D'Arbey was Brood-blood, along with the other woman Heiratikus murdered. He was testing them against the prophecy, against both of the prophecies, trying to discover which of the Brood-blood he could use to break the Prince. If Mervion, put under the same magic, didn't crack, it must be because she fulfilled the terms of both divinations. A sort of magical triangulation.

"You should ask these questions of the Duchess, Gaultry. She'll give you better answers than I can."

Gaultry looked across to where Arnolfo was sleeping, the scruffy dog pressed against his side for warmth. "He's Bissanty-blood, isn't he? He keeps swearing by the Thunderbringer Goddess."

"He is," said Martin. "But he's a good friend, both of mine and of Tielmark's, and he doesn't love war for its own sake. He's spent more than a decade skirmishing with the border tribes in North Bissanty. The Empire's north border no longer has a gods' pact to stabilize it, and Arnolfo is all too aware of the misery that has brought his people. What would the Bissanty Empire gain if it took back Tielmark?

"It's been two centuries since the Bissanties have been wealthy or strong or fanatical enough to wage open war against Tielmark — and they were ill-starred in even their last attempt to reconquer us. What little land they took, they couldn't hold.

"Arnolfo's a practical man, bred of generations of soldiers. He knows who will get sent to the front if another border war opens up. The Bissanties already have a large enough task on their hands, holding onto what they have, without taking on a bonded Principality with a population bred to the belief that they enjoy certain inalienable rights as freemen."

"We're a nation that would be ill suited as slaves," Gaultry agreed. "Even if our Prince lost our freedom, and the Great Twins bowed down before their Mother, no one would be eager to accept that they should just hand their fields or farms over to the Emperor, even if he is Llara Thunderbringer's annointed emissary here in the Sea-Bound Lands."

"That's right. Even if our Prince broke his pact with the gods and lost our freedom, there would be war and tremendous bloodshed before our people submitted to the Emperor."

"Martin," Gaultry said. "I've been thinking on what Tamsanne said when she pulled the Rhasan cards. My card frightened her."

He scowled. "Orchids and Black Wolves? Let's leave Tamsanne's Rhasan guesswork for the Duchess to ponder."

"Guesswork?" An angry wash of color filled her face. "Guessing, as I know you appreciate, isn't part of the Rhasan."

"All right then, let's call it Tamsanne's Rhasan snooping."

She stared at him, mystified by his anger and resentment. "I just wanted to ask what you saw when Tamsanne pulled my card," she said. "I won't mention yours if you don't want me to."

Martin's winter-ice eyes fixed on hers, as unfriendly as ever she'd seen them. "What did I see? I saw a flower of inexpressible beauty, palpatingly ready to open in my hand." An offensive smile curved his handsome mouth. "For all its implications, I doubt that's a forecasting you're ready to hear my thoughts are lingering on."

Gaultry, her face burning, drew away. "If you won't think on helping me understand my card—you can burn before I'll tell you what I saw in yours. Which was something more than a smutty boy's fantasy."

Not wanting to hear his answer, she went to wake the others.

They avoided each other throughout breakfast, ignoring Arnolfo and Hassan's inquiring glances. Gaultry again mounted with Arnolfo, bitterly pleased that Martin, riding a lesser horse, would be breathing her dust.

The sun was high in the sky when they reached the ridge above the wide river crossing that divided Duke Ranault's lands from the Chancellor's.

"That used to be the Duchy of Carlia," Martin said, pointing at the lush hills across the river. "Now it's in Bissanty hands."

Arnolfo snorted. "The last Duke died before Heiratikus even came to Tielmark. It's hardly his fault that your gentry don't breed well—or that you let your land pass through the distaff line. Or that your princes run to the sentimental."

The bridge at the crossing was sturdily built: seven solid masonry piers spanned by wooden sections. Built into the bridge wall on the river's far bank was a stone cottage with a slate roof.

"It doesn't look well patrolled to me," Gaultry said, squinting at the bridge and cottage from her vantage point high on Rodderstand's rump.

"Does it need to be, with such a broad river? Drop out just one of those wooden spans, and no one's going to get across," Arnolfo said. "The Chancellor's got a pair of crossbow soldiers assigned to it. A tough pair, if ever I saw one: a man and woman, to keep each other company. Beriot may have briefed them on his way south. In any case, they wanted to know everything about our business, and how long it was going to take. They're not going to like that we're back so quickly with you and Martin, and the pair of you looking like you've been through a war."

It was true. Martin was particularly shabby, with a dark shadow of beard stubbling his chin, battle-dirt marking his clothes, and his jacket gaping to reveal the slashed rags of his shirt. Gaultry smoothed down her skirt, a little disconcerted by Arnolfo's words. She wasn't much more presentable then Martin: the velvet dress, as she had predicted back at her brother's, was already past halfway to ruined.

"If how we look is so important, Martin and I could freshen up before we head down. I've got a clothes-brush in my bag."

"It can't hurt."

Gaultry retreated behind a bush to put Mervion's abused dress in order. Between blood, muck, and sweat, there was a limit to what she could accomplish with a single clothes-brush. Losing patience, she wove a color casting, spelling the cloth the dusty gray color of the oak at her back, brightening the white of the lace at the wrists and throat with a glimmer of the fresh spring green of the bush's leaves. Despite irregular stiff patches, the garment's appearance was vastly improved. She cleaned her face and bound up her hair.

"Verging on passable. Pity you don't have proper traveling bags," was Arnolfo's only comment when she came out and showed herself.

Martin, despite having managed a decent shave with Arnolfo's razor, still looked like a ragged highwayman.

"Give me your coat," Gaultry said. She was still angry with him for his abruptness this morning, but there was nothing to be gained by not helping him. "I'll get rid of the blood."

"Another color spell?" he asked, stripping down to his shirt. "I thought your dress was looking too good."

"What's too good?" she asked, annoyed, grabbing the coat from him and rubbing the clothes-brush across it.

"You are. Don't bother with the brush, I can see what you're doing."

Angered, Gaultry flung the jacket back, gray and green colors bright and shining, subtly changed to match her own. "Anything else?"

Arnolfo, grinning, took the coat and held it so that Martin, still stiff from the wound he'd taken in Arleon Forest, could easily shrug it on. "Well," the archer said, "you two sound like such happy love birds, I'm sure you'll both appreciate what the Duchess has planned for you next."

"What do you mean?" Gaultry asked. Martin gave Arnolfo a scowl that would have sent a weaker man running.

Arnolfo reached into his jacket, and pulled out a leather wallet that bulged with well-waxed papers. "Here's my pass," he said, thumbing past it, "and Hassan's. And here, as well, is a new pass for Martin, and one for Gaultry."

"Why would I need a new pass?" Martin shot Arnolfo a wary look. As Arnolfo held the paper out to him, Martin's face abruptly lost all color. He reached for the pass, his fingers shaking, as though he had already guessed the news the paper held. "I can't believe she would do this to me," he said, his voice shaking. "I can't believe she'd ask this of me."

"Ask what? Who are you?" Gaultry took her own pass, and folded it open. "I'm the Countess Helena Montgarret of Seafrieg. That's a pretty name. Who am I?"

"You're my wife." Martin shoved his pass back at Arnolfo, turned on his heel, and stalked off into the bushes.

"His wife?" Gaultry asked, disbelieving. "Is this a joke?"

"It's all right." Arnolfo dismounted, and bent to fix a saddle strap, avoiding her eye. "He'll be back once he's got over the initial shock."

"Who does Martin's pass say that he is?"

Arnolfo gave Hassan a questioning look. The quiet man shrugged. "If Martin hasn't told her, you have to," he said.

Arnolfo sighed. "It's no joke. Martin's pass says that he's Martin Montgarret of Seafrieg. That's his birth name."

"I don't understand. If Martin has a title, and lands, what is he doing following the Melaudiere's orders, if they upset him so?"

"Martin and his wife are estranged. Martin has never held the title Count of Seafrieg. It may be the title his pass gives him, but he's not the Count. He's renounced even the Montgarret name. All that's behind him.

"In fact, it's a surprise to me that Martin is indulging himself in a tantrum over it. I'm not surprised he doesn't like what the Duchess has done, but this anger is unlike him."

Since Martin had been intermittently angry for most of the time Gaultry had known him, she didn't know how to respond to the archer's comment. He was truly the self-annihilating Black Wolf. Feeling a little betrayed, she knelt and held Arnolfo's dog. She thought of how she had let Martin hold her in the woods before her brother's, and her cheeks burned, cursing the geas. Her father's spell prevented her from hiding her most intense feelings from him, yet there was no way for her to access his feelings behind the mighty geas that made him dance attendance to her every emotional whim.

While Arnolfo and Hassan were busy arranging the horses and their saddles, Martin returned. His manner was distant and calm. He gave Arnolfo a thin smile. This time he accepted the pass when the archer offered it. "Let's get this over with," he said.

When he turned to Gaultry, she saw at once that he was still furiously angry. "Our son's name is Martin," he said. "And your hair should be golden." His voice was cold and dangerous. He touched her hair where she had pinned it up at the nape of her neck. "Change your hair."

"Not in front of you," Gaultry said, stalling, unsettled to see him so cold, not liking the hard touch of his hand against her skin.

"Don't play with me," he said. "You know that I can't possibly threaten you." She saw the geas-silver rising in his eyes, and saw his pupils, huge and dark, as he stared out at her, fighting against it. "Just change it. I'm not in the mood to have my mind toyed with."

Ashamed, Gaultry did as she was told.

"It looks better fox-colored," Martin told her nastily, as he took his hand off her neck. "But we all must make our little sacrifices."

Arnolfo handed Martin the reins of the iron-spiked horse, tactfully interrupting them. He gave Gaultry the reins to Hassan's horse. Hassan was already up on the pig-mouthed mare that Gaultry had been unable to handle the previous day.

"We're putting you on Hassan's mount," he said, drawing her away from Martin. "It's a good animal and very biddable. You should be able to keep it under control for the pace we'll be taking past the guard-post.

"Just remember, the guards can question us but they aren't entitled to ask about private business. You're justified in turning aside any uncomfortable questions they pose you."

Gaultry nodded, and turned to Hassan. "Thank you for the loan of your horse."

"This is no problem for me." These were the first words Arnolfo's partner had spoken to her. He dropped his dark deer's eyes, and slipped her a smile.

Everyone mounted. They rode over the ridge, and onto the last loops of road leading down to the bridge. Soon after two figures emerged from the bridge cottage. Sunlight glinted off bright hauberks and helms as the pair moved to posts at the far side of the bridge.

The bridge was six wooden spans wide. The guards stood, poised like stern statues, letting them approach. Then, as the party's horses' hooves rang against the boards of the third span, the man raised his crossbow and the woman, her weapon balanced lightly against her leg, put her hand on the handle of an iron lever set in the bridge's parapet.

"Stop right there," she said. "State your business or we'll drop out the spans before and behind." Which would strand them on a short island of bridge where the bridge guards could pick them off with the crossbows at their leisure. Gaultry's stomach dropped with dismay. Over the bridge's parapet the waters that ran underneath the bridge were swollen and evil-looking. She was a strong swimmer, but the river was very wide.

"Our passes are fully in order," Arnolfo called out. His voice had an edge of righteous annoyance, as though he understood the need for formalities, but had little patience for them. "As you well know, having checked them yourselves just yesterday. This is the couple we were sent to escort."

"You weren't supposed to return so soon."

"True enough. But that's our luck, not our fault." He gestured to

Martin and Gaultry. "The Countess and her consort met us on the road."

"Send the Countess to us with the papers."

Arnolfo turned to Gaultry and nodded. "Your cue, Countess."

Gaultry dismounted. She didn't want to risk communicating her tension to the horse, fearing she'd lose control if it sensed her fear. The walk along the bridge seemed endless.

"Put your papers there, Countess." The woman indicated a niche in the bridge's side. "Then stand out of the line of fire." Her manner was more helpful than threatening. Gaultry did as she said. The woman took up the papers, and paged among them.

"What do you think, Mattias?" she asked her partner. "It's all in order. But I can't say I like it. They shouldn't be back so soon."

"You're right." The man's crossbow was unwavering. Sweat broke out under Gaultry's dress. She stood very still, guessing that Helena Montgarret would never have deigned to offer nervous answers. "Not that we've got the authority to stop them."

"No ring, Countess?" The woman's sharp eyes fastened on Gaultry's left hand.

"I'm not fool enough to travel with my jewels," Gaultry answered, coolly as she was able.

Walking around her partner's back, the woman came round to inspect her. "Hold out your hands," she said. "Let's see if you've ever worn a wife's jewels."

"I don't notice you wearing a ring," Gaultry said, folding her hands out of sight, as though the order was an affront.

The woman laughed, cast a brief fond glance at her partner, and brought her weapon up on Gaultry's face with a smooth practiced motion.

"I'm a working woman. Do I look like I need a ring?" There was a pause. Gaultry stared back at the woman, refusing to answer, trying to swallow her fear. After a moment the woman added, grudgingly, "Countess?" Gaultry knew then that she could out-bluff her.

"Are you telling me I need a ring to prove I'm married?" Gaultry raised her chin. "Have my husband across if you doubt my word on it."

The woman didn't like Gaultry's tone. She muttered something under her breath, then let an unpleasant smile flicker on her face. "We'll do just that. Send the Count across!" she called. "We have some questions to ask him!"

Martin came reluctantly over, leaving his horse and weapons behind. Even so, as he neared, the crossbowman, taking his measure, cranked his weapon up another notch.

"This is your wife?"

"What have you been telling them?" Martin asked Gaultry crabbily.

"They want to know where my ring is."

"If you'd wear the damned thing we'd not have this problem."

"Speak for yourself."

The click of a crossbow being nocked quieted them. Martin looked at the woman and drew himself up to his full height, tall and arrogant. "Yes, this is my wife. What of it?"

"Where's your proof?"

"In your hands." Martin gestured to the Duchess's papers.

"There's an order out. The Chancellor's got his eye out for a single lady."

"What does that have to do with us?"

The bridge guards shared an irritated glance.

"Just doing our job, Sir." The woman gave the big soldier an unfriendly look. "Now why don't you just give your lady a kiss and take yourselves along?"

Martin grinned nastily, reacting to something in her manner that Gaultry didn't understand. He clamped his arm on Gaultry's waist, pulling her roughly against him. "That's done easily enough," he said.

Gaultry, not at all liking the turn the pretense had taken, drew away, unsure what Martin was playing at.

"Come, love, give me a kiss and they'll let us by," he said.

"I don't want to," she whispered.

"You're not supposed to want to," Martin said, his voice hard, loud enough for the guards to hear. "But you'll do it anyway."

He bent his dark head to hers, as if determined to humiliate her in front of the guards. Something in his manner suggested he was not in jest. Gaultry pushed him away, furious, equally certain that she wasn't going to let him anywhere near her. They scuffled, and then Martin freed her, so suddenly that she stumbled, and fell on her knees. His eyes were a blaze of geas-silver. Glaring down at her, he clenched and unclenched his fists.

Behind them, the bridge guards smirked, unaware of the charge of geas-magic that roared between them like a physical barrier. "I don't see what other test we can put them to," the woman told her partner. "That's the old story of how Martin of Seafrieg treats his lady. It's said he'll never forgive her for the games she played with him.

"Come over!" she shouted to Arnolfo and Hassan. "On your ways!" They trotted hastily across, leading the empty-saddled horses, then waited as Martin and Gaultry scrambled into their saddles.

"Stop looking so utterly pleased with yourself," Gaultry said sharply, as they drew out of earshot. "You're starting to wear out the benefit of the doubt I'm giving you."

"That's healthy." His features were fixed in a frozen wolf's grin, and there was a challenging light in his eyes. "Now that you have a clearer idea of who I am, we can leave it at that."

"You want me to despise you," Gaultry said, struggling to keep her temper. "I don't know why. It's a little hard."

"You shouldn't have any illusions about me."

"That's a load of crock," she snapped. "Your wife—" Abruptly she remembered his wife's color was in her hair. She stripped the color spell away, letting the fox fire flood back along the braided sweep of her hair, so quickly that there was a crackle of dispersing power. "I have no idea why you have fought with your wife, but the bond between us has nothing to do with her. It has to do with the choice my father made when he rent his heart out on your sword!"

"You know—"

"Don't even try to look guilty!" she said. "Beriot showed me how you did it, back at my brother's house. And isn't it lucky for you that Tamsanne had already showed me a piece of your soul, Black Wolf, so that I could know Beriot's picture wasn't true? You don't want me to play games with you, fine. Afford me the same respect in return!"

Arnolfo, who had been riding behind them, took that moment

to intervene, driving Rodderstand between their two horses' bodies like a great wedge.

"I caught a glimpse of their duty roster. They're expecting a messenger from Ranault at noon. At best we have two hours before news of us catches our heels. Gaultry, how are you doing on Hassan's horse?"

She was doing well.

"It's going to be a race to the border at Melaudiere," the archer said grimly. "We'll have to hope they don't pass a message up ahead and block us."

chapter 9

Great Llara's Bones, that's the end of our luck." Arnolfo reined Rodderstand short and unslung his bow from his saddle in a single practiced motion. "Two days of good fortune, and now this."

They were at the border post between the Chancellor's lands and Melaudiere. It had taken them two days of demanding riding on unkempt roads to reach it, all the time fearing that pursuers from Beriot or Ranault would catch them. After the first day Gaultry was so saddle sore that they abandoned the attempt to keep her on her own mount, and put her back up behind Arnolfo on Rodderstand. But they'd moved swiftly despite that setback, and kept clear of their followers.

The border between Melaudiere and the Chancellor's lands was marked by a sunken track flanked with thick hedges, with a single narrow gap where the road went through. The muddy road they'd traveled for the past day and a half rose up a slight hill to this hedge-marked border. Arnolfo and Gaultry, riding a little ahead of the others, were the first to reach the bottom of the hill, and the first to see the troops that awaited them at the border: six men on lean, muscular horses and four wiry archers on foot. It had been overcast all day, as if threatening to storm, and now there was just enough light left in the dusky sky to glint off the riders' chain mail. Across the border, in Melaudiere, a handful of foot soldiers stood and watched their counterparts, spears ready and eyes intent, but as Martin and Hassan drew up to join Arnolfo and Gaultry on Rodderstand, they made no move to interfere with the gathered force that lay just across the border.

"Someone sent a carrier bird," Martin said. "That's Coyal Torquay up there." He pointed to the leader of the assembled corps, a lithe, helmeted figure on a muscular red-colored horse. "But better Torquay than Issachar Dan."

"Issachar Dan?"

"The Chancellor's military attaché. A pure-blood Bissanty lord, sent over by the Bissanty Imperial court three years ago, when Prince Benet anointed Heiratikus Chancellor. We should count ourselves lucky that the Chancellor didn't send Issachar today. If we can get you across to Melaudiere's land, Coyal will honor the border and call it a day. Issachar, who has no ties to our country and our ideas of fair play, would hound us to Melaudiere's front door." Martin leaned in his saddle to free his sword.

"Heiratikus can't afford to send Issachar yet," Arnolfo said, hands busy with his bow. "Your people won't accept a Chancellor who flagrantly makes use of Bissanty-backed force."

Martin nodded. "Not that Coyal will let us romp past him without a fight."

Arnolfo studied the hill. A humorless smile played across his thin lips. "The hill is with them, but the wind's with us. They're going to wish their archers had a longer range." Gaultry shifted on Rodderstand's rump. The movement reminded Arnolfo that she was there. "I can't have Gaultry behind me while we're fighting," he said.

"She'll have to take a separate mount up through the melee," Martin said.

Gaultry, trying to swallow her dismay, slid down from Rodderstand's back without arguing. Martin dismounted as well, and began adjusting his saddle for her. He had been riding the iron-spined horse. "Hassan is going to need his horse. You should have better luck with this one than you did with the hard-mouthed animal. He's not as hard to control."

They had barely spoken since passing into the Chancellor's lands. Martin had said nothing about her charge that her father had died on his sword. She had hoped he would deny it, that he would tell her Beriot had concocted the whole of the bloody vision to twist her brother's loyalties, that the images she had seen in the ring on her brother's finger had little—even nothing—to do with truth. It was a sword to her own heart that he wouldn't deny the charge. Again and again, she mentally reviewed the geas-impress, trying to discover some hint that might reassure her that the geas had not been passed at the very moment of Thomas Blas's death, to the very man who had killed him.

Martin pushed the iron-spined horse's reins into her hands, bringing her back to the road below the border-hedges. His handsome face was serious, warmer than it had been for the past day and a half, since their argument by the bridge. "It may be that we are parting now, Gaultry," he said. "Even if they take you here, don't lose hope. The Duchess will send more after us if we fail you here." His eyes swept over her, as if committing her features to memory. "I should have told you more than I did," he admitted abruptly. His voice was rough, but not angry. His hands were busy shortening the stirrup straps. "I can feel what you're thinking, and you're right, I should have told you. About your father; about my wife. But I feared if I began, you would storm in anger, so that the geas would force the rest out, to its last gory detail."

Gaultry's cheeks filled with color. "That's not fair. I've shielded all I could of my feelings from you." She glanced at the line of soldiers up above them at the hedge. It was still a shock to know that the five brightly dressed knights and their leader, Coyal Torquay, had been sent to the far reaches of the country, hunting after her. "You say it's hard on you, having to follow my mind, my emotions, to try to shelter me from my own feelings. Imagine how it is for me, having a man I barely know follow my every mood. You're not the only one here who has lost privacy of mind." She pushed past him and put a hand on the stirrup, trying to mount up and make ready for the fight.

"I won't argue," he said, holding the stirrup for her as she struggled with it, clumsy. "We'll get you through and these words will stand between us."

"It's what you've not told me that will stand between us," she said. She stared up the hill at the Chancellor's waiting soldiers, avoiding the sight of his intense face, the strong features revealing a sudden concentrated hunger to justify and explain. What was it he most regretted not sharing with her? The murder of her father? His ambivalence that he, a married man, was forced to play her protector? "I'm ready," she told him fiercely. "Don't make me unready by having me think on things that only weaken my resolve."

Arnolfo and Hassan were behind them, politely pretending not to have overheard their exchange. "Let's get Gaultry safe across the border," Arnolfo said. "The sooner the better."

Neither meeting the other's eyes, both Martin and Gaultry mounted up. Martin, recovering himself, resumed command. "Go shake them up," he directed Arnolfo. "We'll come through on your heels and punch a hole in their ranks for Gaultry to run her horse through." He swung round to Gaultry. "Ride behind us until we make an opening for you. Then, don't stop for anything. Stopping won't help. Your getting across the border will. Once you set foot on Melaudiere's land, they've lost—unless Heiratikus has gone mad and wants to challenge Melaudiere to open warfare."

Gaultry nodded, clutching the sides of the iron-spined horse with her thighs, hoping it would obey her when the crucial moment came.

Arnolfo ducked his head, calling for his goddess's blessing. Hassan unsheathed a strange curved blade. Its hilt was a wicked-looking basket of spikes designed both to protect his hand and serve as an offensive weapon. Gaultry had never seen anything like it.

Martin nodded to the small company, and drew his own sword from its scabbard with a single clean motion. A pale light wreathed the silver of the blade. His eyes were like hard cruel diamonds. This was the demon Martin of the forest, the man who cut down men like ripe corn. He seemed to grow taller, and stronger, and more like an angry wolf, even as Gaultry watched him. Next to Gaultry, Hassan

and Arnolfo tightened their reins, gathered their horses, and prepared themselves for the attack.

"Go!" Martin barked.

Rodderstand darted out ahead of them in a gallop before Gaultry
got her horse to stumble forward in something that even resembled a
trot. Arnolfo stood high in the stirrups, one hand on the reins, the
tip of his great bow pointed into the wind, bow-arm extended. The
men above them took one look and scattered to their positions, the
horsemen dropping into a loose arc, the archers crouching in front
of them.

Rodderstand's silver-white mane and tail rippled like banners as
he ran, his pearly coat glowing with the last rays of the sun. Arnolfo's back was a supple line as he urged the horse up the incline,
his bow-arm a fluid curve. He and the stallion moved as one, wheeling off the road to approach the waiting soldiers at an oblique angle.

Gaultry's horse, stuck on the rutted road, stumbled. As she
fought for control she missed the moment the archer checked Rodderstand's motion, and the stallion reared and twisted his great
body, offering the archer a clear presentation for a shot. Arnolfo
raised his bow with cool precision and loosed a shaft. One of the
waiting archers shrieked in pain. The horse stood, still high on its
back legs, and Arnolfo let fly a second arrow. Another man down.
As the archer plucked a third shaft from his quiver, Rodderstand
pivoted and leapt into a fresh run, this time a swerving, circling
canter. Arnolfo's bow had a longer range than those of the lesser
archers above him—even with the hill in their favor. The great
horse pulled to a second rearing stop. Arnolfo, smooth and deadly,
loosed a second pair of arrows.

The enemy riders, seeing their advantage broken, dissolved their
formation and urged their horses forward down the hill. Rodderstand turned, quicksilver fast, giving Arnolfo a crucial extra pair of
clear shots. This time the archer went for his opponents' mounts.
One horse fell, throwing its rider over its head; another rolled, dashing its rider to the ground.

The rider who'd come off over his horse's head picked himself
up, unfazed, and sprinted on towards the archer and his horse, sword
in hand. Arnolfo sent Rodderstand wheeling away, gaining precious

seconds to put up his bow and free his own sword.

"Cede the lady to our protection and you are free to pass!" Coyal Torquay's voice rang out over the jangle of battle and was ignored as Martin and Hassan closed with the remaining horsemen. Swords flashed and struck, grating together with a horrible tooth-grinding noise. One of the four still-mounted riders, seeing past the melee of soldiers to where Gaultry struggled with her horse, dropped back and circled round the knot of straining bodies. He was large, meaty man, clad in a heavy mail hauberk. Gaultry looked up from her horse, saw him coming, and tried to steer around to the opposite side of the knot of fighting.

Iron-spine, confused by her poor horsemanship, refused to cooperate. He dug his hooves in and pulled up short. Gaultry almost came out of the saddle. She sawed at his mouth with the reins, and managed to get him moving again, but she had both lost precious seconds and failed to turn his head. She swept towards the soldier with a frustrated sense of inevitability, watching as the big rider followed and timed her movements. Then, reining in his mount, he wheeled it around, pacing beside her for a few horrible moments during which her unarmored leg was ground between the two horses' straining bodies, and against his armored thigh. Then he caught hold of her bridle and tried to pull her horse to a stop. Gaultry screamed in angry frustration. He met her scream with a laugh, a deep, unpleasant soldier's laugh.

Their horses moved as one, yoked together by the soldier's hand on her bridle. Gaultry and the soldier stared into each other's eyes. He reached across and took hold of her arm with a hamlike fist, forcing her to drop the reins. The pain brought tears to her eyes. A glimmer of anger flashed through her.

She clapped her free hand over the soldier's wrist. He took a harsh shock as she called the spell, built the power. For a strange frozen moment his eyes, staring into hers, glazed over in fright.

Then she made them glaze over for real. She felt an unfamiliar surge of magic burst within her, deep in her chest, the magic melding with her thought the moment she conceived it. The magic made itself, somewhere outside her own will. It fizzed like a lit fuse up and through her arm, through her hand, into the soldier's body. Gaultry watched with a sort of horrified satisfaction that quickly mingled with frightened astonishment as his eyes washed over, whites and irises both, with a blank milky blue. The magic, only marginally under her control, had fruited as quick as her mind had formed the image.

What was happening to her spell-casting?

As blindness washed over him, the soldier shouted and gave a panicky jerk on her arm, overbalancing them both. They crashed headlong onto the muddy road, limbs and clothing tangling. Gaultry, still sighted, twisted desperately on top as they hit ground. The horses skittered and ran on. Gaultry picked herself up and stumbled after them, up the hill.

"Witch!" the man shouted, flailing in his blindness. "Torquay, help me!"

Gaultry had a brief impression of Martin, and beyond him Hassan, to her left a little below her on the hill. Martin's blade crackled with white and blue sparks as it met that of the Bissanties' Tielmaran Champion, Coyal Torquay. Torquay, a slim boyish figure on a huge horse, hearing his man's cry for help, disengaged and drew back. His helmeted head turned to Gaultry, assessing. Then he pointed at her across the melee. He was wearing silver gauntlets, silver gauntlets that shone with gathered magic fire.

A moment later, a spell hit her, driving her to her knees. It was some sort of a cold spell, or paralysis, and it had Gaultry writhing on the road, quaking, in less than a second. She swore, trying to gather herself, to isolate the spell. Her vision blurred, control near impossible. The stamping horses, the flashing swords, the battle—it all faded. She clutched at the muddy earth trying to ground herself and ease the spell from her body. Nothing worked. The insistent numbness spread from the base of her spine to her legs. Fresh panic gripped her, and she cried out.

A gentle, but tenacious nuzzle in her ribs brought her a little to her senses. She rolled wretchedly onto her side. Soft brown eyes stared at her, anxious. Arnolfo's dog. The ridiculous skinny creature had ghosted after them for days. It was rare that Arnolfo gave it any attention, other than scraps at dinner and a place at his side as he slept, yet it was clearly devoted to him. Now it pawed at her, as though trying to help her regain her feet.

Scarcely thinking, she grabbed it by the scruff of its neck. Before it could struggle or protest, she forced Coyal's spell out of her body and into its skinny frame. It whimpered and sank helplessly back on its haunches, paralysis taking it. Gaultry scrambled to her feet and would have run on, abandoning it, but something in its liquid animal gaze implored mercy. She swore out loud, realizing that it wasn't in her to leave it. She picked it up and bundled it under one arm, lurching to her feet.

Below her, Martin and Torquay were still at it, hammer and tongs. Martin lacked Torquay's bright armor, but despite this the two of them were equally matched, neither able to gain the advantage. Sweat poured down their faces; their horses pawed and neighed beneath them. Torquay's huge warhorse pushed Martin's scrubby guard's steed back, snapping at its skinny throat with curved yellow teeth. As Gaultry watched, the lesser horse stumbled, and would have gone down, but for Martin's superb horsemanship.

Still carrying the whimpering dog, she ran towards them down the hill.

Both men were at once aware of her approach. Torquay backed his horse clear, and raised his gauntleted hand to her a second time. His face was hidden under the visor of his helm, all but his tight red mouth, curved in a sensuous, confident smile.

"Get out of here, Gaultry!" Martin lashed at the opening Torquay gave him, trying to draw his attention.

The young knight parried Martin's thrust, and shot off a second spell. Gaultry, focused now and ready, seized the spell as it struck her and passed it through her body into the dog before it could unfolded and take effect. The dog began to yammer and thrash, terror-struck. Gaultry hugged it to her ribs and kept coming. Torquay had to turn his attention to Martin to stave off a fierce attack. Quite suddenly she was at Torquay's stirrup. His warhorse, trained against belly-attacks, turned on her with snapping yellow teeth. One wicked eye rolled and met hers, and it let out a sharp whinny.

Gaultry returned its glare with a sharp burst of magic, and

slapped the hand that wasn't clutching the dog against its neck. She narrowly missed having her femur smashed by a thrashing hoof.

She pulled the strength from it with a jerk of ferocious power, startling herself with her own strength. As the rock-ribbed war-horse's enraged spirit flooded into her, she whipped it into place with a ruthlessness that made one part of her laugh, remembering the doubt and confusion she'd felt with the first horse she'd spirit-taken, Martin's mare. She wouldn't be letting another horse dominate her so again, not now that she knew this power, this strength.

In front of her the horse's massive body crashed heavily to the ground. The impact shook Gaultry, but it wasn't a running fall and the horse wasn't badly hurt. Torquay scrambled clear of the saddle and had a moment to glare across at the young huntress and her laughing, power-bright face from ground level. She had a brief glimpse of angry blue eyes behind the helmet's visor and the sensuous red mouth twisted in anger. He tried another spell with the gauntlets, but she had the measure of his power now. She slapped the spell through to the dog before it could touch her.

Pumped so full of horse, her spells coming to her so easily, it would have been easy for Gaultry to give in to the temptation to pause to revel in her new strength. A part of her urged her to stay to try to best Torquay. But the border was so near; the fighting would stop if she crossed the border. She spun from the unseated champion and ran, the dog still tucked under one arm—no hindrance to her now with the massive horse she held inside. Someone was running behind her. She didn't know if it was a friend or Torquay's reinforcements. One of the archers Arnolfo had wounded sprang into her path. She brushed him aside. What could hope to stop Torquay's warhorse? It was a superior animal, bred to bring advantage in any battle, and now all its strength was hers.

The barrier of the double hedge loomed ahead. The remaining archers had erected a gate across the roadway. They stood clustered in a loose wall in front of it. Between the palings she could see Melaudiere's foot soldiers cheering, willing her to make it through. Would Torquay's warhorse have balked at the pointed spikes?

She lengthened her stride and threw herself at this last obstacle with desperate courage. There was a rush of air and shouts from both sides. Gaultry cleared the palings with room to spare, then realized in a flash that she was never going to keep her feet as she hit on the other side. She crashed down crooked, curled instinctively around the whimpering bundle of dog, and rolled. The last thing she remembered was a post leaping up in her face as she plunged, out of control, across the narrow lane between the two hedges.

"She was angry with her father for having put the geas on me."

Martin's voice. Gaultry rose slowly to consciousness, to a swaying motion and the sound of horses' hoofbeats. "You remember how furious I was when the geas took me? My anger was nothing compared to hers. Whatever my rage, at least I believed that the old man, however wrongheaded, had a right to protect his young child. In her eyes, he'd forfeited that right years ago. Sending me with the geas to protect her instead of coming himself was an added betrayal."

"Yet the old man died for her." Arnolfo's voice. "She should be grateful that he reached beyond the grave to deed her life."

"I'm not sure I agree," Martin said. "The Duchess sent me to protect a willful child, and that's not what I found in Arleon Forest. I can't believe Gaultry would nurse a grievance against her father unless she had a good reason. Even if it was a mistaken reason."

This wasn't a conversation she was supposed to be hearing. Gaultry coughed, tried to sit up to let them know she'd woken, and found her head hurt too much for her to complete the motion. Something thumped at her side, gentle. She cautiously raised her head and she discovered she was lying in the back of an open cart, moonlight filtering in from cracks in the cart's canvas cover. Arnolfo's dog was curled up at her side. The thumping was its tail. She gave it a weak pat.

"Good boy."

There was a rattle and a bang and Martin was in the back of the cart with her.

"How're you feeling?"

"My head hurts."

"Next time you take a jump like that you might try not to brain yourself on the first available fence post."

"How did you get away?"

"Once you were over the border, Coyal let us go." He grinned. "You impressed him with what you did with his horse. And with Arnolfo's dog. That's the first time he'd seen that."

Gaultry shrugged. "That was luck. His spells weren't named, or particularly well directed. He was calling them from his fancy gauntlets, and not from his own body. So when he attacked me, it was just a loose bolt of magic that had no named center. Running loose magic from one body to another isn't high-magic. A named spell would have been another story. I wouldn't have been able to pass a named spell into an animal that was a fraction of my body-weight."

"You shouldn't have come back down the hill." He wasn't scolding her, but his eyes were serious. "You should have gone on as I'd told you."

"Without Torquay's horse I might not have got past the hedges."

"You still don't accept how important your safety is to Tielmark, do you?"

She fingered the dog's scrubby fur, grateful that it at least couldn't lecture her.

"I'm trying," she told him.

"Try harder," he said. "The next time we may not get so lucky."

"What did Arnolfo mean when he said my father died for me?"

"Your father died at the New Year, Gaultry. The Chancellor had the Prince announce his marriage plans and start ordering the arrest of Brood-blood women immediately after. Who do you imagine must have been guarding the *Twice Fair* prophecy up until then?"

"My father abandoned us," said Gaultry. Her head throbbed with pain. She didn't care that she sounded childish and stubborn. "His fate was not bound to ours after that."

Martin shrugged. "I have no idea what your father wanted. You may be right. He may not have wanted to acknowledge you and

Mervion as his daughters. He may have hated or he may have loved you both.

"Whatever his opinions might have been, the ties of prophecy were above them."

chapter **10**

▼

The Duchess had sent two pony carts to meet them at the border, enabling travel through the night. After Martin left her, Gaultry fell into a fretful sleep, exhausted from the tension of the recent battle. It was the brink of dawn when her carter's voice jolted her awake.

"Lourdes Manor, the Duchess of Melaudiere's stronghold." Gaultry, still tired, could have done without the noisy formality of the announcement. Rubbing the sleep from her eyes, she pushed Arnolfo's dog out of her way, and clambered into the cart's hard front seat.

The Duchess's manor was a new-fashioned building of golden-yellow stone, built on the gray foundations of an ancient Bissanty fortress that, like the ring fort at Tamsanne's, had long since crumbled. Though surrounded by the moat of the old fortress on three sides, the new building itself was only partially fortified. What was left of the old fortress's ramparts had been transformed into pretty terraced grounds. There was a garden between the moat and the manor walls on one arm of the moat, a flower garden with raked gravel paths that led up to the manor's ground floor windows on the east wing of the building.

Despite the incomplete fortifications of the manor's wings, the central hall, along with the building's main entry, was designed to discourage attack. Unlike the graciously open plan of the wings, in the core hall there were no windows on the ground floor, and at the entry, wide double doors opened onto a square stone quay sur-rounded on all sides by water. There was no bridge, only a single small boat tied against one side of the quay.

Notwithstanding the defensive design, the effect at the entry was anything but military. The doors were decorated with painted carvings. Bronze statues the size of living men adorned the front cor-ners of the quay. Despite the early hour, eight guards in Melaudiere's green and gray livery waited on the stone benches that flanked the double doors, shivering a little in the morning cool. The fattest of them held a tall staff with an ornately carved headpiece in the shape of twined lilies. As the carts pulled up onto the paved area fronting the moat, all eight rose and stood to attention, watching as everyone climbed down from the carts.

The dark waters of the moat were cool and serene in the still of the new day. Between the new arrivals and the quay-guards, the sur-face stretched flat as a mirror, broken only by gentle bubbles from an unseen spring. No one moved to untie the boat.

"Let us over, Waterman!" Martin called, stamping his feet. "It's cold!" The fat guard bustled to the edge of the quay, bowed ceremoniously, and tapped the water's surface with the end of the ornamented staff. A streak of light shimmered across the water, ruf-fling its surface. A bright flash of magic followed. The guard sketched an unfamiliar god-sign with his hand.

"Come across, and welcome!" the fat guard greeted them, his round face beaming. Martin and the others stepped towards him, as if a path had opened across to the quay. Tiny waves scuffed away from their feet, but no one sank.

"Come on, Gaultry. It won't wet you." Martin gestured for Gaultry to follow. She hesitated, not sure what she thought of such a profligate use of magic, then tentatively put her toe out to touch the surface. It was soft, like moss, but it resisted the pressure of her foot. She took a step forward, waiting to sink, tempted to run lest the spell break before she reached the others. Another step. She was a yard from the bank now. There were red and orange fish beneath her feet, blowing bubbles as they rose to discover the source of the distur-bance. She quickened her steps, not wanting to be left behind. Has-san was in the rear. Unlike the others, he too seemed hesitant about crossing the water on the back of a spell. "Nice being spared the swim," she commented, a little breathless, reaching his side.

"I don't swim," the dark man said. "Every time I cross here, I wonder how deep it is."

"Every time? They use this magic every time?"

Hassan nodded. "Allegrios, the water god, reigns in Gabrielle Lourdes's holdings. She wants her visitors to remember that. Thus, this." He indicated the water under his feet. "We are at Allegrios's mercy here."

The statues that ornamented the quay's front corners loomed above them. On the left was a fierce bronze god with fin-tail legs; on the right, his female counterpart. The goddess had merry eyes, and was crowned by bronze ringlets that tumbled to her waist, covering her breasts; the god was handsome, with flowing hair, flat, high cheekbones and a laughing mouth. It would have been Martin's image, if Martin's hair wasn't shorn like a common soldier's, or if he ever let open laughter fill his face. Gaultry looked sharply from the statue to Martin, comparing the profiles. The match was too con-spicuous to be missed.

The fat footman, down on one knee, took Martin's hand. His face shone with pleasure. "Martin Stalker. Allegrios Rex brings you safely to us. Your grandmother is waiting in the water salon. She bids you bring her the woman from Arleon Forest at once."

Gaultry's stomach dropped into her boots. She hadn't been sur-prised, back at the Chancellor's bridge, to learn that Martin had been born to a title. Or, if she had been surprised, the news had an-swered more questions than it raised. Common soldiers didn't carry swords with six runes of power forged to their blades, or powerful fire charms that could turn bridges to burning tinder. The title had gone a long way to explaining the big soldier's training, his power, and his arrogance.

But it had not told her that he was blood kin to a woman who sat on the high ducal council, determining Tielmark's laws and yearly goddess tribute. "You still won't accept how important your safety is to Tielmark," he had rebuked her. Perhaps she might have done so if he had told her how close he really was to Melaudiere's ear.

They were past the quay-guards and inside the doors of the manor. The soldiers who had accompanied them from the border left them there, turning off down a side corridor after making their farewells. Martin gestured for Gaultry, Arnolfo, and Hassan to follow him, and set off down a corridor that led through the center of the main wing.

There were mirrors and fine glass fountain-work in every room and corridor; the sound of moving water followed them at every turning. In Paddleways village, the main shrine to Elianté and Emiera was decorated with carved panels and a single crudely carved statue of a double-headed deer. Here, graceful statuary abounded, in bronze, glass, and stone, worked into the paneling and over the door lintels. Mostly it depicted fish or the fish-tailed water god Allegrios, with the occasional cheeky animal or human form mixed in as secondary figures. Staring around at the myriad images, Gaultry felt a very long way from home indeed. Rushing through it all at Martin's heels without getting to see anything carefully made it even more overwhelming.

She trotted to catch Hassan. "Where did all this come from?" she whispered.

"The Duchess makes it," he told her, equally quiet. "With her hands, or her magic. It's in her blood. She laughs sometimes, and throws up her hands, but she can't stop doing it." He smiled. "If it wasn't so beautiful, it would be a curse, no?"

She looked up into the eyes of a glass satyr that crowned an archway overhead, wondering what must it be like to be filled with so much magic that it forced its way out as a constant stream of lovely creations. Tamsanne was like that, she realized, the way she filled the woods around her cottage with wreathing bundles of flowers. What must it have been like to have been part of a fellowship of seven such witches, mingling their powers to create a single great spell?

The water salon was at the very back of the building. After the rich ornamentation of the passages that led to it, the sparseness of this room came as a shock: bare whitewashed walls, a robin's egg blue ceiling, and a rough-hewn font of white marble in the center of the floor. Across the room from where they entered, long mullioned windows opening out into the back gardens, letting in a whisper of a breeze. The floor was gray flagstones, worn with time and weather. The room was part of the ruined Bissanty fortress, a part that had been exposed to the air for generations before it had been overbuilt by the new palace. The plain bowl and stem of the marble font were as worn as the flagstone floor. There were dark stains on the font's stem, scrubbed-looking stains that might have been the remains of old moss.

Despite the open windows, the room was unnaturally silent. It felt like the calm between magic castings; the air rich with the spent charge of an old spell as the new gathered its power. The atmosphere was heightened by the demeanor of the grave-faced woman who stood at the font, one hand trailing on its marble edge, her eyes intent on its depths.

It was Gabrielle Lourdes, the Duchess of Melaudiere.

She was tall, taller than Gaultry, dressed in azure robes shot through with silver thread. Her thin white hair, cropped short at her neck, had fallen forward, hiding her face. With her unusual height, she might once have been a grand presence, but now, though there was a shadow of her grandson's fierceness in her carriage, Gaultry's first impression was of a careworn and troubled soul. Age had been merciless to the Duchess of Melaudiere, stripping the flesh from her bones to render her thin to frailty. She seemed haunted and tired, as if her own ghost was a plague to her.

Then the Duchess raised her head, threw her hair back from her face and looked at them. Amidst the aged wreck of her face, her deep blue eyes were vivid and full of life: calm, powerful, alert, and rich with magic. They did not seem at all to be the eyes of an old person. Her voice, as she greeted Hassan and Arnolfo formally, was strong and crisp.

Leaving the font, she crossed the room to greet her grandson. Her steps were a little halting but her manner was proud. She smiled, and ran her hand lovingly over his cropped hair. "Still the soldier-stalker," she said. "You did well, against worse odds than I would knowingly have set you."

"We were glad when Hassan and Arnolfo showed up," Martin said, kissing her palm. "Grandmère, here is Gaultry Blas."

Gaultry made a jerky bob, somewhere between a bow and a curtsy.

"Twice fair." The old woman's eyes narrowed, and a pleased smile crossed her lips. "Tamsanne's granddaughter."

"Grandniece," Gaultry corrected her.

"If you like."

"I won't be mocked."

The Duchess lifted her eyebrows. Gaultry, defiant, returned her stare. "I see," the Duchess said. "Clever Tamsanne. So clever we almost didn't find you in time." She turned to Martin.

"Take Hassan and Arnolfo and get yourselves some breakfast. Gaultry Blas and I need to talk alone." She dabbed her fingers in the font, and traced a watery figure on the smoothness of the marble edge. "I have news of her sister."

Gaultry, who had been half-willing to protest at being left alone with the fierce old woman, lost interest in arguing. Martin, at first annoyed by his peremptory dismissal, looked from Gaultry's eager face to his grandmother's composed features, and gave a reluctant nod. "Then I'll report on Beriot and his men later, if that suits you. And Torquay. He was at the border where your pony carts met us."

The men went out, leaving the women alone in the echoing chamber.

"Indulge an old woman's fancy. Come see my font." The Duchess beckoned.

The bowl was full to the brim. An image of a dancing fish was carved on its bottom. As her bony old fingers brushed the water's surface, Gabrielle Lourdes's fingers made no disruption.

"Put your hand over mine," the Duchess said commandingly. "Press it down into the water, if you can, and tell me what you see."

Hers was a fleshless, almost skeletal hand, with long callused fingers. Gaultry covered it with her own, feeling clumsy. The old woman's skin was cold and dry. She pushed. The water pushed back.

Under their paired hands, the water's surface bowed a little, and silvered over like a mirror, a strange false mirror that showed a wavery image of inverted trees and a cloudy sky. Gaultry flinched, startled by the power she felt compressed below the water's surface. She knocked awkwardly against Gabrielle, almost drawing their paired hands clear of the water's surface. Whatever it was that had been trapped in the font, it didn't like the disturbance. It sent a whip of magic whirling up, binding the old woman's wrist to the young's, anchoring them both to the font. This time it was the Duchess who took a startled breath.

There was a flutter across the water's surface, then, with no warning whatsoever, her sister's bewildered face appeared before them, framed by the bowl of the font as though in a looking-glass.

Mervion's shoulders were covered with gold cloth. A coarsely forged iron coronet crowned the riot of her red-gold hair. A sapphire necklace, the goddess Llara's sky-stones, winked at her throat, flashing blue fire. Underneath the fine adornments Gaultry's twin looked wearier than the young huntress had ever seen her: face white and strained; lips parched and bruised. She gawked at Gaultry, echoing her surprise. But she was quick enough to recover, grasping at the spell like a lifeline. Her lips formed Gaultry's name, once; twice; and then again, as though she was screaming, but no sound came through.

"Mervion!" Gaultry cried back. "Mervion!" As the words came out of her mouth, her sister's image shattered, breaking into shards. The magic tether that bound Gaultry's wrist to the Duchess's dropped away. She caught at it, trying to recall the spell and her sister both, and her hand went painfully through the water's surface, like a skater breaking through ice. The water beneath was bitterly cold. The image-shards dissolved to liquid ripples. Whatever had been trapped in the font, facilitating the spell, was gone now. "Cast it again and bring her back." Gaultry snatched the Duchess's hand, not caring if it was disrespectful, and thrust it into the coldness of the bowl, trying, and failing, to regain the surface solidity that would bring her sister back. "Cast it again!"

"I can't." The Duchess pried her fingers free of Gaultry's, surprisingly strong, and dried her hand on her skirt. "Not now. Maybe later. But you saw her." Her voice was composed, but her old hands had a tremor in them that had not been there when her hand had first rested under Gaultry's. "That's the important thing."

"Saw her? She saw me. Do the spell again so I can tell her help is coming." Gaultry stood to her full height, aggressive, not quite aware that her stance conveyed an open threat. The despair in Mervion's eyes, her voiceless cry, had pushed the young huntress past care for social niceties.

"The spell won't work that way," the Duchess said, her voice cool, deliberately damping Gaultry's fire. The old woman wiped the edge of the font with the sleeve of her azure robe. "You've seen yourself: a single word will break it. But you could see your sister. That achieves more than you can know."

"Why was she dressed so strangely? The crown, the gold?"

The Duchess stared down at the carved fish at the bottom of the font. "That's a question that begs a deeper question. What do you know about Clarin, Tielmark's first Prince?"

Gaultry shot the Duchess a sharp look. She wanted a straight answer, not new mysteries. But the Duchess, ignoring her, continued to stare into the font, waiting for Gaultry to answer her question.

"Clarin was a Bissanty Prince before he became Prince of Tielmark," Gaultry said, sensing her patience would not outlast the older woman's.

"What else?"

Tamsanne had taught Gaultry everything important that the headstrong young huntress knew about the great Prince Clarin. He was one of Gaultry's favorite heroes, at least in part because Clarin was reputed to have despised court-life as decadent and undesirable. He had forfeited his stake in the throne of an ancient Empire to found a free country, a country without slavery, a country free of the poisonous treacheries of the thousand-year Bissanty noble houses.

"Tielmark used to be one of four Bound Principalities of the Bissanty Empire," Gaultry said. "In Clarin's generation there were five Bissanty princes. Clarin was born the fifth son, so he started as a Prince of no estate. He only got Tielmark when one of his brothers died."

"Died?" the Duchess prompted.

"Was poisoned." Gaultry shrugged. "Do Bissanty princes ever die natural deaths?"

"Go on."

"The year Clarin became Tielmark's Prince, the reigning Emperor died. Gaius Telemedierus, Clarin's oldest brother, ascended the Imperial throne. At his coronation, he demanded a blood sacrifice from the Bissanty princes as proof of their loyalty. Fifty lives from each Bound Principality, one for every year under Llara's grace that they wished him to rule. Three out of the four landed princes sent him the full fifty. Clarin, sensing this was only the beginning of the blood tribute his brother would demand, refused to send even one.

"Instead of sending tribute, Clarin sent soldiers. He declared war and broke Tielmark free from the Empire. That's all," Gaultry said. "That was three hundred years ago. The Empire still wants us back."

"They never stopped wanting us back," the Duchess said.

"The gods were behind Clarin," Gaultry remembered. "Once Clarin had the gods behind him, it didn't matter what the Bissanties wanted. He made a trifold pledge to Elianté and Emiera: he would forsake his blood claim to the Imperial throne; marry Tielmark's soil; and dedicate his nation to their worship. In return the Great Twins succored him from the wrath of their mother, Great Llara, for the insult he'd done her Empire."

The Duchess nodded. "Now, as then, Tielmark's fate will be decided by the gods, not by men—though men have strong influence on the gods' decisions. In Clarin's day, Elianté and Emiera were persuasive negotiators for his pleas, but it's rumored that Telemedierus gained little favor in Llara's eyes by demanding such a bloody tribute. Whatever the case, Llara ceded benefice of Tielmark to her daughters' worship, and pacted with the Great Twins to create our north border, dividing us from Bissanty."

"What does this have to do with Mervion, or myself?" Gaultry asked, impatient.

The Duchess gave her a sour look. "If you don't understand the founding stones of our country's independence, how can you comprehend the current danger?"

Gaultry glared at the old woman. There were some things that every Tielmaran had at least some idea about. "If Clarin or his heirs fail in their pledges to Elianté and Emiera, the Empire — and Llara — could take us back. As a Free Principality we owe fealty to the Twin Goddesses for protecting us from the Great Thunderbringer."

"Very pat," said the Duchess.

"What else is there to know?" Gaultry said. "Isn't it the ducal council's business to ensure that the Prince fulfills his pledges?"

"The ducal council can be corrupted." The old woman showed Gaultry the inside of her wrist. A long, old scar transversed it left to right. "That was put there before I was twenty by my own father. He was dedicated to the Bissanty Emperor, and sent him a yearly pledge of blood — his and mine both. Believe me, he did not wish to see the Prince in my day married to Tielmaran blood."

Gaultry stared at the old scar, trying to imagine the Duchess as a young woman, twisting vainly against her father's knife. "His plans must have failed," she said softly.

The Duchess laughed, a rich, delighted sound that echoed through the chamber. "They failed. They spectacularly failed. And we married the Prince — who was a Princess — to a man of common Tielmaran blood."

By "we," the Duchess could only have meant the Common Brood, the witches who had presided at Princess Corinne's marriage night. "Tamsanne was there too, wasn't she?" Gaultry asked.

"She was. And five others, all sworn and true." The Duchess rubbed the old scar. "After the great peace of Corinne's thirty-year reign, it is hard to remember a despair now fifty years past and gone. The Bissanty obsession with blood was in the open then. Plots laid in Corinne's grandfather's day were ready to bear their poisonous fruit. The Bissanties were bold. Their embassy sent an Imperial princeling to Prince's Night. Their stated intention was that Corinne should accept him in marriage." The Duchess smiled. "For all their professed faith in the Great Thunderbringer, the Bissanty Emperor and his courtiers are a strange folk when it comes to goddess worship.

"Because they are tortured in their own relations to Great Llara Thunderbringer, the Bissanties are blind to the joyous nature of the tie native-born Tielmarans owe to the Great Twins. In Bissanty, priests sacrifice on secret altars, offering blood to Great Llara in the Emperor's name. In Tielmark, there are no intermediaries. Every village offers its harvest to the Great Twins, and when a rich offering is made, the goddesses' bounty is plain to see. The Bissanties can seduce those who are not bound to the land with promises of vainglorious power and wealth, but those who watch the green corn rise in the fields cannot doubt where the true source of Tielmark's bounty lies."

"Then why aren't we safe?" Gaultry asked.

The Duchess smiled, a little grimly. "We aren't safe," she said, "because after three centuries of failing to destroy Tielmark's freedom, the Bissanties are finally beginning to understand both our bond to our goddesses and the weaknesses it leaves us with. If we can't be made to betray our goddesses, the Bissanties must find some other way to break us.

"Elianté and Emiera hold Tielmark in trust from their Great Mother. If they should fail to fulfill certain pledges to Llara Thunderbringer, Llara still holds the god-right that would allow her to reclaim Tielmark's lands for her Empire. And it is here that we consider Clarin's three pledges.

"The pledge to honor and worship the Great Twins has been easily met. Having committed ourselves to the Great Twins, who desires apostasy and a poor harvest? In a nation of free farmers, that pledge will not be broken.

"The second pledge was Clarin's promise to forsake his claim to the Imperial throne. Once Clarin fulfilled that pledge, the right to the Imperial title could never be reclaimed. The blood of Meagathon, Llara's only earthly son, runs in the Bissanty Emperor's line. When Clarin offered himself to the Great Twins for a mystic purging, every trace of the godson's blood was stripped from his body, and there was nothing left for him to pass to his heirs. So the second pledge is done and gone, and not a matter of worry.

"But Clarin's third pledge, his promise to marry Tielmark's soil, is a pledge that must be renewed by each of Clarin's heirs, and this is where Tielmark is vulnerable. Here the spirit of our first Prince's pledge, and its wording, threaten a rift.

"Clarin stood on the great altar of the princes, in the heart of his new capital, and vowed to forsake the High Goddess blood of Bissanty, that he and his heirs would marry common blood, down to the dying of his line. He called Briseis, his bright warrior bride, onto the altar. She was young, healthy and splendid, born of a family of Tielmaran soldiers. The goddesses themselves became incarnate to bless the marriage, then, to Tielmark's lasting woe, the pledge was complete."

"I don't understand."

"The *spirit* of Clarin's pledge was that his line would marry common *Tielmaran* blood. The *words* of his pledge had him promising only commonness."

Gaultry frowned. "Are you saying Clarin made a dangerously inexact pledge?"

The Duchess gave Gaultry a solemn look. "Elianté and Emiera promised their mother a Prince in mystic marriage to his land in return for the dominion of Tielmark. And when the moment came for promise-making, that was not quite the pledge that Clarin made to the Great Twins. Llara would be displeased to see the throne of Tielmark occupied by a Prince bonded in marriage to a consort in whose veins runs not a drop of common Tielmaran blood, a marriage to which her daughters, approving the fulfillment of Clarin's pledge only, have given their blessing."

"The Chancellor wants to marry Prince Benet to a woman whom the goddess Llara won't approve as his consort, even if Elianté and Emiera accept her, and consecrate her marriage to the Prince as a sacral renewal of his ancestor's pledge," Gaultry said. "Is that right? Does the prophecy about the Common Brood point Heiratikus to the consort who can destroy Llara's faith in her daughters' vows to rule Tielmark as a nation that is committed to keeping its promises?"

"My dear, it is the *Twice Fair* prophecy that points Heiratikus the way to an ill consort for the Prince. The Brood prophecy is more complex. It does not simply portend Tielmark's destruction. *The path of the Prince of Tielmark will run red with the blood of the Common Brood.* This hints at new pledges, at a coming end to Tielmark's cycle of dependency on the constancy of a single man's blood heirs."

The old woman's expression was so intense, Gaultry found it difficult to face her. If Tamsanne had been one of the Common Brood, and participated in the mystic marriage of one of Tielmark's greatest rulers, why hadn't she shared these things with Mervion or herself? Thinking on Mervion, and remembering her glimpse of her sister's tortured face, the room felt suddenly stuffy and close.

Out the window, down the garden path, dawn had given way to bright sunshine. Green leaves fluttered, inviting. She was filled by a sudden impulse to dash outside, to run and keep running, to find a deer, a horse—anything—to take from it and run and run, until exhaustion took her, freeing her mind from the mass of worry the Duchess had laid upon her. Outside a shadow danced on the grass, its leaping shape making her feel more trapped then ever.

"I don't want to know about new pledges," she told the old woman. "Or about a great cosmic cycle of hope and doom. The Bissanties will always be trying to destroy Tielmark's freedom. Tell me what this has to do with *now*, what it means for me and Mervion."

Gabrielle of Melaudiere was accustomed to telling a story at her own pace. Making an obvious effort to control her irritation at the interruption, she traced a figure on the rim of the font, keeping her eyes off the young woman lest she betray the full extent of her impatience. "Two prophecies," she said, "hint that you and your sister have been born to a power that threatens Tielmark and perhaps even Great Llara herself."

If Gaultry had not had her eyes fixed on the shadow outside the windows, those would have been Gabrielle of Melaudiere's last words. The shadow leapt in size, and a blast of wind roared into the chamber. Gaultry, her body moving before her wits, dragged the Duchess to her knees as a terrible shriek burst into the room, bringing with it the forequarters of a freakish beaked monster.

It was an eagle, an eagle the size of a draft horse, with blazing gold and crimson eyes, and long metal feathers that scraped like razors against the window's stone framing. Its horrible beak struck, splitting the bowl of the font in two, just in the place where the Duchess's frail body had been before Gaultry had grabbed her. There was a sizzle of released magic as the font-water splashed down. A sizzle, and an unnatural burning smell. The creature gave a harsh grunting cry, and lunged again. It was so large its wings were wedging against both sides of the window-frame.

"Get behind me!" Gaultry tried to drag the Duchess towards the room's inner door. The creature, finding itself jammed, hissed and shifted one wing up so it could force more of its body through the window. Another rattling hiss, and it struck again, seizing a beakful of the Duchess's skirts. It twisted its beak in the heavily embroidered cloth.

Gaultry scrambled, trying to stop the bird from drawing the old woman in where it could more comfortably maul her. She grabbed the Duchess's boney shoulders and pulled, her hands frighteningly close to the thing's powerful beak. It wrenched the old woman relentlessly closer, so strongly that there was nothing Gaultry could do to prevent it. Growing desperate, the young huntress reached for its head, attempting to catch the giant monster's eyes with her own. The metal feathers were as hard and unyielding as they looked, but Gaultry hardly registered the pain as a thousand metal edges rasped her fingers. She threw a channel open in her mind, reckless in her terror, and reached for the animal she knew must be waiting somewhere inside the monster form, the shrieking eagle-spirit that there was a slim chance she could hope to rule.

Bleak predator's eyes locked onto Gaultry's. It knew what she was trying, but it didn't seem to care; she could feel its spirit sucking outwards, see its gold and crimson eyes glazing as the spell took hold. It barely fought her.

Then, suddenly, there was a stranger's voice loose in her mind, a voice that sounded calm, so much like her own, that she knew at once that something was seriously wrong, even as the soothing balm spread, like wide wings, blocking fear.

She could mount this bird and ride the skies, the voice told her. *She could climb on the great monster's back, safe in a nest of steel feathers, and taste the joy, the running ecstasy of riding the wind. Great Gyviere, this bold eagle, would fly her far from care and sorrow. With this creature as her true companion, she would rise, she would rule—*

She would prove herself a fool and willingly deliver herself to the enemy! Gaultry shook her head, trying physically to expel the mind-twisting voice. It was worse than the mare-spirit that had overcome her in Arleon Forest. There were words, seductive words, twined round the impetus to cede control.

Fortunately her fright with Martin's mare had taught her something about regaining control when such madness threatened. She fled to the calm corner of her mind, threw all her strength there, and called to the Great Twins for help. Something deep within her seemed to rip and tear, vivid with sparks of green and purple, and suddenly she was free—albeit on her knees with her head punched down in the Duchess's lap—and the seductive voice was gone.

A hiss behind her ear told her that the monster had not been exorcised with it.

At least the bird had lost its hold of the front panel of the Duchess's skirts. Gaultry staggered to her feet, once again putting herself between the monster and the old woman's frail body. The effort she'd made to discharge the failed spell had exhausted her, but there would be no respite until they'd both escaped the brutal snapping beak.

The bird spat out a rag of cloth, clacked its tongue, and eyed Gaultry evilly, reconsidering its attack. Glancing away, Gaultry spied a fragment of marble, fist-sized yet large enough to serve as a weapon.

As she dove to reach it, the bird lunged again. It caught her by the shoulder. Gaultry howled, the stone forgotten in her direct frantic need to free herself. Her hands raked the creature's barbed feathers and came away bloody. The creature jerked her towards the window, the Duchess seemingly forgotten, one cruel-taloned foot rising to help it get a better grip on her body. Gaultry, reaching now for her lesser spells, grappled harder, ignoring the risk to her hands, and tried to push a color spell into its body, hoping to blind it. A stout shield of magic blocked her. Screaming, she redoubled her effort, and tried again.

This time the creature shook its head, dazed, as though the spell had in some part penetrated its magic shield. Her collarbone, still trapped in its beak, was almost ripped free from her body as the great bird thrashed its head and gargled. Blooming, sheer agony overwhelmed her, and she went limp. Talons closed around her leg. The bird hissed, triumphant. Gaultry tumbled backwards, held only by her leg, as the bird released her shoulder. She threw up her arms, sheltering her head, as she crashed to the stone floor. For a fleeting moment, she found herself looking into the Duchess's shocked eyes. Then the creature pulled back and plucked her out of the darkness of the salon into the sun of the garden with as little ceremony as a lesser bird of prey would have used in wrenching an unhappy rat from a shallow hole.

Turning out towards the garden, the eagle beat its wings, shunting itself forward with short crooked jumps. Gaultry lost all sense of orientation: her body smacked mercilessly across the ground, her blood smearing the grass. Then they were dizzyingly up in the air, Gaultry upside-down, the ground receding beneath her head. She had a crazy view of statuary and fountains and squares of earth filled with brightly colored flowers. Then dark moat-water spread beneath her.

The eagle shrieked with sudden pain, and sprouted a long arrow in its breast. It lurched, and missed a wing-beat. Gaultry screamed anew—the arrow had missed her by a hand's width.

A jolt of white fire flashed along the arrow's shaft. The great bird shrieked a second time, and lost its grip on Gaultry's leg.

She spiraled down like a pinwheel gone mad, striking the water with an impact that shuddered deeply through her body. Mossy water closed over her head.

The last thing she knew before losing consciousness was the gentle press of the water, pushing her upwards to the lovely air, and the concerned faces that loomed over her of those who had run to her across the water's surface. Then the pain overwhelmed her and everything went black.

▼

chapter 11

When Gaultry next opened her eyes, she was on her back, lying in a soft bed. The arm on the side of her bitten shoulder was bound against her body with a leather strap. She wriggled her fingers, and was rewarded with a stabbing pain in her shoulder.

"Ready to wake, child?" The voice was mellow, female, tinted with soothing magic tones. "I wouldn't try moving, if you are."

Gaultry jerked her head round to see who spoke, and immediately regretted not following the advice.

"It hurts," she said.

"I'm not surprised." Sitting by her bed was a woman of middle years, thin as a whip, with pale eyes, a narrow face, and curling dark hair flecked with gray. She wore a long brown dress, double-spirals of gold on the breast and sleeves. A stout, leather-bound book rested in her lap, half-hidden by the folds of her skirts. "The Duchess has called a special healer for your shoulder. And yesterday she sent for me, saying the time had come to take some open risks." Now the woman's voice sounded disapproving.

"Yesterday? How long have I been asleep?"

"More than a full round of the sun. It was for the best when they set your shoulder."

"What was it that attacked us?"

"You have heard of the Chancellor's officer, Issachar Dan?"

"Martin mentioned him."

"It was one of Issachar's eagles."

"He has more than one?" Gaultry pictured the harsh steely feathers, the bloodshot golden eyes. It was unpleasant to reflect that the Chancellor controlled a man who had mastery of more than one such creature.

"Someone panicked. Issachar's eagle should not have been anywhere near Gabrielle's stronghold. But their panic nearly became their success. Gabrielle tells me she would have been killed, if you had not moved so quickly."

Gaultry could think of no appropriate response, and her wounded shoulder prevented her from shrugging.

The woman smiled, not entirely kindly, as if it amused her a little to see the younger woman's confusion. "My name is Dervla," she said. "I am a priestess of Elianté and Emiera. I was once Prince Benet's confessor, before he fell prey to Heiratikus. And you are Gaultry Blas, the huntress-twin of Arleon Forest. How do you feel?"

"My shoulder hurts," Gaultry said. "I'm lucky I landed in the moat."

"True. The Great Twins blessed you yester-morn."

Testing her injury gingerly, Gaultry sat up and swung her legs over the edge of the bed. The priestess watched her, the pale eyes cool, measuring. Gaultry was not sure what to make of the woman. There was a strong aura of the Twin Goddesses about her, and Gaultry guessed that the Great Twins' magic flowed through her with impressive power, but there was something patronizing in the thin woman's manners, something a little cool. Gaultry wondered whether it was simply that the woman knew she was a temporal spell-caster. It wasn't uncommon for priests to disapprove of those who called magic from the gods without first surrendering their life's work to the Great Twins' glory.

"If you want to walk, your arm should be moved into a sling."

"I'd like that, I think."

The priestess helped transfer Gaultry's arm from the bed-strapping into a soft sling, efficiently adjusting the folds of cloth to take the weight off the young woman's bad shoulder. "Your healer won't arrive until morning," she said. "You'll have to make do with this until then. Gabrielle doesn't want me to tend you in the meantime, so you'll have to suffer through until then." There was resentment in her words, as though she would have preferred that the task be trusted to her own hands. "Try walking. Let's see how it feels when you walk."

They were in a splendid bedchamber with long windows and a matched pair of green glass fountains, one on either side of the wide double doors that were the room's only entrance. The mantel was clustered with graceful figurines. An elaborately carved roundel of pink marble faced the chimney. Gaultry had imagined the house of a great Prince would be like this, though a Prince, of course, would not have made his own statuary.

"How is her grace, the Duchess?"

"Shaken, but uninjured. Her concern is all for you." Dervla's mouth set in a disapproving line.

"Her grace didn't get to explain why she thought Mervion and I were involved in the Chancellor's plotting," Gaultry said. "She said we were born to a power that threatened Tielmark, but she never said what it was."

"It's not such a mystery," Dervla said, sniffing. "If it was obscure or deeply hidden, the Chancellor would never have discovered you."

"What do you mean?" Gaultry asked.

"Martin tells us you spirit-take from animals. Have you ever taken it a step farther, and made a blood-beast?"

"I wouldn't describe blood-magic as a step farther from spirit-taking," Gaultry said. The clergy could be annoying, the way they insisted on ranking different magics as though there was a single coherent line of progression in their powers. "They're distinct streams from the river of the goddesses' power. Blood-magic is harder to control than taking-magic, but that doesn't mean it's necessarily stronger."

Blood-magic was in fact the least-biddable power that Elianté and Emiera bestowed, a power so close to creation itself that the Great Twins seldom ceded it with full control. Gaultry played restlessly with the fringe of her bedcover, wondering what Dervla wanted to know. Blood-magic could work enduring changes on living flesh, but it was also a power that could shift and twist as it worked, transforming the spell-caster as well as the object of the spell, making changes so strong they could be passed from parent to child.

"Please answer my question," Dervla pressed.

"I've never made a blood-beast by myself."

"That's no answer."

Gaultry looked into the woman's pale eyes, unsure if it would be best to be honest or closemouthed. "Please," she said, deciding on honesty rather than an answer. "I don't know how much I should tell you."

The priestess laughed. "That's a careful answer," she said. "You must be tired of being chased and questioned. Pray with me. Then decide how far your trust extends. Or not." Dervla traced a circle on her left palm, murmured an invocation of the Great Twins, and offered Gaultry her hand.

To refuse the priestess such a simple thing would have been an open slight. Gaultry, not pleased to have been maneuvered so effectively, accepted the woman's hand, and called a prayer herself.

The well of power that moved in the older woman hit her like a hard, unfriendly slap. Gaultry, looking sharply into Dervla's face, saw that she had been a fool not to recognize at once that the former confessor of a Prince would have tremendous force and power in her. The woman's pale eyes were filled with cold triumph that Gaultry had so easily entered her trap. A surge of magic flooded from the priestess, through her hand, up through her thin arm, pumping Gaultry full to the core with a vivid, generous energy that dampened the pain in her torn shoulder, that soothed the gnawing, barely acknowledged psychic pain of her doubts concerning her father, her aunt, her own self. Gaultry, looking into Dervla's eyes, saw new suffering in their pale almond depths. New suffering and the glimmers of new understanding both. The priestess had lifted Gaultry's pain by stealing it for a few moments, by taking it into her own body. She flashed Gaultry an unpleasant smile, a smile that told the younger woman she intended to hold onto Gaultry's pains, and perhaps to rifle through them at her leisure, learning the young huntress's secret weaknesses, unless Gaultry agreed to tell her what she wanted. The threat was veiled, but Gaultry had seen enough predators in Arleon Forest that she could recognize its ruthlessness, even when it presented a smiling face to her.

"Once. I made a blood-beast once," Gaultry confessed, making her voice as calm as she was able, as if there was nothing in what the woman had done to make her uneasy or stoke new fears. "Mervion had to help. Even then the spell was weak. We made a mouse. It wasn't very nice. I wouldn't do the spell again."

Dervla, having achieved her end, smiled again and withdrew her magic, returning Gaultry's pain. In the moment that the young woman took to regain her composure, she found her mind running back over an old, now painful memory.

Tamsanne had been reluctant to teach her nieces anything of blood-magic, but there had been a time, a time not so very long past, when Gaultry and Mervion together had been foolish enough not to heed her advice. Tamsanne had very probably known what they were about, and decided not to interfere. She was not a teacher who believed in protecting her charges from every burnt finger in the kitchen.

So the young twins spent a week catching mice, and choosing among them. The last day of the week was the first of the month. The moon was full, lending the casting strength. Building a pyre of woodbine and summer roses beneath the light of that full moon, the twins laid a pair of frail mouse-spirits, deep stripped and bloody, in among the flowers. Gaultry, already practiced at animal-taking, did the stripping. Mervion, delicately separating each frightened spirit from the channel it had followed to Gaultry's mind, did the isolation, forcing each delicate mouse-spirit through the fright of the open air and down among the fragrant petals.

Then, with the shivering spirits properly prepared, Gaultry and Mervion clasped their hands together in a single fist, pricked their fingers with a silver needle they'd borrowed from Tamsanne, and let the blood fall, black in the light of the silver moon, onto the topmost of the roses.

They'd only realized how small a part of the spell was under their control when more blood began to fall than they had expected. Far more. They tried to slow the casting, to regain control, but, once started, the spell was too powerful for them to stop or even to stall. The black splotches of blood on the flower pyre widened, then joined in a single bloody mass. By the time the spell forced itself through to its finish, their voices were harsh and sore from chanting, and their throats were dry and painful. At last, frighteningly, the casting rose between them, buzzing like a wasp. A vivid flash of rank-smelling magic cut through the air, and the roses and woodbine crumbled into ash.

A new-minted mouse cowered on the ashes, its skin a hint of crimson red beneath short gray fur. Mervion, moving her foot, made a soft sound. At that instant the creature fled to a nearby pile of lumber. That was the last they'd seen of what they'd thought would be a momentous creation.

Gaultry had imagined that making a new animal would be delightful, like watching the birthing of pups or kittens, or the discovery of young fox cubs in a wild den. The casting itself had taught her such hopes were delusory. Two mice were dead so that one could live. There had been no point, no gain, or at least none that either of the twins could see. Mervion had been unhappy for days afterwards. It had been left to Gaultry to dispose of the tiny corpses of the mice they'd killed. She had burnt them, and that had been the end of the twins' experimentation with blood-magic. They'd both been relieved that they hadn't tried to make a blood-beast of a larger creature. Not the worst lesson for children heady with the idea of magical power, and all the ascendancy it could bring.

"The common blood of two mice made a new mouse," Dervla said, her eyes intent on Gaultry's sad face. "What if you and Mervion pooled your magic to make a human creature in the same way? What do you think the goddesses would make of such a creature, formed of common blood, but not a drop of Tielmaran in it?"

"You can't separate a human soul from a human body the way you can a spirit from an animal," Gaultry said. What Dervla was saying was ridiculous. "That's the essential difference between a soul and a spirit. Humans aren't made the same way animals are. We were formed in the gods' own image, flesh of the gods' flesh. Even if the legends that tell us this aren't exactly correct, I know from my own experience with spells and spirit-takings that a soul works differently from a spirit."

"There are exceptions," Dervla said. "Clarin himself was an exception."

Gaultry smiled. "Clarin was born a Prince of Bissanty. He had god-blood in him, so he started with two souls. He could spare one soul and live."

"There are other ways to be born to a second soul than descent from a god or goddess," Dervla riposted. "You and Mervion were bred on the border near the Changing Lands. You've heard of Glamour?"

Glamour had existed in the earliest ages of the world—the Age of Gods, the Age of Heroes, before the true time of humanity. Glamour-magic was the wild card in the gods' order. Indeed, Glamour-magic had precipitated the end of the Age of Gods. Andion-the-sun and Llara-the-sky, the great father and mother, tiring of their animal creations, had thought to create a new plaything. Intending to create something truly different, they had formed the first man and woman in their own images, using the flesh of Leander, the crafts god, their harpist son, leaving him a cripple with a withered leg. Molding the first human forms of their own son's flesh, the divine parents had given the breath of life to their new creations. Much to the Great Mother and Father's surprise, that breath had anchored in their new creations, and transformed itself into the first human souls. That was the Great Ones' first surprise. There was more to follow.

The first couple was unruly almost from the start. It became apparent that the god-flesh that the eternal Mother and Father had used to form their new creation had retained a glowing whisper of Leander's own god-soul, a soul that was rich with its own magic. The first man and woman soon discovered that they did not need to call to the gods for magic; their second Glamour-soul was a source from which they could call and create their own spells and magic. It had not taken long for the first human couple to declare war against their creators. That had been the Age of Heroes, a shocking epoch during which men and women, themselves semidivine, had fought the gods for supremacy.

Ultimately, the gods had prevailed. They had descended to earth and stripped the Glamour-souls from the great heroes and rebels, as easily as Gaultry could strip the spirit from a mouse or bird. Some of the strongest heroes had escaped for a time, but in the end the gods had made merry, hunting them to earth. Some had been tricked, some had been killed, but when it was over, Glamour was gone, the gods ruled supreme in the heavens, and the Age of Man had begun.

"Glamour's gone," Gaultry said. "All that's left are charms and the illusion of Glamour."

"Are you so sure?" Dervla asked. "We use our souls to bargain with the gods. You speak easily of Clarin having two souls. Yet he made three great pledges to the gods. He guaranteed two of those pledges with his own souls. What do you think he used to guarantee the third pledge?"

Gaultry shook her head.

"He pledged his first soul, his own man's soul, to Tielmark, to make himself Prince; the second, his god-blood soul, he returned to Llara when he renounced his claim to the Bissanty throne. Would the Great Twins have accepted a lesser gift as guarantee of the third of his pledges, even as he offered them his third pledge, new country's worship?"

Gaultry, hemmed in by the woman's intensity, went across to the mantel, as if to take a look at the figurines that crowded it. "If Clarin did have Glamour, so what?"

"So what? Glamour is still among us. Humans have souls which can be taken and combined, perhaps to make a human blood-beast. Do you see the danger that could come to Tielmark through this?"

"You'd have to find not one, but two people with Glamour," Gaultry protested.

"Chancellor Heiratikus thinks that he already has. So does Gabrielle, for that matter."

There were eight figurines on the mantel. A Princess and her court of seven women. Gaultry touched the cool metal of the Princess's head. The silver figure was proportionately stout and dumpy.

The crown looked foolish on the slightly over-sized head. She wondered idly if it was supposed to be Princess Corinne. "You've no proof that Mervion and I have Glamour," she said. "And less evidence. Where are the spells we'd be able to cast if we each had the power of a second soul to fuel us?"

"The power is there," Dervla said. "It is simply not awake. You and your sister have lived quietly thus far, in relative seclusion. Who can say what powers will come as you begin to stir yourselves in the world?"

Gaultry rubbed her shoulder. If only things had stayed quiet! Back in Arleon Forest, Tamsanne must already have known that things were changing for her nieces. She must have known from the moment she had pulled a new Rhasan card for her huntress niece, the strange Orchid card, instead of the Green Goddess Elianté, running and hunting alone in the wood. Why had she not given Gaultry more warning?

Dervla, standing by the bed, passed the leather strap that had bound Gaultry's arm during the night from hand to hand. Her narrow face and pale eyes were hooded, carefully impassive.

"You'll need to believe in Glamour to stand against the Chancellor," Dervla said. "He believes in it, even if you don't."

"What I need to know is how I can help Mervion."

"You'll help Mervion best by concentrating on a greater task," Dervla said. "On Prince's Night, both Clarin's pledge to the Great Twins, and the Great Twins' pledge to Llara Thunderbringer, must be renewed."

"You mean I should help wreck the Chancellor's plans. That's what Duchess Melaudiere told me."

"She's right."

Someone knocked at the door, an impatient triple-knock, twice repeated. Gaultry looked at Dervla.

"It's your door," the priestess said drily.

"I'm awake," Gaultry called. "Please come in."

The door opened, framing a grinning woman wearing green hunter's hose and a fitted tunic in green and gray. A rapier with a silver-wire handle swung from her hip. Wide blue eyes fringed by outrageously long lashes projected a look of innocent curiosity. The woman's delicate triangular face was offset by a mass of blue-black curls. Her direct manners, however, belied the seeming delicacy of her features.

"You'll be Gaultry," she said, crossing the room with a fencer's balanced step. "You don't look too bad for someone who's dropped out of the sky and had her shoulder broken. I'm Mariette Montgarret—Martin's sister." She shook Gaultry's good hand. "Glad to see you're up. Grandmère wants you and Dervla in the water salon. She's got the font fixed and she's ready to risk another scrying—if you're feeling well enough to try, that is."

Gaultry, eager to seize the chance to see Mervion again, said that she was.

"You'll want to dress first, of course." Mariette had brought the young huntress a pair of her own hose and a clean shirt and tunic. "I hope you don't mind wearing Melaudiere's colors," she said, handing them over. "It's a presumption, but they had to give up on the dress you were wearing, after Issachar's eagle tore up the shoulder. In any case, these will be more practical for the traveling that's ahead of you."

She was years younger than Martin—Gaultry guessed Mariette was nearer her own age than his—but the family resemblance was easy to see. Mariette's smile, though more open, had the same proud curve, and there was something in her eyes that suggested they would narrow with the same wolfy look if their owner found herself in a tight situation.

"That's better," Mariette said, when Gaultry had finished dressing. "I'd have brought a jacket too, if I'd been sure of the fit. And you, O Great One, vaunted of our Prince's service. Are you ready?" Dervla answered Mariette's light tone with a curt nod.

"You're the Prince's High Priestess," Gaultry said, then immediately wished she could have bit back her surprise. Small wonder that Dervla had stripped away her pain so easily, and had performed such a smooth casting that Gaultry had been well on her way to accepting the spell before she even knew it had been cast. Her eyes narrowed. Dervla returned her gaze with a pale stare. She looked not at all disconcerted.

Mariette didn't seem to notice the exchange. "I've been to

Princeport," she told Gaultry, as the trio left Gaultry's room and entered a mirrored corridor. "The news isn't good. Your sister is confined in the Chancellor's quarters—that's half a wing of the palace.
No one can get in to see her. The Prince has all but withdrawn to
the Chancellor's quarters himself, and one of the Chancellor's servants is always present when anyone does gain an audience to see
him. A Bissanty embassy has already arrived to witness the marriage—that's traditional, but this time they've had the nerve to
bring a Priest of Llara with them. They're calling him an observer,
but Grandmère thinks they're just getting cocky, and want to make
a point of showing us that Llara's eye is on this wedding."

They descended a marble stair that Gaultry could not remember
from the preceding day, turned a corner in a passage, and were at the
water salon's door. A servant told them there would be a delay
before they could enter. "Her ladyship is speaking with her grandson," he said. "She begs you wait."

Mariette shrugged. "First it's all a rush, now it's delay." She shot
Gaultry a speculative look. "Martin is angry with poor Grandmère
for making you pretend to be his wife at the Chancellor-land's border. Did you mind as much as he did?"

"Your brother's pledged by magic to protect me," Gaultry said,
hedging her answer. "It wasn't a voluntary attachment on either
side. It feels invasive to me—even knowing that without Martin's
protection I would be prisoner with Mervion in Princeport now. If
Martin doesn't like his marriage pledge being exploited without his
permission, I don't blame him."

Mariette grinned. "My brother's less unhappy about protecting
you than he pretends. You should have heard him arguing not to be
left behind when they take you to Clarin's barrow."

"Who's taking me to Clarin's barrow?" Gaultry gave Dervla a
bewildered look.

"You haven't told her?" Mariette said to Dervla, shaking her
head impatiently. "I thought you were supposed to tell her."

"I was doing that when you brought Gabrielle's summons,"
Dervla said coolly. "Besides, we're not agreed Gaultry's going to
make any such trip."

Mariette gave the older woman a dangerous look. "You and Grandmère both are being far too careful trying to control what you're telling her." She swung round to Gaultry. "I'm sure they've been filling your head with pretty stories of how terrible the Chancellor is for this country, how noble it will be to war against him. They're ashamed to tell you about the specifics of their own responsibility for his successes—however unwitting."

"That's not true," Dervla said. She gestured at the servant guarding the salon's door, indicating that he should leave them. Mariette laughed.

"Why shouldn't he stay? Gaultry is the only one here that doesn't know the foolishness of old Princess Lousielle's Common Brood."

"Mariette—"

"You didn't even know your own grandmother was one of them, did you?" Mariette turned to Gaultry.

"Tamsanne is my aunt, not my grandmother."

"And you don't even know that you're blood of the Common Brood!" Mariette hissed. "I'm sure they're trying harder to convince you of your Glamour-blood than to make you understand the truth of that!"

"Mariette!" Dervla made a warning gesture as if she would summon a spell. "Quiet yourself!"

Martin's sister put her hand on her sword's hilt, suddenly deadly calm. "Don't threaten me, Dervla," she said. "I won't have it." She turned to Gaultry. "Did Martin tell you about our friend, Louisette D'Arbey, the woman Heiratikus drove mad and killed? It was Dervla's clever idea to let Louisette put herself into Heiratikus's power."

"That was when we didn't know about Thomas Blas's prophecy," Dervla said.

"What do you mean, my father's prophecy?"

"Didn't they even tell you that?" Mariette said, disgusted. "There's a second prophecy. It's how they found you and your sister. *Twice fair*—"

"I heard the prophecy," Gaultry said. "But no one will tell me what my father had to do with it."

"*Gaultry,*" Dervla said. Her voice was heavy with magic. She reached for Gaultry's hand. The young woman jerked away.

"Don't try calming me with your castings, Priestess. I need to know what my father's involvement is here. Didn't any of you stop to think that this is something I'd need to know?"

Mariette, aware that she'd stirred something stronger in Gaultry than even she had intended, gave her a surprised look. "You didn't know your father was the second prophecy's keeper? After all the care he took to hide you and your sister in Arleon Forest?"

"I don't know what you're talking about," Gaultry said. "He abandoned us when we needed him most. Hiding had nothing to do with it."

"Gaultry." That was Dervla, her voice at its gentlest, most sirupy smooth. "On the Great Twins' immortal breath, it's true. Your father risked his life to warn the Prince the Tielmaran throne was threatened by a prophecy, a prophecy apparently known only by himself since the death of his wife in parturition. Thomas Blas's ill fortune was that Benet had fallen sway to his Chancellor when the old man's petition to be heard by his Prince came through. By speaking to Benet then, your father unwittingly gave up the prophecy to the enemy. But he made his own amends for that error. Indeed, he paid out his life's blood rather than lead the enemy past the prophecy to you and your sister."

Gaultry closed her eyes. Dervla's words invoked her wildest nightmare, and yet, remembering the geas-impress, it made a certain horrid sense. She thought back to the very first image Martin had shown her: Thomas Blas's moment of pain and anger when her child-self had run after him, alternately raging and begging that he not leave. Revisiting that wretched day in the geas-impress, even knowing she saw it finally through her father's eyes and mind, she had been unable to understand anything other than her own pain. Now, with remorseless clarity, she understood the pain in that vision had been that of a father tortured by the knowledge that he had to leave his children, had to allow a child's bewildered anger stand, lest he compromise the very safety he wished to protect by "abandoning" them to Tamsanne and the obscurity of Tielmark's southernmost woods. His most enduring memory of his daughters had been a stark moment of bereavement, as Gaultry-the-child had scourged him for what she imagined was his betrayal.

"I didn't know," Gaultry said, her voice dull. "Neither Mervion nor I knew. He let us think there was a bad reason for his having left us."

"He must have decided it would be safer for you both that way," Dervla said, folding her hands piously. "You can't blame yourself because he wanted to protect you."

The door to the water salon opened.

"What's going on out here?" Martin was there, with a younger man whom Gaultry didn't recognize. Seeing Gaultry's down-turned face, anger blazed across his own. "What have you been saying to upset Gaultry?"

"She's upset with herself," Dervla said, with deliberate mildness. "Too much truth too quickly. Calm down, Martin. She doesn't need you rattling your sword in her defense as well."

The water salon was still damaged from the eagle's assault. The window-frame was gouged with talon marks, as was the flooring near the window. A grayish cast tainted the formerly white walls and blue ceiling. Though the marble font had been pieced together and mended, it was a clumsy repair. The mortar was the wrong color.

The Duchess stood by the font as she'd been when Gaultry had first seen her, looking, if possible, more frail and ethereal than ever. Her obvious bodily weakness only made her eyes the more bright and alive. "Gaultry. It's a relief to see you on your feet." The left side of the old woman's face was grazed and swollen. "I am twice in your debt: once for your bravery, and once for my shame. I would not be here today if it were not for your courage. And—" Her piercing blue eyes bore deep into Gaultry's "—And you are a guest, and in my protection, and my host-pledge has been broken. I will answer for that, you know. It will not pass unanswered."

Gaultry bobbed her head, embarrassed.

"I see you've met Mariette. This is Gowan, Melaudiere's heir." She nodded to the slender boy at Martin's side. "He has words for you himself."

The Duchess's heir was younger even than Gaultry's brother Gilles. Like Mariette, he'd inherited the vivid blue of Gabrielle

Lourdes's eyes, but there was a shy cast to his features. Gaultry guessed he had grown up in the shadow of his strong-willed cousins, Mariette and Martin, and perhaps also that of his fierce grandmother. Whatever the case, he was down on one knee, the hilt of his sword extended. "I want to pledge you my service," he told the young huntress, his young voice high and nervous, just short of cracking. "Grandmère would do it herself if she were any younger, to honor her broken host-bond. Please accept my service in her place."

"You don't have to accept him," Martin interrupted, looking displeased. "I'm pledged to you, and you don't need two members of this house dancing you attendance. Unless you fancy having a ducal puppy at your heels."

"Martin!" the Duchess said angrily. "We've discussed this." Gowan's ears, visible as he knelt at Gaultry's knees, went red. The extended hilt was ever so slightly trembling. Gaultry had no idea what she should do. Gowan was little more than a boy, and she had no desire to expose him to dangers. But neither did she desire to cede ground to Martin, not least because of the arrogance of his attempted intervention. After all his complaints that her father had forced him to serve her, it seemed a bit much that the big soldier should champ like a spurned suitor when another freely offered his protection. Glaring at Martin, she grasped the boy's proffered sword hilt.

"Offer me this pledge after Prince's Night, and I'll accept it," she told Gowan. "Martin's geas will run its course by Prince's Night, and then I'll need your service. Will that satisfy your honor here?" The Duchess, hearing Gaultry's compromise, looked relieved. Gowan lurched to his feet, his expression carefully neutral, but clearly pleased that she hadn't outright rejected his offer.

"You're supposed to give him a token," Mariette interjected. "I could lend you a handkerchief."

Gaultry shook her head. "I'll give him a lock of my hair." Martin's obvious disapproval at this suggestion somehow made her more determined that this was the right pledge. "Here." Before Martin could stop her, she clipped free a long lock of her hair, and thrust it into the young man's hand, a gleaming swatch of red-gold silk. "Protect that until Prince's Night, and I'll trade you for something better when I formally accept your service."

"You honor me, Lady," Gowan said, finding his voice.

The Duchess watched her heir fold the shining lock of hair into his kerchief. "There's a first for you, grandson-mine." The old woman smiled a secretive smile.

"Now for a final scrying." There were silver mercury waves painted around the rim of the font's bowl, and eight silver eyes. "Gaultry, we're going to have to take your arm down from that sling."

Mariette helped her, unbending Gaultry's elbow, which had stiffened, and carefully arranging her fingers over one of the eyes. The mercury made her skin itch. "Your second hand goes on that one," Mariette said, pointing. Gaultry complied, the discomfort making her reluctant.

The Duchess, Mariette, and Dervla took up the other stations round the font's edge.

"We owe this scrying to Mariette," the Duchess said. "She tells us Heiratikus is taking Mervion back to the Keyhole Chamber today. He's been preparing a new spell for a week."

"The Keyhole Chamber?" Gaultry could not conceal her surprise.

"The Prince's Chapel."

Gaultry ducked her head. "I know, of course, I know." Every child in Arleon Forest knew of the Keyhole Chamber, and the powerful magics that the Prince's magicians could work there. "I'm just forgetting." Forgetting how powerful the magics ranged against her and her sister would be.

The carved fish at the bowl's bottom had cracked, and been mended with the rest of the font. One yellow-mortared crack ran across its head, making it look like it was smiling.

The Duchess touched the surface of the water. "By great Allegrios's nine secret names, by the Great Twins of Tielmark, I call all here to witness and join this casting." The water's surface turned silver, obscuring the fish, then flashed to show the familiar sky and trees Gaultry had seen at the beginning of the previous day's spell.

Then there was a burning crackle of magic, and the view of trees and sky vanished. With Dervla supporting the spell, the magic was palpably stronger. Everyone in the room could see Mervion now: not just the image of her face and shoulders, but a compressed view of the entire room in which the Chancellor had imprisoned her.

Mervion, dressed in gorgeous cloth of gold, and still wearing the rough-forged iron coronet, sat on a low stool, her back pressed against a bare wall. An embroidery frame sat in her lap, and she was working furiously, stabbing the thread through the cloth with clumsy, overlarge stitches. The sapphire stone necklace Gaultry had seen her wearing the previous day was in pieces, the wires that had supported the stones bent and mangled. As they watched, Mervion stitched the pieces of the setting, with the stones still attached, onto the cloth. Though thin and pale, Mervion was somehow more beautiful, more ripe with life, than Gaultry had ever seen her. Her unbound hair swirled down past her waist in silky waves, a copper-fire cloak which competed with the gold-colored silk of her dress. Her eyes, catching light from an unseen fire, glittered like emeralds. After a moment it became clear she was sewing a spell into the cloth. Every seventh stab of the needle made an odd loop as it entered the cloth, and Mervion's lips moved, calling magic or praying, setting the spell.

"Do you know what she's casting?" the Duchess asked, in a flat voice.

"I've never seen anything like it," Gaultry said, equally toneless, hoping her voice would not upset the spell. "It looks strong." Stronger than she was confident that Mervion could control.

"Are you sure they're moving her today, Mari?" the Duchess asked, when they had watched Mervion sew for longer than they wanted, and the strength of the spell had begun to make their heads ache.

"It's today," Mariette answered. "Tonight's the half-moon. They'll bind her onto the altar in the Keyhole Chamber and wait for the moon to rise, to give the spell strength."

Mervion tied a last knot in her thread and threw down her needle. Standing, she smoothed her skirts, and picked up the embroidery frame, holding it in front of her like a shield. Her stitches formed a blue spider-web of thread, sparkling sapphires and bent pieces of silver wire studding the web's threads where they intersected.

The Chancellor had sent four men for her, burly soldiers in polished armor. Mervion's lips curved in a shouted insult. For a moment the soldiers hesitated, casting one another uncertain looks. The boldest, a man with red hair, opened his mouth to shout, and reached for her. She slapped his hand away, whirled round, and flung the embroidery frame into their faces.

It burst into a spreading web of blue fire, a web of living tentacles of light that writhed outwards, consuming her tormentors. Two were driven to their knees, writhing and screaming; the remaining pair, standing behind their fellows, fought their way free, grabbing for Mervion's skirts. She threw herself into the melee, her hands reaching for one man's head, mouth open in a shout as she called another spell. There was an awkward flurry of action, hard to follow through the limited font-window. Then one of the soldiers had Mervion in a headlock, and the other, in front of her, drove his fists into her stomach. Gaultry's sister screamed, and fought to get away.

Something changed. The man pounding at Mervion dropped his fists, the other released her shoulders. The unlucky soldiers bound in her glittering web ceased their struggles.

Mervion stood, her face suddenly impassive, staring at a point beyond the font-window's frame. One hand clutched her stomach, and she took a shuddering swallow. Her eyes seemed huge in her face. She took an unwilling step forward, and then another, her body stiff with reluctance and fear.

A fifth man moved into the picture, a tall, powerfully built man like a figure from a nightmare. Long black hair flowed loose down his back, coarser than a horse's mane. Sword-cut scars, jagged like thunderbolts, marked his cheeks. Sinewy muscle was packed onto his frame under pale, parchment-tight skin. He walked confidently to Gaultry's sister, ignoring the soldiers. At his approach Mervion shivered, and ducked her head.

Why didn't she strike out at him? As Gaultry watched, horror-stricken, he cupped Mervion's chin in his hand, and raised her eyes to meet his. Did magic pass between them? Gaultry was struck sud-

denly by the memory of the allure of the steel-feathered eagle, calling to her the day before, the rush of glorious power that it had
promised her. But she had found the strength to resist its call. Why
wasn't Mervion, her twin, pushing the man away, repulsing his spell?

"*Mervion!*" Gaultry cried, desperate to break her sister's thrall to
the monster. "*Mervion!*" A wave of magic seemed to leap down into
the font-water, calling out to her beloved twin. The shocking
strength of Gaultry's cry knocked the Duchess's hands from the
font's rim, dimming the spell, but the image did not break. Gaultry
knew, suddenly, that only she could hold the casting together, that
she could hold it, would hold it, all by herself, if that was what her
sister needed from her. "*Mervion, don't!*"

Then, crazily, Mervion responded, her head turning to Gaultry
as though she struggled to wake from a dream. At first her eyes were
dull, flat as chips of ice, then she shook her head, saw Gaultry, and a
new light flashed in her.

The man, frowning, turned as well. For a strange moment, his
eyes too seemed to focus on Gaultry's. A black look crossed his face.
He made a quick wiping motion with one hand, mouthed a sound-
less word, and the image vanished.

chapter **12**

▼

Gaultry stumbled back from the font, reeling with the intensity of emotion and magic that had briefly linked her sister to her.

"That, my dear, was Issachar Dan." The Duchess pried Gaultry's good hand off the rim of the font and patted it. "Mercury helps the spell, but it won't help you, will it?" She wiped the heavy metal off Gaultry's skin with a damp cloth. "Is your shoulder bothering you? Should Mari take you back to your room?"

Bereft of speech, Gaultry shook her head. Why had Mervion not struggled against the Chancellor's aquiline officer?

"Perhaps, Gabrielle," Dervla said, coming to Gaultry's other side, "now that you've had your vision, we can retire to comfortable quarters and discuss our next move. Gaultry should be off her feet, and so should you."

They settled in a music room on the manor's ground floor, a room furnished with tall wooden chairs and a long chaise. The Duchess, looking a little pale, stretched out on the chaise, insisting that Gaultry pull a chair near.

Martin paced restlessly between the windows and the chairs, in no mood to sit still. "We must get Gaultry to Haute-Tielmark quickly now we're certain Heiratikus wants the Blas twins for Benet's marriage. Judging by what we saw today, Mervion won't fend off Issachar's magic much longer. Gaultry won't fare any better if we can't wake the Glamour-power in her."

"What do you mean?" said Gaultry, affronted. "Mervion had enough free will that she could answer my call." Even as she spoke, she knew there was little to justify her reflexive defense. The spell in the great eagle had been alluring enough, a day's ride from its owner in Princeport. Would she be able to maintain her equanimity, and hold herself free, if confronted by the spell-caster himself? She doubted it.

So did the rest of them. "Don't be a fool, Gaultry," Mariette waded in, blunt as ever. "Martin's right."

"I'm not trying to insult your twin," Martin said. "I'm just trying to be realistic."

"Realistic! Maybe I don't like your idea of reality!" Gaultry spat back, wounded.

"Just because Gaultry has thrown her lot in with us," Dervla interjected, putting a possessive arm around Gaultry's uninjured shoulder, "it doesn't mean she has to agree with our every point. Martin, you'd best let Gabrielle explain our plans."

The big soldier made an impatient gesture. "Grandmère—"

"Be quiet, Martin. I need to hear myself think." Gabrielle Lourdes pressed a thin hand to her brow, as though she felt all the weight of her years and it hurt her to see her grandson pacing and angry. Her hair hung forward, hiding her eyes. When she spoke, her voice was weary. "From what we have witnessed, we know Mervion Blas is in danger, perhaps even on the brink of succumbing to the Chancellor's spells. Some fight remains—turning the magic of the necklace that bound her into a weapon shows imagination and fire are with her still. But she faces a powerful and experienced opponent. We don't know how she will fare in the Keyhole Chamber tonight. The last time I saw the Prince, although his mind was whole and healthy, his will was no longer his own. I fear that what has been done to Benet may also be done to Mervion.

"Prince's Night is only nine days away. Tomorrow, Mariette and I leave here for Princeport. We'll take part in the week-long festival that has been planned to lead up to the grand event while we try to get help to Mervion. The balance of power is such that the Chancellor's allies and Tielmark's loyalists are trapped in pretense. Together we sustain the deceit that we are not enemies; that the Chancellor is not plotting to destroy Tielmark's independence; that those ranged against him are not plotting to undermine a Chancellor who has yet to commit open treason.

"I have plans," the Duchess said in a tired voice. She shifted her frail body fitfully, and reached for Gaultry's hand. "I have had plans for near fifty years now." It was as if she were talking to the young huntress alone, as though there was no one else in the room with them. "This cycle of fraught marriages for our Princes must be broken. Fifty years past, I offered my life—and others gave their lives— that our young Princess, Corinne, might marry well, and Tielmark prosper. The Brood fought after Corinne's marriage, we were inexcusably stubborn, and we broke to go our separate ways. Corinne's sweet reign lulled us into the false belief that our failure to resolve our differences had no bearing on Tielmark's future. As for myself, my lands and my people prospered. I flattered myself that I had helped achieve something more for Tielmark than a passing victory. Then Corinne died, and the true price of our arrogance was exposed. Brood-blood such as ours is irredeemably bound to our princes. Two of our turbulent seven died with Corinne. When Roualt, her oldest son, died, he took my first son into the grave with him. Prince Ginver's death robbed me of my second. I was not the only Brood witch to find I was paying for my princes' deaths with those of my own children.

"When, just three years past, Heiratikus was elevated to Chancellor, I understood at last that the triumph of Corinne's wedding was tainted. Heiratikus did nothing to betray himself, but a man of half-Bissanty blood, half Brood-blood in the role of prime councilor to the Prince of Tielmark could not mean anything other than disaster for our country—particularly with the great three hundredth Prince's Night and a crucial princely marriage just three years away.

"As Chancellor, he did nothing overt to advance the Bissanty cause during his first years in office. Nevertheless, it's been appalling to me to see how fast the Bissanty rot at court has spread, like relapse into disease. It seems half the Prince's court need only be promised riches, and they agree to stand to the side and let Bissanty agents guide them. I have not witnessed anything like it since my youth." She rubbed the old scar on her wrist.

"Dervla and I have thought long and hard how best to waken your latent powers, Gaultry. From what Martin says, they are already beginning to rouse. Is this so?"

Gaultry thought of the strength of her recent spirit-takings, the way her spells had begun to leap to life out of the briefest impulsive flickers of her thoughts. "One or two things have come out more powerfully than I had intended," she said, trying to give a cautious answer.

The Duchess nodded. "And Tamsanne pulled a Rhasan card for you, a card that hinted at budding power."

Gaultry gave Martin an unfriendly look. He had the grace to look uncomfortable. "You were unconscious for a full day," he told her, defensive. "You would have spoken of it yourself if you had been awake for Grandmère to have asked about it."

Gaultry would have spoken, but the pressure of the Duchess's hand on her own forestalled her. "I'd like to pull another Rhasan card for you," the Duchess said, her eyes intent. "Would you agree to that, Gaultry?"

Did Gabrielle Lourdes think pulling cards from the Rhasan deck was a pretty parlor game, a game to be played at any difficult turn-ing? Gaultry could forgive the old woman that she was profligate in her use of the water god's magic. It was surely pleasant to be petted and praised by a powerful old woman grateful for swift reflexes. But Rhasan magic was another matter. The young huntress couldn't keep disapproval from her face as she answered. "Because you wish it, Duchess Melaudiere, I'll agree."

"You remind me of Tamsanne when you make that face," the Duchess said, not at all insulted. She released Gaultry's hand and smoothly pulled a deck of cards from a hidden pocket. She shuffled them slowly, then opened their backs to Gaultry in a neat fan.

Shifting waves blurred before Gaultry's vision: the cards' backs depicted a ship tossed on a stormy sea. "Take a card," the Duchess said. "Try your own fate."

Gaultry hesitated. Sitting in the elegantly appointed room, with its fine carved furniture and walls hung with silk and fine linen, Tamsanne's cottage, and the crude flashing woodcuts of her Rhasan cards, seemed very far away. In Tamsanne's cottage, it was easier to believe the Rhasan could mold fate.

"Did you make these yourself, your Grace?" she asked, stalling.

"I made the twelve god-cards," the Duchess said. There were more than twelve cards in the deck. Many more.

Gaultry snatched a card at random and flipped it, flinching in the expectation of the consuming torrent of magic it would invoke.

It was a lovely miniature painting. The orchid-flower, cracked open in bloom, gold leaf glossing the anthers that peeped from the lip of the blossom, the blossom itself blue and white—Tielmark's royal colors—veined with purple.

A lovely painting, and nothing else.

"Tamsanne's deck—"

"If this were Tamsanne's deck," the Duchess said, "I would not have asked you to pull for yourself."

Gaultry stared at the delicate image, admiring. "It's beautiful. I'd like to see the rest of the deck," she murmured. "Are the others like this one?"

The Duchess stared at Gaultry's card, and let out a long inheld breath. "Look at the card's number," she said.

Gaultry, preoccupied by the lovely image, had not noticed the card had a number. Tamsanne's cards did not have numbers.

The Orchid card was number thirteen.

"After the twelve gods, Glamour is the thirteenth power," Dervla said, coming to look over Gaultry's shoulder.

The Duchess, darting an annoyed look at the priestess, retrieved Gaultry's card, closed the deck, and slipped it out of sight under her robes. Her lank hair had fallen in front of her eyes again. She pushed it back. "Gaultry, I am sending you to Haute-Tielmark. I want you to visit Prince Clarin's barrow."

Haute-Tielmark was the westernmost province of the country. "That's what Mariette told me, before we joined you. Why send me there?"

"Since yesterday's attack, I've made offerings to the gods, asking where I could send you, to secure you in a place of safety. I sent Allegrios my strongest prayers. Dervla called a circle for the Great Twins, seeking her own answer. The answer we received, though inconvenient, has been consistent. You must travel west to Haute-Tielmark, and visit the burial mound of our first Prince. There you must pray to Clarin himself to offer you council."

"You want me to confer with a man who's been dead for almost three hundred years?"

"Gaultry, these are strange times, and they call for stranger measures. I know the Orchid card, but until today I didn't know it was there in my own Rhasan deck. I've only ever seen a depiction of it once before today." The Duchess met Gaultry's eyes candidly. "It was a pictograph carved onto the entrance stone of Clarin's crypt."

"I'm not wholly convinced we should send Gaultry west," Dervla interrupted. "She'll be exposed to the Chancellor's men anywhere she journeys now. The passage to Haute-Tielmark will render her particularly vulnerable to Bissanty attack. The portents were not so clear as you suggest, my Gabrielle. There are less wild schemes we could follow, and still protect the Prince."

"Every portent we have seen has Mervion and Gaultry Blas standing on the Prince's high altar on Prince's Night," the Duchess retorted, rising up a little on the chaise. "It would take little short of a miracle to prevent that from happening. We need Gaultry strong, so she can control the outcome of the ceremony. Sending her to Clarin's barrow will make her strong!"

"Perhaps, Gabrielle. I'm sure that's what you would want to do yourself, if you still had your youth and vigor of old. But Gaultry may have no desire to expose herself to such a reckless venture. There are rites that can be cast to help her, meditations and bonding that may bring out her Glamour-strength, without exposing her to the claws of another of Issachar's eagles. What does Gaultry want?"

"She'll want to go to Haute-Tielmark."

"Why not let her choose?"

Gaultry stared at the two older women. Dervla met her eyes with an encouraging look. Gaultry wasn't sure that it was encouragement that she wanted. The magic of the Great Twins was strong in the thin priestess, but the woman herself was not above manipulating people to her own ends by magic. The huntress sensed that the woman's power had always come to her a little too easily, dampening her ability to understand the honor she had been gifted. It was easy for Gaultry to picture Dervla in devout genuflection before Elianté and Emiera's high altar, her strong face proud, certain that she followed the goddesses' will, the magic flowing to her easily, each casting a familiar joy. Magic never came so easily to a hedge-witch that followed the Great Twins.

Gaultry turned to look into the Duchess of Melaudiere's worn face, the brilliant, deep-set blue eyes, the wasted length of her body. As a child, Gaultry had thought of the Common Brood as gloriously beautiful and privileged enchantresses, arrogant and sure of their success, spinning their blood-spell around a young Princess like a veil of crimson silk. Now, looking at the Duchess, remembering the deep scars the old woman had showed her on her wrists, Gaultry could guess that the blood-spell that had enabled Corinne's marriage had been neither a splendidly beautiful casting, nor a victory of which they had been certain when they had called the spell. Blood-magic was wild, it would have threatened their lives even as they called it. Yet despite the evident dangers, the Duchess and her peers had gone forward with the casting.

"I'll go to Clarin's barrow," Gaultry said. "I can't guess how it will help me, but I'd rather take the risk than not."

Dervla frowned. "Well, Gabrielle, then you'll have to do all you can to ensure our young huntress here doesn't regret her decision."

The Duchess gave the High Priestess a cool look of her own. "As you will too, Dervla. Gaultry's made a wise choice. Your rites and bindings weren't much help to poor Louisette D'Arbey, were they?" She turned to Gaultry. "Not that Dervla isn't right about the dangers posed by the Haute-Tielmark journey. Talking to Prince Clarin will be the least of your problems. Your most pressing concerns will be of a less transcendental nature. Victor, the Duke of Haute-Tielmark, is the member of the ducal council most heavily under Bissanty influence. Haute-Tielmark is almost cut off from the body of Tielmark by an outcrop of Bissanty territory. You will travel with a war party, to help you fight your way through any obstacles that come in your way.

"If you are taken before you reach Clarin's barrow, every man who accompanies you will be slaughtered. You will be spared death, at least until after Prince's Night. And I—I will be hung for treason." The old woman gave Gaultry a proud look. "I will mount the scaffold knowing I have served Tielmark well."

The Duchess's grandchildren shifted uneasily. All three had listened patiently while the others had spoken, but now they cut in, all three speaking at once. "That won't come to pass," Martin said.

"I'll avenge your death," said young Gowan.

Mariette met Gaultry's eyes with her own as she spoke. "Gaultry won't let herself be taken," she said, making her words an encouragement.

If she was going to throw her lot in with a family of fanatics, Gaultry smiled to herself, at least it would be a family of fanatics who were determined to hang together rather than separately. Thinking of her own loyalties to Mervion, she was a little reassured. "I understand your commitment," Gaultry said. "I mean mine to be as lasting."

"Then that's settled," the Duchess said. "I'll give Allegrios Rex thanks for that.

"We've called a healer for your shoulder, Gaultry." The old woman grinned at Dervla, openly pleased with her triumph. "He'll arrive tonight, late, and fix your shoulder first thing in the morning, before you set out for Haute-Tielmark with my soldiers. Now, if you will excuse us, Dervla and I will retire to make some preparations for your long journey. Enjoy the freedom of my castle and its grounds. It's safe enough—I've taken fresh precautions against unexpected visitors. Heiratikus will regret it if he orders a new attack."

"I'll show Gaultry the gardens," Martin suggested. "She looks like she needs some air."

"I'll come with you." Mariette linked her arm into Gaultry's, grinning when Martin met this suggestion with a dark look. "Come on. Let's go see Grandmère's flowers from the nonaerial view."

It was easy to warm to Mariette. She had Martin's charm and fire, and a near-perfect replica of his threatening edge of temper, but there was a generous humor in her with which the young huntress felt an easy sympathy. Gaultry accepted her offer with little hesitation.

The gardens, rich with the Duchess's magical invention, were a delight. Sea motifs crowded every turning: statuary of deep-water fish, shells, boats, and strange branching corals. "Grandmère's blood is from the Sea-Counties," Mariette told Gaultry. "She agreed to marry Melaudiere and come inland only when he agreed to build this new house for her."

"Does your entire family follow Allegrios?" Everywhere Gaultry looked, images of the great water god peered out at her.

"We do," Mariette said. "You know he was Tielmark's god of old, before even the Bissanty Empire took us over?"

"I suppose I did," Gaultry said. "But that's a millennium past, or more! Are you telling me you trace your line so far back?"

Martin snorted. "My sister has water on her brain if she believes that." Mariette laughed, let go of Gaultry's arm, and ran ahead to turn on yet another fountain.

Gaultry gave Martin a searching look. "I've never been to the sea," she told him.

"Many of those who live in the Sea-Counties owe their second allegiance to Allegrios, after the Great Twins. They'll tell you that they were born on the land of the Great Twins, but that they earn their living from the water god, and the bounty of his province, the sea. It's rough country. Tall cliffs, rocky beaches." The gray wolf's eyes took on a faraway look.

"Is that what Seafrieg is like?"

"It is." His eyes came back to sharp focus, and he favored her with a suspicious look. "Why do you ask?"

"When did you become Count of Seafrieg?"

"I've never been Count Seafrieg."

"Then how did you come to be married to the Countess of Seafrieg?"

"I'm married to the Countess of Seafrieg," he said, his voice bitter, "because my older brother was a fool and he didn't father an heir before he died."

Mariette trotted back from the fountain, a broad smile on her face. "What's got Martin's back up now?" she said. "What are you talking about?"

"We're talking about Morse," Martin said.

Mariette's smile faded. "Morse has been gone a few years now," she told Gaultry. "It's hard to believe he's gone. Your trip to Haute-Tielmark would have been a real adventure, if Morse was still here. He was the wildest of the three of us."

Gaultry said she found that hard to credit.

"Martin," Mariette said, "no one has told Gaultry the whole story of her father's death."

Gaultry swallowed. "That's not quite right. Aquilles Beriot did, back in Arleon Forest."

"The Baron of Blamire? He's one of the Chancellor's favorite puppets. What did he say?"

"He wanted me to think badly of Martin." If she stared very hard at Mariette, she didn't have to watch Martin's expression. "He had built a memory for my brother, a memory of Martin laughing as he tore my father's heart from his body with his sword. It was a very clear image: blood, the edges of the wound—everything."

Next to her, Martin was absolutely still.

"Beriot was there when Martin did it," Mariette said shortly. "So it's not surprising he at least got the wound right. Are you going to tell her what happened when the geas passed to you, Martin?"

There was a long silence before Martin answered. "It jumped onto my sword," he said. "His heart jumped onto my sword, like it had its own life. I didn't know what was happening." He took a deep breath and met Gaultry's eyes. Something curdled in her suddenly to be able to see so clearly the scorching pain that he had hidden from her, all the time they'd been together.

"We were off the horses, right on top of the boar. Gerrard Tobys—he's not important, but he took first blood—Gerrard was there, he broke the point of his spear against the big bastard's shoulder, and suddenly it charged at the pack of us who had the bad fortune to be down on the ground, right in that old boar-pig's path, and we were slipping in the deep winter snow, trying to get out of its way. I took a hit at it, then I swung round to get out of its way, and your father was right there. My sword went in him as if the man had no bones. I had no idea what was happening. The runes on my blade lit up like blazing brands, trying to fight off your father's geas; but it overcame them one by one, and shot through the blade's hilt and on up into me like a lance of silver lightning. One moment I was watching an old man's death agony, the next—you know the next. My sight was blocked by the impress, and I found myself being berated by the vision of an angry fourteen-year-old who felt certain her father was abandoning her for no good reason.

"Beriot cried out that I'd murdered the old man; fortunately for me everyone else who was there could see it wasn't my fault. The boar tore up Gerrard's leg, and half-disemboweled another man—causing enough confusion that I would have stood acquitted even without four men swearing your father was proud and smiling as he welcomed my blade into his body."

Gaultry turned away, angry tears squeezing from her eyes. "My father abandoned us before we reached womanhood. Now I'm supposed to believe he died for us. If he was so concerned for us, why didn't he at least warn Tamsanne about our birth prophecy?"

Brother and sister shook their heads, unable to answer her. As they walked, they reached the fountain Mariette had run ahead to turn on. A pair of bronze figures surmounted a sparkling froth of water: a horned merman reared out of the foam to grasp the waist of a pretty nymph with flowing hair as she busily turned herself into a rosebush to evade him. The mood was comic rather than dark: the merman had hurt his hand on her thorns. He stared at his injured hand with a bemused expression that made even Gaultry smile. That was before she recognized the figures: herself and Martin. Her smile dropped.

"What's this?" she asked.

"Grandmère made it yesterday," Mariette answered. "She had a blackout after the attack, and when she woke she came out here and made this."

"How dare she!"

"Are you upset?" Mariette said, a hidden but not unfriendly laugh in her voice. "When one of Grandmère's fits are on her, I assure you, she doesn't choose her subjects."

"I don't understand any of you people!" Gaultry spat. "You all know too much for your own good. You're all fighting battles that go back half-a-hundred years, battles that I don't know anything about. You tell me I don't even know anything about my own family. No, all of you know better than I! My aunt isn't my aunt, you slyly say. My father never abandoned me! My magic would be working now if only I hadn't lived all my life in Arleon Forest! Well, I did live in Arleon Forest. And I wouldn't change that for all your wretched intriguing!"

Not wanting to hear another word, Gaultry turned and dashed away towards the manor. Mariette made a move to come after her, but Martin, geas-bound still, stuck out a foot and stopped her, knowing Gaultry wanted to be alone.

She got lost in the confusing corridors of the great house's ground floor, and had to ask a servant for directions to her room. Once there, she threw herself down on the bed, clasping her injured arm and shoulder. To her further frustration, tears refused to come, leaving her more miserable still. She thought of her brother's wife Anisia, trapped somewhere in Princeport, no one cared where, because she wasn't a player in the game to marry the Prince; of her half-brother, abandoned to a mendacious tether of magic; of her sister with a deadened expression in her eyes, shrinking from the ominous scar-face warrior who had seized her hand and forced her to follow his bidding.

Now she must add to this the certainty that her father and Tamsanne both had lied to her. Lies of omission, to be sure, but lies nevertheless, lies that left her innocent of destiny. *The path of the Prince of Tielmark will run red with the blood of the Common Brood.* The words of old Princess Lousielle's prophecy pounded in her mind. What had possessed Tamsanne to pledge herself to the Common Brood, knowing that she condemned her bloodline to dance to the Prince's service?

She heard a gentle knock at the door.

"Who is it?" Gaultry wiped her nose and sat up.

It was the Duchess. "I've come to apologize for letting Mari surprise you. And for not having been more careful of my creation. May I come in?"

Gaultry, trying not to sniff, nodded assent. Her shoulder hurt. She'd strained it during her run from Mariette and Martin.

"I've brought something to make you sleep," the old woman said. She set an earthenware cup down next to the bed. "Have you seen my figures here?" she asked. "I put you in this room so you could see them."

"I didn't know who they were," Gaultry said. "How could I have known?"

The Duchess frowned. "I asked Dervla to show you. No matter. Come and look now."

Gaultry had guessed the identity of seven of the figures on the mantel, but she had missed with the eighth. "It's not Corinne," the Duchess corrected her. "Corinne was beautiful and generous, open-faced and full of life and grace. The figure here is her mother, Lousielle, the woman who brought us all together." Gaultry stared at the silver image. The old Princess had been slightly built, and unimpressive.

"Yet she bound you all with a prophetic oath," she marveled.

"No one ever caught Lousielle's likeness," the Duchess murmured, touching the metal edge of the Princess's skirts with a bony finger. "No one ever caught anything of Lousielle. But look who she caught—" The old woman gestured at the other figures. "These were Tielmark's finest young spell-casters, and every one swore her faith to this dull-faced Princess. She didn't have flashing eyes, a mystic air of command, or anything outward to tell us what was in her. Perhaps her voice—perhaps her words. Somehow she knew something to make each and every one of us pledge our faith and the blood heirs of our bodies. Here—look at Marie Laconte. There wasn't a prouder woman in Tielmark."

The Marie Laconte figure was beautiful, fine-boned, everything that Gaultry would have expected in a Princess. "She would find it hard to bend to another's command," Gaultry guessed.

"It was true of every one of us!" The Duchess laughed. "Now look at Tamsanne."

Gaultry hesitated. Her great-aunt? Her lying grandmother? Her curiosity overcame her sense of hurt, and she glanced shyly at the figure the Duchess held in her hands.

It was Tamsanne. She was young. And very clearly pregnant. Gaultry looked at the Duchess, shocked.

"Two of the Common Brood were pregnant on the day of Corinne's marriage," the old woman said, matter-of-fact and dry. "One of them miscarried just hours after the ceremony and the spell-casting, proving the oath we had taken wasn't a matter of mere words and light promises. Much to everyone's surprise, Tamsanne held her baby. She must have spelled her womb shut so that she wouldn't lose it. When I asked her, she told me she would name the child Severine."

Severine. Her mother. Gaultry touched the bulging metal curve of the figurine's stomach, trying to fuse this image of Tamsanne with that of the old woman she had thought that she had known so well all her life.

"Why were all of Lousielle's spell-casters women?"

"Lousielle's father failed to protect her from the Bissanties, and Lousielle was bitter for it. He had married her to a Bissanty pawn, and she was bitter about that too. She didn't believe men would understand what they were pledging when they stood up and made an offering of their life and blood." The Duchess shrugged. "She got that a little wrong. Perhaps only Tamsanne and Delcora knew what she asked of us. The rest couldn't see so far into the future."

"Delcora?"

"The woman who lost her baby." The Duchess pointed at another figure, this one thin and hollow-faced. The figure's dress had double-spirals molded on the breast and sleeves. "You are right in what you said to my grandchildren in the garden. Every one of these women spawned a family battle to last half-a-hundred years. Tamsanne didn't want to be a part of it. Princess Corinne was never sure whether she'd lost the best or worst of her allies when Tamsanne retreated to Arleon Forest."

"How could Tamsanne have hid all this from Mervion and me?" Gaultry asked.

"Perhaps she thought the burden of knowing would stunt your strength and growth." The old woman gave Gaultry a sympathetic look. "You're tired now. You should lie down, drink your sleep draught, and rest."

"I want to know about the others."

The Duchess sighed. "Drink your draught, and I will tell you one last story."

The sleeping draught tasted of honey and sweet sorrel. Gaultry lay back against the pillows, and the Duchess brought a last figure to her. "This is Melaney Sevenage. She was Lousielle's last inductee. And she was the woman who sacrificed the most to her Princess. She has a smiling face here, a reflection of her brave heart." The Duchess pressed the figure to her cheek, as if it were a child rather than rigid silver metal. "In the last months before Corinne's wedding, Lousielle was dead. The Brood feared not knowing what the Bissanties were planning. Melaney was beautiful. She was the Duke of Carlia's only daughter. The Bissanty Ambassador had been sniffing at her skirts. He had made an offer of marriage to Melaney's father. We took a vote. Three for, three against. Melaney cast the deciding vote, and accepted his offer. She became our eyes within the enemy's camp.

"Was this price worth the success of our blood-spell, of Corinne's marriage? Would the Great Twins have seen our spell through to triumph without Melaney's sacrifice? Her husband bound her in sorcerous chains and absconded with her to Bissanty after Corinne's wedding. We heard only that she died early, only that she had given birth to a son—Edan Heiratikus."

The Duchess's voice was softening as Gaultry slipped towards sleep. "It seems that the Common Brood has birthed at least one son who wishes to free himself of Lousielle's prophecy by bringing the path of the Prince of Tielmark to an abrupt closure."

Even drugged and half-asleep, Gaultry could hear the ring of truth in that.

She woke with a searing pain in her shoulder. A pad was pressed over her mouth, stopping her screams. A man with fire-colored hair bent over her, applying a spell to her shoulder. The magic rent her flesh like the touch of a red-hot poker. She almost threw him clear off her body with her surprise.

"Keep still! Keep still!" It was the voice of a fanatic, a madman.

Gaultry screamed into the gag.

"Meld the bone, fire-faced god. Meld the bone. Bone to metal, metal to bone." The pain increased, it was harder and harder to bear. Gaultry spit out the gag. She howled and dragged her hands at the man's, trying to tear herself free. Then, as the first wave of darkness took her, the man let out a triumphant cackle. The agony dropped away. The madman laughed, shoved her deep into the bedclothes, mad eyes sparkling inches from her own, foul breath fanning her face. He stood away.

"The pain is gone," Gaultry said, testing her shoulder.

"Of course it's gone!" The man glared at her with his angry, somewhat bloodshot, eyes. "Andion won't suffer to see his work undone, except by Lord Death!" He touched a sun-shaped gold disk at his throat. A priest of Andion, the father god.

"How do you feel, Gaultry?" Dervla asked. She stood by the door, a disapproving look on her face.

Gaultry scrambled out of bed, bursting with energy, then snatched at the sheets, embarrassed. Someone had undressed her during the night. "How do I feel?" she said. "I feel like I'd better put some clothes on."

The mad healer ignored her as he packed his tools and powders into a strange patched bag. Gaultry, answering him with the same manners, turned to pull on the hose, shirt, and tunic she'd worn the day before. Her shoulder was completely recovered. Even the scabs on her hands where she'd tried to grab the eagle by its serrated feathers were gone.

Her healer finished packing his bag, pushed past Dervla, and went out.

"Not even a good-bye?" Gaultry asked. After the agony she'd woken to, it was such a relief to be free of pain, she found herself in a good humor.

"Andion's clergy are strange men. But Gabrielle insisted that no one else would do for you."

The thin priestess threw a packet into Gaultry's lap as she sat on the bed to pull on her boots.

"What's this?"

"A gift," Dervla said, a little coldly.

The young woman tore the paper open. A string of flashing green stones, stones that danced with the Twin Goddesses' power, spilled out onto the quilt.

"This is your own power," Gaultry said, touching the smooth surface of the stones. "You're giving this to me?"

Dervla grimaced. "I had a long conversation with Gabrielle last night. Do you think it's pleasant knowing that the future of all you hold dear depends on the conduct of a pair of untried girls? Let me assure you, it isn't pleasant. But I am the Great Twins' High Priestess, and I must submit to the goddesses' choice.

"This is a gift, Gaultry," the priestess said. "Because I am loyal to Tielmark, and there is no escaping the truth that I must do anything that is within my reach to help you."

The beads were smooth and warm in her hands. Gaultry looked at Dervla carefully, remembering the figures the Duchess had shown her the night before. "You're Delcora's daughter, aren't you? The Brood-woman who lost her first child after Corinne's wedding. Is that why her Grace called you here?"

Dervla's pointed chin lifted proudly. "I am Delcora's heir, blood of the Common Brood. My fate, like yours, is bound to my Prince's."

Gaultry put on Dervla's necklace, then tucked it out of sight under the tunic's collar. The touch of the beads on her skin was like a soothing hand. "Thank you," Gaultry said.

"It is the best I can give you." Something in Dervla's manner told Gaultry the priestess did not exaggerate.

Breakfast was a formal affair. Martin and Mariette sat at opposite ends of the table, casting ill-tempered looks at each other. The Duchess and Dervla simply looked tired. Arnolfo and Hassan, whom Gaultry hadn't seen since arriving, were also there, both in somewhat higher spirits than the rest of the company. Hassan would be traveling to Princeport with the Duchess, while Arnolfo would head west to Haute-Tielmark with Gaultry's party.

The Duchess and the priestess accompanied the westward-bound party to the manor's entry quay. Across the moat, horses waited, accoutered with saddles that were gaily trimmed in green and silver and saddlebags that were heavy with provisions.

"Dervla tells me she gave you a present this morning." The

Duchess turned to Gaultry and fastened her glittering blue gaze on her face.

"She has been too generous."

"I should hope so." The old woman smiled a little grimly. "I intend for this venture to succeed, and there's no use in any of us giving you half the force you will need to make it. Besides, I suspect Dervla owed you an apology."

Gaultry nodded, not trusting herself to speak.

The Duchess made her good-byes to Arnolfo and Martin, shaking the archer's hand and giving her grandson a swift hug. Her final words were cautionary. "Go as fast as you can. Brook no delays. As soon as the Chancellor has wind of your intent, the Duke of Haute-Tielmark will be set against you. You must try to reach Clarin's barrow before this happens."

This time, Gaultry stepped down to cross the water of the moat with no hesitation. She was as eager as the others to be on her way.

BOOK TWO

▼

Prologue

Lily Rowes crouched in the nook behind the stone staircase of the great tower. It was a good place for a short while's hiding, and she needed a short while by herself to cry. A basket of soiled laundry stood, temporarily neglected, at her feet. She had been crying for some time now, using one of Prince Benet's shirts to mop her tears. The scent of him that lingered in its fine chambray folds was all that she had to give her comfort now.

It had been so long—months now—since the Prince had been himself, and she, it seemed, was the only one who marked the difference.

Lily was a slight woman, little more than a girl, small and fine-boned with the hard living of her youth. She had been the youngest child in a fisher's cottage. There had been ten before her, and children for the oldest children even before she was born. Life had been hard and lean, until one marvelous day, a day, two summers past now, that had changed her whole life.

That day had started terribly. Lily, scrambling on the Princeport quay side for the half-pennies that the great lords sometimes threw into the chill harbor water for the pleasure of watching the fisher children scramble and dive to retrieve them, had been expecting nothing better to come from the day than a ducking, and, if she was quick and lucky, a copper coin.

It happened when Lily had been in the water twice already, missing the coin both times. She had stood on the quay in her wet chemise, her lips purple from the cold, and patiently worked her way up to the front of the pack, waiting her next turn in the water. A coarse code of conduct had evolved among the dockside divers: no more than four in the water after each coin, and certainly no less than three. The fine lordships would tire of the sport if it was less than three.

Suddenly it was her turn again. The coin, a copper flash as it hit the water, had been thrown very far out. At first Lily had thought that was good, because she was fast and nimble, and she easily reached it first. It was only when she resurfaced, coin clutched triumphantly in her fist, that she found out it was bad. One of the rougher dockside girls had been there when she came up. She had grabbed Lily's fist, coin and all, in her own, and struck the smaller girl on the scalp with the razor edge of a broken shell. Another girl had forced Lily's head under. Half-drowned, she'd relinquished the coin and dragged herself, blinded by her own blood, back to the landing. The noble lord had thrown his half-penny very far out.

Then the miracle had happened.

Arriving on the landing, sputtering, streaming blood, water, and tears, she had been greeted by a servant in the Prince's shining blue and white livery.

The dock children loved the Prince, what little they saw of him. He had his own boat, a small, lively craft with blue and white sails, and he used it often enough in the summer that the dock folk were accustomed to his presence among them. He never threw coins, except on state occasions, but he honored a soup house on the dock with his patronage, and he knew how to sail his own boat. He was young, and shy of his own people; but no one minded.

He'd seen Lily in the water, and perhaps watched her before she'd gone in, and he had taken an interest. An interest that went well beyond the impulse of providing a thick warm cloak to huddle under on a chilly quay.

He wouldn't let her go back to her parent's parsimonious household. Overnight her world changed. She began to work in the palace, first in the kitchens, then in the laundry. During that first year of service, her Prince—how she adored him!—was a distant figure. That first year, unaccustomed to the generous rations of palace living, she ate like a horse and tried to make herself fat, not quite believing that she wouldn't be thrown back into a life of gnawing hunger when the Prince's whim had passed. He saw her twice to speak that year, and teased her both times that she'd got plump—but not meanlike, to make her embarrassed. She slowly came to understand that, at other times, he was watching her.

In the second year, her growing caught up with her food. She had a spurt of growth and got taller by a little bit and returned to gamine and slender. The Prince's smile subtly changed. Suddenly her laundry duties included collecting clothes from his rooms. She seldom saw him in chamber, but there were always small presents waiting for her to find. Small, unimportant things, to let her know he did not mean to buy her. In the castle, at court, the prince would flirt with the fine ladies, laugh and play-offer them his favors—but his feelings for Lily were different.

"Chancellor Heiratikus reminds me daily I must take a common-blood bride" the Prince told her, just before the New Year. "I'll come and claim her on Prince's Night," he whispered. "Who do you think she will be?"

I hope someone who loves you, her eyes told him. She tried not to let herself hope. Chancellor Heiratikus, Lily guessed, would have an idea like no one else's of what common blood entailed.

In January, something changed. Benet became distant, his fine dark eyes became haunted. He stopped flirting with his fine ladies. The court was full of gossip. A woman died, and then another, and it was murmured that they'd died for jilted love, that it was Benet's fault for not having announced his bride-choice publicly.

Then, as the last snows of March faded, Mervion Blas came to court. The Chancellor had sent out all the way to the southmost province for her. She arrived the night of the full moon, at the turning of the month. Lily watched from the shadows when she first came before Benet for her formal presentation. The woman from the South Border was so proud, and tall, and fine-looking, Lily's heart hurt just looking at her. Red-gold fire seemed to stream from her hair as she'd curtsied, her skin glowed like creamy satin, her mysterious green eyes glittered with intense inner light. She had a friend with her, a pretty, slight woman with curling white-blond hair—someone said it was her brother's wife—but all attention was on Mervion Blas. They said her father had been born an ostler, and her mother was a farm-girl.

Lily could only believe that she was looking at Chancellor Heiratikus's idea of common blood.

She dashed away, and went to cry in her special hiding place, the nook behind the great tower stair that she'd taken to hiding in when she was particularly miserable.

That was how she discovered that the Chancellor and his frightening officer, Lord Issachar Dan, were taking Mervion Blas up to the Keyhole Chamber. Either Mervion Blas had not wanted to go, or the Chancellor had not wanted to give her the choice. Four hulking guards had pushed her up the stairs, even as she fought against them.

A laundry girl can go almost anywhere she wants to, in a Prince's palace. Jealous tears still staining her cheeks, Lily went to the Prince's chambers, to warn him the Chancellor bode his intended ill, that he meant to twist her with magic. She had hated the way Benet had looked, so intently, so fascinated, at Mervion, as they had been introduced at the great state dinner, but she was desperately sure that her loyalty to her beloved should be above such petty jealousies, that he should be warned.

So she found her dear Benet, alone in his rooms, and told about the Chancellor and Mervion. Whatever sorcery the Chancellor had bound him with, it had weakened this night, and Benet was hers for a time again. Her Prince looked at her seriously and told her, "Mervion Blas is to be my doom, dearest; not my bride." He offered no explanation for his words, only held his arms out as though he saw himself drowning, and this time she was to be his savior.

They lay together that night. He held her body to his own, somewhere between despair and tenderness, until finally he fell asleep, still clutching her to him.

She crept away before morning.

She did not seen him again after that night. His body was there, and the smell of him on his shirts, and his tone was light, and he flirted still with the court ladies, but he, her dearest Benet, was gone. It was as though someone else was playing his role, someone who knew how he acted in public—but not someone who knew the secrets of his private life. There were no ribbons hidden among the linens, no flowers tucked into the leaves of the clothespress, no secret glances, no caresses.

There was no one with whom she could share this. They'd laugh at her foolishness and tell her she had been taken and rejected, like many a young girl before her. Only Lily knew that this was not rejection, that something worse had happened to her man.

Steps on the stone staircase warned her to muffle her sobs. Steps, and then mingled voices. It was Mervion Blas, the Chancellor, and terrible Issachar Dan. Mervion Blas had been forced up into the tower once again.

To Lily's surprise, Mervion was laughing, lightly quizzing Lord Dan about his terrible eagles. Her voice was teasing, relaxed—even playful. What was it like to ride them, the border woman asked. Would his favorite mount, Gyviere, be soon recovered—it had been wounded—so he could take to the skies again? They reached the last step.

"Three days—a week? Who knows." The dark lord's voice was impatient, disinterested.

"And then you go for my sister?"

"And then I go for your sister." A pause. "Perhaps she will fight better than you have done."

"Don't confuse her!" That was the Chancellor's voice.

"You've ripped her totally open," Issachar said. "What does it matter?"

"Appearances—"

"Damn appearances!"

"Appearances are all," the Chancellor snapped. "If we don't hold to them, the court will block us. Take the Prince—"

Lily didn't mean to make a noise. It was only a little noise. No one should have heard it. But Issachar Dan—sometimes she wondered if he were even human. With his fierce darting eyes, he was like one of his own eagles or hawks, bound into a human shape.

Now, he appeared around the stone spiral of the stair like a black-fire demon, seized her arm, and dragged her out.

"What have we here?" Lily, spun into torchlight by Issachar's powerful grip, burst into fresh tears. The dark lord laughed. "An eavesdropper! We'll soon teach her better!"

"Lord Dan!" That was the Chancellor, making the dark lord let her free—perhaps to assess her better. Lily looked up through her tears. The Chancellor was a tall man, with a mane of silvery hair like a bard's. Long-lashed dark eyes dominated his face. Tonight, standing half in the torchlight, those eyes were magic bright. There had been rumors in the kitchens that he was an adept of the Great Goddess Llara. Trapped within his intense gaze, Lily could only believe they were true. She dropped a curtsy, and tried to stem her tears.

"Your lordships." She tried not to look at Mervion Blas, but she could not help but notice her, as she hung back so shyly from the torches. Her proud head was tilted at the same defiant angle she'd presented to her Prince—but something was different. All her color seemed to have faded, as though she had greeted the Prince flushed with magic, vigor, and life—and now those things were lost to her. Lily did her best not to let the Chancellor see where she was looking. She bobbed and curtsied, as though her life depended on them not guessing at all what she was thinking.

"What were you doing there?" the Chancellor demanded.

Lily flushed, and sobbed anew. She could not find the words to answer.

"You're frightening her, Master. Shall I try?"

"Issachar!" The Chancellor's voice was sharp.

"A little persuasion—"

"I haven't done nothing wrong!" Lily blurted. "Please, Sir—your Excellency—I was crying."

"We can see that." Now Heiratikus's voice was purring silk. "Now, why were you there?"

Lily turned her face to his, trying to read what he intended. All she could think of was the cold day on the docks, the cut of the shell on her scalp, the blood, the noblemen laughing on the quay as she panicked and clawed her way through the water, desperate to reach the safety of the dock. The man had thrown the coin too far out, toying with the dock children's need.

She ducked her head, and told him the truth. "I've lost my man. I've no one to tell it. They laugh at me in the kitchens, Sir, but I can't help crying."

He thought it was pathetic, worth at least a sharp laugh. "Nothing to cure here, Lord Dan! You're not the one to fix a broken heart! Nor am I!"

He didn't even bother to dismiss her. Issachar hesitated, then he too turned and was gone.

She was alone. In so many ways more than one. There was no one to help her, or her Prince, or anyone.

chapter **13**

▼

I t would take them four or five days of hard riding to reach Haute-Tielmark. For the first three days of travel, the Duchess had arranged horses and open passage through her western neighbor's land. The logistics were impressive: fresh mounts at every way station for Gaultry, Martin, and Arnolfo, and the troop of ten soldiers the Duchess had assigned to accompany them. Their own endurance—which meant Gaultry's endurance—set the limit on their speed of travel.

For the first two days, Gaultry put all her focus into her riding, pushing herself to exhaustion on the road, abandoning herself to heavy sleep each evening. She didn't want to think about the implications of anything she had learned. The first night, her ploy was a success. She slept solidly the night through with no bothersome dreams. The second night she was not so lucky. She was haunted by dreams of Mervion, waking three times during the night to an intense sense of loss.

"You look exhausted," Martin told her, as they saddled up the next morning in the inn's stable yard.

"I'll manage," she said, fumbling with her stirrups. She had avoided him since they'd left Melaudiere's manor. Despite the Duchess's apologies, some part of the young huntress was still disconcerted by the figures she'd seen in the fountain, herself and Martin, clasped in each other's arms—however comically, however unwilling— among the jets of water. After having scrutinized the sculptured portraits of the Common Brood, she knew that the Duchess's figures depicted something more than mere caprice or whimsy.

"Do it this way," Martin said, untangling a wayward strap and showing her. "This way you can adjust it from the saddle."

"Thanks."

"Long day today. We'll reach the border of the Bissanty Fingerland before it ends."

"I don't like it that we're traveling through Bissanty territory at all." When it was explained to her that they were actually going to have to cut through Bissanty territory to reach Clarin's barrow, Gaultry began to understand why Dervla had been so set against the plan. "It seems so risky."

"There's no help for it." Martin traced a quick map on the smooth leather of the saddle. "The Bissanty Fingerland juts into Tielmark like a narrow inland peninsula. We could avoid it by circling round it to the southwest, but we'd add two, maybe three days to our travel—as well as having to pass through the territory of another member of the ducal council whose sympathy the Chancellor has bought with promises of power. All of which means we'd only get to Clarin's barrow just in time to celebrate Prince's Night."

"How long will it take us to travel from Clarin's barrow to Princeport?" Gaultry asked, counting over the days left to Prince's Night in her head. "Does the Duchess really believe we'll reach the Prince's capital in time for his marriage?"

"Getting to Princeport will be the least of our worries," Martin said cryptically. "Our worst will be Victor, the Duke of Haute-Tielmark. He's an ambitious man, and he's ruled the most troubled province of Tielmark for fifteen years. Rumor has it that Heiratikus has promised him a nice soft County in the east for one of his sons. Whether that's true or not, it's certain enough that Victor will be set against us. Worse, Grandmère's information has him actually at home *in* Haute-Tielmark as we ride towards it. We'll have trouble avoiding him once we cross into his territory out of the Fingerland."

"So we take the high road across the Bissanty Fingerland into Haute-Tielmark's realm, and then ride on until we reach Clarin's tomb?"

"That's right."

"Won't that draw undue attention?"

Martin shrugged. "It will. But there's really no viable alternatives. As you just pointed out yourself, time is short."

"We could go cross-country."

"Impractical. From here on the land gets marshy—it's wild paddy-fields all the way through the Bissanty Fingerland. Not the terrain to take a horse through."

"But if we go on the high road we know we'll alert this Victor Haute-Tielmark. How close is Clarin's barrow to the border of the Fingerland, once we reach Haute-Tielmark?"

"Not close. Another day? Less if we don't run into trouble." Martin made an unhappy gesture towards the soldiers who had come out to saddle their own horses as they spoke. "Grandmère wouldn't have given us such an escort if she thought it would be easy. But you at least will be able to get through. It should play something like our crossing into Melaudiere, when we fought against Coyal and his men. But with more blood."

Gaultry shot a horrified look at the men and women of her escort. "You mean that the Duchess has sent them along as fodder for Bissanty swords?"

Martin lifted his brows, disapproving. "They're not unblooded children, Gaultry. Do you imagine that my grandmother would have told you that her own neck would be for the block if there wasn't a very good chance of there being serious trouble?"

Gaultry had to shake her head.

"Besides, as a party of thirteen, we'd be just as obvious foundering overland through swamps with our horses as we would be taking the high road."

"We could disguise me so they didn't know I was part of your company."

"Don't be ridiculous, Gaultry. You've not got the looks to pass for a page boy." He smiled, as if at some private thought, and finished adjusting the saddle. "Let me give you a hand up."

"What if I went overland by myself and met you again after you'd crossed back into Tielmark?"

"What would you have us do in the meantime? Wait for you at the first inn over the border while you went and mired yourself in some swamp?"

"Why not? Besides, I wouldn't get myself mired in any swamp. Martin, it makes better sense the more I think of it." Gaultry put her foot in his cupped hands, and swung herself up onto her horse. She was pleased to have devised a plan she could feel genuinely enthusiastic about. "If there's one thing growing up in Arleon Forest taught me, it's how to move through wild brush without getting myself into trouble. Think about it: if I go cross-country, that removes the bother of having to pass me across two borders, and, if the Bissanties are sharing news with the Duke of Haute-Tielmark, it should put some doubt into his mind as to whether—or when—he should attack. What would be the problem? You've seen how fast I can move on foot—wild brush is my element. I wouldn't even need to fuss with a horse."

Martin shook his head. "You're not trying to understand me, Gaultry. This is rough country we'll be passing through. Difficult to hold on to and not much worth having when you've got it. There's a reason that Clarin left it to the Bissanty Empire three hundred years ago while he annexed the land around it to Tielmark. Three hundred years of being the backwater of a dying Empire hasn't improved it."

"So long as I don't run into troops—which doesn't sound likely, if the land is as rough as you're suggesting—I don't see where the problem lies. How much ground are we talking about? Twenty miles, and then back into Tielmark?"

"What would happen if you were alone and one of Issachar's eagles came down on you?"

At least Martin had the grace not to rub her face in the point he'd won. As she struggled to come up with any sort of a convincing answer, he looked away, and stroked her horse's neck, running his fingers gently under its mane. It whickered softly, and tried to shove its ears into his hand for more scratching. "The geas is fading, you know," he said. "I'm losing the impress."

"Good," she said, her surprise making her sharp.

"I'm losing sight of what you looked like as a child."

She'd grown comfortable, knowing he was there to protect her, that she could turn his mood when he threatened her. "That sounds about right," she said. "When it's gone you can leave me too, just as my father did, and have everyone think you noble for doing so." She dug her heels into her horse, starting it moving, her face burning with regret that she'd allowed herself to say anything—let alone something that sounded so wounded and childish.

Her mood, hanging sullenly on her, did not clear with the morning's mists. She brooded as she rode, not sure whether Martin had meant to warn her that that he wouldn't always be there to protect her, or whether he had meant only to say that even without the geas, he would continue to protect her. At the lunch hour, when they changed horses, she was uncomfortably aware of the young soldiers and their good-natured bickering as they argued among themselves about which of the fresh horses they should choose for Gaultry. After her display of poor horsemanship during their first morning of ridding together, it had become a point of honor among them to single out the most-biddable animal for her every time there was a changeover. This time they'd narrowed the field to a white mare with touches of gray at her muzzle and hooves, and a big bay gelding. The gelding looked like it had a better temper, but two of the young men had taken it on themselves to defend Gaultry's riding skills, arguing that she was ready for a more spirited mount. "The mare's just right for her," one of the two, whose name was Daurat, argued. "The bay's too wide." Gaultry allowed herself a crooked smile. Despite the poor riding and unladylike manners that she had shown to him, however inadvertently, since he'd first ridden as her escort, Daurat had been consistent in his formal manners towards her from the first morning. She suspected the boy was arguing for the white horse because it better fit his picture of the proper mount for a lady.

Seven out of ten of her escort weren't much older than her brother Gilles. With their hair cropped close under their helmets and their open camaraderie, they seemed even younger. When Martin came to settle the dispute over the horse, there was a chorus of dismay when he told them Gaultry would take the bay after all. Daurat blushed to his ears when Martin told him if he liked the mare so well, he should ride her himself. The others roared, taking Martin's words as a crude joke.

"You shouldn't tease them," she said, as they got going again.

"Why not? It keeps their spirits up." Martin grinned, a thin wolf's grin that showed her she wasn't the only one in a bad mood. "I don't need a geas to see what you're thinking. If you want me to give the boys their way, because they'll soon be risking their lives for you, I can think of more effective means of obliging them. We could un-bind your hair, and crown you with forest roses, and fire them up, telling them they were fighting for the queen of May. That would make them far happier than having them think they were imperiling themselves for the sake of a grim-faced nag of a vixen."

He had brought his horse very close to hers, making her grateful for the solid, tall body of the bay gelding.

"Don't take your anger out on me because you don't like your own plan either," Gaultry said.

He glared at her, fury coloring his face, and reined his horse away.

She stared after him, a little shocked in the realization that her angry guess at the cause of his bad humor was likely correct.

In the smokey, low-beamed public room of the inn where they stopped that evening, Martin was once again the professional sol-dier, teasing and provoking his men, but letting little of the deep concern hidden behind his composed face show itself. His contin-uing coldness to Gaultry told her, more than words, that his wor-ries were greater than ever. A traveler coming eastwards from the Fingerland had told the inn's mistress that the high road's border post had been reinforced two days before and he'd seen, as he'd put it, "enough pigeons winging messages to feed a family for a week." All the jokes in the world were not going to make that news en-couraging.

Later, in the privacy of the pallet room where the men were bunking, the soldiers sat close by, cleaning their weapons while Martin and Arnolfo discussed strategy with their corporal, Anders.

"Someone—maybe even a pair of men—will have to hang back and destroy the bird-coops," Arnolfo suggested.

"That shouldn't be a problem," Anders said. He gave Gaultry, who was leaning against the wall behind Martin's chair, a wide smile. "We know how important it is that Gaultry get through. What about when we cross back into Tielmark?"

"That depends." Martin reached into his coat and pulled out a leather document wallet. "If the Chancellor is very desperate to get Gaultry, he may finally show something of his colors, and arrange for the Duke of Haute-Tielmark to come try and take us there at the border, where we'll have no place to run."

He took out a faded map that had been folded so many times it was limp at the creases, and laid it carefully on the table. Gaultry, staring over Martin's shoulder, felt her throat go dry and scratchy.

Past the border, the high road took a long horseshoe bend to the north, before winding back south and crossing into Tielmark. As a crow flew, the way across the Fingerland was less than half the distance of the road. There was a swamp marked in the body of the horseshoe—a difficult crossing for a horse or horsemen, but if Gaultry could find a deer or some other animal to borrow speed and agility from, the way straight across would be easy enough.

Martin turned and caught sight of Gaultry staring at the map. He frowned, and moved his hand so it covered their intended route. "Why don't you go up to your room?" he said. "You're going to want a good night's sleep for all the riding you'll be doing tomorrow."

"I haven't checked my own weapons yet," she said. The Duchess had supplied her with a new bow and a nicely balanced knife.

"I'll bring them up after we're done here."

"Don't you think I have a right to help plan what we're all going to be taking part in tomorrow?"

"That's a reasonable request," Arnolfo seconded. "It's as much her battle as ours."

"I'll let her know what's going to happen tomorrow when I bring up her weapons." Martin stood abruptly and took hold of Gaultry's shoulder. "Say good night, Gaultry."

She looked into his hard gray eyes. "I want to stay," she said, trying to understand his sudden stubbornness. "You have no right to bully me."

"It doesn't take much to establish rights." For just a moment, a vein of silver geas-magic seemed to flicker across his irises, a minute strike of lightning. Then it was gone, and he was looming threateningly over her. "Go up to your room," he said.

Arnolfo sighed, and turned the map so it faced him. Anders, openly shocked, gave Martin a furious look, and put his hand on the hilt of his sword.

"I'll go," Gaultry said, seething, but not quite angry enough that she wanted to see Anders and Martin in a fight. "Don't make me wait long, or I'll come back down."

In the privacy of her own room, she went to the small window and stared out, her quick glimpse of the map fresh in her mind, imprinted all the more clearly for Martin's horrible bullying. After all they had been through together, it was maddening that he suddenly expected her to submit to being ordered about like a meek child.

The map had showed that this inn was less than three miles from the border. To the south lay a small river, running east to west. She squinted out past the inn buildings, across night fields, and saw the silver of water running dark behind a line of poplars. If she followed that river cross-country until she reached the place where a smaller tributary joined it, that, according to the map, would be the border. She could head west from there—and perhaps a bit southward, to avoid meeting the high road where it looped down from its northward horseshoe-shaped curve. That would be the shortest route to Haute-Tielmark.

She pressed her face against the cool glass of the window, wondering what she should do. If Martin and the others were to cross into the Bissanty Fingerland without her, would the fighting they met with be less severe?

A knock at the door made her start guiltily away from the window. "Come in," she said.

It was Martin. Though he still had his sword with him, he'd stripped down to a shirt and trousers for the evening, and was looking surprisingly calm. He came in, dropped the bundle of her weapons on the goose-feather mattress of her bed. "Cooled down yet?" he asked.

"How many men did you decide to sacrifice to the bird-coops?" she asked, still bitter.

"It won't be like that, Gaultry."

"I don't see why you can't just let me go cross-country and have us meet up in Haute-Tielmark. Can't you see how easy it would be for me to cross a wild place like this? Would you have to fight at the border if I wasn't with you?"

"Nothing fazes you, does it?" Martin said, crossing to the window. "Not even the prospect of getting scooped up by one of Issachar's eagles. What have you been up to? Staring out the window and trying to make up your mind when you're going to leave?"

Gaultry pressed her hand to her shoulder where the sun-healer had closed the eagle's wound. "Yes," she finally admitted, defiant. "I can take care of myself, you know, and if the Duke of Haute-Tielmark is likely to know we're coming, going in along the high road is a rotten plan."

"Gaultry," Martin said, smiling and sitting down on the edge of her bed. "There are times when you make me feel the weight of my age."

She looked at him, bewildered, not understanding where all the tension had gone in him. It was hard to be furious with him while he was in the grips of such a strange, sunny temper. "Why are you in such a good mood?" she asked, suspicious.

"If you went along cross-country," he said, "do you realize the nightmare it would be for the twelve of us, waiting for you to make your appearance, and praying to the gods that you weren't drowning in a lonely quagmire somewhere that even the Chancellor's men wouldn't find you? Grandmère would never forgive me—not that never would be much of a long time, with Prince's Night just days away."

"I can protect myself," Gaultry said hotly, starting to pace.

"I'm not asking you if you can protect yourself," Martin said, deceptively mild. "I'm just asking you to imagine what it would be like for the rest of us, if we let you walk out that door to make your way to Haute-Tielmark unaccompanied. All those young men down there have sworn on their honor to stand as your shield against all dangers. Do you see what you are asking, demanding that I let you go off alone? Imagine what you would feel if Mervion wouldn't accept your help in these troubles, if she insisted she could beat Heiratikus by herself. Even if you knew it was in her power to crush him, how would you feel to be denied the chance to aid her?"

Gaultry paused, and gave him a sour look. "We're twins. I can't not help her. That's the difference." He had somehow twisted her round, so that she had begun to sound unreasonable, and even petty.

"The geas on me is fading as I pay you the coin of my protection," Martin said. "But it's still very much there. Are you telling me I have a choice as to whether or not I should be trying to protect you?"

"So what are you saying?" Gaultry said. "That it's better for the men downstairs to die protecting me, than for them to risk suffering the dishonor of having allowed me to fail to fend for myself?" Martin picked up her bow, and turned it over and over in his hands, not meeting her eyes. "Tell me!"

Frustrated, she leaned over and jerked at his shoulder, making him look at her.

"We won't have to fight at the border if you aren't with us, Gaultry," he said, putting his hand over hers. "Which is why I'm telling you now that I want you to head out for Haute-Tielmark tonight."

"What?" She tried to pull away, but he folded his hand over hers, and wouldn't let her go.

"Not that you should put much store by my map, mind you. It doesn't even show the north-south track that runs up through the Fingerland into the Bissanty heartland."

He was sincere in wanting her to go. Now with the prospect of actually undertaking a lonely trek through the night looming in front of her, a stab of fear pierced her. "What about Issachar's eagles?"

"Only Gyviere would be big enough to get you up off the ground—Gyviere is the eagle who attacked you at Grandmère's. And Gyviere is in Princeport, recovering from the arrow Arnolfo put in his breast back over Grandmère's moat."

"That earlier warning was a lie?"

He narrowed his eyes and stood up, coming close so that she could feel the warmth of his body. "Will you do this, Gaultry? If you do, it will be a secret between the two of us. Anders and the others—" He smiled, the laughing wolf's smile that made him seem so dangerous. "They'll be hot to get across the Fingerland to rejoin you, but I'll keep a tight rein on them while we cross the border posts."

"You're making this seem like a dare," she said, giving him a look that was half-smile, half-scowl. "You were being rude down there to make them feel sorry for me, weren't you?" She put her free hand around the back of his neck, feeling the strength of him, the proud curve of his body.

His smile deepened. "I was."

"And now you're being nice to me to make me hurry across the Fingerland and find you again," she said, her voice low and teasing. She should be feeling more shy than this. She should step away, and leave him alone, and remember that he was married to the Countess of Seafrieg, remember that her sister and her country both were in danger, and needed her full attention. She stroked the hair at the base of his neck, happiness piercing her at the trust he had given her.

He put his free hand around her waist. "Maybe."

A strange joy passed between them, something that was not the geas, or a casting. It might have been the simple recognition that both wanted their imminent parting to be brief. She turned her mouth to his. He welcomed her advance, drawing her to him more tightly than ever, one hand winding in her hair, letting her feel all at once the fierce heat of his desire.

"This is a tangle." Martin sighed when he let her free. "I'm mad even to think of letting myself touch you." He gave her a wry look. "Get through to Haute-Tielmark safely, and perhaps we'll untangle it together, after Prince's Night."

"I'll get through," Gaultry said, stepping away a few paces to pick up her new bow and test its bowstring. She smiled to herself as he unconsciously followed her, not wanting to leave the circle of her body's heat. "I want to do what I can to save you and the men having to fight."

He gave her a grave look. "Don't misunderstand me. This isn't a matter of saving men, Gaultry. It's our best chance to get you safely to Clarin's barrow." He shrugged. "Perhaps I'm being a fool, sending you off secretly, with no support. I have to believe that's not true. If the men think you've acted alone, if they don't know what we've planned—not only will they have better motivation to catch up to you, but it will be safer for everyone. The Bissanties like to torture their prisoners."

As he spoke, she was examining the kit he had brought her. Besides the weapons, there were some rations and a small pouch. She buckled her knife belt around her waist, gray leather with a green enameled buckle. It was good to feel the short blade, in its sheath, resting familiarly at her hip, as though she were back in Arleon Forest, preparing for some late-night hunting. "I'll see you in Haute-Tielmark," she promised. "Just get yourself through in one piece."

▼

chapter 14

E scaping unnoticed from the inn was not going to be easy. Martin warned her as he left that he intended to set some-one to watch the stairs. "If you can't sneak out of the inn without my men catching you," he had said, "I'm not going to let you risk the Fingerland."

Gaultry thought that was a reasonable condition.

She waited in her room, listening to the sounds of the inn clos-ing for the night. Finally satisfied that all had settled, she blew out her candle, sat on the bed in the darkness, giving her eyes a moment to adjust. When she quickly opened her door and poked her head out to check if the landlord had finally retired for the night, she caught sight of the head and shoulders of the man Martin had posted on the first landing, silhouetted by the light of the damped-down fire in the public room below.

She hissed, annoyed that Martin had taken his promise to make it hard for her to leave the inn so literally. There would be a servant stair, she knew, but the idea of stumbling round through the dark-ness in search of it did not appeal.

A soft sound near her feet startled her, and the whisper of a touch against her knee. Looking down, she saw the inn's large orange tomcat standing back from her knee, pausing to clean a paw, pretending to ignore her now that it had her attention. Night vision, she thought. Night moves. She muttered a fast prayer to the Huntress for sending it to her. Then she hissed again, this time gently, to call it to her.

Luring it into her room was easy. Getting the supple strength out of it was less so. Gaultry was clumsy where cats were concerned. Tamsanne's preference for a canine familiar had meant no cats around the cottage on which to practice the taking craft. From Gaultry's standpoint of wanting to borrow energy and spirit, they were the most selfish, stubborn, and difficult animals she had ever encountered.

Tamsanne had once said to her that this was because she and they had too much in common.

It cost her a nasty scratch on one hand, and was a rather nosier and longer process than she would have liked, but she finally fixed the spell and stripped loose the animal's spirit. There was something sordid in borrowing the spirit-strength from such a small animal: it made her heart race, and would leave her nervous and headachy when finally she set it free. But as the cat-spirit settled into her, her color vision dropped and the edges of the room cleared, the murk of the shadows contracting. She knew having it in her would be worth the effort and the pain.

She plumped up the ticking of her mattress to make it look like she was still in bed, and curled the cat's warm body up on the pillow where it would be comfortable. Unfortunately she had no paper to leave a message, but her room had a fireplace that hadn't been swept entirely clean. Using an arrow as a makeshift quill, she wrote "1st Inn" with ash on her pillowcase, leaving it where a cursory inspection would reveal it in the morning.

Dropping the remnants of her writing ash back on the hearth, she took a closer look at the fireplace—and the chimney. It was built of hand-molded bricks, and, fortunately for Gaultry, had been built broad. Curious, she stepped onto the hearth, and looked up. The rough sides of the flue framed two stars, and a piece of the night sky overhead. Even without cat grace giving a balanced polish to her movements, it wouldn't have been difficult to clamber up.

A few dusty minutes later, she cautiously poked her head out at roof-level, completely soot-covered, suppressing a cough. About fifteen feet along the ridgepole, hunched sleepily on another chimney pot, she saw the dark silhouette of a large hawk. Even with the moon behind a cloud, its feathers glinted, unnatural and metallic.

In the first shock of her dismay and surprise, Gaultry almost lost her toeholds on the sides of the flue. Had it been shadowing them since they'd left Melaudiere, or had it been sent from the Bissanty border, to pinpoint when their troop would be arriving? Whatever the case, Gaultry doubted that Martin would want her to set out alone, across unfriendly territory, knowing that one of Issachar's birds was watching.

The moon came out from behind the cloud, and she saw that the bird's back was to her.

Before it could spy her, she drew her head back into the flue, fumbling with her toes for lower holds.

Martin would want to know it was there so he could decide for her whether or not she should reconsider her lonely trek through the Fingerland swamps. She rested her head against the chimney's rough brick, thinking. Martin had enough intelligence and will that he had forced himself to see the sense in letting her range outside the shield of his personal protection. What with the geas and the personal vows that bound him to protect her, it had cost him much to let her go. She wanted to honor the trust he had put in her. But she also wanted to prove by action that she was worthy of that trust.

Then again, the silver hawk's back had been to her. If she could kill it, and kill it quietly, there were pressing reasons to go on. If she couldn't—or if she tried and missed—she'd risk her neck dropping back down into her room just as fast as she could go and face the embarrassment of calling in reinforcements and explaining what she'd been doing crawling up her chimney past midnight.

Scarcely daring to breathe, she wedged her feet in two good holds at the chimney sides, and, twisting, fumbling, and concentrating desperately so she wouldn't drop anything or make a noise, she managed to get an arrow nocked in her bow.

The bird let out a horrible shriek when the arrow took it. It neither died nor lost its grip on the chimney pot. Its squawks cut through the night, terrifyingly loud. Gaultry panicked. Her borrowed cat-spirit, seeing something with feathers fluttering, hearing its screams of pain, crowded eagerly into the front of her brain and took over. The young huntress pounced forward along the ridgepole, surprising herself with her own agility. She grabbed the squawking bird and broke its neck. Then, panting, she slumped down on the ridgepole to steady her nerves. A dampness on her hands, then pain, told her she had cut herself on its razor-sharp feathers. Below her, in the inn's yard, nothing moved, no alarm was raised. It seemed, amazingly, that no one had heard the hawk's death cries.

Recovering sufficiently to think, she stuffed the bird's body down a small flue pipe at the side of the chimney. It wouldn't do for Martin to find it and know that she'd set out with the knowledge that the enemies' creatures had found them and were watching.

She scanned the inn's yard and the trees that surrounded the inn, grateful again for the cat-vision, which made every branch stand out, distinct, and seemed to catch the smallest of motions. Nothing. She hoped that meant there had been only the one sentinel bird.

The cat-spirit made the tricky jump down onto the stable-yard wall ridiculously easy. Gaultry briefly considered exchanging the cat-spirit for that of a horse, but, guessing that Martin might have put a watcher on the stables as well as on the stairs, she decided not to risk it. From the wall she dropped to the ground and made for the river. Soon enough, she'd have to find some large animal from which to take the stamina she would need to keep herself going through the night, but for now the feline energy would have to do.

Crossing the field and reaching the line of poplars she'd seen from her bedroom window, she met the river. Where it ran by the inn it was more stream than river: narrow, lively, with weeds and thick brush choking the banks, except for the thin strip of mud, studded with stones, at the water's edge, where flooding had swept the bank clean. Although her heart was hammering uncomfortably with the cat's nervous energy, the small animal's agility helped Gaultry make good time along the slippery bank. She guessed the creature was used to night prowling along this river. The moon, a bare five nights away from full, gave her a little light, though the thick rafts of cloud that had been moving in since late afternoon made it less a help than it might have been.

The fields faded into scrub, and the trees began to get taller, wilder. She veered away from the water to avoid a broad oxbow loop, wondering if she had missed seeing the ingress of the second river, which would have meant she'd crossed into the Bissanty Fingerland, and left Tielmark territory. It was hard to know how far she had come in the dark.

"Why we can't have a light is beyond me, Jaquim."

"Spade for spade pulling night duty."

They were a bare thirty feet away, dark silhouettes in a clump of trees on a knoll to her left.

She must have crossed the border into Bissanty territory without knowing it. Stopping short, she hunkered down behind the trunk of a broken pine tree.

Only the cat and her camouflage of chimney soot had saved her from discovery.

"The captain tells us to watch without a light, we watch without a light." A new voice. Three men. Or more.

"Why does he expect them to come this way?" That was the first man.

"It stands to reason they'll come this way, if they don't take the high road. I wouldn't want to bring a troop of riders this way, but it could be done. Then again, I'd fancy even less the odds I'd be meeting on the high road. Charnor says there's a call come all the way down from Bassorah bureau ordering us we'd better take them." The man spat, loudly. "Pack of spies. They have a cushy lot up there in the capital. What do they want, riding down and lording it over us out here, making our life hard for us to no good end?"

Gaultry's blood went cold. It sounded like Martin and the men were going to have to do battle on the road even if she wasn't there to provide a focus for the attack. They could all be killed, down to the last man. She pictured herself waiting raggedly in the courtyard of some inn; Martin and the others never showing. What then?

Then, she thought grimly, she would have been proved correct in arguing to make her own way into Haute-Tielmark, and Martin would have been proved right in sending her, while he and his troops mounted a diversion for her on the high road. Martin must have guessed that the Bissanty reinforcements on the road would be more than his ten men, plus Arnolfo and himself, could handle. Realization dawned that he might have sent her off so he could get himself killed without her. Her stomach, already queasy from the cat-spirit, began to feel downright nauseous. Her memory of Martin's fine mood, as he came to her room, ready to surprise her with his decision to trust her judgment above his own, was like a physical blow. Surely he would have given her some hint if he had believed that he was heading into potentially deadly battle the next morning?

If Martin and the others were killed or captured, she would have to continue on to Clarin's barrow by herself. The Duchess would expect it of her; it was the only way she could help Mervion.

"Where's Piet gone with the dogs?" That was the first speaker, the nervous man. "You'd think he'd be back by now."

"He'll be checking the headland. Don't you worry."

Dogs meant she had no choice but to move on. The moon was temporarily behind another cloudbank. It was time to risk movement. Forcing the cat-spirit to obey her, she used every whisper of the cat's finesse in creeping quietly through the bracken away from the guardpost. She could feel the cat-spirit, spitting and angry, throwing what it could of its strength around in her brain, clawing at her temples, seeking constantly for some crack in her concentration that would allow it to pry itself loose.

After her brush with the border post, she headed due west. The clouds which had threatened throughout the afternoon and early evening now gathered in thick bands across the sky. A wretched hour or two followed. Increasingly swampy ground meant she couldn't release the cat until she found something to replace it. The stars were hard to see through the maze of vines and branches overheard, and it was easy to trip and fall when she made the effort to look up from her feet to view them. After wasting minutes retrieving a boot that had been torn off for the third time by the muddy clutch of an unseen root, Martin's comment that he and his men would end up despairingly waiting for her at some roadside inn while she mired herself in a lonesome Fingerland swamp began to seem like an unpleasant probability. What devil had gotten into her that she had flattered herself that she could cross unknown wild lands so easily?

A crackle in the brush ahead of her brought her back to earth.

It was an enormous wild boar.

It was minding its own business, rooting in the mud at the base of what must have been a tasty bush. A huge creature, with bristling spines on the crest of its back and cruel-looking tusks.

In Paddleways village she'd taken from pigs, as a sort of childish joke, but she'd never risked a wild boar. They weren't common on the border near Tamsanne's cottage—and she'd avoided them on those few occasions when she had come upon them in the woods. One year, not long past, she'd been tracker for a boar hunt with the local villagers, looking to catch some winter fat. The fury of the creature at bay had been the most frightening thing she'd ever seen—now excepting the attack she'd suffered from Issachar's monster eagle. Martin's description of how such a beast had come at him through the snow, on the afternoon of her father's death, had been equally chilling.

But this creature—peaceably rooting for a late-night snack—surely taking from this creature would save her from wasting time and energy hunting for deer? It didn't look threatening. After two hours of being chased through forest and field, any animal at bay was frightening and angry. All she needed to do was surprise it.

If she hadn't just spent two frustrating hours making poor headway in the swamp, she never would have been fool enough to try it.

Waiting until it moved around the bush, still chomping, and presented her its rear flank, she made the spiral-sign of the Great Twins and kneeled to call the fresh casting. She took her time, weaving in extra flourishes so the cat-spirit wouldn't disrupt the new spell when she loosed it. Then she stepped cautiously forward into the soggy clearing where the boar, its high, skinny bottom turned to her, was vigorously breaking open the thick roots of the bush for their pulp.

Halfway across the clearing, one foot broke through the mud underfoot and plunged into a knee-deep hole. She gasped and jerked herself free, but it was too late.

The last vestiges of cat strength and cat agility saved her life.

Alone, her reflexes would never have been good enough to escape the creature's first savage run. Throwing herself to one side, she felt a flashing pain sear along her ribs: the thing had just missed goring her with its glinting tusks.

Like a complete fool, she hadn't even unsheathed her knife. She'd wanted her hands free for the spell, and she'd assumed she could sneak up on the creature, seize from it, and be off. Now, too late, she knew better. Clutching her side, she stumbled away, tripping over half-submerged roots and bracken.

Its little piggy eyes fixed on her, gleaming red with fury. Scared as anything, she glared back, and raised her palms, showing it her spell.

"Come at me now pig, and you're in for a surprise." It tossed its great head, hesitating as it sensed the casting. Trying to ready herself against the frightening animal, she let go the last of the cat. The feline presence shot from her like an arrow released from a bow, leaving a great empty channel, a void that made her reel and waver as her magic shifted, unbalancing her.

The great boar swung up its tusks and charged. Her choices were to jump and be gored or to fall and be trampled.

The boar's head hit her with a force that left her astonished to find herself still both alive and conscious. She was half under the creature's massive body, pressed deep into branch-filled slurry. It had over-run her. A prayer to all the gods sprang, unbidden, as she twisted beneath the boar's legs, not finding the chance to force her spell on it. One razorlike hoof, striking at random, slashed her arm, and the creature lowered its tusks to savage her shoulder.

The shoulder that had been spelled to health by the Priest of Andion. "Andion won't suffer to see his work undone," the Priest had said. It felt as if she had armor on that shoulder, all along where the eagle had wounded her. By rights, the great boar should have severed her arm from her body in the first seconds of its attack. It hadn't. The pain she could feel was distant and strange, as though it was happening to someone else's body.

There was no time to marvel, no time for relief. Gaultry threw her taking-spell at the boar with all her remaining strength. "All gods aid me!" she cried. "My life is in your hands!" The spell broke loose and exploded into being. It washed across the heavy creature like an enveloping wave, a dam burst by flood.

The boar dropped onto her as if it had been felled by an ax, driving Gaultry deeper still into the bracken, muck, and half-submerged broken sticks. She lay quietly, in shock, barely conscious of the great weight that crushed down on her. Inside, the space the cat-spirit had left empty bulged with a great porcine force that was more enraged than chastened. Beneath the still of her body, the physical shock, her mind worked furiously to subdue it.

After a moment the boar-spirit quieted a little and she became aware of her surroundings again, the spiked sticks beneath her like lances in her back. She tiredly shrugged the mountain of quivering pig flesh off, and peeled herself carefully off the soft muddy ground, waiting for the stab of pain that would tell her she had broken a bone. Shucking mud from her tunic and wiping her face, she stumbled five paces to a felled tree where she could sit. If the ground beneath her had been any harder, the weight of the boar as it landed on her would probably have crushed her rib cage.

She stood shakily and drew some deep breaths. Boars, she thought, and stooped to shift the great beast's head so its rubbery nose was safely up out of the watery muck. A boar had been the vehicle of her father's death. She should have taken that as a sign, and left the creature alone. She tenderly rotated the shoulder that the creature had so ineffectually savaged. Although Mariette's jacket and the shirt beneath were in ribbons, the skin was broken on neither the shoulder nor the arm where the boar's hoof had seemed to slash her.

The healing that the Priest of Andion had lain on her was more powerful than anything she'd seen of its kind. She owed the Huntress thanks that the boar had gone for that shoulder instead of the other; if it had gone for the other she would have been dead seconds after it reached her.

She hadn't been so fortunate with her ribs. There was a deep slash on her left side. Not quite down to the bone, but it hurt. She bound it, clumsily, with what was left of her torn sleeve. Her spirits began to revive. The fight had been a shock, but she had full control of the boar-spirit now. Its strength was already waking her up, revitalizing her senses.

The remainder of the journey across the swamp was almost too easy. Along with its hulking strength, the boar-spirit gave her surprising delicacy of movement. She brushed through undergrowth with new confidence, intuitively sensing the line of least resistance, and she stopped losing her boots off her feet at what seemed like every fourth step. Above her, the sky lightened a little. Long wedges of cloud transversed the sky like great pointers, leading the way west. How could she go wrong now? With the boar's spirit in her, the throbbing pain across her ribs seemed negligible, her tiredness was banished to a small, plaintive corner of her brain. The calm corner of her mind was there, more insistent than ever, reminding her that this reckless confidence, no doubt, was something she was getting from the boar as well.

It was still dark when she came to the worn pavement of a road that ran north to south. She'd long since lost track of time's passing. This had to be the road north to the Bissanty heartland of which Martin had spoken, not the loop of the high road she had seen on the map.

Whatever the answer, there was no finding it by hanging about waiting for a patrol to come up on her. There hadn't been pavement on the east-west road from Melaudiere. Unless the Bissanties had paved the tolled section of the Tielmaran high road that ran through Bissanty territory, which seemed an unlikely courtesy to a state that had revolted against them, this would be the north-south road that connected the Fingerland to the Bissanty capital. The high road into Haute-Tielmark would be to the north. Right or wrong, all she could do at the moment was continue forward, and try to get back over the border into Tielmark's territory.

The ground began to stabilize soon after she crossed the paved road. Swampy gave way to a mossy surface, then to outcrops of thin, knife-edged rock. She kept finding false paths, open trails that went on for a little way, petered out, and ended. Tiring of falling constantly offtrack, she began to push forward through the brush in earnest, sensing her goal fast approaching. Even so, she was unprepared when the trees suddenly opened up.

She was at the bottom of a cliff. It was eighty feet high, a broken wall of dark gray shale, stretching north to south in an undulating stretch of shattered canyons and arêtes. Haute-Tielmark was a table-land above the marshy Bissanty Fingerland. She stared up dully, the initial surprise of the new obstacle sapping her courage.

She could climb it, she thought, if the shale-stone wasn't so frag-ile that it crumbled under her hands, and if she took her time and hunted out an easy route to the top. With such broken, jagged stone, at some point along the cliff's line there would be enough handholds that she'd be able to claw her way up. But not until she had more light. She would take an enforced rest, wait until dawn before she made any attempt. Feeling wet and more tired than she'd yet felt in the night, she found a place under a tree to bed down for a few mo-ments of sleep. Around her, everything was still dark and cold. If this was the border—and she had little doubt of that—she'd traveled at least eighteen or nineteen miles in the short dark of the spring night. Huddling into herself, she sent up a final prayer before giving herself up to rest. "Andion, Sun-Father." She closed her eyes, spoke through cracked lips. "You preserved me tonight. May your dawn light shine on me soon."

She tried to settle, but she was too cold, too full of nerves. There was a new harshness to the land around her. The sharp spurs of shale-stone that jutted up among the rough vegetation cast eerie shadows in the moon's fading light. Soon she would be in Haute-Tielmark, her country's most westward and most troubled province, a high Dukedom flanked to the north by the Bissanty border, to the west by mountains that were populated by the rough, warlike Lanai tribesmen, and to the south by the westmost border of the Changing Lands. The Lanai were a wedge that the Bissanty would force into Tielmark's side, those summers when they could muster gold and soldiers enough to drive the mountain tribes towards Tielmark. Gaultry's father had earned Blas Lodge by fighting on the western border; Prince Benet's father and his father's older brother, rulers of Tielmark before the young Prince, had lost their lives to the summer warring, taking the Duchess of Melaudiere's sons with them, and perhaps others of the Brood-blood as well. Haute-Tielmark was a province torn by constant fighting. Perhaps, then, it was right that she should travel there, to learn some secret that might bring Tielmark lasting peace.

She grimaced. Probably every Tielmaran soldier who had marched west to confront the Lanai had hoped that their efforts would finally stabilize Tielmark's border there, but without a god-pact to sustain the boundary, there would never be a lasting accord with the wild tribesmen. And if there were a pact, what then? It would only mean new pledges for Tielmark's Prince to uphold. Gaultry would not have found herself, mud-covered, crouching in the chill of a predawn morning, if the Prince was not having trouble enough keeping his great forebear's old pledges.

Troubled by these disturbing thoughts, Gaultry turned inwards to confront the boar-spirit, hoping to revive her own spirit by learning from a power that she could have some hope that she could control instead of worrying about one that was beyond her.

Gaultry rested her head against the tree, and forced herself to concentrate on the beast-spirit within her. Slowly, carefully, she let first one of its senses, and then another, supersede her own. The creature's sight was dim, its hearing was sharp but untextured. A branch snapping was the same as the scuffing of a foot. With its massive strength, bold temper, and toughness, the boar had little need of acute sight and hearing. It was only with the boar's sense of smell that Gaultry began to feel the pleasure of what it meant to be the great, iron-skinned animal. She could smell early-spring onions, the delicate balms of moss and bark, the sharp turpentine of the pines. The smells reminded her she was hungry. She opened the pouch that Martin had given her—it seemed so long ago now—and ate ravenously of the provisions he had supplied her.

Finishing her rough meal, she felt her heart lifting. So much of what she'd learned in the past days challenged her understanding of her childhood and upbringing. Tamsanne's lies of omission; her father's. To learn that the life she'd lived in Arleon Forest had its roots in the heart-soil of her country's struggle to retain its freedom from the cruel Empire to the north had been a great shock. But feeling the range of the great boar's senses reminded her that the life Tamsanne had given her had not been misspent. Gaultry knew little of court trickeries, of plotting that spanned generations, but she knew what it meant to inhabit another creature's senses, to share its outlook. Back in Arleon Forest, Tamsanne had given Gaultry and Mervion a simple life and encouraged them to understand the basic emotions that motivated all life and gave it connection. Now, squatting at the base of a shale-cliff, Gaultry could only hope that her aunt—her grandmother?—had raised her and her sister to such a life because she had intended it to help their survival as they faced forces of prophecy greater than themselves.

She slept a little.

She woke to a deep amethyst-blue sky, streaked from the east by the first rays of dawn. The night's strange bands of clouds had dissipated. It was going to be another clear day. With luck the air would soon warm and she'd be able to dry herself. Martin and the others would be just waking up now.

Would it be Martin first who came to her room and discovered the cat and the empty bed; or would he send Anders, or one of the others? She pictured the chaos: ten young soldiers dashing up and down the inn's stairs, calling for their horses, their arms; Martin would shout louder than them all to recall them to order. Then they would scramble for their weapons, saddle up, and turn their horses' heads towards the border. Gaultry sketched the double-spiral of the Great Twins with her hand, wishing them safety on their journey. She stood quickly and stretched, not wanting to think about the Bissanty force that waited for them at the border. All she could hope was that there would be great confusion as the Bissanties looked for a woman matching her description among them, that they would let them past without engaging them in battle. She hoped that wasn't too much to wish for, and sketched the Great Twins' spiral sign again.

She paced along the bottom of the cliff, waiting for the first rays of sun to rise above the trees and strike its face. The dark gray rock was wet, gleaming almost black in the early light. Here the cliff was utterly sheer and featureless, there a broken canyon where the shale was so fragile it crumbled, rather than crunched, beneath her feet. The walking warmed her a little. She tried swinging her arms briskly, to further warm herself, but the motion made the boar's slash on her ribs hurt.

Rounding a last arête, she looked up. The breath caught in her throat. She'd stumbled onto a deep but narrow canyon. One wall was unclimbable, the other was broken and treacherous. At the canyon's back, separating the two walls, a jagged vein of white rock ran through the stone, from the top of the cliff to its base. The white streak shone silver in the morning's damp.

It was as if a streak of lightning had come to earth and been frozen in stone. Llara Thunderbringer, the great thunder-goddess, could hardly have made her stamp on the great cliff any more obvious. Stroke for stroke, it was Llara's symbol as any of her priests would have painted it, or as any of her warriors would have carved it on their own cheeks.

Gaultry, awed, spread her hands in prayer. Amongst all the cliff of friable, sliding layers of shale, she could not have found a better place to climb. To climb the pure white stone here would be little more than ascending a steep staircase, the way the vein jagged and wended its way up the canyon's back. But would it be apostasy against the Great Twins to turn to their mother for aid at this juncture? Did Llara mean the ladder as temptation? Or was this a more subtle god-sign, to remind Gaultry that her movements were in the gods' hands, that it was fruitless to fight against the gods' predeterminations?

She remembered what the Duchess had said to her about Glamour-magic. The gods had not expected humans to have their own will. Destiny itself had surprised them. When the gods had sought to stamp out Glamour, it had refused to die. Even without Glamour, men and women both had gone on to choose their own course — men like Clarin, who had turned his back on the Great Mother herself and lived on to rule the Free Principality he had founded.

If she continued to search, she might eventually find a place to climb, but the gods were offering her a challenge here, and if she sought their favor still, she would have to answer it.

She stared up at the deep clear of the blue sky over her head. "Mother," she said, in the low voice she used most often for prayer. "I want to be back on Tielmaran soil, and out of this marshy Fingerland of yours. I'm going to use your staircase here, and offer you my thanks in sacrifice at the next temple I find. But I want Tielmark to be free of your Empire. I won't pretend otherwise. If you don't like that, I offer you now the chance to break your stairs beneath me as I climb. You can break me now, and stop me from doing my all to oppose your followers' plots against our Prince. But I here commit myself freely to your care, and trust you will hold me as I climb. Blessings on you, goddess, but it's not in me to pretend I can bow to your Empire's rule."

Her entire body was shaking, as though with an intense fever. The boar-spirit, calmed after its jaunt out through her senses, had become unquiet again. It seemed to be squealing, somehow distressed by the determination in her words. Gaultry, wanting to be totally calm during her ascent, abruptly let it free.

She knew she was committed now, more than ever before. Gaultry had listened with half an ear to all the Duchess and the priestess Dervla had told her, trying to concentrate on what she could do to save Mervion. Perhaps the cold invitation of this stone stair was the gods' way of reminding her that it was impossible for her to focus on so small a goal.

The white stone was icy-cold under her hands and feet, far colder than the dark shale walls on either side. She took one step up, then another. Before she knew it she had risen twice her height up the wall, too far to stop. Her hands burned where they touched the stone; the soles of her feet felt as if they were burning too. She tried not to look down, conscious of the green wall of scrub at her back as it sank away beneath her. She came level with, and then moved above the top line of the trees. A strange humming filled in the air. Her concentration was so intense that she only slowly realized the sound came from her own throat. Near the top, she ran out of handholds. She teetered, pressing herself against a shale buttress to one side of the cold white ladder, and tried not to think what would happen to her if she fell, if Great Llara chose that moment to knock a single chunk of rock free from beneath her foot. Her groping fingers touched a hidden spur of rock, high above her. Its edge was razor-sharp, a cutting tooth. Ignoring the pain she gripped it tighter, moaning a little as she felt it cut her flesh. But there were no other holds. It was this or nothing. She pulled herself up.

That was the final ledge.

At the top of the cliff there was a gentle hill. Bare stone gave way to a lush carpet of moss. At its crest, she found a line of border stones, great gray guardians with rough-hewn faces turned to look out over the cliff to the rising sun.

She sat for a moment and rested with her back against the nearest stone, waited for the sun come up over the trees. Gaultry was cold, mud-covered, and exhausted, but also light-hearted and full of exhilaration.

Back over the Bissanty lands to the East, the sun finally emerged above the trees, the great golden chariot of fire dazzling to the young huntress's sleep-deprived eyes. Gaultry spread her arms wide to its wonderful first-morning heat, and rose to her feet. "You answered my prayer," she told the sun. A strange fancy moved in her then, to tell the gods of her night's triumph. She shouted out a prayer to Andion, to Llara, to all the gods who had been with her through the night. Her prayer was a long ululating cry, wordless, but full of triumph and light and life.

When she was done, she huddled down again at the base of the standing stone, and tried to find a comfortable place in the soft moss.

Her palm throbbed a little where she'd pressed it on the last white spur of rock. In her excitement at gaining the cliff's top, she had forgotten it for a moment. For all the pain she had felt as she'd made the last move up, she was surprised to find that the skin was smooth, undamaged. Yet the gently throbbing cold spot reminded her that there had been pain.

Sighing, she tucked her hand inside her shirt and closed her eyes. The sun felt lovely. Her hand was undamaged. For now that would have to be enough of an answer. Closing her eyes, she soon dropped into a deep and pleasant sleep.

chapter 15

Some hours later, her muddy clothes, drying and beginning to itch, woke her. Gaultry sighed, rubbed the backs of her
legs where her borrowed boots chafed her, and sat up. The sun was
already high in the sky. The air around her was unseasonably heavy.
It was a brooding sort of a day. Not a breath of wind wrinkled the
still of the morning air. A storm was coming, Gaultry thought.
Maybe not today, but it was coming. She checked her food pouch,
hoping for a morsel she might have missed the night before. Nothing. She sighed. The porcine impulse that had been in her as she ate
had made it a certainty that she would consume every scrap.

She looked back towards the east, curious to have a better look
at the land she had crossed. From her vantage point on the crest of
the hill, the land, seen under the full light of day, looked dauntingly
rough. Martin had been right when he told her it would be paddy-
fields and waste. A veritable maze of hummocks and coarse brush
stretched eastwards, seemingly to the horizon. It was the Huntress's
blessing on her that she'd found the boar, with its great strength and
bush-cunning. And Andion's grace that she'd survived having
found it. She fingered the rags of jacket and shirt over the arm and
shoulder that the boar had so ineffectually savaged, marveling once

again at the power of the healing that had saved her life. She wondered at the Duchess's foresight, in forestalling Dervla's offer to heal her, insisting that Gaultry's wound be tended by the strange sun-priest. Was Gabrielle Lourdes led by blind intuition, or did she have some closer link with Allegrios, her potent water god, that helped her see what course was best to follow?

If the latter, Gaultry could only wish that her own link to Elianté–Emiera would over time become as strong.

Around the standing stones, the thick but delicate pelt of moss that covered the ground had lain undisturbed for many seasons. Before she left, Gaultry smoothed down the torn brown marks where her own feet had damaged it, erasing the most obvious of the signs that she had been there. The thickness of the moss was disturbing. Duke Victor of Haute-Tielmark must have come to a comfortable arrangement with his Bissanty neighbors to let his border become so overgrown. That didn't bode well for the leg of the journey that would take them through Haute-Tielmark to Clarin's burial place.

Them. She patted the last clump of moss in place and scrambled to her feet. It would be "them" only if she managed to catch up with Martin and the others. It was past time for her to be on the move.

It was hot work, moving uphill through the brush with the sun on her back. The land rose in a shallow series of shale ledges, each just a little higher than the top of her head. Her hunt to find the easiest places to clamber up lured her a little farther south than she wanted. It was a relief to get up the last ledge and discover the gentle curving land of Haute-Tielmark's high plain. She crossed an overgrown hunter's track there, and turned onto it, heading north, relieved at this hint of civilization. It was not long before she came to a fallow field, with young rabbits nibbling at the tender shoots of the rough new growth gleaned from the fallings of last year's crop. She stopped, unslung her bow, and managed to bag two of the fattest before the rest sighted her and fled to the hedgerows. The fresh meat could prove useful currency, she thought, hastily gutting the coneys with her knife, if she came upon an outlying farm where she could ask directions.

Not long after the fallow field, she came to a strip of cultivated forest, every second tree neatly pollarded and the brush beneath carefully cleared, and then, in quick succession, two plowed fields. Beyond, tucked into a curve of the land, was a weathered farmhouse, part timber, part stone, with a stave-fenced yard, sheltered by mature trees. Smoke coiled up from one of the building's three chimneys. A woman, accompanied by two children, stood outside what Gaultry took to be the kitchen door, a bicolored dog begging at her knees for scraps. Gaultry decided to join him.

"Spare an egg or two for a hungry traveler?" Gaultry paused at the gate, a little relieved to see the double-spiral of the Great Twins carved into the wooden posts there. She could make the traveler's sign to these people and here, on their own ground, they would have to honor it.

The dog whined. The younger of the two children, shy, ducked behind the woman's skirts. The woman, who had been feeding the dog something greasy, wiped her hands on a checkered cloth, and gave Gaultry an intent look from eyes set deep under dark brows. Her hands, broad and strong, were of a piece with her wide face and sturdy frame. She had gold hoops in her ears, a little fine for a farmer. Her hair, which was thick and dark, was massed untidily in a ragged bun at the back of her head. She'd been working, and perhaps not expecting visitors.

"Where have you sprung from?" Rough, but not hostile.

Gaultry made the traveler's sign, palm up, fingers spread, and offered the woman the gutted rabbits. "The Great Twins blessing on your house," she said. "I'm heading to Princeport. I've lost the high road."

The woman raised her dark eyebrows. "Indeed." Her eyes said she thought Gaultry was coming from the wrong direction if she had wandered off the high road. But she indicated that the ragged traveler should enter her yard. "The high road's easy to find from here. Follow our lane and you'll fetch up there. But break your fast first. There's no rush to the day."

"If you can spare it, I'd beg a bucket of water before eating," Gaultry said, handing the rabbits over and wiping fur from her hands.

"I'll go in and warm something for you. The well's there." The woman pointed. "Arcadie, bring the traveler some soap!" Her daughter, a blond sprite of a girl in a much-laundered smock, darted inside, bare legs flashing; her mother followed, somewhat less rushed. The girl soon popped out in the yard again, her hand full of an oily pine-scented soap, which she slathered over onto Gaultry's hand, grinning and curious. A little to Gaultry's dismay, the girl stayed to watch as she scrubbed down her face and arms, and picked the worst of the bracken and twigs out of her hair.

"That's swampwort," the girl said, watching Gaultry unwind a tassle of green-leaved plant from her hair.

"Among other things," Gaultry answered.

The young huntress shucked her jacket, and beat what she could of the night's muck out against the stone edge of the well.

"Were you fighting?" the farm-girl said, scrutinizing the tear in Gaultry's shirt, the crusted bandage beneath that concealed the gash the boar had made on her ribs.

"Only a bush or two," Gaultry answered. "I was moving in the dark last night, and clumsy."

The girl gave her a level look, clearly disbelieving. "Mother's seen your face before," she said.

"What do you mean?"

"You'll see." The girl tripped away, disappearing into the house, and, save for the bicolored dog, left Gaultry to finish her wash in solitude.

In the absence of a needle and thread to make even the most basic of repairs, Gaultry shortened the jacket's sleeves with her knife, evening up the good one with what remained of the one the boar had torn. Then, her curiosity to discover what the girl meant hastening her ablutions, she wiped the much abused garment over with her hands, calling a casting to alter it: dirty green and gray dulled to mustard yellow and washed-out blue. It wouldn't do to be spotted by unfriendly eyes with the Duchess's livery on her back.

By the time Gaultry reached the kitchen, the farm-woman had taken the heavy iron pan off the kitchen hearth, and the food was ready. She'd fried sweet forest mushrooms and pork crackling with the eggs, and there was as much good coarse bread as Gaultry could get down her throat.

"That's some appetite," the woman commented, joining her at the table.

"It's lovely," Gaultry said, between mouthfuls. "Your land is lovely too." The rolling strips of tilled earth that ran deep into the woods surrounding the farm reminded her of the fields around Paddleways, near Tamsanne's. Perched on a rough-hewn wooden bench, polished smooth by years of service, in the plain, comfortable kitchen, eating from a wooden plate, a wave of homesickness washed over her.

"The Great Twins willing, it will stay that way," the woman said. "It may happen that it's on your shoulders to keep it so." She laid a burnt piece of paper on the table in front of the younger woman, and, folding her arms, awaited Gaultry's response.

It was a crude woodblock print, a page torn from a roving tinker's picture book. Such things were common enough in Tielmark farmhouses, this scene particularly: the huntress and the lady dancing arm in arm under a spreading tree. Not a Rhasan card, rife with magic, but a Rhasan image nonetheless. Gaultry took a closer look. Her knuckles, where she was gripping her knife and fork, went white, and she hastily put the utensils down, furious with herself for having betrayed herself with this obvious response.

The artistry was crude, but there were details in the figures that made them good likenesses of herself and Mervion. Straight nose, arching brows—the shape of the face was alike too. The likeness alone was disturbing, but it was worse than that: the image had been mutilated. Half the lady figure had been burned away.

"How did this happen?" Gaultry asked, throwing the page down on the table. "When?"

"Four nights past." The night Mervion had been taken to Heiratikus's tower the second time. "That was the burning. It fell into the fire, which might have been chance—save that half the sheet wouldn't burn, when we were slow on our feet to rescue it. But it fell again last night. This morning, it was on the floor when we came in." The woman picked up the page and tilted it towards the light, so Gaultry could see the small gash in the paper, just over the huntress's ribs. "Arcadie says you're hurting."

"I'm fine," Gaultry said, staring into the woman's dark eyes. "But the other," her voice faltered, "the other is my sister. My twin. Where did you get this image? Who put the magic in it?"

"Your sister? Things are changing indeed for Tielmark. Even our witches see trouble coming." Young Arcadie came and pressed her hand against her mother's shoulder. "When things change for Tielmark's Prince, the land feels it first, especially here in Haute-Tielmark. We were the last land Clarin freed from Bissanty, and we're the first to be threatened when change occurs. Our first Prince knew that. He made his burial ground here as his best talisman against future losses. The ones after him forgot. Saving Briern, of course."

Gaultry could not help but smile to hear the woman's bias. Briern, Tielmark's greatest warrior prince, had married a farm-girl from Haute-Tielmark, a girl who'd beaten her plowshare into a sword when the Bissanties had invaded.

"Laugh if you will," the woman said, seemingly picking the thought from her head. "Briern was married on Tielmark's first centenary. It's the centenary again this year. I don't see today's Prince in his fancy capital making as good a wedding."

Gaultry flushed, feeling caught out. "You don't know that," she said, raising her chin: "Prince's Night isn't on us yet. Who knows who Benet will marry?" She glanced from the burn-shadowed figure of the lady on the page to the composed face of the farm-woman. "Who are you?" she asked, sick with worry for her sister. "And who gave you the picture?"

"You climbed Llara's Ladder to get here," the woman said, again ignoring Gaultry's question. "Don't deny it. I saw the stain on your hands as you came from the fields."

"What does that mean?" Gaultry asked, folding her hands guiltily in her lap. The cold place on her palm where the spur of rock had seemed to pierce her at the top of the climb was pulsing, but there was no mark on her hand that she could see.

"The Great Thunderer wants you here in Haute-Tielmark. You wouldn't have found her ladder, or climbed the border cliff, if she hadn't desired it."

Gaultry swallowed, remembering the crumbling shale. "What shall I do?" she asked. "I'm pledged to serve Elianté and Emiera, not their mother. I don't want to serve Llara, or the Bissanties."

"Nevertheless, the Thunderbringer's mark is on you. You must have pleased her."

"She must have done something brave," Arcadie said softly. "Llara likes heroes."

Gaultry squirmed. "Nothing like that. I'm just trying to get my sister out of trouble. And doing a poor job of it, if what this picture shows is anything near truth." She stood, and crossed her knife and fork on her plate. "I have to go. I'm supposed to meet my friends at the inn near the border."

"That'll be the Black Man. It's to the east when you hit the road. Less than a mile from our lane."

So she'd come far enough into Haute-Tielmark to have passed the first inn after the border. That was useful — surely the Chancellor's minions wouldn't expect to meet her heading east towards Bissanty territory.

Pretty Arcadie remained behind to clean the kitchen while her mother followed Gaultry out into the lane. Gaultry wasn't sure what to make of either of them, but, once outdoors, her mood took a quick turn for the better. The sun beat warmly on her head and the exposed skin of her arms. A mile and a half to go. With food in her belly and a smooth road to follow, it wouldn't take her long. At the second gate, with the farmhouse out of sight behind the trees, and the track roughening, she thanked the woman for her hospitality. Then she couldn't help but repeat her earlier question. "Who are you?"

"You haven't guessed?" the woman said. "I'm Tielmark's common blood. Arcadie and I, young Piers and my husband — we're the ones the Bissanties hate. Take the turning into the next farm — you'll find us again. Perhaps," she said, "not so clear-sighted as I, but we'll be the same." She kissed Gaultry on the forehead, and clasped the younger woman's hands. "You want to know who gave me the Rhasan image. I can't tell you. She helps the crops here, and she likes to hold onto her own secrets.

"But this at least I will say: when she gave it to me, she told me it was a picture of Tielmark's greatest living shield against Bissanty force. I see now that it was not the great goddess twins of whom she spoke, but rather a pair of earthly twins, one with the Great Thunderer's mark on her."

Gaultry looked at her hands as the woman set them free. For a moment she thought she could see a spider-light sheen of white on her palms. Then it faded. "How do you know—" She looked up. The road was empty. The woods seemed to shimmer, and draw close.

Then, quite suddenly, she realized that she was on the high road, broad, muddy wheel-cuts running a deep course below the banks of forest on either side. Around her the trees stretched bony branches wide, as if rebuking the young huntress's impulse to tear back among them, and search out the strange woman and her farmhouse. If it hadn't been for the tautness of her full belly, the encounter would have seemed the stuff of dreams.

She rubbed her palms together, worried. There *was* a coolness in her palm where she'd touched that last spur of rock. That at least hadn't been her imagination. Yet another strand of threat she wasn't ready to face, or even had the tools to comprehend. She sighed, and turned her face eastwards. She was going to have to focus on finding Martin and the others. This new mystery would have to wait.

Showing her face in a public inn would be as perilous as all the night's lonely travels, on some level more so. Lies never came easily to her, and she was going to have to arrive with a more convincing story than she'd told at the farmhouse. Gaultry smoothed her coat and rolled the cropped sleeves up high to conceal the rough job she'd made of undoing the boar's damage. The color-change had been a good idea. She'd have to repeat it with her hair. Her bright red mane was too obvious a flag to be left untouched. Without much thinking, she called a fresh casting, only to discover that she'd somehow chosen to turn it dark. Dark but not black. Martin's color. She brushed at it with her fingers, thinking of him.

The road broadened as she followed it, the trees thinning, taking on a more cultivated look. The incline was in her favor. She passed turns to a couple of farms. Soon after, she crossed a shallow ford. The land around the road opened out to plowed fields. Further still, was a grouping of horse paddocks, and some small cottages. At the top of a small rise ahead, a large, rambling inn dominated the small hamlet. The building had a slightly military character, as though soldiers might often billet there on their way to the border. There were half a dozen horses in the yard, and a cluster of leather-aproned ostlers, working with currycombs. The signpost overhead showed a smith at his anvil, red letters underneath. The Black Man. One of the inn's many outbuildings would be a forge.

"Busy day?" The ostlers glanced up as she came near.

"I'll say." The head-ostler, distinguished by his long mustaches and harassed demeanor, stood away from the horse he was attending, and began to work the horsehair out of his full curry comb with his fingers. "We weren't thinking His Grace was going to be through, riding hell-for-leather, half his ruddy court at his heels. And him wanting fresh horses and sup when he comes back. How're we supposed to do it, I ask?"

She mustn't let her dismay show on her face, she thought. How long had it been since the Duke and his men had been past the inn? Minutes? Hours? One horse turned a tired head to her, rolled its eyes and champed its teeth. Its breathing was a little heavy. Not hours, Gaultry thought. Not with the way that horse was standing, still strained and wild-eyed. This had to be the tail end of the Duke's entourage. No wonder the ostlers were busy.

"What's their hurry?" If she had not stopped for breakfast with the farm-woman, they would have run her off the road.

"Word was a state visit. But who can say? I've never seen battle armor for a state visit."

"I guess I'd best get something to eat before they come back for their horses."

The man grinned, suddenly friendly, and curled one of his mustaches. "That lot will eat the master out of house and home. Go on in, lass. Best get something before his Grace comes back and claims it all as his frankpledge."

She thanked him, and went in, wishing she could ask how many had been in the Duke's party. Certainly more than the six with the horses in the yard, but how many more?

A feeling almost of paralysis gripped her. Without Martin and the others, how was she to complete the journey's next leg? It had given her a warm feeling to prove to Martin—and to herself—that she could cross the Fingerland alone. But to immerse herself in a night forest had been, on some level, to regain her element, to return herself to the woods huntress that she had been as she'd ranged the woods around Tamsanne's. By contrast, her very first meeting with Martin had amply demonstrated to them both her vulnerability when faced with a pack of determined men—and it would be men, not boars or bracken or crumbling cliff faces, that would be the hazard on this road.

The public room of the Black Man Inn was bright and cheery, with wide windows that overlooked the front yard. There were comfortable high-backed benches against the walls, intimate nooks and booths under the stairs and gallery, and a wealth of broken farming tools laid by for a rainy day's fixing. Gaultry took a chair by the kitchen door and waited, wanting to draw the attention of one of the serving girls. A young boy brought her a cup of cider. Half of her wanted to flee, to disappear into the woods before the Duke returned from the border. The stronger half wanted to stay, to be there to find out if Martin had made it alive across the Fingerland.

Beyond the door, she could hear shouting, and the clashing of cooking preparations being hurried forward. She wasn't surprised that it was some time before anyone came out to give her service. The inn's only other customers were a trio of merchants waiting for a traveler from the west. They played cards by the window, oblivious to all else. After a time a young woman banged noisily in through the kitchen door with a basket of flowers. She sat down on a bench near Gaultry to make nosegays for the tables.

"Does the Duke stop in at the Black Man often?"

"Not as often as the master'd like." Gaultry's new companion grinned. She was brash, fresh, and pretty, with a coppery brown mop of hair and a snub nose. "All the fuss that's on, I ask you!"

"I could help you with these if you like." Gaultry put her hand over one of the flower bundles.

"If it's no bother—"

"None."

"Would you? I had my hands full in the kitchen even before the master thought to fuss over decorating the tables."

"Leave me to it, then. I'll get them done."

"Thanks. I'll ask the master if he'll fix you some lunch in return."

"I'd appreciate that."

The little bouquets were soon finished. Gaultry got some tankards from the barman to use as vases and began to put them on the tables. She was about halfway through when the sounds of horses and men filled the road outside. Soon the shouts were in the yard. Someone let forth a blast on a trumpet. Laughter and more shouts followed. Gaultry worked on. It has nothing to do with me, she said to herself, trying to keep calm. Hiding in plain sight would be her best cover, the last thing the Duke, staring among Martin's troop for her face, would be expecting.

She was not sure she believed her own reassurances.

The noise in the yard grew ever louder. How many men? Twenty? Forty? A stoutly built man with heavy arms and shoulders came in ahead of the others, his face red and sweating from unaccustomed exertion. He was unarmed and finely dressed. A member of the Duke's retinue rather than one of his soldiers. A boy in scarlet livery tagged at his heels, struggling with a heavy, leather-bound accounting book. "His Grace's company want their lunch!" The inn's landlord, followed by Gaultry's new friend and a pair of thin girls in starched aprons, hurried in from the kitchen.

"Sir Lawrence!" the landlord welcomed the newcomer, wiping his hands on his apron. "Back so soon, yet we are ready. There's plenty to go on the tables, Sir, plenty, I say."

"We'll see." The Duke's retainer scanned the room with an unimpressed and disapproving air. "At least it's cleaner than the sty we found here this morning." He slapped the boy lightly on the arm and took the heavy book from him. "Tell them to come in." The boy, relieved of his burden, darted away. Sir Lawrence disappeared into the kitchen, accompanied by his nervous-faced host.

There was a stamp and a jangle and suddenly the room was filled with laughing soldiers. In a knot at the crowd's center was Victor, the Duke of Haute-Tielmark. He was golden-haired, a great, thickly bearded bear of a man, standing a full head taller than any of the men around him. His riding coat was cut from bright scarlet silk, with the silhouette of a stag's head sewn on the breast. He had a great booming laugh, matching his giant's body. Gaultry guessed he was used to intimidating those around him with that laugh alone — goddess forbid he ever got really angry and started striking with his hamlike fists.

Behind him, surrounded by guards in the Duke's bright scarlet livery, were Martin, Arnolfo, and four of the ten guards who had accompanied them. Anders was there, with a bloodstained bandage on his head. One of the other soldiers had his hand tightly wrapped, as if he was missing some fingers. The others simply looked shocked and lost. Arnolfo and Martin's faces were so pale and grim it made her sick. Where was the young romantic, Daurat, who'd wanted to see her riding the white horse? Where were the other young soldiers who had vied so cheerfully to choose her mounts? Where was Arnolfo's scruffy dog? She looked away, her hands, as she fussed with the placing of the next nosegay, trembling.

"A good thing I stopped by the border to pick up the lot of you." The Duke of Haute-Tielmark's voice boomed as loud as his laugh. "The Governor of the Fingerland has some crack men. When he decides to cancel free passage, there aren't many who'd make it through."

"It was good of you to negotiate for us." Martin's voice was cracked and harsh. "Even if our passes were in order."

"Yes, those passes. Pity you lost them at the border post. Getting an early start on the summer warring, were you?" When Martin didn't answer, Victor of Haute-Tielmark grinned, and clapped him on the shoulder. "Plenty of time to kill Lanai mountaineers when the summer comes properly. What other reason do you Easters have for coming out to my humble domain?"

He turned from Martin, not expecting an answer. "Lunch, Sir Lawrence!" he bellowed. "I must give my guests some lunch!"

Sir Lawrence popped from the kitchen like a clockwork toy, assuring his great bear of a master that everything was ready, or at least that it all was on its way. The Duke settled himself, with Martin and the others, at a table at the room's center. "I'm flattered by your visit," he told Martin. "How's old Melaudiere? Still cosseting her nursling?"

"Gowan will make her a fine heir. No one's in a rush to see it happen."

"Send him west to harden him up," the Duke advised. "War will man him for you."

Gaultry, moving away, distributed the last of the nosegays. With the Duke's rough crowd of men, she wondered why the landlord had even bothered.

"Enough of that, girlie. We want drink, not flowers."

"I'm not regular staff," she said, plunking the last nosegay down. "But I'll see what I can do."

She threaded through the crush to where the landlord was fussing by the kitchen door. "I've been helping with the flowers," she told him. "I wouldn't mind getting back to my own drink. But if the girls need a hand—"

The man glanced across to the woman Gaultry had spoken with earlier, and the two younger girls, who were struggling through the crush of soldiers. He nodded. "There's supper in it for you. And drink and a pallet for the night if you're wanting it."

"That sounds fair."

"Drop into the kitchen for an apron before you start at the tables."

With the apron tied around her middle, she cut a more convincing figure as an improvised inn-maid. The other girls gave friendly nods when they saw her. Soon they were all pushing their way among the tables with heavy trays of tankards. The soldiers' rough manners were unpleasant, but they were not ready to provoke a confrontation with any of the inn-staff in front of their master. So instead they kept the women skipping to meet the demands of their drinking. For a time Gaultry was almost too busy to worry about the risk she was running.

The innkeeper served at the Duke's table, so she had little

chance to get near. Fortunately, she didn't need to linger to hear the conversation. The Duke of Haute-Tielmark's booming voice made it impossible not to catch scraps of the conversation even from the furthest corners of the room.

It was Arnolfo who spotted her first, as she risked pushing past his back to reach a table just beyond. His jaw dropped open, and she had trouble hiding her dismay in return, certain that discovery was imminent. Then he recovered, and slopped his beer on the table to cover his mistake.

"It's been a long morning," the archer told the Duke, answering the man's curious look. "Unhealthy for me to be fighting men of my own country."

"And putting arrows into more than one of them." The Duke grinned. His deliberate, loud heartiness was like a rasp against every feeling.

When Gaultry next risked a look at the table, Martin's eyes were on her. There was a gleam in him that went beyond smiling. She couldn't help but grin in return, even as her heart hammered, so loud she feared the men around her would hear it.

"Who're the men with the Duke?" she asked, trying to cover her reaction.

"An envoy from the Duchess of Melaudiere. The Governor of the Fingerland decided he didn't like their looks. Not that we're so sure that our lord likes their looks either. He's had their weapons confiscated."

Amidst the cheery clatter of the inn, rising panic gripped her. She had only the vaguest notion how to get to Clarin's barrow. A day's ride to the west, Martin had said. Were those directions enough that she could make her way there on her own? Worse, how could she possibly reach Princeport in time to help Mervion—let alone the Duchess and her country—once she had done her best to invoke the High Prince's aid?

It was another three hours before the Duke and his company departed, taking Martin and the others with them. Three grueling hours of keeping herself busy and moving, avoiding questions and the men's increasing aggression, as they drank deep and lost the inhibitions that had kept them polite. One of the two young girls serving the tables broke off early, and retreated to the kitchens to cry. Gaultry didn't blame her. No one seemed to have any suspicion of her connection to the Duke's prisoners. Just as clearly, with no one to protect her, Haute-Tielmark's soldiers felt they had a license to harass. It was lucky, Gaultry found herself thinking, as she pushed away another man's groping hand, that Martin's geas had faded. If it hadn't, he would have been hard-pressed to restrain himself from interfering.

After the Duke and his men cleared out and departed westwards, Gaultry stayed on, clearing tankards while the others mopped the floor. Long after the last sounds of the Duke's retinue had faded, she was still stuck in the inn's kitchens, scrubbing plates with only the promise of a hot dinner and a warm bed as a reward.

"What do you make of this?" The woman she'd helped with the flowers, her work temporarily finished, came over with a crumpled scrap of paper. "I found it on the floor under the Duke's table."

Martin's map. Gaultry dried her hands and put away the last dish, her heart beating with renewed hope. It was all she could do not to grab at the crumpled scrip. "A map. Quite a good one. This is where we are." She pointed to the spot along the high road near the border.

"Would it be useful to you?"

"Well, yes, I guess it would."

"Take it."

"You sure?"

"Gemma, Laure, and I could never have handled those trays alone. Even at the Duke's table, they were all trying to get each other drunk. Not friendly drinking, either. One man said there was fighting at the border, they wanted to relax after it. Some people were killed." She shook her head, disapproving. "Strange way to relax."

There was no note, just the critical piece of crumpled paper with its lines and directions. The way to Clarin's barrow was clear. Another half-day's travel on the high road, then a road branched north. Clarin's barrow was depicted by a little drawing, standing stones on the top of a hill that faced towards the Bissanty border. On the map the location looked nastily exposed. Worse, Duke Victor's stronghold was situated less than a mile away from it.

Once again, it appeared that her choices lay between bumbling her own way cross-country or following the public roads.

Gaultry put her head in her hands and sighed. She'd give it a thought on the morrow. For now all she could think was that she'd lost a night's sleep and she wanted it back. The innkeeper's offer of a pallet was one she simply didn't want to refuse.

chapter 16

The innkeeper's generosity extended to breakfast in the morning. Gaultry ate it in the kitchen with the rest of the inn's staff.

It wasn't a comfortable meal. Things had settled from the previous day's confusion of trying to give good service to thirty-odd soldiers who had arrived on the inn's doorstep without giving decent warning. In that confusion, Gaultry had been a convenient extra pair of hands. Now, the ruckus over, people were beginning to be curious.

The ostlers were the worst. Working around the entourage's horses, they'd heard more gossip than the troop had felt free to air inside at the tables, where their master might have heard them. One of the ostlers, a ruddy bear of a man who smirked too much for Gaultry's taste, was particularly pressing.

"The Duke was out searching for a bride — so his men told us. Whether it was his or another man's no one was saying. A pretty girl like you — why didn't you put yourself forward?" When she tried ignoring the man, he persisted. "Handy that you were here to give Bess and the girls some help."

"Your master seemed to think so."

"Where have you come from then? Did our great goddess twins send you to help us?" The man's sly eyes flicked down her body, assessing her rumpled gear and torn sleeves. Bess, her flower-girl friend, broke in and rescued her.

"Leave her be, Mikal. It was easy enough for you yesterday, out in the stables. We had work to do in here."

"They're still looking for the woman," a second ostler added. It was the prime topic of discussion at that end of the breakfast table. "They say there's a reward from the Prince himself for the man that finds her."

Gaultry, increasingly uncomfortable, bent over her food, wanting to finish and be gone. If there was a search going up and down the road for her, perhaps her safest plan would be to travel cross-country again.

She'd lost the heart for it. Seeing Martin and the others trapped in the Duke's retinue, knowing she would be denied their protection for the final leg of her journey, she couldn't help but linger on the comfort it had been for her to travel in their company. At the very least she hadn't needed to worry about insinuating louts at their food and lodging stops!

Even after Bess had shut him up, the ostler who had questioned her exchanged looks that made her nervous with one of his fellows. She was grateful when the landlord came in to scold them all for lingering in the kitchen, and broke up the conversation. She made her escape from the inn as quickly as she could.

On the road, the weather was as wretched and uneasy as her mood. The sky was dark, full of thickening clouds. Wind raked the trees, occasional hard gusts tearing at the young foliage. About a mile past the inn, as she was passing the stretch of woods near where she guessed the hidden lane ran to the preceding day's farm, a light rain began to fall, rounding out the day's unpleasantness. The wind swept in sharply from the north—Llara's wind, from Llara's land. Nervous as she was, she began to imagine she saw great faces above her in the sky, peering down through the cover of restless clouds to spy on her.

The next hour was increasingly wet and miserable. Beneath the driving rasp of the wind, the road was unnaturally quiet, everything hidden under shelter, keeping out of the rain, save herself. She passed two eastward-bound horsemen on skinny nags, hooded figures under umbrella-tents of some dark-colored oil cloth, and then a trio of huntsmen on foot with their dogs. Then the road became stark and empty, a lonely ribbon of mud running between wet fields. The fields were poor, striated by slate outcrops like long ribs, dark stone turned to black with the scouring rain. She felt she was seeing the bones of the earth, laid bare before the rising storm. Her unease deepened, remembering what the farm-woman had said about Haute-Tielmark feeling changes in the Prince before the rest of the land. If the gods were unhappy with Benet, all Tielmark would suffer a failed crop. The black, starved-looking ribs of the land here were like a rude omen of that future peril.

Taking cover under a tree, she unfolded Martin's map. After another three miles on this road, she'd reach a lake, on the right—the north—side of the road. If she meant to go cross-country to Clarin's barrow, it would be sensible to turn off the high road just before the lake and follow its shore around to the north-west. It was a puzzle. After the lake, the map gave no details until the mount of Clarin's burial ground. Would the land be rocky scrub, similar to the fields she was passing now, or would it be harsher, more dangerous?

"Fancy a ride on to the next inn? I'm sure they'll have work for you there." It was the ostler from the Black Man, and a companion. "Where have you sprung from?" Gaultry snapped, startled. She hadn't heard their horses. Already they were very close to her, and moving in.

She slipped her knife from its sheath.

"She has claws." The ostler smirked, dismounting and looking at his companion. "Are we surprised?" The pair of them were dressed for the rain, in long oilskins. Their horses were rawboned but sturdy looking. She'd been so intent on the map she hadn't heard them coming.

"Why are you here?"

"A little bird told us it might be worth our while to come after you."

"It's worth your while only if you can take me. If you can't, it's worth your life to try me." They had planned how they would approach her, she realized with dismay, as the first man drew her attention while the other circled round.

When her eyes flickered to follow the second man as he dismounted, the ostler whipped off his oilskin and, bundling it in front of him like a shield, made a grab for her. She tried a lunging swipe with the knife, missed, tried again, and got her blade tangled in the oilskin's folds. Seeing his comrade's success, the other man joined the fray. In seconds, they had her down on her knees in the mud, her arms twisted so hard behind her back her shoulders were nearly wrenched from their sockets.

"So much for taking you." The ostler, panting a little, took hold of her chin. "Now I'd say the question is can you make it worth our while? Or do we trot you straight along to our good Duke?"

She lunged at him, trying to free herself, to stall and gather her strength.

"You've made a mistake," she told him, fighting to keep her voice calm. "If you had any idea what I am, you'd die rather than risk raising a hand against me." She stripped the color spell from her hair, and was pleased to see the man blanch as the fox-fire red of her hair slipped through the dark of her dying color spell like rising flame. "You're risking blindness, or impotence, or worse. Did your bird tell you that I'm a witch, that I have the strength to cripple you?" Maybe her hands weren't free, but he had contact with her skin where he had hold of her jaw. She'd never channeled magic through her face before, but that's where she needed the spell. *I'll blind him*, she thought, staring up at him angrily. *I'll call the spell and I'll blind him, whether or not my hands are free.* Her head spun with the unfamiliar sensation as the spell rose in her and she forced it up through a new place in her body. Her eyes started with tears, painful as though the spell she meant for him was going to turn back on herself.

Then the man released her chin, shaking his hand like he'd been stung by a bee.

"Huntress help me! You are a witch!" Whether the spell had worked or not, it had touched him enough to scare him.

She lunged out again—not getting far, with the man behind her still holding her arms, but it made a good effect.

"You're getting the picture?" If he was out of reach and she couldn't cast on him, she'd cast another spell on herself. She blanched her hair almost to white. "Care to lose twenty years of life?" She tried to make her voice crackle like an old woman's. The coward behind her let go of her arms.

"Mikal! You didn't tell me she was a witch!"

More fool him, setting her free. She spun and caught him by the neck. With her fingers on the bare skin at his throat, her thumbs on his pulsing jugular, she filmed his eyes over with color. The spell came more easily than she could have imagined. He shrieked and staggered away, clawing at his face.

The ostler, Mikal, stumbled back. She took a few steps towards him, stumbling herself.

Something strange was happening. The spells that she'd called into her head, her face, had struck a strange resonance, and she was trembling and disturbed, shaken by a rush of rising power. Simple magics. Coloration and projection. They should have brought only a light buzz, a cool tingle of satisfaction that they had gone off with success.

Instead she was fairly pulsing with gathered force.

From the moment she'd called the spell into her head, something had gone wrong. Her vision was blurring. The ostler seemed to recede and shrink before her. The beads of Dervla's necklace were like hot coals burning against her throat. Tamsanne's charm, given to her so many days back now, was a lump of ice at the base of her throat. The flesh of her hands felt leaden, heavy. She could feel every detail of her clothes as they rubbed against her body.

"You were fools to come after me, alone and with no weapons of steel or magic." She lunged, almost drunkenly, towards the cowering ostler. Her color-vision faded, as she reached for him, as if she'd taken on the night vision of some great unknown animal. The landscape and the man before her dulled to gray and black silhouettes. "Would your Duke have sent a call out for a simple traveling girl? How could you think that taking me would be so easy?" She stared about, muzzy, and saw that she had come up next to the men's horses. Scarce thinking what she was doing, she grabbed up the trailing reins. Anything to steady herself.

"Take the horses and they'll be onto you before you can hide yourself, witch!" The man's voice trembled somewhere between fear and anger.

Take the horses. The man's frightened call brought the thought to blossom in her mind. She slipped her heavy hands up round first one arching neck, then the other, gripping the thick tuft of mane at the base of each curving equine neck. One of the pair gave a worried whinny. She thought of the animals she'd taken from the night before: the boar with its frightening power, the cat with its stubborn will not to share. Compared to those wild creatures, horses were pliant and easy. Frightened, and nervous of her, but easy . . .

Blotting out the ostler from her awareness, she began to call the taking-spell. Her vision closed off completely as she called deep within herself to focus the power, to focus it, to feel only the quiver of a frightened horse under each hand, and the trembling of her own body. She opened a deep channel in her body, to ready herself for the taking, and suddenly the walls of the channel were bright with color: gold, scarlet, and a vivid vein of purple, twisting like water on the sides of a whirlpool. Somewhere deep in her chest, she felt the taking-spell gather and move. It had goddess-magic in it, that she could tell. Potent and familiar, like every calling since she'd been a child. But then, deeper still, she felt something ripping, like a rent of metal foil, something pushing itself out into the open through the rent. The spell she'd called from the goddess leapt, twisted, and then she could feel it twinning itself, the energy growing, parting, and rebuilding itself, twice strong. Both halves fully fruited, the twinned spell drew apart, and bucked with a sudden burst of power. The bipartite spell channeled, like searing irons, down her arms. The horses balked and fought, but somehow she managed to keep hold of both, managed to hold herself open for the power she knew was coming.

It hurt. The horse's twin strengths pumped up through her arms into her body, swelling her with more animal power than she'd ever yet experienced. The spiral of color that blocked her vision collapsed, and suddenly she could see. Everything was sharp edged and bright, from the collapsed bodies of the two horses at her feet, to the horror on the face of the single man who still faced her.

She felt she had gained a foot of height. Blood rushed in her ears. She was a giant, wielding a giant's powers. Her heart felt it would burst — but she had both creatures in her.

Mikal was staring at her, horrified. He seemed small and scared. She laughed at him, and tossed her head.

"If I were you, I'd run," she told him.

Abandoning his blinded partner, he took to his heels. Gaultry watched him for a moment, her heart pounding. Tamsanne had told her that taking the strengths of two animals together wasn't possible. The Great Twins wouldn't support it: it wasn't possible.

Tears were running down her face. Tears and rain mingled together. Gaultry did not want to look up at the gathering gray of the sky, did not want to think what was possible, what was not. She turned her face westwards, brushed her hair away from her face, and began to run, leaving the blinded man to keen to the wind behind her.

The day swept past in a hazy delirium. The horse-spirits were racing each other, racing her, pushing her body on past the point of endurance. Part of her was numb, beyond fright or terror. It didn't want any part of the channeling or the controlling of either frightened creature; it couldn't accept that she had the right to do so. They waged a fierce animal competition in her body, pushing her legs forward whether she would or no. She had little awareness of the passage of time or miles. The first time she fell, the surprise that her legs weren't running brought her a little to herself, but even this faded. The small corner of her mind that was still Gaultry shut its door, denied what was happening. The way she was stretching, the way all her skin and body felt it was expanding, reaching outwards — if this was what the gods felt every moment of their lives, she was grateful at least a part of her was mortal.

Some time later, she thought she passed a hamlet. She had an impression of pale faces pressed against cottage windows as she went by, her hair tangled in a coarse white flag over her shoulders, her clothes in wet tatters. The clearest image she had from the day was a view of the lake and herself turning northwest to follow its shore; the rest of the time passed in a haze.

Above her the gray sky dimmed. The land curved upwards in harsh ribs of stone to a scrubbily forested ridge of sloping hills. Seeing the steep ledges, she was just conscious enough then that she began to be frightened, began to want to stop, to take back control.

Halfway up a band of coarse scree, the rush abruptly ended when a shattering pain saturated her body. Her legs seized up and she crumpled with ghastly surprise. She howled in rage and rebellion against the pain and her seeming helplessness, her numbed apathy to her peril brutally broken.

Someone was attacking the horses she'd left behind her with the ostler's companion. It was as if she could feel the knife, stroke for stroke, biting into her flesh. The sympathetic torment cut her body like a razor; the doubled horse-strength she held plunged in convulsive agony. A mind-shattering turmoil wrenched through her body as she fought, with sudden focused strength, to shuck the horse-spirits from her body—she had to separate one from the other as they fought and roiled, tangled together, interlocked in her flesh. Panic seized her, giving her the will she needed to force them apart, to reject them from her body. As she thrust first one, then the other, from the gaping channel in her mind, she was stung by a last, agonizing shock. At least one of the horse-spirits had no body to go back to.

When she came to her senses, she was lying on the band of loose scree, her knees drawn to her chest. Her body was shaking with cold and horror at the echoing memory of the dying horses. If their slaughterer had chosen to kill the horses more quickly, more efficiently, she would be mad or dead herself now. Gaultry clutched her knees tighter, trying to calm the involuntary quaking that wracked her body. The ghost of the animal whose spirit had been trapped within her could have driven her to madness. Indeed, madness must have taken her already—she had been insane to invoke such a potent spell, with no preparation; to rely on intuition, rather than on knowledge, as her guide.

Or possessed. She shuddered. Was this what it meant to have a Glamour-soul? Loss of the self to a greater, more charismatic power?

After a few minutes, her head felt clearer. The pain in her body was all her own: overworked legs and sore joints. No more taint of sympathetic agony. She sighed, and stumbled to her feet, assessing the damage.

Another pair of boots ruined. Her hose were in rags. The spell that had whitened her hair was gone, as was the spell that had altered her jacket's color. Something inside her shirt scratched her throat when she moved. She thrust her hand in her shirt to bring out Dervla's necklace. All that remained of the glowing green beads was cinders on a blackened piece of string. She thrust her hand deeper. Tamsanne's charm was a black cinder-stain where its leather thong had rubbed her shirt. Gaultry stared at the destroyed charms, then dropped to her knees, shaken by the realization of the force these amulets had consumed before they'd self-immolated.

They'd absorbed power from the magic she had invoked, protecting her from her fresh, untrammeled strength. Finally they'd burnt out, like wood consumed by fire. Without them her own power, breaking so catastrophically free, would have burnt her to her bones.

She had worked a power stronger than she could control, and lived.

She tore both amulets from her throat, and threw them as far off into the scree as she could. To loose her Glamour, Dervla had counseled training, and meditation; the Duchess had counseled action, and an interview with a long-dead Prince. Back at Melaudiere's manor, if she had believed the Duchess when the old woman had said she had Glamour-power in her, would she have chosen the terrors of this latter course?

The young huntress crouched on the barren hillside, exposed to the wind and rain, and felt the smallness of herself within the bare hills and limitless sky.

She looked up at the great gray sky. The rain beat down on her face like cold tears. The storm was still moving in from the north, from Bissanty.

Wiping her eyes, she stood once more, and turned her face into the wind.

Whatever her fears, she was going to find Clarin's barrow, where she would confront the Prince who had torn Tielmark free of Bissanty bondage. Her will was free: she could strive at least to save herself.

If the Duchess had sent her on a fool's errand, where she would meet her death trying to open her power, this at least would not be the death of a slave—the death that faced Mervion and her both if Gaultry was captured and taken to Princeport with her power still quiescent.

But if she did reach Clarin's burial place, and something was changed in her so she could use her power without destroying herself . . .

Then she would head east, and try to reach Mervion before Prince's Night. She would try to save Mervion, and hope that in saving Mervion Tielmark would be protected too. That was the focus Tamsanne had taught her, that was the focus that she would now exploit. Her legs ached, her joints ached—but she would continue.

▼

chapter 17

The sky hung heavily overhead, sheeted with gray storm clouds that threatened rain. Smaller white clouds scudded underneath in a fast wind, like vapory white birds. The bare bleak hills glinted wetly, mirroring the stark sky. In all her journey, Gaultry had never felt so sure of Great Llara's presence. The young huntress was coming to the edge of Tielmark, nearing the Thunderbringer's dominion.

Martin's map had disappeared somewhere during her spell-maddened run—not that it would have been detailed enough to help her through the rolling foothills amongst which she now found herself. Looking around at the harsh scrub growth of the landscape, she decided her best prospect lay in gaining high ground, and trying to see her way from there.

Unfortunately, in practice, this meant thrashing up the thorniest of the available hills. Her legs were almost spent, but she forced herself to continue. The rain restarted, and the ground under foot, already saturated by the morning's downpour, became even more slick and treacherous.

Two false summits didn't help her mood.

When she reached the crest of a third hill, the landscape opened in front of her, and she understood why she'd thought she'd felt the Great Thunderer's presence.

Across the steep valley below her, a smooth-sided, evenly shouldered hill stood apart from all its neighbors.

She had found the High Prince of Tielmark's barrow.

There had been magic in the forming of the hill. Its steep, curving sides were as regular as a geometric form. In contrast to the barren clay and rock of the land that ringed it, glossy green sward covered the whole of the hill's body. The top was crowned by a low mound of stone. A rough stone table or throne topped the mound facing northwards to the Bissanty border.

Motion on the Prince's hill caught her eye, down below the hill's crown. Horses. Someone had set a guard on Clarin's holy hill. Biting her lip in anxiety, she waited, counting. She stopped when she reached six. Six horsemen circling the hill, maybe more, their heads bowed against the rain, but still stoutly armed, still alert, ready for an intruder who was seeking the Prince's counsel.

Like herself.

There would only be one entrance to the barrow, most probably beneath the stone throne on the hill's opposite side. With six men between her and it, it might as well have been back in Arleon Forest, or on the moon, for all the good it would do her.

She glumly sank down on her haunches, kneading her sore legs through the tattered rags of her hose. It was ironic that she'd got free of Martin and his men, proved to them and herself that she could come all this way on her own, only to find her way blocked at last by a force that could have been easily dealt with by the strong guard the Duchess sent out with her! Martin and his men would have punched a hole through the flimsy shield of horsemen like a stone going through glass.

Her only chance would be to wait until night. She'd find a sheltered spot on her scrub-covered hillside and wait.

As she turned away, a faint sound reached her ears, a sound that didn't fit with the landscape. A keening wail.

Overhead, the storm worsened. The wind and rain picked up, the sky darkened. Thick, ropelike bands of thundercloud moved in—from the heartland of the Bissanty Empire. A shiver went through her. It was said that Llara's eyes were in her storms, in her thunder and lightning.

The sky was thickening so rapidly, she couldn't believe the focus of clouds, all over the barrow, was the hand of the goddess on nature. Someone else, someone mortal, was calling magic. Gaultry could almost feel the air thicken with a great gathering of power.

Still the rain intensified, striking her skin now like cold daggers of ice. Gaultry, up to her shoulders in brush, had little shelter; this was even more true for the riders on the open barrow-hill. The horsemen ducked their heads, and reined up their horses to a slow, cautious pace. Now angry gusts of wind were accompanying the rain. As she watched, one of the horsemen's mounts stumbled, shying and slipping on the soaked turf. She could hear the edge of fear in its rider's voice as he sawed at the reins, trying to steady it on its feet.

Then her eye caught movement in the sky, at the corner of her field of vision. A sudden gust of wind brought her a lonely shriek, higher than the wind.

The single speck, so high in the sky it was almost beyond the range of her vision, was Issachar's steel eagle.

She was miserably tired, and the grass looked terribly slippery.

But now there was no choice. If the eagle had known where she was as she had stood by the Duchess's font in the water salon, it was sure to find her, on the great open curve of the hill. Trying to make herself small, invisible, she called the last spell that she had any energy for—a simple color spell to camouflage herself as she went up the slope.

Her hair muted to a wet grassy green color and her skin went splotchy and dark. She'd have to hope that she was mud-besmeared enough that she wouldn't be noticed until she was the best part of the way up the barrow-hill's slope. She made a last prayer, and began to creep forward.

She timed her ascent so that she started up Clarin's hill just behind one of the horsemen, clambering up where she thought he was least likely to spot her. The grass was horribly slippery and long, full of hidden tangles. A tussock trapped her foot and she took a nasty slip. She managed not to call out, but the violent motion attracted the attention of at least one rider.

"She's here! The witching girl is here!" The call rang out from behind and slightly above her on the slope. In his excitement the man applied spurs to his horse's sides. The animal jumped and slipped, neighing with fear as it half-skidded, half-fell down the slope, its hooves roweling up long strips of mud. It shot past Gaultry and on down the hill, rider and horse struggling together to regain control.

There was nothing in her that wanted to run. There wasn't a spell left in her to give her help. She slipped and fell a second time, rising slowly, hacking mud out of her mouth. She looked tiredly at the approaching horseman, and moved another slow step upwards. The wind slapped the rain against her face like a whip, and she tasted salty tears. Her defeat felt sour, but she straightened her back, and tried to face it proudly. She could go no further.

A too-close shriek from Issachar's eagle snapped her head up. High above the hill, the great steel eagle was circling, close enough that she could make out wings, its massive head, its tail, flared and ready for a dive. Today, hunched low between its wings, the bird had a rider.

The Chancellor's officer, the dark-maned warrior with the scarred cheeks, Issachar Dan.

The bird shrieked and plummeted, talons outstretched. A horse that had almost reached her panicked, tossed its rider, and bolted down the hill, neighing with terror. Gaultry threw herself flat on her stomach and pressed her face into the wet grass. The bird swept over her head, claws raking inches above her back. Its rider shouted angrily and twisted in the bird's saddle, trying to force it to bank in to the hill for a quick landing.

Raw fear banished her tiredness, her sense of numb defeat. She scrambled onwards, clutching at tufts of grass when her feet slipped and slid beneath her. Her heart hammered in her throat, everything in her dreading the first bite of the creature's dagger beak into her back.

Before she knew it, she had reached the first ring of stones that marked the barrow. If she went straight over the top, she'd come down near the barrow's portal, and maybe there would be sanctuary inside the Prince's own walls. That would mean climbing over the

huge stone throne. Hands on stone, she started the scrabble up, slipping and half-sprawling on the slick wet rock.

Don't run. The spell took her in the back and flushed along her
spine into her brain like a warming fire. She froze, her hands numb
against the oily-wet stone. *Don't run.* The spell took her as easily as
it might have taken an unshielded child, blocking her vision with a
bright image of herself riding in shining glory on the eagle's back, an
image that blotted out the hill, the throne, the whole of Llara's
stormy gray sky. *Up in the air, full of grace and splendor—as beautiful
and full of glory as her overvaunted sister Mervion could ever hope to
be—Mervion would envy Gaultry, rather than Gaultry Mervion—*

The slight to Mervion saved her. Furious and insulted both,
Gaultry found the will to tear aside the vision—or at least to tear
enough of her mind clear that a foggy impression of the real landscape around her superimposed itself on the image of herself
crowned in triumph. She stepped forward, forcing herself ever upwards, and stumbled against the stone skirts of the throne. A few
yards further and she'd be on her way down the barrow on the portal
face of the hill.

Stop now, Gaultry Blas.

The spell was back, stronger than before. Double vision confused
her sense of direction. That might have been the end, but Gaultry,
forcing herself forward despite her spell-dazzled vision, took a last
step onto the great seat, thinking to cross it with two steps, and jump
down on its other side. Issachar's new spell caught her just as her
second foot joined her first on the great stone slab. She cringed and
doubled over, blind to her surroundings once again.

The stone was gone—where had Issachar's spell taken her? She
flailed out with her hands, trying to regain her balance, and the
spell, without her volition, shattered like glass. For a moment, she
had a crazy fish-eye view of the expanse of landscape that swept
away down the hill towards the Bissanty lands. Then she realized
that the throne's stone seat had turned to water, and she was sink-
ing, losing Issachar's influence as she did so. The stone rose to close
in over her head, to shut her into horrible, airless dark. Struggling,
she tried to strike for the surface. She was suffocating, dying; to be
taken by Issachar was better than this—

One foot, kicking out, stubbed against solid ground. She could breathe. She had found the bottom. The darkness around her became absolute as the last afterimage of the scene aboveground, of Issachar's flight picture, faded. Magic hung thick in the air, pressing her skin. A burnt dirt and spice smell filled her nostrils. Relieved as she was to be able to breathe, she soon found herself coughing.

"Gods!"

This is not the place to seek the gods. A whisper. A rasping ancient-toned whisper. *Welcome to my barrow, Gaultry Blas.*

She went down on her knees. She thought of Dervla's burnt-out beads and her aunt's demolished charm, and the fear that she too was destined to twist and burn to a cinder clawed at her. Perhaps the magic around her was stronger than mortal flesh could bear. She could smell death all around her. Old, powerful death.

"Prince Clarin?"

It has been fifty years since I had my last visitor. And never a one so lovely as yourself, Twice Fair.

"Where am I? How is it that you can see me?" Fear made her voice skip.

Do you want to see me, to know me as I am?

She hesitated, hugging herself in the dark. Did she want to come face to face with a three-hundred-year-dead Prince? "I do," she said. "More even than I want light."

A sharp flood of white radiance sent her cowering, hands over her head. Angry and humiliated both, she decided that she had had enough of being on her knees. She blinked back tears and stumbled up. The room was small, musty, with bare flagstones underfoot and moldering gold and green tapestries taped to the walls. The tapestries depicted the first Prince of Tielmark's career: a battle scene with Clarin striding head and shoulders above his troops; Clarin's enthronement; Clarin kneeling at an altar, with two enormously tall women—Elianté and Emiera?—extracting a pair of shadowy figures from his body. The fourth image showed Clarin once again, but now—if the pictures were in sequence, it would be the scene following the altar picture—he was no taller, and depicted in no brighter colors, than the men who surrounded him. This last picture showed

Clarin on a silver throne in a garden, surrounded by servants, children, and fruiting trees.

My life. She thought there was a whisper of longing in the ancient's voice.

The room was light and white as day, but the brilliance had no discernible source or lantern. Everything in the room emitted its own light, even her own body. There was no shadow under her feet. Her clothes felt strange and light, spun of air and silk.

The wall that held the scene of Clarin's battles had a tall, featureless door in its middle. The surface gave back nothing of the room or the tapestries. It reflected only her own image, as clear as the finest mirror. In the door-mirror image she stood, isolated, in a field of black: a filthy, mud-plastered figure with her hair in strange green clumps dangling down on her shoulders like wet snakes. Her skin was speckled, froglike. Self-conscious, she stripped the false color away, and wiped her lank hair back from her face. She tried to stand tall, as though she was unafraid. She wasn't fooling herself, and she doubted she fooled the ancient Prince either.

Her vanity amused him. She thought she heard a low sigh, like laughter. *So here you are. Here too am I.*

The outlines of her reflection wavered, remade themselves. The planes of her face broadened, twisted, transformed themselves into the boney skull of a stern old man. Beneath the proud skull-face, he was dressed in long burial robes, double goddess spirals embroidered in gold on the shoulders. A rough-forged iron crown rested on his head, a match to the coronet Mervion had worn when Gaultry had seen her with Issachar. His body was thin underneath the rich robe, and she sensed a skeletal brittleness in his folded arms. But despite the age that deeply lined his features, despite the parchment pallor of his skin, he was strikingly beautiful of face, indeed the most beautiful man she'd ever known. A trio of goddesses — the Great Twins themselves and their illustrious mother Llara — had favored him, and it was not hard to see why.

The old Prince's attentive, unfathomable eyes fixed on the young huntress, drinking her in. She stood before him, quivering, dazzled.

If my current heir was so well loved among the Great Twelve as I was in my own day, you would not be here, and my heir would not be playing puppet to a slave.

"Benet is much loved in Tielmark," she assured him, feeling a fool even as she spoke.

He is Prince and heir to the Twin Goddesses' realm, but he has not yet earned their favor. If he had, Great Llara would not toy with the thought that now might be the time to bring a strayed realm back into her own domain.

"You want to stop Llara from seizing power?"

Now she could be sure she was amusing him. *From beyond the grave?* There was definitely a smile in the Prince's creaky whisper. *It was hard enough to push the Thunderbringer back in my lifetime. But I had no choice but to break with my Imperial brother, and I could not break with my brother unless I broke too with Great Llara. But it is not for me to keep or break the god-pact now. I have had my share of defiance of the gods.*

He had been bold as a lion to set himself against them. "Was it worth it?"

He answered with a creaky chuckle. *It would be something to have the answer to that question in one's own lifetime.*

She lowered her eyes, embarrassed, but it seemed Clarin was still considering her question.

Was it worth defiance to free Tielmark from Bissanty slavery? Irrepressible pride burned, unrepentant, through the spell that was his voice. *That answer will always be yes.* His depthless eyes seemed to scorch her with his passion and heat. *For Tielmark's sake, I should have demanded more. I thought it would be enough for me, for my land, to make myself a free Prince. Instead of tying Tielmark to a Prince's god-pledges, I should have made myself King. Or I should have birthed an heir who had the mettle to do it for me.*

"King?" Gaultry asked. "Does Tielmark need a King?"

Lovely Gaultry. You have risked much to come here.

The thick smells of the room were like heavy wool against her skin. Every inch of her itched, and felt hot. As he spoke, with his rough, seductive spell of a voice, Clarin was working magic on her. She could feel it; she couldn't stop it, she didn't want to stop it. The tang of spice mixed with the magic pressed against her. The longer the figure of the aged Prince spoke, the more her head spun, the more languorous and weak she became. Though she sensed his every word was prophecy, desperately important, she was too weakened to attend to all he was saying. Coming to herself a little, she found she was down on her knees, head bowed. The itch on her skin began to burn. She tried to swallow, but the fumes hardened in her throat, and she was hard put to keep herself from gagging and choking. Yet she was happy here, and warm. The aches had gone from her abused legs. For all her nausea, here she was safe, here there would be no eagle's claws to rend her.

Your presence here will make it harder for Llara's minions to betray my marriage pact. He watched her intently, his figure growing taller as hers drooped and wavered.

"My presence here?" She gulped back involuntary bile. "I thought that my visit here was meant to spark the Glamour-magic in me into action."

The Glamour in your body has found its life. There was a wistful note behind the Prince's words. *Golden, beautiful, it will blacken if it goes.* Gaultry glanced at the tapestry that depicted the goddesses pulling the twin shadow figures from Clarin's body. Was that the symbol of the magic the goddesses had taken from him, the god-blood and the Glamour?

"I thought you were supposed to tell me how to use Glamour so I could help Mervion."

He laughed, mocking. *An old fox sent you here in the hope that your power wouldn't kill you before we spoke.*

"I don't understand." Her head spun. Prince Clarin's image in the door-mirror now towered above her. Was the image wavering, or was her sight going? Had he touched her? Had she merely imagined the caress of a hand on her throat, on her chest, the brush of lips against her cheek?

Your Glamour is open, Twice Fair. It is yours to use. Prince Clarin's voice and image faded, leaving her in darkness. The overpowering scents suffused her senses. She lurched blindly forward, hands brushing for the mirror, and knocked her elbow against the smoothness of its face.

"I don't understand," she mourned, facing the dark glass, wanting the sight of him once again. "I don't understand." An unearthly flame blossomed on her breast, searing her body with flickers of pale green and blue fire. For an instant she saw the imprint of a man's hand on her breastbone. Clarin's rasping laugh broke over her in the dark. Then the strange fire spread, sheathed her entire body. In the light of the new flames her reflection had reappeared: body outlined in the dancing blue-green flames, hair a dark corona fringed in blue. With some corner of her fuddled mind she remembered that the mirror was also the room's door. She reached out a hand to her own image. Through the lit-up skin of her hand, she could see the darkness of her own bones.

Strength, Twice Fair. You will need it. Clarin's last words—his blessing?—were a muffled echo in her head. His presence was all but gone now. She opened her mouth to ask one last question—

A gauntleted hand broke through the surface of the mirror, easily, as if it was rising through a flat plane of water, and seized the hand she had raised to her reflection. Closing its fingers on hers like a vise, it yanked her forward viciously. Screaming, she found herself slammed against the mirror, unable to pass through its surface as the hand was doing. The metal rings of the hand's gauntlet cut her flesh. The mystic fire that sheathed her body like living armor intensified, so bright she put a hand up to protect her eyes from the glare.

You will come to me. This was not Clarin's voice. It was the great eagle's rider. How had he got into Clarin's barrow? Why wasn't the great Prince protecting her? She was supposed to be the hope of the realm! The command spell her enemy was casting seemed shades weaker than the first one he'd attempted, but its force was nothing to sneer at. Neither was the physical power that smashed her against the surface of the mirror for a second bruising time.

"Let me go! Let me go! I'm spelled to not pass through the door!" Her unseen foe responded by giving her wrist another vicious tug, slapping her once again against the unyielding plane of the mirror.

As she crashed once more against the mirror, the pain was countered by a euphoric rush of pleasure. The magic that sheathed her was reaching its peak, the green fire changing color, flickering to gold, entering her skin. Some barrier in her had finally burnt open.

A warm rush of power swept through her body, invigorating it, wiping away the last trace of stiffness in her legs. A gross contrast to the sick crunch of her wrist against the mirror's surface!

The fire that cloaked her body suddenly flickered out, casting her once again into darkness. Gaultry, dazed, thrilled with a new sense of power and life. Her unseen foe gave another jerk on her wrist. With the flame gone, the mirror made no resistance. She flew through its surface into light, and slammed up short against the body of the man who had reached in to pull her out. They were in a shallow passage that led out of the barrow. Turning back, she had a glimpse through the silvery-white shield of light that filled the door to an unfamiliar space: a vaulted chamber with a massive stone casket in its center. The tapestry chamber in which she'd seemed to stand and converse with Prince Clarin was nowhere to be seen.

The silver shield over the door had left a shimmering film on her clothes and body. She was still stunned, half-reeling from the power that had been loosed both on and in her.

The dark warrior released her wrist. "Daughter of bitches," he swore. He wrenched his gauntlet—similarly silver-coated—from his hand. Under the gauntlet, in burnt black tatters, were the remains of a leather glove, and beneath the glove, blistered flesh.

Seeing that he had her attention, the man gave her a fierce glare. "It may be that I can't hold you at the moment, girl, but try to run, and have no doubt, I'll bring you down quick enough."

At least he wasn't being falsely respectful or friendly. As she watched, transfixed, he held out his undamaged hand to the gauntlet where it lay on the passage's stone floor, shining with its coat of silver magic. His dark brows drew together in a moment of concentration, and a crackling bolt of eldritch fire burst from his palm. The shimmer on the glove clouded over, then went dull.

I'm next, Gaultry thought, swallowing nervously. The man retrieved his gauntlet and pulled it back on. If he hadn't been standing between her and the entrance to Clarin's crypt, she might have been tempted to try to duck back in out of his reach through the white film of protection. It was obvious he wouldn't be able to follow her.

Seeing her longing look at the crypt door, the man gave her a contemptuous glare. He raised his palm to her, his eyebrows gathered fiercely as he focused, calling a spell.

She had only the feeblest of magic bolt spells to counter him—enough to curl a mustache or divert a spell, no more—but she found herself giving it a reflexive call as the dark magic fire burst from the warrior's palms for a second time. White bolts lanced out from her raised palms, equaling and even pushing back the warrior's eldritch flames. The man's eyes narrowed in anger, and he dropped the spell.

"I came late." His voice was flat and ugly.

"Issachar Dan, I presume." Gaultry's voice broke as she named him. In life, the man was not so large as she'd expected. When she'd seen his image in Melaudiere's font, he had seemed to loom above her sister. Perhaps that had been because Mervion had seemed so withdrawn, so shriveled. She stared at the man's flowing black hair, his sharp black eyes and brows, the jagged lightning-bolt scars that marred his cheeks, making his cheekbones appear chiseled and harsh. His mail shirt was finer than any she'd seen in her life, and there was a long sword in a silver-wire scabbard at his hip. At his throat there was a steel torque ornamented with ram's heads.

The most frightening thing about the man was his almost complete lack of color. His skin held a waxy gray pallor. Even his lips betrayed only the faintest tinge of color. If Gaultry hadn't seen the enflamed blistering on his hand, she could have easily believed that he was formed of metal or stone, instead of flesh and blood.

"Gaultry Blas. I had thought to meet you sooner." He was calling another spell, keeping her talking as he brought it to being.

"Don't bother," she told him, trying to make her voice sound confident. "I'm not a gauntlet to have the magic battered from it. You'll humiliate yourself if you try to overcome me with magic on the doorstep of my own Prince's tomb."

He stared, trying to gauge whether or not she was bluffing, then shrugged. "Then I'll take you to a place more conducive to breaking your will."

"I won't bow to you."

"You will. Your compliance is requisite at a wedding. Whatever power your petty Prince has given you, *you will come with me.*" His

last words were a sudden snapping call of power. It took all she had
in her to resist taking a step forward.

Gaultry drew back against the cool stone of the passage, trying
not to show her fear. She knew she would have to go with him. He
could make her come by physical force alone, but he was bastard
enough that it wouldn't satisfy him. He would want to dominate her
with spells as well. Looking into the dark warrior's scarred face, she
guessed that taking her by spells would be a point of pride for him,
proof of his power.

"I'll come with you, Lord Dan. I'm one against many, I'll have to
come with you," she told him. "But I won't be a slave to your
magic."

As coolly as possible, she turned her back and walked towards
the patch of light that led back out on the hill. A cocky gesture. As
she reached the passage's entrance and looked out down the hill, her
heart seemed to die in her. She wished she hadn't bothered with the
bravado.

While she'd been in the barrow, the sky had thoroughly darkened over. There was lightning in the thick storm clouds. The rain
beat down more fiercely than ever. On the rough terrace on the hillside in front of the tomb's portal, a clump of horsemen waited miserably in the rain. They wore the Duke of Haute-Tielmark's scarlet
jackets. Opposite them, bobbing its fierce head and frightening their
horses, crouched the military officer's great eagle, its feathers fluffed
out against the rain, an unfriendly gleam in its eye.

"Your goddess has a funny way of smiling on your successes," she
said, pausing before moving out into the drumming rain.

"You will not remain inviolable for long."

The man was an animal, a dangerous animal. Delaying leaving
the barrow one last moment, Gaultry took a last look at the dark,
hawkish warrior, as they stood together by the door of the crypt. His
black eyes probed deeply into hers, fishing for some advantage, some
weakness. Gaultry stared back, asking herself the same questions.
She didn't want to go out under that bleak sky and face the rain and
the full force of the storm.

The leader of the horsemen stepped forward nervously, his eyes
averted. With the white sheen of magic still coating her body,

Gaultry realized suddenly that she looked like a ghost, rising anew from her Prince's crypt.

"The Great Twins will haunt you for betraying their trust here," Gaultry told him. "Or have you already submitted to the collar of the Bissanty goddess?"

"Your saddlebags are ready for you, Lord Dan. What would you have us tell our master?"

"Tell him he need hold Melaudiere's men no longer. I have what I came for."

"My master will want his reward." The man sketched the sign of the Great Twins, and licked his lips, unhappy.

"He will have it after the wedding."

The Duke's man frowned. He looked at Issachar Dan as though he wished to press him further, then his eyes flickered to Gaultry's white-sheathed figure, and he thought better of it. "The Great Twins' Blessings on you, Lord." Looking away from Gaultry, he called his troops to rally, and remounted. With another salute, Haute-Tielmark's men headed off down the hill, leaving Gaultry and Issachar alone on the high terrace.

"So now what?"

"Now, woman, you discover the wonders of flight."

The world exploded in a shower of stars as Issachar clubbed her with the hilt of his sword. "Llara curse you," he swore, as the protective spell on her iced over his sword, penetrating through his gauntlets to his hands. Ignoring the effects, he hit her again.

As his fists struck her, again and again, each blow searing his own flesh, Gauntry saw the stubborn pride in him that drove him on. Rather than allow her a shadow of hope that she was following along with his plans of her own volition, for her own cause, he was taking damage on himself, proving his determination to break her. Despite the strength of her new magic, she was now utterly in his power.

chapter 18

While she was groggy from the blows, Issachar dragged her across to his eagle and dumped her on the grass near its claws. Ignoring the pain in his silvered hands, he swung into the eagle's saddle. "Up Gyviere, up!" he called.

The creature shrieked and beat its wings, taking to the air as though Issachar's weight was nothing to it. Why was he leaving her? Gaultry lurched, befuddled, towards her feet, slipped on the slick grass and fell back. Staring dumbly, she watched the great eagle coast off the hill into a long loop, wings beating against the rain and buffeting winds. Issachar, busy on its back, cast another spell of eldritch fire, cleansing the venom of her protection spell from his sword and hands. Then, as the eagle swung back towards the hill, he bent low on the eagle's neck, and wove sheaths of eldritch fire on the bird's feet. She still hadn't guessed what he intended. As she watched, the great predatory bird turned in a slow, graceful arc towards the hill, talons outstretched. Then she knew. She threw up her arms to ward it off. It plucked her off the hillside, as easily as a falcon going down on a rabbit. The ground receded, her screams mingling with the eagle's shrieks. Somewhere above her, Issachar Dan was laughing.

The white film of protection on her body fizzled and steamed against the eldritch spell that coated the bird's feet. One of the great steel-feathered creature's claws hooked her arm, the other, more painfully, gripped her by the soft flesh of her thigh. Gaultry tried not to look at her leg as, excruciatingly slowly, the silver-white sheath faded and the eagle's talons, still thickly armored with dark fire, began to sink into her flesh.

Mercifully, she blacked out. When she came to, nothing, save for the level of her pain and the further fading of the white magic that had protected her, had changed. Her leg was rank with clotted blood, and she was cold—so very cold. Below them was a bleak gray plain that she took at first for the strange landscape of dream. The realization that it was water, her first view of Tielmark's great bordering sea, came slowly.

They flew on for numbing hours, the storm clouds following them, the wind at their backs, pushing them forward. Gaultry hung from the bird's claws in a half-conscious state: to struggle would be to risk being dropped. She had no leeway to pose or bluff or threaten: her plight was every inch the crushing defeat that Issachar intended.

It was night, utterly dark, and still the eagle flew on. Above her, Issachar seemed to have fallen asleep in the saddle. As the pain in her thigh increased, Gaultry went through periods of complete blackness, a release from growing nausea and cold. Despite the lashings of rain, in her diminishing moments of consciousness, she was terribly thirsty. She thought she would die. She wanted to die.

It seemed as if they had been flying forever.

Prince Clarin's last words had been to tell her that she must be strong. Rain cut through her clothes and tears tracked down her face, mingling with icy rain. She didn't feel strong.

When the eagle finally released her, it dumped her unceremoniously on hard cobbles. Gaultry was so cold, the press of stone against her cheek was warming.

"What do you mean by this, Lord Dan? The girl was to be brought in good condition. What need have we of a half-naked corpse?"

"She'll live." Issachar's voice was a cruel purr. "It's her own fault if she's suffered hard treatment. She communed with the spirit in the barrow. I had no choice but to weaken her." A toe prodded her leg. She gasped and rolled away. Her thigh, where the hawk had pierced it, throbbed, agonizingly painful. "A ride through wind and cold is not enough to kill a strong adept like this. The barrow-spirit gifted her with a protection spell of awesome power. A rough ride was the most effective way strip it from her." She cracked her eyes to see if he spoke true, shuddering to see the unwholesome purple blotchiness of her skin. There wasn't the slightest hint of protective white sheen left anywhere on her. She coughed miserably, and covered her face with her hands.

"We've a bare three days to get her into condition," the new voice complained.

"You, Excellency, have only three days to get her into condition. I have fulfilled the terms of my contract."

"By Llara, you have not, Lord Dan." The new voice took on an imperious tone. "Think of the glory the Great Llara will lay on you at the reparation of her Empire."

"What Llara wants may not be what you want, Excellency. You may be Chancellor here, but you would do well to remember my deepest alliance is to Her."

"Don't push me, Eagle Lord. I know where your deepest alliance lies." The Chancellor's voice was mocking.

Gaultry, curiosity overcoming her urge to curl up and hope that the sweet darkness of unconsciousness would take her, coughed, and raised her head. Issachar's eagle was near her, looking a little worn, feathers ruffled and head drooping. Issachar was nearer still, his hand on the hilt of his sword, a look of constrained anger suffusing his features.

At his side was Edan Heiratikus, the Chancellor of Tielmark. He had a fine profile, long spidery hands, and a rough brush of prematurely silver hair. He was a rapier to Issachar Dan's jagged broadsword, lean and graceful, and infinitely dangerous, smiling unpleasantly at Issachar, the palms of his spider-hands bridged together. To her surprise, Issachar turned away rather than meet the Chancellor's eyes.

"Your wishes are mine, Chancellor," the dark warrior grated.

"And so Llara is served, Lord Dan. My faith is yours."

Issachar turned and noticed that Gaultry had recovered enough that she could follow their talk. "Excellency," he said, meeting her eyes with a look that augured new cruelties, "we should secure the prisoner before we discuss this matter further."

"Can she stand? Her leg seems very bad."

"Call some guards to take her to the tower."

"Now? The state she's in — ?"

"However pathetic she looks, Excellency, don't put it from you that this ragged piece of flesh is an open channel for the most potent magic below that of the gods."

Heiratikus looked down at her, eyes narrowing. "It's late," he said, the spider-hands fluttering. "The altar is not ready. The tower must wait."

"If you must coddle her, Excellency, put her in the lodge rooms. And tomorrow, don't delay. Put her through the tower before the evening," Issachar advised. "Preferably while she's still weak."

The Chancellor nodded. "I want to see her face," he said. Two guardsmen stepped out of the shadows and hoisted Gaultry up off the cobbles. One grabbed her by the chin and forced her to look into the Chancellor's face. Meeting his dark eyes, she squinted a little beneath the intensity of his stare.

"Do you know who I am, girl?"

She stared at him dully, too tired to answer. The agony she'd been through hanging from the bird's claws, the numbing ride through the night, were too close.

"Do you know who I am?" The guards gave her a nasty shake, letting her neck snap.

"Sir, you're Tielmark's Chancellor, Sir."

"I am Edan Heiratikus, the Chancellor of your nation. Tielmark's highest court, the ducal council, granted me this high honor in accordance with all the laws of our nation. Anyone who opposes my will is betraying their duty to Tielmark." He nodded at the guards. They loosened their grip, leaving Gaultry to stand by herself, swaying, all her weight on her good leg.

It was mad. He wanted her to curtsy. She was in rags, and cold, and her thigh had begun to bleed again.

When she attempted a half-bob, one of the guards kicked the back of her knee, and down she went, in a proper full curtsy.

She found she couldn't rise again by herself. When the guards dragged her to her feet, she refused to lock her good knee again, and the guards had to hold her, swaying, lest she drop again.

Heiratikus bent and put his face close to hers. "Your duty is to your country, Gaultry Blas." There was a spark of madness in his eyes. "Despite what others might have you believe, your duty is to comply with my orders." He straightened, and smoothed back his hair, the threat in his posture melting to honey. "You will of course be amply rewarded for your service."

Gaultry could not keep an expression of disbelief off her face. "Rewarded?"

"You may have been frightened by events of the past days." He nodded to her guards, and suddenly the hands that held her were gentle. "I understand that you may even have felt we were your tormentors. But I will assure you here, now that you have arrived in Princeport, your safety is guaranteed. There has only been violence in your life since you fell in with the traitors. But it is not too late for you. If you cooperate, the highest honors await you."

Only a madman could have imagined that such an offer, made to a woman who had been beaten so long she could no longer keep her feet, could possibly be timely. It was not deceit that made her head roll on her shoulders and her body slump, it was tiredness and despair. She sensed rather than saw the Chancellor moving away.

"Take her in. Tell the women to let her have a good night's sleep. I'll want her on the morrow. Don't give her breakfast." Then a pause. "If she's conscious after the women have settled her, you can let her see her sister."

"That would be a mistake, Excellency," said Issachar.

"Nonsense, Lord Dan. It can only confirm that we mean her and her kin no harm. What could be better?"

The dark warrior gave him no answer.

The guards took her to a bed. More accurately, they took her through a bewildering number of passages and up and down an uncountable number of staircases and through at least one magically warded door. But the bed was the only thing of which Gaultry was in a state to notice.

She was dead to the world before her head hit the pillow.

*   *   *

Gaultry woke to the scent of roses. Improbable silk under her fingers, and the scent of roses. Unwilling to leave such a lovely dream, she cracked one eye open.

She was lying in a sumptuous bed; and she was indeed smelling roses. Mervion, dressed in green and gold silks, was sitting by her bedside. "Mervion!" Gaultry was out of bed with her arms around her beloved sister before her heart took another beat, dragging her leg in her eagerness. "I was so frightened for you," she said. "In Haute-Tielmark, I saw such terrible omens—"

Mervion smiled, and traced Gaultry's cheek with her smooth fingers. "Omens can have many interpretations," she said. Then she laughed, a light, chatter-of-bells laugh that made the hair rise on her sister's spine. "Were you frightened for me?" Mervion said. "I was frightened for you, and, it seems, with better reason. Let me look at you. You're skin and bones!"

"Issachar wanted to break me." Gaultry sank back on the bed, the pain in her thigh suddenly bitter and hard. "He came close to succeeding." Inwardly she cringed from the stranger who wore her sister's face, who held up a mask to mimic a sister's concern.

Mervion's mouth twisted in a fleeting moue of distress. "Issachar can be naughty," she said. "The Chancellor was very angry. Sit down, Gaultry. Rest yourself. They're sending for a priestess to fix your leg, and then you and Issachar can make your peace."

"A priestess?" Gaultry said, a little dazzled by her sister's leaps of logic.

"Gyviere, Issachar's eagle, pierced your leg. The Chancellor insists that it be tended. He wants you well and walking, Gaultry."

"I met the Chancellor last night," Gaultry said. "Well and walking is not how I'd say he wants me."

In her wafting green and gold dress, Mervion seemed more beautiful than ever, Gaultry thought, taking her sister's hand. Her twin's hair glinted with red and gold lights, her green eyes shone with life. Concern for her little sister was written plainly on her face. But beneath the glitter and color, Gaultry sensed a mounting emptiness. She reached out, trying to sense some bond of magic, some shield that might have bent her from her innermost loyalties, but, it seemed, there was nothing to find, not even a veil of spell that could account for her sister's eerie lightheartedness within the darkness of their imprisonment.

The image of the marred picture the Haute-Tielmaran farm-woman had showed her seemed to loom up, brighter than memory: the huntress with the gash over her ribs; the lady with half her figure burnt to ashes.

"How are you, Mervion?"

"I? I'm happy. How could I be otherwise, now you're here?"

"Mervion!" Gaultry grabbed her sister's shoulders. "What are you saying? Great Twins! I saw you fighting and angry less than a week past. You cast a spell through your embroidery frame and fought like a fox in a trap."

Mervion's lashes fluttered, masking the confusion in her eyes. Her voice, when she finally spoke, was halting, as though Gaultry had asked her to remember a secret history long since forgotten. "You can't know why I was fighting," she said. "You haven't been here."

"You left me a very worrying letter," Gaultry answered, softly, trying to keep her rising panic out of her voice. "In the letter you were afraid for our brother and our marriage-sister's lives. Are you saying now that you've sided with those who have threatened your own family, Mervion?"

She flushed. It brought delightful color to her cheeks.

"Do you want to see Tielmark enslaved to the Empire again?" Gaultry pressed her.

It was the wrong question. The queries about Gilles and Anisia had almost reached her, but Tielmark's fate—Mervion had been taught to answer confidently every question about Tielmark's fate. "You're wrong to see this as Bissanty against Tielmark, Gaultry. If you could see the Prince—you'd know his bride would have to be very special to bring the line back to power."

"Bring the line back to power? What do you mean? All the Prince needs to rule Tielmark is the blessing of the Great Twins."

"You'll meet with the Chancellor in the tower and he'll convince you. Or Issachar will. Be nice and he'll take you up on his eagle."

"I don't think so." Gaultry shuddered. "Once was enough for me." How did Mervion imagine that her leg had come to be mauled?

"You're on the traitors' side, Gaultry." Mervion had her hand now. She spoke earnestly, intensely, patting her sister's leg as she spoke. "That's a terrible thing. You owe your allegiance to the Prince. Both of us do."

"My allegiance is to my Prince," Gaultry said, her temper fraying. "Not to the Chancellor who has twisted your goodness."

"Gaultry!"

"Did they tell you about the prophecies? Did they tell you we were born with Glamour-power, a power not seen in Tielmark since Clarin's day?"

"Gaultry, you're frantic for no reason. How can you talk of Glamour? The Age of Glamour is gone, Gaultry. It's gone. It went by with the Age of Heroes."

"Did it?" Gaultry took one of Mervion's lovely smooth hands between her rough tanned ones. "Mervion, listen to the power in me. It's the twin of your own. Mervion, listen to me." For a long, seemingly frozen moment, Gaultry strove to touch her sister's soul, to show her everything Clarin had opened, the great barrier that had been burned open, the raw power that now coursed free in her body, free for Gaultry to use to power her spells, her castings. For two heartbeats, as Mervion left her hand in Gaultry's, she almost seemed to listen. For two heartbeats, the sisters shared a warmth of communion, a familiar presence, the sweetness of shared magic. Then Mervion pulled her hand away. Her face was grave and stern.

"You have always been harder than me, Gaultry. You followed the Huntress Elianté while I followed Emiera the Lady-Queen. But playing among beasts in the wild of the woods has given you more strength than wisdom."

Gaultry reached for her sister, stricken, but she pulled away.

"Sleep, Gaultry. I'll come and see you tomorrow. After you've been to the tower, and have come to see what's right." Mervion smoothed her dress, made a sharp sketch of the goddess twins' spiral with her hand, and walked briskly to the door.

Gaultry lurched to follow her, reaching the door just as it clicked shut, and a key turned in the lock. "Mervion!" There was no answer.

Too tired and too distraught to return to the bed, the young huntress sank down by the door.

If her night with Issachar Dan had not already wrung the last tears from her, she would have cried. Mervion had always protected her, always backed her in a fight. They were twins: they had shared spells, love, and Gaultry had long depended on her sister to help her make the right choices—counsel better fitted to her than even the wisdom Tamsanne could offer. Even though Gaultry had been warned that her sister might buckle beneath the Chancellor's power, she had not fully understood that her sister would be actively set against her. Despite the warnings, the young huntress had yearned for their reunion, trusting that once together, they could share the burden of choice-making.

It seemed stupid now that she'd not expected it. When Melaudiere had described her fruitless attempt to speak to the Prince, and warned Gaultry that Mervion too might fall sway to the Chancellor's castings, Gaultry should have understood the implications.

Her last protector, her closest advisor, had been turned against her. In the gilded cage of the lavish bedchamber, Gaultry kneeled by the door, feeling utterly foresaken.

At least, she decided grimly, she knew who her enemies were. Issachar Dan. The Chancellor. The men whose names Mervion spoke with such fondness—and even a shadow of love, however coerced. Gaultry ran her hand down her injured leg, and winced. They were going to try to coerce her too.

Her thoughts turned to the Duchess of Melaudiere, standing and staring into her font in her palace of water and light. Gabrielle Lourdes had made no effort to conceal the fact that she'd dedicated her life to a more ambitious end than Mervion's rescue, but the help she'd offered the young huntress had been genuine. She was an old fox, bound by a fifty-year-old pledge to serve her Prince. She'd defied a High Priestess's counsel to send Gaultry to Clarin's barrow.

Clarin himself! Gaultry could still feel the raw newness of the depth he'd opened in her chest, a depth from which—once she'd recovered her strength — she could call vivid magics. She thought of her wild run with the two horses: imagine controlling the power raised by such a spell; imagine having the power not to be immolated by it! Clarin's potent, noble face had been like a beacon of truth appearing before her — a beacon above a skeletal body hidden beneath princely robes. He had not been able to tell her whether defying the gods had been worth the risks, and his disappointment in his heirs had been most keen. Yet he had told her that for Tielmark's sake, he should have asked the gods for more.

It was easy to offer one's land one's life, she thought. Melaudiere's young men had shown no hesitation. How many of them had already given their lives, making a heroic but fruitless crossing of the Bissanty Fingerland. Was that what the goddesses wanted? She shook her head, sure that it couldn't be so. The Great Twins had asked Clarin's line to seal and seal again their country's pledge with a marriage, not with a sacrifice of blood.

She was on the cusp of sleep, trying to settle her thoughts. The door was cold against her cheek.

A hand on her shoulder shook her awake. She was on the floor; stiff and chilled. Above her, a hard-faced woman stared down. She was an exquisite beauty, with pure Bissanty looks: raven black hair, pale skin, and dark eyes. Her dress was thick silk, the color of dark wine. A look of open displeasure marred the fineness of her face.

"Get up," she said, her frown deepening. "I've come to heal you." She stood and watched, but would not help, as Gaultry dragged herself across to the bed.

"Bissanty-blood, eh?" Gaultry couldn't bring herself to be pleasant. "Perhaps you'd better leave my leg alone."

"I'm going to heal you," the woman gritted. Despite her obvious anger, her hands were calm and smooth as she pinned up her sleeves. "Chancellor Heiratikus has instructed healing, so you will be healed."

"You're a priestess?"

"As Llara is my mother."

"She isn't mine," Gaultry said.

They glared at each other, like angry cats.

"Go ahead," Gaultry finally told the woman. "As Llara is your mother."

The healer gave her a resentful look. "Stretch your leg out, then. Don't lock your knee."

She put her pretty white hands against Gaultry's leg. Her eyes stared down into Gaultry's. Her dark irises sheeted to a lighter blue, sapphire blue, as Llara's magic flooded her. Behind the woman's eyes, Gaultry felt a great emptiness opening, as though the woman's eyes were windows to a distant sky, a distant sky where white birds were flying, thunderbolts under their wings, chilled by magic, vast creative magic.

The skin of her thigh beneath the healer's fingers went cold, then numb. There was no pain. The sun-priest's healing had hurt— hurt almost more than her wounding. The sun-priest had been so noisy as he worked, so angry, so full of passion for his god. This woman was cold as ice, and just as still.

The sense of cold—and with it the dull pain of her wound— was suddenly gone. The woman closed her eyes. When she opened them again, the pure sapphire blue was gone, and the resentment had returned.

"There," she said, sketching the Thunderbringer's bolt with one hand. "That's done." She snapped her fingers. A serving girl, who had been waiting unobtrusively in the doorway with a bowl of warm water, brought it over. The healer washed her hands, elegant and fastidious, taking a long time with the soap. Gaultry didn't miss the implied insult. It made her angry, probably angrier than the gesture deserved, but she had been so helpless against Issachar and the Chancellor the night before, so powerless when her sister had left her, that the chance to get her own back was a little too strong.

"Hold hard a moment," she said. "I want to ask you a question."

The healer shot her a nasty look, dried her hands on the clean cloth the girl had given her, and tried to turn away.

"I said I had a question." Gaultry grasped the woman's wrist, and twisted the towel out of her hand. "Given that you're a guest here in the Great Twins' country, you're going to answer it."

"Let go." There was no fright in the woman, only coldness.

"It seems to me," Gaultry said, "that there is hardly consensus in Bissanty as to whether you want to own our fair country. Yet you all worship Great Llara. How can that be? Do you think maybe even Great Llara doesn't know if she wants us?"

"I won't answer your questions." The woman made a gathering gesture with her free hand.

"And I," Gaultry said, "I don't want Llara here in Tielmark, yet something tells me—"

The serving girl backed away, clearly terrified. The two women were openly struggling now, the healer trying to free her wrist, Gaultry trying to catch her other hand, both of them gathering magic to call spells, trying to force the other to give in.

"Something tells me that Llara can't hate me, for I have climbed Llara's Ladder, and Llara herself has marked me!" Gaultry pressed the palm that she'd caught on the sharp spur of Llara's Ladder to the woman's throat. A sharp tang of magic burst between them, a blaze of blue light. Gaultry, in her surprise, lost her hold on the woman's throat. The healer fell back, panting, her cool air of disdain broken.

"The goddess knows her own mind," the woman said, hate lighting her eyes. "Answer your own questions." She was out of the door and into the corridor.

Gaultry, panting, sank back on the bed, staring into the palm that had touched the woman. There was nothing on to see. But the woman had felt something, something had been there.

The girl with the water was sidling towards the door.

"Don't go—" Gaultry told her, waving the towel she'd grabbed from the healer. "I want a wash too." The girl cast a doubtful look out into the hallway, as though fearing rebuke. Then she shrugged thin shoulders and brought the basin back over to the bed.

"You need a wash more than that one." Her voice was little more than a shy whisper, but beneath her shyness Gaultry sensed something other than fear.

"Huntress help me, you're right. I do."

The girl watched solemnly as Gaultry scrubbed at the crusted spatters of blood that were all that remained of the wound on her leg.

"Do you think you could get me some fresh things?" Gaultry

asked, eyeing with distaste the clothes she'd worn almost constantly since leaving Melaudiere's. "I'm not putting those things back on for any price." That brought a ghost of a smile to the serving girl's face. She was a small, thin girl, with a tidy manner. Gaultry guessed she must agree that the filthy rags were too revolting for words. She'd probably thought Gaultry was too revolting for words, at least until she had washed. "Go on," Gaultry said. "See if you can get me some clean things. If you can't, it's not your fault." The girl bobbed her head, and agreed to ask the warder if she could fetch a clean dress.

She reappeared some time later with a simple gray smock, just as two more officially despatched housemaids arrived with what they must have thought would be appropriate attire: an elaborately cut gown in rose-pink silk with a cascade of lace down its front. Gaultry stared at it, not sure if this was someone's crude idea of a joke. Looking into the young huntress's face, the shy girl broke into a nervous giggle. The other two, who hadn't seen Gaultry before she'd washed, didn't seem to understand that anything was so funny.

"Lady, if you could see your face!" the girl gasped.

Gaultry scowled. "Am I supposed to wear the pink thing, then?"

"I couldn't say, Lady." The girl choked back her laughter, seeing that Gaultry didn't think it was so funny.

"Someone has a twisted sense of humor. I'm going for an interrogation, not a garden party." Her shyness broken, the girl started giggling openly, an infectious laughter that set Gaultry smiling—albeit grimly—with her. Liking the girl's humor, Gaultry shot her a closer look.

She was older than her slight appearance suggested, and perhaps not so simple.

"I'm wearing the plain dress," Gaultry told the late arriving housemaids. "I'm not going to argue about it, either." They looked disapproving, but when they saw that she meant what she had said, they acquiesced.

"You might as well help the lady dress, Lily, if she doesn't mind your service."

"Lily?" Gaultry asked. "Is that your name then?"

"Lily Rowes."

"Lily Rose?" Gaultry said, mishearing her. "Your mother must have liked flowers."

The girl—no, she was more than a girl, Gaultry thought, she had a woman's sense in the dress she had brought her—the young woman looked down shyly and did not answer.

She let Lily help her with the plain dress, relieved at her narrow escape from the rose-pink silk.

"Do you know when the Chancellor is sending men for me?"

"I don't, Lady," Lily said softly. "Soon, I think."

"They're taking me to the Keyhole Chamber," Gaultry said, shivering. Two woman had been driven to madness there before her, and Mervion had narrowly escaped being the third—if her strange manners now weren't to be counted madness.

Gaultry looked over at the young woman where she fussed with the ruffles of the fancy dress, tidying it away for another victim. She had a pretty, gamine face, and her small body was graceful and lively, but her expression was closed, even secretive. Gaultry couldn't guess her thoughts.

"You wouldn't know a man named Martin Stalker, would you?"

"Countess Montgarret's husband?" Lily dimpled, then frowned, as if memory had intervened. "He was nice. He was popular at court, until the recent trouble. He's on the Chancellor's list now."

"List?"

"Enemies. Enemies of Tielmark."

"It's the Chancellor who's Tielmark's enemy."

Lily shrugged, something a little wistful in her. "Your sister wasn't keen about helping with the Prince's wedding either, until the Chancellor explained things."

"Mervion's only helping because the Chancellor has twisted her," Gaultry spat.

The young serving woman gave Gaultry an odd look. What would you have me say? her gentle eyes seemed to ask.

"Don't you know anything about Tielmark's history?" Gaultry demanded, not liking the woman's look of rebuke. "The Prince is supposed to marry a common girl, not a creature of high witchery as the Chancellor has planned for him." Not, Gaultry admitted to herself, that she had been fully aware of the importance of this before the Duchess had opened the matter to her.

"I know Tielmaran history."

Gaultry could see that she had hurt her. Lily's chin was trembling.

"The Chancellor promised the Prince and the court that the Prince's bride would be of common blood," Lily said.

"He did?" Gaultry couldn't keep the surprise from her voice.

"Benet wants to marry a girl of common blood."

"He does?"

"He does." The girl looked away. "Benet is very nice. He sees things that no one else does. It's just too bad everyone has decided that he has no head for matters of state." She smoothed her hand lovingly over the lace on the front of the detested pink dress. "He can be silly. He brought this style in. He likes seeing girls wearing pink."

Gaultry stared at the dress, newly dismayed. If Benet could express fondness for girls in pink as the power of the gods that supported his nation was draining from him, perhaps it should not come as a surprise that the Great Twins should turn their faces from him. She noted with a bitter eye that Lily's own bodice was laced with tulip-pink ribbons. Was she trying to attract the eye of the Prince? She spoke of him more familiarly than Gaultry would have thought was proper from a house-girl to her Prince.

"Well, Lily, I'll tell you this." Gaultry gave the slight woman a stern look, and was embarrassed when Lily drew back, intimidated. "If I return from my visit to the Chancellor's rooms touting the appropriateness of my sister and I sacrificing our Glamour-souls to form a common-blood bride for Prince Pink-Pretties, you can be sure it won't have been a voluntary conversion."

"Please. I don't know what you're saying."

"You don't? Three hundred years ago a great Prince fought with all his soul to create this country. He forfeited two souls to the gods to secure Tielmark's freedom. Mervion and I," her voice cracked as she pronounced Mervion's name, "Mervion and I are not going to give up another two souls just so Tielmark can fall back under Bissanty rule—"

"A fine defiance." Issachar's purr cut across her tirade. "I'll be more impressed when I see you sustain it before Heiratikus. Or were you merely rehearsing your speech for the benefit of this young wench? A valuable convert to your cause, no doubt." Gaultry whirled, and there he was, framed in the door. Lily scrambled to her feet, clutching the fancy dress, a frightened look crossing her face. She bobbed a curtsy to Issachar. "Go on then," he dismissed her. She slipped out of the room without a backwards glance.

"A valuable convert?" Gaultry said. "I don't see why she shouldn't be. She'd be a better bride for our Prince than anything Mervion and I could come up with. And probably more to his taste, with her pink ribbons." She wasn't hanging helpless from his eagle's talons now. She could fight his supercilious condescension.

The dark lord's mouth set in a cruel line. "This mockery has no purpose. Use it against Heiratikus if you must, but don't attempt it with me, or your punishment will be swift. Your ancient Prince is not here to protect you, whatever he might have promised you."

She closed her mouth. There was no point in inviting violence from a man who would sooner clout her in the face than listen to her talk.

chapter 19

P assing her through the tower" started with the ascent of more stairs than Gaultry had any enthusiasm to try on her
recently healed leg. Issachar walked behind her, a menacing presence at her back, as they went up and up, passing old-looking doors,
until at last the stairs opened out into a spacious twelve-sided
chapel. The ceiling was a shallow dome, with an oculus window at
its center, an open eye to the gods. The walls of the room were dedicated to the twelve gods, one god for each wall, their symbols decorating an elaborate band near the ceiling. Directly beneath the
oculus there was an austere stone altar with a shiny metal rim.
Scorch marks crisscrossed the altar's surface within the circle of
metal. Two sturdy metal rings curved up from the altar's surface, just
where leg shackles might be conveniently clipped. Something about
the look of the metalwork suggested that it was a recent modifica-
tion.

There was an arched doorway in the corner where Elianté and
Emiera's walls came together, and a darkened room beyond. The
Chancellor entered through this door as they mounted the last of
the steps and came into the chapel. He had a controlled and self-
consciously noble expression on his face, an expression that befitted

the High Chancellor of all Tielmark, but his eyes were agleam with a suppressed frenzy of eagerness for the coming spell.

"Well, Gaultry Blas. You're looking fresher for a few hours' sleep." Heiratikus was robed in flowing sky-blue silk, silver lightning bolts patterning the back and shoulders.

"You're looking worse," Gaultry said. "I don't know how you could have become Tielmark's Chancellor."

"*Twice Fair,*" he said, tasting the magic of the words in his mouth, laughing as she shied back. "If only you knew the troubles we've faced to bring you here. You're just like your sister. She had the very same words for me. Once. And worse. Now you'll bend — or perhaps break — just as she did."

"I'm Mervion's twin, not her double," Gaultry told him, trying to be brave. "Your spells have no power to hold me."

"We shall see." The Chancellor turned to Issachar. "Set her on the altar, Lord Dan, and we'll fix her to us."

Issachar pounced, steel shackles ready, shackles formed of metal shot through with the now-familiar eldritch fire. He was desperately strong. There was nothing she could do to prevent him from securing her wrists in front of her. A moment later she was standing, shaking, her feet locked to the rings on the altar. As the dark lord fastened the last chain, Heiratikus came to stand in front of her, a rough-forged iron coronet clasped in his hands. "Llara crown her with new wisdom," he intoned, and handed it up to Issachar, who clapped it onto her head without further ceremony. She tried to shake it off, only to discover that she was wasting her strength. The coronet's rim had a spell on it. Resigning herself to the impossibility of shaking it off without a counterspell to aid her, she stood angrily before them, frustration and rage written plain on her face.

"Open your mouth." Heiratikus's manner had altered for the worse now that she was safely shackled to the altar. He held a dried, blood-colored wafer in his hand. It looked foul.

"Half-blood bastard." She spit in his face. There was no way on this earth that she would allow them to feed it to her. Heiratikus wiped her spittle away with a sleeve, his movement deliberate, and artificially calm.

"Lord Dan?"

Issachar moved forward. This time Gaultry had a spell ready, and it was the dark lord's turn to be caught off guard. She hit him in the face with a white bolt of fire. It seared his thick black brows, and he threw up a gauntleted hand in an angry gesture. Heiratikus gave the dark lord an anxious look, startled.

Shaking his head to dispel the shock, Issachar grabbed for her. The struggle that ensued cut her bolt-spell short. Issachar caught her by the throat and there was a nasty moment when she thought he'd crushed her windpipe. She raked at his hands, trying to free herself, but in a matter of seconds he had pinned her head under his arm. Blocking her nose so she had to open her mouth, he forced the wafer past her teeth as she sputtered and spat and tried to shut her mouth against it. Dry crumbs seared her throat. Closing her eyes, she drew all the power and magic she could find it in herself to muster away from her attack on Issachar, and tried to concentrate it on the magic poison that was so swiftly spreading in her throat and stomach. She wouldn't let it take her — gods she wouldn't let it take her. The roil in her stomach grew. She coughed, her throat heaving at the intrusion of unfamiliar magic in her gut.

"Llara's blood," Heiratikus said with satisfaction, watching the color drop from her face as she struggled to bring the crumbled wafer back up. "Our Prince's bride will be a creature of marvels."

The light of the sky over her head seemed to reach down to her. Her roughly wrought coronet was a focus for some great airborne power. Her body seemed to expand, to open, to bloat with the power, an unfamiliar channel opening in her, veined with purple and black. Death's colors. Her vision sheeted with silver mist. She had barely enough consciousness left to perceive Heiratikus standing in front of her, a silver ewer in one hand, an unformed lump of metal slag in the other. Issachar was but a step behind him, his sharp brows, though thinned and scorched by her magic bolt, drawn together in a black line, his eyes intent and curious as blast after blast of power funneled into her, wrenching her concentration into scattered threads, unmaking her ability to concentrate, to defend herself.

In a flickering moment of lucidity she saw that her hands, now in

front of her, were pressed together, cupped, her palms forming a little bowl. Cold clammy sweat beaded out from her every pore, a wet-
ness was running down her face. Heiratikus held up his vessel. Her
hands dipped in response, some force in her readying to channel
into the silver ewer.

"Not yet, fool." Issachar's voice was hard as iron. "Don't warn
her."

There were two thunderstorms charging through her body. One
was her own, leaping from the deep place in her chest to engage the
other, an alien torrent of a whirlwind, awesomely great. Both forces
spasmed her arms, battling for supremacy. Her hands were pressed
together so hard, so bruisingly, it felt as if the bones of her wrists
would snap against their own reciprocal force.

There was a searing sensation. Her hands pooled with dark, almost purple liquid. She peered woozily down, trying to see what was
happening. The little bowl made by her palms was already full to
brimming.

The spider-hands held up the ewer, their master eager—her
palms involuntarily dipped. Her gaze dropped beyond the ewer,
focusing on the lump of metal he held clasped in his other hand.
Since the starting of the spell, it had changed. It was a crudely
shaped figurine now, the tiny face an unfeatured blank, except for
the mouth. The mouth was shaped like a spout.

The sight of the blank figurine brought renewed purpose to her
struggles.

Her hands tilted slightly upwards. Whatever the whirlwind was
that had filled her palms with blood, it didn't like her resistance. But
it was a spirit force, akin to something she might take from an animal, and she was concentrating on it, willing control as she'd never
willed anything in her life. She was being torn to pieces: her heart
pumped in her chest hard enough to burst, blood roared in her ears,
the bones of her wrists threatened to crack under the strain of the
cupping-spell. She gathered her will to push harder. Yet what was
this pain, compared to what she'd suffered hanging from Issachar's
eagle, to dueling with the wild boar, to experiencing two horses'
death throes in her body?

Something seemed to break loose, and there was a faint retreat. Gods! She was winning—

Lower your hands, Gaultry. Lower your hands. She had shut her eyes when she'd begun her effort. Now she snapped them open. The mist had marginally thinned, and she stared past Heiratikus's jerking figure to meet Issachar's snapping black eyes. The command spell was as strong as when he'd first cast it on her at Clarin's barrow—if not stronger. The sky whirlwind that wracked her body, sensing her attention had been distracted, redoubled its force. Her hands tilted relentlessly downwards. Issachar's cruel mouth curved into his familiar bleak smile. He liked to see opponents twist in the agony of defeat. Now she couldn't prevent the downward motion of her hands, the first drop of purple brimming free to spatter in Heiratikus's ewer, the second—

Before another drop could fall, she dipped her head to her hands and opened her lips. The first mouthful was unspeakably foul, worse than bile, but she drank it nevertheless. Heiratikus squealed with rage. She gulped down another swallow, and then another. Gods, she wasn't going to stand there like a passive fountain sculpture, watching the life force drain from her!

They'd done it to Mervion. This ritual had to be what they'd done to Mervion. A fit of trembling wracked her body—the sky whirlwind taking its revenge on her disobedience as she sucked the last of the purple blood from her fingers. The taste of it stung in her mouth, hot and tangy, but she felt deadly cool, and angry, thinking of deep purple blood dropped into a silver ewer and then fed to a faceless statuette. Her sister's blood. Her sister's will. Drained away like unholy wine.

The sky whirlwind—it was unlike any animal she had ever taken in her body. She could sense no spectral image of its shape or size. But it was a spirit to be excised like any other. She moved deep inside of herself, trying to find a thread. If she could catch one thread of it, she could unravel the rest and exorcise it from her body. Directionless at first, her search gained momentum as she went on. The whirlwind's color deepened, intensified, almost vivid enough to grasp. On her palm, just under the place where Llara had marked her, she finally found the thread. It was easy then. She blocked it out of her fingers, her hand, her wrist, her arm, laughing with the craziness of her triumph. She didn't care whether it had a shape or not, it was not going to stay in her body! With methodical anger, she forced the whirlwind into retreat, even as it raged and tried to retake her. The rage did it no good. Her rage was greater.

Suddenly Gaultry was free, she'd driven it up into the wrought coronet that encircled her brows. "Take back your own, Llara!" she cried, and gave her head a fierce shake.

There was a crash of thunder. The coronet tumbled from her head. In front of her, Heiratikus stood with the ewer in one hand, a featureless lump of metal in the other. His face was ashen.

The dampness of blood mingled with sweat on her chin. Panting, she wiped her face with a hand, scarce believing the evidence of her senses that she was free.

A long silence grew in the tower room. Issachar Dan was the first to break it.

"You really should have listened to me, Excellency. The girl didn't need rest, she needed breaking. Any test of magic that fails against her now can only serve to heighten her power."

"She can't have resisted!" The Chancellor's voice was an angry squeal. "Too much is riding on her compliance!"

"Too much, indeed." Issachar stared up at Gaultry where she stood on the altar, his eyes black and intense. "But again, what is compliance? Broken spirit, or broken resolution?"

"What do you mean?" The Chancellor glared, his eyes wild, all pretense of being a rational courtier dissolved into crazy rage. "We need to break her! The other can't form the bridal creature on her own."

For all her triumph, when she looked at Issachar, Gaultry felt a chill raise the hairs at the back of her neck. His eyes seemed to strip at her resolution, her posture of courage, to reach for the truth at her soul. This wasn't a spell, it was the power of his warrior's judgment racing to outguess her.

He let loose a short laugh, the same she'd heard above shrieks, screams, and thunder at the moment his eagle had seized her in its merciless claws.

"We have her sister. So long as we have her sister, we have this one's spirit too, don't we? Gaultry?" He spoke her name, so softly, so surely, the young huntress quivered.

"Don't be so sure," she grated, still trying to fight him. But she'd hesitated before answering, the crucial moment had come and gone. Even Heiratikus could see that she'd flinched, could see the truth of his dark warrior's statement. The Chancellor's laugh raked her ears. He clapped his hands together, triumphant.

"Such an easy bait, and I couldn't see it! Issachar—Lord Dan— you are a marvel! We shall have our Princess of common blood!"

"Along with the benefit of a Glamour-witch strengthened by fire and fight. A woman of amazing force and fortitude. As well as sentimental foolishness." Issachar's voice was silky soft. He touched her foot where it was clamped onto the altar, and looked up along her body to her bowed face.

"One more battle and I'll have strength beyond your imagining," she gritted. "I'll make you regret your threats."

"There won't be time for another battle." The dark lord smirked, his thumb on the catch of the clip that held her ankle. "After Prince's Night the Glamour will be gone from you—from you and Mervion both. And Tielmark will have a new Princess. Blood of the common blood."

"I'll see myself dead first!"

"That's not the question, sweet one. Would you see your sister dead first?"

"Of course she won't, Issachar, of course she won't!" Heiratikus was crowing. Gaultry, glaring, had no rebuttal to give him.

"Keep her under heavy guard until the time," Issachar said, warningly.

"So long as we have the other, what's the risk?" Heiratikus gloated, a happy wriggle running up through his tall scarecrow frame. Then he met Issachar's eye and came back a little to himself. "Of course, Lord Dan," he said haughtily. "Are you suggesting I would do otherwise?"

She stood rigidly above them, blood smeared on her face and hands, eyes closed tightly, the taste of defeat sharing the stain of blood in her mouth. She was a fool not to have known from the beginning that her efforts could only end in a complete breakdown of resolution once Mervion's life was threatened. So much for her vaunted pride and independence.

chapter 20

Heiratikus agreed with Issachar that the safest place for her was a cell beneath the newer part of the Prince's castle. Issachar and the guards escorted her down, the dark lord coming into her cell to lock his eldritch-fire shackles to a metal ring in the cell's wall. The large dungeon chamber was split into smaller cells by metal grates. Her cell was opposite a guard post, lit by two guttering torches.

"Haven't you done enough already?" she asked Issachar wearily, as he bound another pair of locking-spells on the cell's barred door.

There was a pause as the dark warrior stared back at her through the bars. "No," he said. "No I haven't." His eyes were evil and cold. "There's no reason you should have been able to resist Llara's Wind of Possession. Lord Heiratikus worked it easily enough against your sister."

"Maybe the Thunderbringer likes me."

He sneered, and didn't deign to answer.

"When Mervion is safe, I'll come after you."

He shrugged, dismissive. "Without Glamour to power you, I'd crush you like an insect. After you cast the spell that makes the bride, Heiratikus may be fool enough to let you and your sister free—but you won't have the strength between you for more than a good cry at the wedding."

"Don't underestimate us, Lord Dan. Our Glamour will be gone, but we'll still have the strength of the Twin Goddesses."

"A girl's foolish trifle against the Thunderbringer."

His contempt fueled her anger afresh. Anything not to stand, beaten, before him!

"I'll believe you mean that when you say it again before Elianté and Emiera, when they make themselves incarnate to sanctify the wedding—it's the Prince of Tielmark's divine right, stronger than any mere symbol."

"Gods come to earth? Do you think to alarm me?" Issachar asked. "We'll see magic on Princes' Night, not gods." His voice was silky, and he looked deep into her eyes, his mouth going hard and cruel. "Rest assured, if there is any fight in you after Prince's Night, I will relish the chance to crush you once again."

She scowled. "Don't sleep easily in the anticipation of it."

He turned on his heel and left. Gloom settled over the ill-lit chamber. She gave her chains an experimental rattle and sat down on the bench that was to serve her as a bed.

"You must have done something to annoy him, Gaultry. It's not often Issachar Dan slips up and admits he's capable of feeling pleasure."

Gaultry whirled angrily, tired of being mocked. The cells on either side of her were empty, but a figure three cells down from her waved a hand and grinned, parched lips revealing a newly chipped tooth that did little to detract from its owner's jaunty good looks.

"Mariette!"

Martin's sister made a sweeping bow. "And not even in chains."

"What have they done to you?" Besides the chipped tooth, Mariette's clothes were torn and ragged. Despite her still playful manners, she was in rough shape.

"I made the mistake of trying to talk to your sister, assuming that her sympathies had gone unchanged since the time we saw her in grandmother's mirror." Mariette rubbed a scabbed-over scrape on her cheek with torn fingers and gave a rueful grin. "She'd somewhat changed her attitude."

"I know. They let me talk to her before they took me up to the tower to try to work the same change on me."

"Which, according to what Issachar just said, you quite impressively resisted." Mariette gave her a curious look. "Not wanting to insult your skills, Gaultry, but how did you get out of it?"

"I don't know," she said. "Maybe because my Glamour has been opened. We made it to Clarin's barrow. Maybe that's why." She looked thoughtfully down at her palms, tracing the cold spot on her skin where Llara's Ladder had touched her. Llara's Wind of Possession. That was the name of the whirlwind she had resisted. "Or maybe it's because I prayed to the gods loudly enough that they decided to listen. I don't know." Or maybe, she thought, Llara Thunderbringer is tired of her empire of cowards. She kept this last thought to herself.

Mariette laughed. It was a good sound to hear, brightening the close dark of the dank cellar. "So that's done it for their plotting. They won't be able to make you go along with them now."

Gaultry didn't answer. Mariette looked at her, alarmed. Gaultry turned away, her cheeks flushed guiltily bright.

"If they can't possess you," Mariette demanded, "then how are they going to cast a spell that needs both you and Mervion to work it?"

Gaultry's mouth felt nastily dry. "They don't need to possess us both, if we both agree to do the casting."

The jaunty air dropped from Mariette's posture. Gaultry got a sudden ugly sense of what it would be to face her in battle. Not unlike her brother.

"What do you mean?"

"I'm sorry, Mariette. But come Prince's Night, there's going to be a fresh blood casting, and Mervion and I both are going to be a part of it."

"Allegrios Rex! What have they offered you? Martin said we could trust you. Why else have you risked your life these past weeks?"

"I know," Gaultry growled. "I've suffered unholy pain, fighting the Chancellor and all he stands for."

"Then why? You know the Bissanties are evil—"

"Don't push, Mariette." Gaultry cut her short. "I've been to Clarin's barrow—I've talked to Tielmark's greatest prince. I'm under no illusions as to how the Bissanties would treat this country once they held it. I'll give my life—or my power—to sustain the realm Clarin built."

"Then why—"

"Some things are not mine to give. You're asking me to sacrifice Mervion."

"If Mervion was in her own mind, don't you think she would agree—"

"It's not in me to make that choice for her. I can't lie and fool myself that it is." Gaultry's voice was hard and angry. "Mariette, unless you believe that you could take a dagger in your hand and thrust it through your brother's chest in the name of supporting a greater good, don't tell me that's what I should do with Mervion."

"Gaultry—"

"Please, Mariette. I won't lie and pretend that when the moment came, I could force myself to make the sacrifice. It would be what you wanted to hear, but I'd be lying."

As the words left her mouth a guard came in to take up his post opposite her. Mariette gave her an angry look, obviously having more she wanted to say, but she didn't want to share it with the guard. A grim silence stretched between them.

Gaultry, whose cell was nearest the jailer's station, fixed him with an unpleasant glare, willing him to disappear so she could find out more about Heiratikus's decision to imprison the Duchess's granddaughter. She wondered if the Chancellor had declared open warfare against the Duchess, branding all her followers as enemies of the state. Was it a good sign that Martin's friend, the dark-skinned warrior Hassan, was not in the cell next to her? The bruises on her face suggested that the young woman hadn't been taken without a struggle.

The day passed slowly. Mariette shot her an occasional stormy look. Day slipped into evening, the difference marked only by a rotation of their warden. Mariette and herself were the only prisoners confined to the twelve cells that she could see from her own. A boy brought them a pail of dinner: bread and water. Now that Heiratikus had her secured, he apparently saw no need to try to bend her to his side with bribes or sweeteners. She wondered how they were treating Mervion. If Llara's Wind of Possession had taken her, she'd little doubt her body would have been sitting comfortably by a pleasant fire feasting itself on a lovingly cooked meal.

Another hour passed—maybe two. The guard opposite yawned, and settled for a nap. There was a rat in the cell next to Gaultry's. She wondered idly where it had come from.

"Come here then." She held out a crust. It came reluctantly, greedy but cautious, whiskers aquiver. She'd taken from a rat a couple of times in her life: they were cunning, and agile, but too small to use with any degree of comfort. "If only I could take your size instead of your strength," she told it. "Then I could get out of these shackles, as well as out of this cell." It wouldn't take the food from her hand. She had to drop the crumbs on the floor.

As the rat scampered away with the last crumb, she looked up. Mariette was gazing at her intently. Her sharp blue eyes, a young version of her grandmother's, were sternly disapproving. Gaultry's gaze flickered across to the guard. He was sitting at his post, his back slumped against the wall, the breath regular in his throat.

"Where's Hassan?" Gaultry whispered. The anger in Mariette's look melted to not entirely pleased surprise.

"Why do you want to know?" she replied, suspicious.

"Why would you think?"

"Well, if you've turned on us—"

"There's a wide range between turning traitor and protecting lives, as I would hazard to guess that your grandmother knows." Gaultry glanced at the guard, who was openly snoring. "I'm going to do what I can. But I'll need help. Will I have it?"

Mariette tipped her head in an infinitesimal nod. "But not from me." Her smile was back as she tapped on the bars of her cell. "I'm going to be shut in here for the duration, more's the pity."

"Would that I were so lucky," Gaultry told her.

"If you could just—"

"Don't ask for promises."

They lapsed into silence.

The night slipped away with sleep and rest. Gaultry was exhausted. Defeating the attempt on her spirit had deeply drained her. She thought of the silver ewer and the faceless statuette and shuddered. Somewhere in Heiratikus's possession there was a twin statuette, complete with Mervion's features. Likely there was one somewhere of the Prince as well.

It was an uncomfortable thought to fall asleep with.

chapter **21**

▼

It was Prince's Night. All day they'd heard the jubilant tolling of bells and the cracking of fireworks. Now joyous day
had given way to the quiet of evening, and it was finally Prince's
Night. An hour after dark, Issachar came down to the dungeon to
unlock her shackles. He had a formal contingent of guards with him:
ten men dressed in the Prince's royal blue and white livery. Issachar
himself was wearing neutral gray with gold piping. Only the blue
armband on his sword arm hinted at any allegiance to Tielmark's
throne.

"I was beginning to think you'd decided against using my services."

Issachar, concentrating on dissolving the spell on her cell's lock,
ignored her feeble sarcasm. Gaultry looked suspiciously at the flimsy
bundle of white he had brought with him. A dress?

"Your wedding dress." He dropped it in her lap. "Put it on."

Spun silk like silver ice.

Her wrists had swollen during their confinement. She tried to
chafe them back to life, without much luck.

She wasn't enthusiastic about dressing herself in front of eleven men, Issachar included. "Turn away," she said. The dark warrior looked at her, amused.

Turning her back, Gaultry stripped off the gray dress the little serving woman had brought her, two days back now, and slid the fresh white gown on over her head. Its clean white color emphasized her own grubbiness. Two and a half days locked in a rat-infested cell had not done much for her hygiene.

"Am I supposed to be playing priestess?" she asked Issachar, displeased.

"This is Heiratikus's orchestration, not mine." Issachar gestured for her to exit the cell in front of him. "Today marks the fruition of many years of his planning. He has hopes of being rewarded by the Emperor." He shrugged. "It may happen."

"He's half-Tielmark blood," Gaultry said. "Won't that make a difference to the reward they give him?"

Issachar's deep, impenetrable eyes and cruel mouth told her nothing. Nevertheless, she found it hard to believe that a proud warrior like Issachar would enjoy dancing to the tune called by a crowing maniac like Heiratikus. "You hate serving him, don't you?"

"The Empire and I are loyal to Llara." Issachar shunted her out of the cell with an abrupt hand. "However the Emperor chooses to reward Edan Heiratikus's services is not my concern."

Gaultry risked a sideways look at Mariette as they went out past her cell. It was a mistake.

"You can't do it, Gaultry!" The dark-haired woman was up at the front of her cell, her hands white-knuckled as she gripped the bars of her cell's door. "It won't be worth it! What guarantee do you have they'll keep their word? You can't trust them! Would you lose your country's freedom and your sister both?" She rattled her cell door fiercely, her eyes bright with emotion. "Once you've sent your power from you, what's to keep them from breaking their word?"

Gaultry's footsteps faltered. Issachar jogged her elbow to keep her moving. As she cast a last look back at Mariette, he bent his head and spoke low in her ear.

"If you don't keep walking, I'll have one of the men skewer her where she stands."

"You wouldn't!"

"Will you test my resolve?"

Gaultry kept walking.

Mariette's exhortations followed them up out into the prison court, dimming only as they moved away from her.

It was a relief to be out in the open air. Overhead the sky was a clear star-filled bowl, shot through with the last pale of twilight. Not a cloud in sight. She silently prayed that that augured ill for the Thunderbringer's minions.

Prince's Night, the night of the full moon, the eve of May, and all the summer celebrations.

The castle seemed eerily quiet, the air unnaturally hushed and calm. Issachar, with the guards packed close around them, led Gaultry along a narrow wall-walk towards the oldest part of the castle. Rounding a corner, her breath caught in her throat as her first comprehensive view of the Prince of Tielmark's palace seat opened before her. It was a grand collection of buildings: turret rising above turret; wall above wall; climbing gardens that added patches of color. Rich wafts of scent drifted up to them from hidden gardens beneath the wall. The tall tower in which Heiratikus had tried to spell her two days before was adjacent to the great hall they were now fast approaching. She thought of the workroom and the fouled altar in its highest chamber and shuddered.

Overhead the preternaturally large, milk-white disk of the full moon hung low on the sky's rim. The four evening stars sparkled in a girdle just beneath it. A quiver coursed down Gaultry's spine. Issachar hurried her along, seemingly oblivious to the beauty of the night all around them. All the noise and business of the realm had stopped, as if in worried expectation of the night's events.

They descended a little staircase in the wall and came to a stone portal set into the side of the great hall. Mervion was there, standing golden and lovely in the light let out through the open door. Gaultry's heart went into her throat; a surge of pain took her in the chest. Goddess save her! She couldn't sacrifice her sister.

Mervion wore the same white silk as Gaultry, but there the similarity ended. Where the huntress twin was drawn, nervous, and stank from her confinement, Mervion was composed, majestic, and coolly pristine. Gaultry had never seen her looking more beautiful. Her hair rippled past her waist in shining red-gold waves, her mouth curved in a sweet smile of welcome. Mervion was all that Gaultry wished to be, all that she almost was. There was nothing in her older sister's pose to show that some vital piece of her spirit was missing.

Then Heiratikus stepped out through the door to stand at Mervion's side, and the illusion that Mervion could possibly be free shattered. He cut a majestic figure—the Chancellor was certainly grandly dressed, in richly embroidered robes that sat well on his tall, narrow figure—but all Gaultry could see now in his face was his unpleasant gloating triumph that he'd won, that all his plans had succeeded. He had the smug confidence of a man who knew power was in his hands.

If she'd convinced herself that Mervion was free—even for a moment—the only person she'd fooled had been herself. Heiratikus held some part of Mervion—some part that he could crush if Gaultry didn't obey him. She drew herself up and narrowed her eyes. Mariette had been right in saying she couldn't trust the man. Not that that left Gaultry much room to bargain.

"Not quite a matching pair, are we?" Her voice came out harsher than she'd intended. The young huntress crossed to her sister's side. Mervion gave Heiratikus a worried look, taking in her sister's tangled hair and general dishevelment.

"Lord Chancellor—Excellency—you assured me Gaultry was comfortable."

"I've been fine, Mervion, it's not a problem." Gaultry took her sister's hand, and felt the coolness of Mervion's fingers against the sweat of her own palm. "I'm going along with the Chancellor's plans now."

Mervion's face lit up, the color flushing prettily in her cheeks. "The Prince will be grateful, Gaultry! To think of all the trouble you went to before, not knowing who to trust—but Issachar tells me it will serve in the end to rally the strength of the casting. So it was for the best, it was for the best—I'm so happy now that all is well."

"I'm not sure the deaths of good men were for the best," Gaultry muttered, not quite under her breath. Mervion, her attention distracted by the approach of a pair of page boys dressed in deep royal blue, seemed not to hear.

"They've brought the coronets! Gaultry, look at the coronets!"

Each page bore a pillow which cushioned a wrought-iron coronet—a matching pair, one for Mervion, one for her. The coronet she had worn in the tower; the coronet she'd seen Mervion wearing in the vision. Replicas of the first crown of Tielmark.

Gaultry shivered and looked at Heiratikus. An eager light burned in the man's dark eyes. He could almost taste the success of his whole life's plotting.

"What are you offering me as guarantee for Mervion's life?"

"Gaultry!" Mervion flinched and withdrew her hand. Gaultry, torn by the withdrawal, did her best not to show her reaction.

"I ask the question again. What will you give me to guarantee Mervion's life?"

"Gaultry, how can you ask such a thing? You promised—"

"I promised under duress." Gaultry met Heiratikus's eyes and held them. "Tonight is a magic constellation of god-driven events, the night a three-hundred-year-old pledge may be broken or renewed. If you were born to bring Tielmark's land back to the Empire, this is your night. The pieces you've plotted so long to join will never fit together after tomorrow's cock crows. Tonight marks your one chance to break the Great Twins' hold on this realm and return it to the Great Mother Llara's holdings."

Mervion would have interrupted her, but Gaultry waved her aside. "My sister is right—I have agreed to help you. But I'll need a guarantee of her safety first."

"Surely my word—"

"Is worth nothing." Gaultry cut the wretched man short. "Since you can't think of anything I'd value to offer me, I'll set my own price." She drew herself up as tall as possible, trying to look imposing, not guessing how her tall, lean figure, shadows and torchlight striking off the hard bone of her face, had a look of deathly determination to it.

"For me to cast the spell for you, you're going to have to give me the Prince's life," she said. "Whatever you've taken from Mervion, you've taken from the Prince of Tielmark as well. Well, I'm claiming his life as guarantee of my sister's safety."

"Impossible!" Heiratikus's voice was a squeal. Unfortunate for him that his voice went squeaky when he felt himself losing control.

"Not at all." Gaultry gained confidence as she spoke, her voice hardening. "If your purpose is to break the Twin Goddesses' hold on Tielmark, the spell Mervion and I will create will accomplish that goal. Llara will see the blood-pact broken, and she'll sweep into our land." Gaultry didn't want to imagine the storms that would wrack Tielmark as the once ousted Thunder-Goddess, the angry mother, took back her own. "If that's your goal, I'll help you and you'll gain it.

"But if you're hoping to get a puppet Prince on the throne as well as breaking the blood-pact, a Prince who will allow Bissanty troops to walk over our borders unopposed—well, there you'll have to think again."

Heiratikus's eyes glittered with hate. "I can't allow it. And you— Why, you won't know how to work the Prince to your favor. What good can his life be to you?"

She stared back at him. There was nothing more she wanted to say.

"Lord Dan—" Heiratikus turned to Issachar, his voice shrill. He hadn't expected opposition this late in the playing.

That was worth an interruption—Gaultry didn't want Issachar in on the bargaining if she could avoid it. "What can Lord Dan say here? He'll see his goddess Llara in power in Tielmark—why should he support a coward's ploy to pull the strings of puppets?"

Heiratikus, infuriated, swung on her. Gaultry did her best not to flinch. Issachar stood to one side. If anything, he seemed amused.

"She has you, Excellency," the dark warrior said. "You don't have time to argue with her—the night draws on. Give her the Prince. Perform the ceremony. Serve Llara's power, and the rest will follow. With the goddess backing them, the Empire's power will prevail, puppet Prince or no."

Heiratikus almost choked on his own tongue. He grabbed at his dark officer's arm, as if to shake him. "The Emperor wants new lands, not a new battlefront!"

"You don't have faith that Llara will reward your efforts?" Issachar's voice went dangerously cold. Heiratikus dropped his hand.

"I have faith," Heiratikus said faintly.

"As to Gaultry Blas keeping the Prince," Issachar continued, turning his attention to the huntress and drawing his eyebrows together threateningly, "she hasn't asked that—*she's looking for a guarantee of her sister's safety, not to build her own power.*"

The command spell struck out like a lightning bolt. Elianté's arrows! It felt stronger than any spell he'd yet tried. As it flared and sought to envelop her mind, to blot away her thoughts, Gaultry seized instinctively at Mervion's hand, and pressed the spell towards her.

Mervion soaked it up like a sponge takes up water. Easily and without hesitation. Issachar's spells had made an impression on her, each new casting taking more easily than the next. Though the spell had been named for Gaultry—well, Mervion was her twin, very nearly her exact double. Gaultry wasn't surprised by her tactic's easy success.

The blissful smile that crossed Mervion's face as the spell hit her was something else again. Gaultry hadn't expected her sister to enjoy the possession by Issachar's spells.

"You'll just have to hope that command echoes my own view without the presumption of a spell, you hawk-faced Bissanty bastard." Fear for Mervion's mind lent her words an angry edge.

Somewhere within the hall, a trumpet sounded. Issachar shifted on his feet, impatient. "Take her offer, Heiratikus. Give her the Prince. Play your hand well and you'll have him back again soon enough."

"But the Emperor—"

"Why do you delay? Regain the realm for Llara and she will reward you past your wildest imaginings."

A ray of hope jumped in Gaultry's heart. If they were that concerned about giving her what they had of the Prince, Gaultry had to assume that whatever was wrong with Mervion could be set to rights as well. As the Bissanties bickered with each other, she looked woefully at her sister. For all Mervion's aura of gathered composure, it was becoming easier and easier for Gaultry to sense a distance in her—a distance which allowed the open threats passing between the Bissanties and Gaultry to go by her ears as meaningless sounds. Mervion seemed deaf to half the words that were being spoken.

Gaultry would do anything to have her sister whole again.

Behind the sisters, Heiratikus and Issachar had come to an agreement.

"The Prince's life for your cooperation, then," Heiratikus finally agreed. "Your sister's life for your opposition." Gaultry nodded, noting that the Chancellor didn't ask her for her word on the matter or offer his own.

The Chancellor brought a heavy handful of black velvet from under his robes. "Take it, then." A single object rolled inside the cloth, a figurine of silver no longer than one of Gaultry's fingers. If it had once been a match in size with the statuette in the Tower workshop, it was now strangely shrunken. Gaultry, trying to get a better look at it, brushed it lightly with her hand. She almost dropped it and the cloth when she felt a painful jab of what she at first thought was heat.

Folding the cloth carefully so it insulated her fingers from the metal, she took a closer look. It was a likeness of a young man, handsome enough, but not particularly distinguished. The mouth was strange and wide, opened in a mournful "O" that disfigured the features. The heat she'd thought she felt—it was not heat. It was pain. The strange pain of a human creature, communicating itself straight through her skin.

The silver figurine was a living effigy, some fraction of a man's soul held in constant torment. Small wonder it burned to touch it.

Gaultry looked up and met Heiratikus's eyes. The man shifted nervously beneath something he sensed in her expression.

"You mistake the spell, Lady Blas. The recipient feels nothing, remembers nothing. There is no awareness of the entrapment when the spell is reversed."

She grimly wrapped the figurine in its cloth, not wanting to look at it any longer than she had to. "You'd better be right about that. Get me something so I can carry it."

One of the footmen brought a pouch. She stowed it and the figurine under her skirt. Mervion gave her a sorrowful look. She couldn't understand the trouble Gaultry was putting the Chancellor to, the delay she was causing.

The seriousness of her situation and concern for Mervion aside, Gaultry's heart beat like a drum in her chest at the success of her stratagem. Her bluff had succeeded. She literally held the freedom of Clarin's heir in her hand—the knowledge gave her a heady feeling. With a free Prince on the throne of Tielmark, perhaps, as Clarin had done three hundred years before, the country could unite to find the power to force a new pact among the gods. The Princess she and Mervion would create with the blood-spell would be a creature of pure Glamour-magic. Surely such a Princess's power would enable Tielmark some strength to bargain with the gods, even if Clarin's pledge was broken?

"Are you ready, Lady Blas?" Heiratikus brought Gaultry back to herself.

"I'm ready."

The pages advanced and presented the sisters with the coronets. Mervion grasped hers in both hands, raising it ceremoniously over her head. "Lady Emiera bless me that I might perform this work of magic. I call for her strength." Gaultry swallowed nervously as her sister intoned the familiar formal invocation to the goddess Lady. Neither Mervion nor she possessed the spell for creating a blood-creature. That didn't mean they wouldn't be able to take the spell from Heiratikus's book—but it did mean they'd need the goddesses' help to call the spell.

She took the other coronet from its pillow, and held it high above her head. "Huntress Elianté bless me that I might perform this work of magic." The crown was heavy. Gaultry straightened it with one hand. "I call for her strength." Even if the call was to an ill end, the words of the goddess-calling were a familiar comfort amidst all the strangeness.

Heiratikus gave a satisfied smile, pleased to see events proceeding once more. "Join hands." Gaultry looked doubtfully at Mervion, who held out her hand, eager.

"We'll process in." Heiratikus was back in stride now, giving hasty instructions. "The altar and the lectern are in front of the throne. The spell is not complex. You've performed similar magic in

the past. With your combined strength, the spell will simply un-
fold." The Chancellor put his face close to Gaultry's. His eyes were
cold and hard as stones. "Don't forget, Lady Blas. This is a great oc-
casion. The highest lords of Tielmark are attending. Make any move
to disrupt the ceremony, and your sister won't last the moment. And
don't think that I won't give her a conscious taste of agony before I
kill her, should you disobey me."

His hand went to his breast, just where there might have been a
pocket beneath his robes. Gaultry tried not to let her eyes flicker to
follow the motion. Elianté's arrows! He was carrying the figurine
that held her sister's will with him. If Issachar hadn't been standing
by, she might have jumped on the rail-thin Chancellor then and
there, and fought him for possession. Heiratikus was tall, but he
didn't look strong, for all his sorcerous power. Her body trembled
involuntarily at the thought that Mervion's chance for freedom—
the only power Heiratikus held over her—could be so close. The
thoughts crowding her mind made it hard for her to follow the man's
instructions—until his last words.

"The priestesses who represent the Great Twins are standing by
to read the vows and sanctify the marriage."

Two priestesses to sanctify the marriage? Gaultry had thought
the goddesses themselves were supposed to make themselves incarnate to perform the ceremony. Her heart dropped to realize that the
promised visitation was mere hyperbole. Clarin's ghost had been
real enough. Why shouldn't the goddesses present themselves? Did
Heiratikus imagine that the promise of the goddesses to come and
witness the wedding was a myth, a mere story for children? The gods
appeared often enough in dreams and visions, they gave humankind
magic, they watched human toils and triumphs. Why should
Heiratikus imagine that they wouldn't make themselves incarnate,
to honor the terms of a pact they themselves had confirmed three
hundred years past?

Whatever the answer, it was not in her control. Gaultry looked
at Heiratikus and forced herself to smile. "Let's get this over with."
She took Mervion's hand. Her sister's eyes were bright as stars.

"You've had your power opened, Gaultry," Mervion whispered
as they stepped forward into the great hall, Heiratikus preceding

them, Issachar behind. "You'll have to lead the spell." She paused, a glint of memory flashing behind her eyes. "Just like you did the time we borrowed Aunt Tamsanne's spell book and made the mouse."

Just like Gaultry had done the time they borrowed their aunt's spell book and made the mouse. Back when Gaultry had thought that Tamsanne was her aunt, that the human soul could not be twisted to form a blood-creature, that life would always continue happy and content. As they came out into the full light of the hall, Gaultry's stomach was churning.

By the Huntress, by the Lady, by the great Prince Clarin who had broken them and the land of Tielmark from the Thunder-bringer's power—by all the powers of the Great Twelve Gods—what was she to do?

chapter 22

The great hall was a shock of light and noise. Every rafter was festooned with spring flowers, and the brilliance of thousands of candles brightened every corner. She'd never seen so many people gathered under a single roof. A wave of irritation swept over the young huntress. So much that had happened in the past days had been beyond the limited realm of her experience, quietly hunting in the borderland woods.

Now she held the self-will of the Prince of Tielmark, heir to Prince Clarin the Great, in a pouch tucked under the folds of her skirts. There was no reason a crowd of overdressed nobles should take her breath away.

All the same, that was exactly what they were doing. Disregarding the temperature that had built up in the hall, rich brocade and gold embroidery abounded. Half of those in attendance, men and women both, wore burnished armor that glinted in the light, dazzling to the eye. Mervion's hand in her own and her cool acceptance of the scene were a comfort—even knowing she wasn't in her proper state of mind. Mervion had always been the one to deal confidently with the crush on a market day back in the quiet village of Paddleways oh-so-faraway now on Tielmark's southern border.

The hall dated back to Clarin's time. The walls were rough-hewn stone, the beams and gilding of the lofty coffered ceiling stained with centuries of soot and age. Triumphal banners that dated back three centuries hung down from the ceiling. Heiratikus had brought them in through the west door. They came out on a secondary aisle to make their way to the main central aisle. The great aisle led down from the great southern door to the blank wall at the hall's back—blank except for a row of windows at the top. Outsized eagles glowered in every one of these windows, alert and fierce. Issachar's mount, Gyviere, was perched in the place of honor, the large center window. The great metal-feathered raptors were a dismaying show of Issachar's power.

At the end of the hall a double-tiered dais built of stone was set against the blank wall. The top tier was strewn with flowers. In front, on the lower tier, was a small altar and lectern. Sharing the lower platform, in front of the altar and lectern, was a huge stone throne, a mate to the great weathered chair that had stood on the hill of Clarin's barrow.

The rank of seats nearest the throne was packed to overflowing with Heiratikus's supporters. Gaultry recognized a few faces in that crowd. Coyal Torquay, the knight whom Martin had fought at the border of the Chancellor's and the Duchess's lands, stared down at her with calm blue eyes, familiar even without his helm. Out of battle, Torquay had a good look: his face open, honest, confident of a life well lived. For a moment, meeting the knight's gaze, Gaultry was tempted to scream out to him for aid. Then she recognized the man seated next to him in the same row, and the impulse died. It was Aquilles Beriot, Baron Blamire. The man who'd played her brother like a fish on a hook, and threatened her marriage-sister's life. Gaultry hoped Anisia was safe, now that Heiratikus had both twins in his grasp.

Heiratikus's scoundrels had seats raised well above the level of the floor so that they could get a good view of the dais. She scanned the crowd for the imposing figure of the Duke of Haute-Tielmark. The great booming bear of a lord should have been easy enough to spot—and if he'd reached Princeport for the ceremony, perhaps Martin and Arnolfo would have made it back with him. The Duke was nowhere to be seen, dashing another hope. No doubt Victor of Haute-Tielmark didn't have access to a magic eagle to speed his passage. Martin and Arnolfo wouldn't have had the time to arrive either. If the Duchess had sent help, it would have to be in some other form.

Below the nobles, standing behind a low wooden barrier, were the castle servants, mustered in their best finery. Amongst them were the Llara priestess who had attended Gaultry's wounds, her cold face still sneering and disdainful, and Lily Rose, the pretty serving woman who'd brought Gaultry the plain dress. Lily wore a serious look and a cluster of fresh pink ribbons, obviously her idea of doing herself up fine in honor of her Prince's marriage day. Gaultry wished the evening could have been so easy a celebration for herself and Mervion! The simple clothing of the servants contrasted with the richness that cloaked the nobles who were seated just above them. At first it seemed curious to have given the servants a place of honor so close to the Prince's throne. She guessed it had something to do with honoring the common blood of the land.

Then, just to Lily's left, she saw Hassan's dark face. A wild hope surged in her breast. She gave him a beseeching look; he frowned back at her, and moved his shoulders in an inconspicuous shrug, acknowledging that he had seen her. If only they could have exchanged words! Too quickly their entourage passed him and was climbing the steps up to the first platform.

Heiratikus took up a place by the throne. Her sworn sovereign, Benet, Prince of Tielmark, sat rigidly on the throne's edge, dressed in a cloth-of-gold dalmatic, the iron crown of Tielmark sunk low on his brow. He was a moderately good-looking young man with dark hair. Remembering Clarin's striking looks—even as an aged man—it was hard to believe that this soft boy was his heir.

The Prince stirred nervously as they approached, and inclined his head to the Chancellor. "Heiratikus! We've been waiting for you! Where have you been?"

"Great Twins and mortal twins together bring you your bride today," Heiratikus intoned. Benet's complete faith in his Chancellor was obvious: he quieted without hesitation at Heiratikus's bidding and assumed a more formal pose. Gaultry was tempted to take the figurine of the Prince out of her pocket, to take charge of Benet herself or even give him back his own will. Heiratikus had said she wouldn't know how to work the Prince to her favor. Was he right?

Mervion pulled on her hand and led her across to the lectern.

Resting on the lectern was an ancient book with vellum pages. It was open to a page illuminated with colored pictures of small animals; the text hand-lettered with elaborate black and gold penwork. The magic in the tome was so potent that it sent a crackle through her hair. Mervion's hand tightened in Gaultry's, as she too felt the power.

The young huntress swallowed nervously, waiting for the signal to start reading. Blood throbbed at her temples. She began to feel an increasingly familiar expansion in her chest as the Glamour in her stirred. "Huntress help me!" she murmured, softer than a whisper. To feel the loosening of such power and to know that she had to let it go!

Behind her, the trumpet call blared once more. There was a last sighing susurration through the crowd, and then silence. Then another trumpet blast called the magic to begin.

At the back of the top platform, the wall pulsed, its surface contracting, altering to reveal a pair of dark holes—doorways—that framed the figures of two tall, strongly built women, dressed in the same white as Mervion and herself. They were made up to seem preternaturally large, their faces and hair obscured behind outsized masks, painted white, and huge curling wigs woven of gold wire coils. Another trumpet blast, and they advanced to the front of the platform, their movements as stiff and formal as clockwork. When they turned their faces to address the young twins who stood before them, their voices boomed, as if from a single throat. Each motion was so exactly choreographed that it was hard to believe that there were living women behind the masks.

"Twice Fair. Likeness of the Goddess. Have you come here on this Night of the Prince to present Us with his Bride?"

"We have." That was Mervion with Gaultry, not quite in unison, stumbling to follow her sister's lead.

"What is the Lady's Blood?"

"We will read a spell and tell you." That was Mervion. She read out the first line of the spell, her voice clear and unhesitant. "Great Emiera, weaver, lady of the new moon, behold the night of Tielmark's greatest triumph and witness here a spell . . ." Looking down at the book to see what she'd read, Gaultry found a magic had seized her already. She could understand the words on the page before her.

It was a spell for two practitioners of craft. The first line called Emiera to witness the building of the blood-creature. The second line—Gaultry's line—called for the same witnessing from Elianté. They were words of great power—they stung her throat as they rolled from her mouth. Gaultry spoke the first word as a whisper, the last as an involuntary shout. Mervion, beside her, blanched. A surge of power, a frizzing white wave, bolted forward from their hands, setting the altar above them on fire. The light around them dimmed to a bluish haze. The priestess figures dropped back, the woman on Gaultry's side making a warding sign with her hands.

Heiratikus's directions flashed through Gaultry's mind. They'd covered every political eventuality. "We'll have two priestesses on hand to read the wedding ceremony," he'd said. But it was the goddesses themselves who were meant to appear to perform the ceremony. They had to approve the bride. What was happening? This was nothing at all like the mouse spell—

Mervion read out the next line. Something about the fire of the mother birthing the child. A pain shot through Gaultry's body, so intense, she didn't know what she next read from the text—her lips were moving without her volition, pronouncing the terrible words. Mervion shuddered. Her hand clenched Gaultry's in a terrible, ruthless grip. If Gaultry didn't have other pain to worry her, she would have thought Mervion was trying to crush her bones. Perhaps her own clasp of Mervion's hand felt the same.

Goddess save them! Two lines into the poem and already she thought the spell was going to kill them both!

Gaultry was blind with pain. She couldn't see the book or the lectern or the priestesses through the blue haze that obscured her vision. Her chest pulsed—her ribs seemed to rip apart, or rip open, and blinding gold light flooded from her. She had turned to face Mervion—Mervion's figure was the only thing Gaultry could still see with any clarity. It appeared that Mervion was facing her. When had she let go of Gaultry's hand? Now Mervion's arms were stretched high above her head, her face ecstatic. The open throat of her dress revealed the skin over her heart, haloed in gold. Her eyes were closed and there was a dreadful smile on her lips.

How could Mervion smile? Gaultry's own body—the heat was centered over her heart, she could feel that now—her own body was being wracked with fire. Ecstasy was far from her mind. She reached out to Mervion, and discovered that the golden light from her sister's breast was warm and soothing, an anodyne to the horrible pain that tore her flesh. Some part of Gaultry was still reading at the lectern. She could feel the next line of the spell working itself—and she was somehow wiping open Mervion's chest, thinning the skin over her heart so the light within shone forth like a warming sun. Beneath the surface of her sister's skin was another, golden, Mervion. A flickering memory of the tapestries in Clarin's tomb touched her—but the Glamour-figure taken from the Prince's body by the goddesses had been black, not gold and shining. What she saw in Mervion was what Glamour-magic looked like when it was live and held within the body. It was the Glamour-soul that would combine with her own to form a living, golden Princess.

Somewhere far away, Gaultry read another line of the spell. In answer, the outer shell that was Mervion reached out a hand. Alarmingly, a shapely golden hand and arm reached from Gaultry's body to clasp it.

Mervion read the spell's next line. Gaultry found her hand reaching out in involuntary response. One of the golden arms of the inner Mervion moved forward to clasp it. Then there was a gentle pulling—gentle yet it caused such pain that Gaultry wept—and Mervion began to pull the marvelous golden creature that had been hidden for so long in Gaultry's flesh out into the open, as Gaultry did the same for Mervion.

It should have hurt more, Gaultry thought. The thing that was the Glamour in her shouldn't have slipped so smoothly from the warm sheath of her flesh. Already its torso was free—a lovely creature of golden light, shaking loose its hair like sheets of golden flame—Mervion's was half into the open as well. Great Twins, how could it be that they were not resisting the departure of their Glamour-souls? Somehow, neither could refuse a sister's request.

A very worldly screaming interrupted the delicate irresistibility of the spell, snapping Gaultry's attention away from this strange otherworld in which twins were twinned. The blue haze that blocked out everything that wasn't Mervion diminished a little and suddenly she was again aware of her surroundings.

She still had hold of Mervion's hand: bones and flesh. On the altar in front of them a rich gleam of gold flamed up from the white fire that burned upon the altar: the head and shoulders of a glorious creature with an imperious expression on her face. Their Princess. A partial combination of their Glamour-souls. Half-formed and already regal. She would make a perfect triplet to the Blas twins, cast in living gold.

But beyond the altar, on the stage of the top platform—that was where the screaming was coming from.

The two priestesses had swollen to an immense height—their heads were halfway up the wall at their backs, towering a good fifteen feet over Gaultry and Mervion's heads. It was worse than watching a thief be tortured on a rack. Every dimension of their bodies contorted unnaturally outwards and upwards, yet still they lived. One clutched her mask at the neck as though she was strangling, the other—the other's face had swollen so grotesquely large that it had burst the mask. Gaultry could see the woman's freakishly stretched features, her mottled skin, her screaming mouth.

When both figures had reached a height of about thirty feet— their heads opposite the band of Issachar's now-shrieking eagles— there was a thunderclap of magic and power and light and the tortured skins split and sloughed away. Blood and skin spattered onto the dais, disregarded.

Standing side by side behind the altar, their heads brushing the ceiling, were full-fleshed incarnations of the Great Twin Goddesses, the Lady and the Huntress.

They were impossibly beautiful. Silver-gold hair skeined down past their shoulders. They were sylph-bodied, eyes brighter than sparkling stars. They were impossibly majestic. Diamond-frosted skirts swished down over their graceful legs as they twitched their skirts and settled themselves, looking sternly out over the assembled crowds.

There was a roar in the hall, then silence. The crowd recoiled in delight and horror both, awestruck by the wondrous fright of the moment in which the divine became corporeal and appeared in the worldly realm. The Lady and the Huntress. Twin figures, like as great as like. Gaultry stared up into the wise beauty of the great faces, too astonished to cower or kneel or bow or anything. The goddess on the left rewarded her with a sly, womanly smile. There was an arrow in her hand, an arrow with a point like shining fire. The Huntress.

—HAVE YOU FORGOTTEN THAT THE HUNTRESS IS ALSO THE TRICKSTER?—

"Elianté. Goddess!" Talking to long-dead Clarin hadn't been anything like a preparation for this.

—DON'T TEASE HER, SISTER— That was Emiera, kind and level of judgment. —HER BUSINESS TODAY IS NOT IN JEST—

The Princess—the thing—Mervion and she were building on the altar—it was nothing, a mortal flame that would live and die in an instant. Mervion and herself—they were substanceless shadows. Despair shot through the young huntress at the pride she'd nursed, imagining that she could offer her own goddess any sacrifice that might drive her and her sister from power. While their beloved goddesses stood before them in the fullness of flesh, Mervion and she could not think to complete the spell they'd started. Only the demanding power of the half-cast spell detained her, held her back from an attempt to slink guiltily away. Goddess, what to do with the power already raised?

Unbelievably, Mervion was unaffected by the divine appearance. Her head down, her eyes on the page, she was already reading the next line of the spell. Gaultry felt the pull of the spell recommence, inexorable, blue haze leaping up to dim her vision of the goddesses before her.

That was too much—twin or no, empowered of her own will or no, Gaultry slung the weight of her will against her sister's, straining to regain the vision of the Great Twins. No, Mervion, Gaultry thought, fighting her twin, they were not born to cast this spell, whatever the personal cost. She would not let Mervion deprive her of the vision of the goddesses. Gaultry dug into her will, and fought against the casting.

Something broke loose, and Gaultry's sight once again sharpened. Mervion gasped as though she'd been punched in the stomach. Whatever was possessing Gaultry now didn't feel inclined to feel sorry for her.

The goddesses beamed down on the twin mortals. There was a pause, and then, in a single booming voice, they repeated the query the masked priestesses had made just moments before when Gaultry and Mervion had begun the spell.

—TWICE FAIR. LIKENESS OF THE GODDESS. HAVE YOU COME HERE ON THIS NIGHT OF THE PRINCE TO PRESENT US WITH HIS BRIDE?—

"We have." That was Gaultry. Mervion should have joined in, but she didn't have the breath for it.

—WHAT IS THE LADY'S BLOOD?—

What was the lady's blood? Gaultry's gaze flickered to the half-formed Glamour-figure on the altar. Though incompletely formed, it already stirred in dawning life. Flashing golden eyes stared inhumanly across at her. Except for the color, it was Mervion's face—or her own, in a living golden mirror.

Here she was, allowing Mervion to pull life from her as Gaultry pulled it from Mervion. For what? For the sole sake of her sister's body, the mortal body of flesh and bone that stood by her side, sucked dry of one life force after another?

Issachar had told Heiratikus to trust in the Thunderbringer Goddess over the Emperor. She despised the Chancellor for his lack of faith. But where was her own? With two goddesses standing incarnate before her nose, she could either trust that Heiratikus would honor her sister's life, or she could put her faith in the Great Twins and trust that they would reward her if she served them well. But she didn't want a reward. She wanted Mervion, free and whole. She stared up into the beautiful faces, so high above her head. The grave, impassive faces offered no answers.

Mervion chose that moment to repeat the next line of the spell.

To maintain equilibrium, Gaultry had to strike out at her. Mervion's counterthrust was surprisingly weak.

That decided Gaultry. What was it she had been told had been pledged to renew the power of Clarin's pact? Common blood— common blood—the Glamour Princess was being formed of the common blood of herself and Mervion. But common blood—surely now that the goddesses had manifested themselves there was another way that this could be accomplished.

Mervion repeated her line a third time, and this time, the blue light swamped Gaultry like a wave, and she could not resist. Horrified, Gaultry found that rather than answering her goddess, she had read another line of the spell. Even though she had shaken free of the blue blindness, the spell, inexorable, was still trying to get itself said. Raising her eyes to the goddesses, she shouted something that wasn't the spell:

"The Lady's Blood is as common as that which Clarin pledged you three hundred years past! We of Tielmark here maintain the spirit and flesh of the pledge both." She tried to drop Mervion's hand, and found that it was bound to her own with magic. The spell they'd called wasn't going to let them loose so easily.

That didn't mean anyone could force Gaultry to present the product of the spell as the Prince's mate. She wheeled around, still holding Mervion's hand, and looked past the astonished faces of Heiratikus and the guards as they stood, seemingly frozen, in their places.

"Hassan!" The dark man was out in the aisle, ready. She was grateful for his lack of hesitation. Her gaze skimmed the assembled servants, fastening on young Lily. She was small, Gaultry thought. Hassan could bully her up onto the dais, or force her, if necessary. "Bring me the girl by your side." Lily Rose's mouth opened in astonishment and shock, but Hassan moving quickly, seized her by the waist and bundled her over the low barrier. The young laundry woman was hurried up the steps to the lectern before she could formulate any objection. Issachar made a move to stop her, but a warding from the sly-eyed Huntress froze him in his tracks.

—THE THUNDERBRINGER DOESN'T CALL FOR YOU, HAWK-HEART. TIELMARK'S CHOICES ARE NOT FOR YOU.—

Hassan shunted the girl forward. His face was pale under his dark skin; hers was white as paper. She dropped to her knees next to the altar that still held the unbodied head and shoulders of the half-formed golden Princess, audibly praying. There was a candy-pink ribbon tied in the girl's glossy brown curls.

—WHAT IS IT TO BE?— The Lady's face, infinitely mild, looked down on Gaultry, serious and grave. —WHICH BRIDE DO YOU OFFER US?—

There was more than a hint of gravity in the goddess's question: was Gaultry to offer Lily Rose and prove sororicide? The spell Mervion and she were halfway through—more than halfway through—she could hold it, but would she have the strength to reverse it? Which bride did she offer—

The shriek of Issachar's eagles as they swept down from their perches to attack cut short Gaultry's frightened dithering. Now there was no time for choice—

▼

There were nine windows in the rank overhead, and nine eagles to fill them. Gyviere, Issachar's mount, had held the center window; now it led the attack. It swooped down, talons outstretched. Gaultry flinched. This time there was no place to run.

In the split second in which Gyviere plummeted down, Gaultry's cower of fear jerked her into the realization that it was Lily the great bird aimed for. The young huntress would have thrown herself forward to protect the young serving woman—at least Gaultry thought that she would have thrown herself forward to protect her—but a flaming arrow blossomed suddenly in the creature's neck. The bird spun out over Gaultry and Mervion's heads, and crashed amongst the assembly. "The Prince! Protect the Prince!" Shouts rose all around, mingled with cries of fear and distress. Soldiers moved in the crowd. The Duchess's forces had finally come to the Prince's aid.

Gaultry shot a quick look up into the goddesses' impassive faces. A pony-sized eagle was attacking the shoulder of the Twin she thought was the Lady. The Goddess gave it less attention than if it had been a fly buzzing over her head. It beat its frustrated animal energy in vain against the goddess's dress, seemingly incapable of doing any harm. If only the rest of those assembled in the hall were so invulnerable. The goddesses had stopped Issachar from interfering—why not his eagles?

Gaultry looked at Lily's bent head with its candy-pink ribbons, and then at the proud crown of the golden Princess-to-be's flaming hair. A gold Glamour-figure where Prince Clarin's Glamour-figure had been black.

"The Bride is this girl, long of the Prince's service!" Gaultry shouted, clasping Lily's hand and raising it to the goddesses.

"Fool!" Somewhere behind her, Heiratikus found his voice. "Then die, Mervion Blas!"

A new sizzle of magic fouled the air between them. Mervion's face turned sickly green. Gaultry still had her sister's hand—there was a horrible rush as the half of the blood-spell that Mervion had been controlling surged into the young huntress's body. Gaultry remembered what it had felt like, touching the Prince's imprisoned life for just one moment with her finger—that must be what Mervion was feeling now, all through her body. Curse Heiratikus! As pain overcame Mervion, pushing her towards the black edge of death, the spell the sisters had called together pulsed up into Gaultry's arm, not ready to die with her twin.

Alone, Gaultry didn't have the strength to check the spell's power. She couldn't control it. The blood-spell was a mass of destructive power scouring her body. The yet unspoken words of the spell from the page in front of her popped and spit sparks of green fire; the vellum was on fire—not the best way to handle a book of power. The heavy tome jumped and bounced on the lectern, then spurted with a surge of frenetic magic and crumbled into a mass of black ash. Its spells, burned from the pages, pumped free into the air in bearded showers of sparks—goddess, Tamsanne had warned Mervion and Gaultry not to misuse book magic, but this . . .

Gaultry had half a second to realize that the fragments were following the remains of the first spell that had been freed from the book, as if down a flood-channel broken in a dam, and another half a second to realize that her body was providing the flood-channel. Then the second had passed and all she could do was scream with the sick realization that she was about to learn firsthand what the

two priestesses whom the Great Twins had destroyed by their coming had experienced. Already her body bloated horribly, over-
stretched with magic. How was it that she was still alive?

The head and shoulders of the Glamour Princess rotated so
the creature stared dispassionately into Gaultry's eyes. As uncontrollable magic force pumped into the young huntress, some last
rational corner of her mind looked back at the thing, so oddly
separated from her body—yet half at least of the power that ani-
mated it was her own.

Gaultry had gained an agonizing foot of height. A moment
more, and it would be too much for her poor frame. Mervion, her
hand fused to Gaultry's, slumped to the ground, almost pulling her
sister off her feet. Gaultry was so tall now that she was holding Mervion up: first on her knees, then on her feet. A moment more and
Mervion's corpse would be dangling from Gaultry's hand. All
around them pitched battle roared as the assembly rose up to protect
the Prince, the eagles swooping ever nearer, Heiratikus's men trying
to clear a space in front of the dais, but for Gaultry there was nothing but the Glamour-creature and Mervion and herself—and the
pain.

If she could take the Glamour back into her—both Mervion's
and her own—it might balance the power. Perhaps she would even
live. Maybe—oh, goddess, it hurt, it hurt—

—IN THE NAME OF OUR GREAT MOTHER, LLARA THE THUNDER-
BRINGER, WE FIND THE BRIDE OF TIELMARK A WOMAN OF COMMON
BLOOD, FIT TO CONTINUE THE LINE OF CLARIN. LONG LIFE TO HER,
AND STRONG PROGENY FROM HER WOMB. BENET PRINCE OF TIEL-
MARK, DO YOU ACCEPT YOUR BRIDE?—

Long life to Lily!—what about the goddesses' humble servants,
being torn to shreds before their eyes?

With a desperate effort of will, Gaultry reached out for the
Glamour Princess, knocking over the lectern. It had more substance
than she expected. *You are dying,* the Glamour Princess's golden eyes
seemed to tell her. *Like the mice you killed on the pyre of woodbine, you
have given me so much of yourself that you are already dead.* The young
huntress jerked the figure of golden light back towards herself, trying
to inhale the thing, to channel it back inside her—anything to re-

gain the power she'd spent on it and save herself. It responded at once, thank goddess, unravelling to a faint shadow. The gold eyes, staring into her own with reptilian calm, gave no hint of regret as they faded. The half-spoken spell and the crowd of other spells redoubled their power at this new invasion of strength, as she pulled the Glamour back into her, Gaultry felt a surge of relief. In a moment she'd have retrieved her own Glamour-magic, and with it, an unexpectedly large piece of Mervion's. There was a moment of intense relief—and then a flood of new agony. Half of Mervion's Glamour-soul was still locked in her sister's body, and sympathetic pain from her dying sister was rushing through to her across the tie, just as it would have done if Gaultry had taken the spirit from an injured animal. Gaultry skated near to fainting. She would have to pull the Glamour fully from Mervion to seal herself off from the pain Heiratikus was twisting in her.

Gaultry looked down at her sister's green face through a haze of tears. There was perhaps a heartbeat or two of life left in her. Gaultry would have to work quickly, or she'd be pushed far beyond the fit of madness she'd experienced when the two horses were almost killed while their spirits were within her. Her own twin to die while inside her flesh! That pain, that burden, could not be borne.

But there was another choice. If Gaultry gave Mervion back her Glamour, combined with her own, perhaps it would leave Mervion with enough strength to hold her until the goddesses had finished performing the wedding. Or were they already done with the wedding? Had Benet accepted the bride that she'd chosen for him? There was fighting in the hall—surely the Duchess's allies, reinforced by the omen of the goddesses' appearance, would win out against the Bissanty side? In the aftermath, surely someone could bargain with Heiratikus to make Mervion whole again? She could see by Mervion's face, by the blood at her ears, that her sister was a pulse from death—

Scarcely knowing what she was doing, Gaultry thrust the whole brightly tangled mass of Glamour-souls away. Let Mervion have it, she thought fiercely, pushing it at her. Let Mervion be the one who lives.

There was an unbearable flare of gold flame. Gaultry's heart contracted as if a hand had given it a vicious squeeze. She found she could release Mervion's hand. She stumbled forward, tripping over the fallen lectern with its ancient book—now ashes, its magic spent. She reached weakly for the edge of the altar, trying to steady herself as yet another painful explosion of power burst inside her. How long did it take to die this way? How long?

—GREAT-HEART—the voice was infinitely gentle—THE WEDDING IS OVER. YOU MUST FINISH THE SPELL NOW, GREAT-HEART—

Gaultry blearily raised her head. Her vision had degenerated to a strange double focus. She saw four goddesses, then two, then one, then two again before her. "What spell?" she asked, hugging her tortured body as another ancient spell wracked her with its power.

—LOOK AT US.—

Her vision steadied and she saw that there were indeed two goddesses. Each held a frightened and struggling eagle. As one, they seemed to offer her the birds.

—THE BLOOD-SPELL, GREAT-HEART. FINISH IT AND BE FREE—

Mervion and she were small, and they had made a mouse. Two make one, and one scampers under the woodpile and is gone. Mervion and she were grown, they had made a Princess. Two make one, and one gives Mervion life—was that right?

—*FINISH THE SPELL AND BE FREE*—

This time the words were a command—a spell Gaultry could not resist. She struggled through the tangle of spells that was destroying her body, looking for the loose end of the blood-spell. Then her mouth was moving of its own volition, the words spilling out, drowning her, choking her, power words that left her no chance even to draw breath—

In front of her, the two eagles that were trapped in the goddesses' hands shrieked despairingly. White flames flared across the altar. An immense new eagle, its spiny feathers undermarked with crimson, mantled over it. It flared and hissed, like a phoenix in a nest of white coals. There was a rush of power as the confusion of spells that wracked the young huntress's body burst free, focusing on the altar, fanning the flames so the great blood-eagle the ancient blood-spell had formed was engulfed in a shimmering cocoon of light and fire. It shrieked angrily—more bloodcurdling than anything she'd yet heard—and launched itself free from the flame. Then it was up in the air, out over the assembly, scattering gobbets of flaming magic on the ranks of seats. It dashed itself against the glass of a high window, seeking to escape, rebounded, then struck the glass again. A shower of glass and wood rained down, adding to the confusion.

Gaultry wobbled uncertainly to her feet, touching her body, thinking to find great stretched grooves in her skin. She felt, she felt—she felt alive. Trembling with gratitude, she looked up into the great faces of her deities.

One sister looked at the other. They clasped hands, hands that seemed to merge as one at the fingers. They stared one last time out over the crowd.

—BEHOLD YOUR PRINCE, BEHOLD YOUR PRINCE'S BRIDE. A GREAT PRINCE'S PROMISE IS NOT BROKEN. WE HAVE APPROVED A BRIDE THAT OUR MOTHER, TOO, WILL ACCEPT. WITNESS THIS AND REJOICE. TIELMARK IS FREE: ELIANTÉ AND EMIERA ARE YET ITS GUARDIANS—

Lily and the Prince were crowded together on the great throne. The former serving woman was huddled on the Prince's lap, her arms around his neck, and her face buried in his shoulder.

The upper dais was empty—save for trampled flowers and the burnt remains of the eagles that had been killed by the blood-spell. Without even a thunderclap, the Great Twins had gone. An awed hush passed over the crowd. The lights of the thousands of candles seemed suddenly dull.

Issachar was the first to move. He drew his sword, and swung it at the Prince's neck.

But Martin was there, gripping his blade in both hands so that it absorbed the full force of what had been intended as Issachar's killing blow. If Martin hadn't been wearing gauntlets, the hand that supported the double-edged blade would have been severed at the fingers. As it was, the big soldier grunted in pain and stumbled inelegantly back into his Prince's lap, squashing him and the new Princess both.

Lily screamed; the hall, which had quieted during the goddesses' speaches, degenerated into a morass of confusion. The remaining eagles shrieked and swooped. Soldiers fought to reach the dais, trying to quell the confusion—soldiers who were unsure whom they should be fighting, but certain they should reach their Prince to protect him.

Hassan helped Gaultry to her feet, dragging her towards the edge of the dais. "We can't stay here."

"Mervion!" She flailed out, grabbing for her sister's hand.

"I don't think there's anything you can do for her."

"That's not possible!" Not with two shares of Glamour-magic pulsing beneath her skin. Gaultry shook her head, trying to orient herself. She felt terrible, but if the goddesses had deigned to give her the power to purge the excess of spells from her—she wasn't done fighting yet. Not with Mervion's life in the balance. "Where's Heiratikus?"

Leaving Issachar to face the outraged mob, Heiratikus had skirted the throne and scrambled up onto the stage above them. Rage and fear twisted his face. Without a glance right or left, his robes fluttering behind him, he disappeared through one of the dark doorways behind the altar.

"We must follow!" Pushing Hassan aside, Gaultry clambered onto the top tier of the dais.

"Gaultry! Stop! If there's a trap on the door—"

She was already through and falling into blackness, having missed a step on the other side of the door. She went down on her hands and knees, and touched the stone underfoot. The light and noise of the hall had ceased, as though a door had slammed shut. Wherever she was, it was absolute black.

There was something with her in the darkness. Something terrified, and panting; something that scuttled, crying to itself, through the darkness above her.

If it was Heiratikus, he was moving as though he could see in the dark, which was more than she could say for herself. She began to call a spell to throw a white blast of power after him so she could see where she was going.

Then she remembered, and cut the attempt short.

Her Glamour-magic was pinned in Mervion's body, keeping her flesh alive. Gaultry couldn't help but swear. All she'd have in her now would be a weak fizzle of power. She swore, and began scrabbling after Heiratikus through the darkness. If he was above her, there'd have to be steps somewhere.

As she smacked her forehead against a wall, her outstretched fingers touched a step. Above it another, then another. She climbed up through the absolute black, her eagerness to catch Heiratikus overcoming her caution. Soon the stairs had wound into a tight spiral—she could no longer hear Heiratikus in front of her, but it was a comfort to have a hand on each wall.

The floor dropped out from beneath her feet with a clatter of falling masonry. She plummeted frighteningly through the darkness, screaming. The fall was short, one coil of the steps only, but she landed badly—or if there was a good way to land on stone steps, she didn't find it. A simple trap, but an effective one. For a very nasty moment she lay in the dark on the rubble of broken masonry trying to recover herself. When she staggered up, there was blood in her mouth, and one of her ankles felt wobbly.

Gritting her teeth and spitting, she resumed her climb—this time more cautiously, stooping with one hand outstretched to feel for the risers in front of her. Seventeen steps up and she was back at the gap where she'd fallen through. Fearfully, she clung to the last solid step and stretched a tentative hand out through the dark, almost weeping with relief when she discovered that the gap was only four treads wide. It was a challenge to traverse in the dark, but not impossible, even blind.

She was beginning to wonder how much further the ascent would take her when she burst into a narrow chymistric workroom—no warning as she passed from the black of the staircase into the light of the workroom. Beyond, through an arched door, she could see the Keyhole Chamber, the round chapel torch-lit and eerie, the oculus to the night sky a dark eye in the roof that let in a chill wind. As for the Chancellor—Heiratikus stood by the altar throwing many-colored powders onto blue flames. His shoulders were shaking, his movements hurried. The metalwork that had once bound her had been stripped from the altar, leaving only the stark bareness of scrubbed stone.

Instinct told her it was an escape spell. If she didn't attack at once, he could be gone, taking Mervion's spirit with him.

She passed quickly through the workroom, and paused at the door to the chapel, uncertain how to stop him.

"Excellency!" she called.

He swung to face her, his dark eyes large, filled with hate. A fresh powder, orange crystals that crackled as they touched the stone, joined those already on the altar.

"Your sister ruined everything," he complained, rubbing his hands and choosing a new powder from a green-glass bottle. A hastily made pile of bottles and boxes cluttered the floor near the altar. "You should have warned me that she was mad; that she had no sister-feeling." His voice was unnaturally calm. "The Great Twins came, it's true. I didn't believe that would happen, but it did. I would have prevailed nonetheless if your sister had any sense of blood or family."

The young huntress swallowed, realizing that Hieratikus, in his mounting madness, had mistaken her for Mervion. Deciding to play along, she took a careful step towards the altar. "She had higher feelings for her gods, I'd hazard."

"Stay where you are!" The Chancellor's spider fingers were busy among bottles and flasks, but the dark eyes followed her, mad and intense. "I should have broken her, you know. I should have trapped her soul as easily as I trapped yours, pretty one."

Gaultry cupped her hands together, feeling the cold place where she'd cut herself on Llara's Ladder. "The Great Mother spared her for another fate," she said. "Who can know why?"

Heiratikus threw another ingredient on the altar, gesticulating over the small mound of powder. "The gods should not show their faces to mortal men. The Great Twins should never have come. It wasn't fair. I watched. The Huntress changed her face to Lady—" He peered at Gaultry through the gloom of the chamber, squinting to make out her face. "As you have done. When will you change back?"

"When you return to Bissanty—"

"The Brood-blood dominates in me. I fought all my life against it, but it's my fate, my destiny. Red path before the Prince—"

Gaultry stared at him, torn. The sight of the goddesses whose rituals he had profaned had unbalanced his already fragile sanity, yet his body was still working, busy with the spell that would spirit him away to Bissanty, to safety. His creeping madness frightened her.

"My mother betrayed my father; her blood in me betrays him again." His eyes fixed on hers, he began a shuffling circle around the altar, spinning as he went and craning his head so he always faced her. "We have more in common, you and I, than you know. Our mothers died in the toil of childbirth, and prophecy formed in the viscera that was extruded with their wombs. Imagine what it meant to our fathers, to be touched by the glory of the gods at that moment!"

"What do you mean?" said Gaultry, shocked, forgetting to stay quietly by the door.

"Poor Thomas!" Something in Heiratikus's gaze shifted, and Gaultry felt suddenly that he was seeing her, clearly, perhaps for the first time since she had joined him in the room. "Like your pitiable huntress sister, he thought his first responsibility was to his Prince and gods, and not to the daughters that he had hidden so carefully in the depths of Arleon Forest. Too bad for him that Benet was already my puppet when he came to confess his secret to his Prince and Master!

"Twice Fair, on the sixth run's closing night may bear
A Bloody Fruit, to bride the Prince to ruin.

"Imagine your father's face when he realized he had betrayed his secret to Tielmark's worst enemy! I would have had you then, you and your sister then, and all the time I needed to break you to my service for the closing night of the sixth cycle, but I left a chink in his guard of spells."

"What do you mean?" Gaultry asked, fascinated despite herself.

"Suicide was out of the question. But there was a hole in the wall of spells I built around him. The old man was more inventive than I credited him. I never imagined he'd use my hole to get himself murdered."

In his madness, Heiratikus had pushed too far.

"You tied magic-strings to him to make him your puppet, and you didn't even do the job well enough to keep him alive?"

Heiratikus shrugged. "He was a poor-born knight, a man of no importance. How could I have known he'd married Brood-blood;

that the name he sought to hide was his own?"

Gaultry, screaming, threw herself across the last gap that separated them, and closed her fingers on his throat.

"You can't!" Heiratikus choked, beating at her hands. "I have
your soul; you can't fight." He sobbed, tore free, and ducked behind
the altar.

Gaultry seized one of the heavy bottles Heiratikus had left
stacked beside the altar, and came after him.

"The Huntress! The Huntress!" Heiratikus screamed. "She's
back! Oh Llara, save me!"

A force was moving in her, a red, angry force that focused everything on killing him. She hit at him, brutally, breaking his arm. "He
died for me!" she raged, tears streaming down her cheeks. "I hated
my father these five years and he died for me!"

"Lord Dan! Lord Dan!" Heiratikus was weaker than his height
suggested, and her anger made her unnaturally strong. She threw the
whole of her weight into him, forcing him away from the altar.

"Issachar can't help you now." She clubbed him with the bottle
a second time. This time he saw the bottle she was belting him with,
and his struggles intensified.

"Lord Dan! Lord Dan! *Come at once!*" A spell!

"Issachar can't help you—" There was a thunderclap of magic, a
horrid ripping sound, and Issachar was there in the room, blood
streaming from a scalp wound, but his sword still strong in his hand.

"Lord Dan! *Save me!*" Heiratikus gave another scream for help—
his final mistake. Knowing she hadn't the strength to fight them together, Gaultry smashed Heiratikus in the face with the bottle, hoping to knock him cold. The glass, which had survived the impact
against his shoulder and his arm, shattered against his skull.

She dropped the broken neck of the bottle—and Heiratikus—
in horror.

Whatever the bottle had contained, it had been magical, and
fiercely corrosive. Half Heiratikus's skull was gone, and a good part
of the brain inside as well. His pale silver hair melted into an unpleasant foulness that steamed and dripped from the remainder of
his head onto the floor.

Issachar grinned, an unpleasant death's head smile that

stretched the scars along his cheekbones. "A bad way to go." He hefted his sword, but did not attack.

"Did he deserve better?" She kept her eyes on the dark lord, her hands busy in Heiratikus's robes. Issachar had his sword in his hand, but he did not advance. There was a strange expression on his aquiline features. Gaultry, wondering why he was holding back, could only guess that it was fear.

"Lucky for me he proved a coward," Issachar said, touching the wound on his scalp. "If he hadn't called me, I'd be dead below."

"Nothing pulls court factions together like an open attempt on their sovereign's life." Looking at Issachar, Gaultry saw a bloody stain spreading along the front of his tunic, and another on the sleeve of his sword arm. The thick mane of his black hair was lank and wet from the scalp wound. The dark warrior took a tentative step forward just as her hand found Heiratikus's inner pocket. As she pulled free a handful of cloth he retreated. He was grinning again— Gaultry had never seen a grin less reflective of pleasure.

"The Great Twins have bested their mother twice today," he said.

"What do you mean?" As she spoke, she unwrapped her bounty, eager to confirm that she'd found Mervion's figurine.

Not one but two figures clinked together in the cloth. She risked a look, not wanting to take her eyes off Issachar, but curious. Mervion and—Issachar. The figurine of Issachar wasn't so well formed: the face was indistinct, the figure awkwardly formed—stooping, stumpy-legged, the arms obscured in wing-shaped sleeves. But it featured Issachar's distinctive mane and the lightning-bolt scars on the cheeks. Gaultry let out a breath she hadn't known she'd been holding.

"No wonder you stayed to give Heiratikus a hand."

"We both serve the Thunderbringer."

"Served, you mean." Gaultry gestured to Heiratikus's corpse.

"As you like." Even with blood creeping down from his shoulder and his soul-effigy clutched in her hand, she felt rather like a smallish white mouse to his black cat. Or perhaps it was just that he had more experience than she at hiding fear.

Behind them, on the altar, Heiratikus's last spell sputtered and took form as a halo of blue light that began to oscillate over the altar.

"What is that spell?"

Issachar hesitated.

"What is that spell, curse you. If you know, tell me."

He winced, and gave her an angry look from under his thick brows. "It's a door to Llara's high temple in Bassorah, the Bissanty capital."

"How does it work?"

"You stand on the altar and it takes you there." Heiratikus's last escape route.

She looked the dark warrior straight in the eye, considering.

Then she dropped the cloth that had protected her hands from the power in the figures and she took Mervion's figurine in one hand, Issachar's in the other.

▼

chapter 24

The pain—it was as intense as she remembered it from Prince Benet's figurine. Mervion's hurt, but even as it pained her, it was a welcome assurance that her sister still lived.

Issachar's pain was unlike anything she might have expected. It was angry pain, thrashing like a wounded animal trapped in a wire snare. Like an animal. Perhaps that aspect of the pain should not have been so unexpected. Gaultry looked into Issachar's dark eyes with a new awareness. The goddess— was she the Huntress or the Lady?—had been in earnest when she had called him Hawk-Heart.

"Half your soul is gone." She stared at him, awed by the power of the sorcery that had been worked on the dark warrior's soul. "And half a hawk's soul replaces it. Who under Llara's sway owns such power?"

Issachar glared at her, angry, helpless—and exposed. He had been able to best her physically—but it was no wonder he'd never quite been able to impose his will on her, for all the strength of his command spells. The ruthless animal-spirit in him would be an advantage against many an opponent—but not against Gaultry. Fighting her, any touch of animal was a weakness.

With her Glamour gone, she had only a handful of spells left to her, but still, she did have her own experience. And that wasn't limited insofar as animals were concerned. Deciding what to do with Issachar was suddenly easy.

"Go stand on the altar."

The dark lord hesitated.

"Go stand on the altar, Issachar." Her voice was low, threatening. "You saw what I did with your eagles below. I forced the blood-spell to accept their spirits over the two souls it had first been offered—and I didn't need Glamour-magic to do it. I've taken and possessed animal-spirits since I was a child. Test me and I'll have the spirit out of this piece of metal in less than the time it takes to ask you again. You won't like what I do with it then."

"Lady Blas—"

"Don't call me by a title I don't want, and don't observe. Just do as I tell you."

The dark lord's face was livid, his mouth set in an angry line. He sheathed his sword, and stepped across to the altar. The blue halo obligingly rose towards the oculus to give him room to stand. His face was impassive, but Gaultry, knowing what to look for now, sensed fear in him. Animal fear that he couldn't quite control.

The halo hovered, then descended. It passed down over his head. His head did not reappear on the other side of the ring of light. Then his shoulders had disappeared up into the descending circle, and his chest, his arms, his hips, his knees—at the last possible moment she tossed the dark lord's half-human, half-eagle figurine onto the altar. It landed between the toes of his boots with a metallic clank.

"Fly free, Issachar."

The halo of light grounded against the altar. There was a searing blast of blue fire—and then it, and Issachar, were gone, and all that was left was a scorched black circle burnt on the altar's surface.

Save for Heiratikus's corpse, Gaultry was alone in the Keyhole Chamber.

She retrieved the cloth she'd dropped on the floor and carefully wrapped Mervion's silver figurine away, tucking it into the pouch with the figurine of the Prince. Only then did she let out a long breath and lean against the nearest wall for support.

Heiratikus's corpse was a hideous sight. She averted her eyes.

That was when she discovered that when she had stumbled back against the wall, looking for support, somehow she had come to rest against the Great Thunderbringer Llara's wall.

"I let him go," she whispered, staring up at the silver lightning-bolt symbol. "I hope that's what You wanted."

"**D**on't hurt me!"

"Idiot!" Martin lowered his sword, and pulled her into a half-angry embrace. "I could have killed you."

They had surprised each other coming round a turn of the twisting stairs: Gaultry had heard a noise, dropped her light, and Martin had attacked, only just managing to pull his blow so that he hadn't beheaded her.

She buried her head against his shoulder, shivering, grateful that the big soldier had been the first to reach her. "Heiratikus is dead," she said. "I killed him." Her fingers fumbled for the pommel of Martin's sword; the sword her father had died on. "He killed my father, Martin. It wasn't you."

Martin turned her so they were heading back down the stairs, and snagged the dropped lantern. "What are you saying?"

"I let Issachar go," she said. She wanted to tell him everything that had happened in the Keyhole Chamber, and it all came babbling out at once, in no particular order. No matter. Martin was only half-hearing her in any case. The geas-light was burning bright in his eyes, his body still shocked by the near brush he'd had with shedding her blood. "With Heiratikus gone and the wedding completed, Issachar didn't have a stake in usurping Tielmark's throne."

Martin sheathed his sword. "You're going to regret your generosity one day."

"I don't think so." Gaultry leaned against his arm, letting him support her as he turned them both round to hurry her back down the steps. Beneath his battle-readiness, fatigue marked his face. "I saw you save the Prince. Were you hoping to come dashing gloriously to my rescue too?"

"I was." He rubbed his hand over his cropped soldier's hair, managed a grin. "Tell me that you still have the Prince's soul figure."

"Did the page boys let on that I took it from Heiratikus?"

Martin nodded. "With a bit of persuasion to jog their memories."

With a light, the gap in the stairs from the four missing steps barely slowed them. They rounded the last twists of the staircase and reached the last room before the Great Hall.

"We're almost out of this," Martin told her. "Wait. Before you go—" He stopped on the step in front of the black-masked door that led to the Great Hall.

"What is it?"

"The geas is slipping." She thought he wanted to touch her, to hold her, but he kept his hands by his sides. "I doubt it will last the night."

"Oh." She looked at him, trying to read what he wanted in his face. "You'll be happy to be free."

He shook his head. "Maybe."

"What are you asking?"

"I want you to kiss me before it goes."

She gave him a sharp look. "Why?"

Then she answered her own question by pressing her lips to his. When they had finished, the geas was gone.

Stepping onto the dais, the noise and brilliance of the hall struck Gaultry like a physical blow. The lower tier was crowded with soldiers and gentry. To one side sat Hassan, supporting Mervion's head in his lap. She gave him a grateful look. Unfortunately, with the entire court assembled before her she was going to have to attend to the Prince first. She looked over the confusing sea of heads and managed to catch the new Princess's eye.

"Princess?"

"Lady Blas!" Lily's cheeks were flushed a pretty pink, but the Prince's new bride looked more concerned than happy.

"Please let me through."

"Get out of the lady's way!" Lily stood up and waved both hands at the crowd. "Quickly now!" Lily's voice was crisp and commanding—far more so than Gaultry would have expected. A path opened between the young huntress and the throne, as the crowd, awed by their new Princess, drew back. Lily waved Gaultry forward. "Please," she said. "Help him."

Prince Benet was slumped over, his face pale with a green tinge, his hands clenched in fists. Lily gave him an anxious look as Gaultry neared. "He was fine when he told the goddesses that he'd marry me. Then when the Great Twins went and you ran to go after the Chancellor, he fell down in a fit."

Benet's face was the same miserable color Mervion's had been when Heiratikus had released the torment of the spell on her. She hastily brought out the handful of velvet in which the Prince's figurine was wrapped. Unwrapping it, she offered it out to the Prince.

"Your Highness. Perhaps if you took this in your hands—" The Prince lifted his head, listless, his eyes dull. "Please take it, your Highness."

Like a man in a dream, he reached out. She pushed the figurine between his fingers.

As he touched it, his face flushed with healthy color, and a broad grin broke across his face. He raised his head, weak but alert, and reached out for his new wife's hand. "The Great Twins are kind," he said, as his gentle brown eyes filled with life. "It's all come right then. I've made an honest woman of you. Heiratikus will be scandalized."

Gaultry stared at Lily, her jaw dropping. What was it the slim woman had told Gaultry about the Prince? "He sees things that no one else does. It's just too bad everyone has decided that he has no head for matters of state." She had thought the young woman had seemed over-familiar with her Prince, but she had never imagined that there was any understanding between them. "He likes pink ribbons," Lily had hinted, laced in with a lover's gifts. Not that Gaultry had had any idea what she'd been going on about.

"It's Gaultry's doing, dearest," Lily was telling him, much to the young huntress's embarrassment. "I spoke to her—just once mind you, before she went off to the Keyhole Chamber—and she knew immediately how we felt. We wouldn't be together but for her bravery."

"Then I owe you my all, Lady." The Prince took Gaultry's hand, his face flushed with feeling. Gaultry tried to stammer out a denial. This was perhaps the first time she had been accused of exercising intuition, and never more erroneously. She remembered the despairing moment when she'd looked down from the dais, and chosen Lily at random from the crowd—it had just happened that she'd been the girl standing closest to Hassan. Random, unless some deeper force had been at work. The Huntress had reminded Gaultry with her first words that she also played the role of the Trickster. Gaultry wasn't sure what to think.

"I, I don't—Your Highness, would you allow me to attend to my sister? She's sorely beset—just as you were."

"Of course, of course." The Prince craned his head. "Clear the way, gentlemen." Lily whispered to him and he cleared his throat and tried again. "Clear the way for Lady Gaultry Blas."

Hassan looked up as Gaultry approached. "I don't know what's keeping her with us," he said. "She's very low."

Gaultry bent and touched her cheek to Mervion's. Her sister's breath was slight, her body slack. Gaultry had to take her hands and clasp them loosely around the little figurine. It meant feeling Mervion's pain once more—but the pain was life, and for that she was grateful.

"Come on, Mervion." Her sister's lashes fluttered against her cheeks, but there was no other movement. "Mervion, come on!" Gaultry's voice rose to an anxious cry. Something was resisting. Gaultry thought of the imperious look in the Glamour Princess's eyes, even while hovering half-formed over the altar. Alarmed, she forced open one of Mervion's eyes, and none too gently.

An unfamiliar golden iris stared out at her, unwinking. An unfamiliar, unfriendly golden iris.

One and one had indeed come together to make one. Gaultry's Glamour had spontaneously merged with Mervion's to create something almost like a living soul. The thing didn't entirely have control of the husk of Mervion's body. It couldn't move her limbs, it could only shallowly pump her lungs, keep the beat of her heart moving. But what little control it did have, it intended to keep.

"Bitch," Gaultry shouted down into the thing that was inhabiting Mervion's eye. "Bitch. Let go of her. Let go of her, damn you."

"Gaultry—" There were hands on her shoulders, ready to restrain her. She shrugged free.

"That's not Mervion. It's a thing, not my sister at all." She stared frantically down at her sister's body. "The Glamour has taken her. Look!" The single eye had remained open. It stared up, malevolent and unnatural. Mervion's eyes were properly green—living emeralds, warm and shining—not this vile metal gold.

"You bitch creature," Gaultry snarled. "You're letting my sister back into her body if I have to send you in halves to ghost this castle for the rest of eternity."

She put her fingers on the corner of Mervion's other eye and forced it open as well. Remorseless golden eyes met her own. "Keep the figurine between her hands," Gaultry snapped at Hassan. "You don't need magic, you just need to hold it there. But it may be more difficult than you think. It may hurt."

Gaultry stared into the creature's eyes, and called to the Huntress. The power rose in her, sweet and sharp. This was the magic Gaultry had called through her years in Arleon Forest, the magic the goddess gave her, the magic she'd worked to earn.

The creature saw what she was about. The threat focused its power and gave it enough control that it could make Mervion's limbs move. Mervion's body lunged, almost throwing Gaultry off onto the floor. Hassan knocked into her, trying to keep the possessed woman's hands clasped around the figurine. Brave of him, Gaultry thought. Surely where he touched the metal, he felt Mervion's pain.

Gaultry forged a channel forward, reaching into the creature with her mind. It was worse than a cat, withholding itself with more than animal selfishness. A cat was a simple animal. It could be enticed into the open and seized. This creature—it was like trying to grasp the shadow of a shadow. It barely seemed to exist. Again and again the young huntress grabbed for it, again and again it eluded her. Gaultry had a bleary sense of others moving in to help hold

Mervion, to pin her body still, but somehow she couldn't quite catch the creature—either Mervion's half of it or her own.

Her failures, grimly enough, seemed to give the creature strength. If the thing had had any humanity in it, Gaultry would have said it was laughing. Gaultry was tiring, and getting clumsy. Control of her own flesh was going. She felt her body spasm and slump against Mervion's, and there was little she could do to gather herself. The day's earlier exertions had taken too much out of her.

One last effort, and she'd have to concede defeat. Gaultry tried to focus herself, to gather herself for one last try—but the creature was heaving and moving her sister's body jerkily away, and it was an effort just to stay in contact with her flesh. It tried to push Gaultry away with Mervion's hands—Hassan was still holding the figurine against her hands, and she brushed against the metal by mistake so that her fingers felt an uncomfortable aching stab of her sister's pain. Mervion's pain was worse than it had been earlier. What they were doing was hurting Mervion. She looked down at the creature that was occupying her sister's eyes and smiled grimly. Last gamble.

"All right, then," she told it, grinning like a fox, pushing Hassan's hands aside so Mervion's figurine was awkwardly cupped in all four of the sisters' hands. "As Huntress I've failed. I can't seize you and pull you back. I know myself well enough to know I'll not succeed by calling on the sweetness of the Lady, so—" Gaultry paused, and took in a deep breath "—let's see how I do as Trickster!" She made a sudden mental feint—farther than she'd ever dared before. There was a vivid flash of magic, she broke through some level of resistance—and then her poor abused body sagged and crumpled behind her.

The creature in Mervion gave a howl of anger, a terrible contortion of Mervion's lips. Gaultry, blinded, feeling herself tumbling through darkness, was not there to see it. Her entire world now was the creature, as it cringed out of her way, unable to stop her, frightened by the craziness of a woman who had ripped her own soul free from her body, and charged forward with it across the terrifying void of the air into her twin's suffering flesh. Gaultry's soul-being, driven by her frantic urge to save her sister, bore down on the Glamour-being, tearing at it with a terrible psychic power. Her vision flushed over gold, the color of Glamour, and then went black.

The young huntress blearily opened her eyes. She was staring up from a sprawled pose on the floor, her head resting in Hassan's lap. For a moment she wasn't sure what had happened. Then Mervion—Gaultry knew it was Mervion, it was her smile and her sparkle that were looking down at her—loomed between her and the ceiling.

Mervion—but incarnate in Gaultry's flesh.

"We both had hold of the soul-figure," Mervion said. "When you emptied yourself into my body, the piece of me that had been trapped in the figurine finally had a body to go to. So this happened." Gaultry's own eyes—an unusual, almost animal green with yellow centers, one of the twins' few marked differences—were filled with Mervion's sweet expression, as her worried older sister looked down at her sibling and tried to smile.

"Gaultry, Gaultry. Say something." That was Martin, shaking Gaultry's body by the shoulder. Mervion turned her head and smiled. It was rather a pleasure to see the big soldier blush and flinch away. At least he had the sense to know immediately that something was wrong.

"Gaultry is there." Mervion pointed at her sister, a question lighting her—Gaultry's—eyes.

"That's Martin Stalker. He's the Duchess of Melaudiere's grandson." Gaultry looked to where Hassan was gripping the hands of Mervion's body. "You can let go now, Hassan. I've more or less sorted things." More or less! She'd rended the merged Glamour-Souls back into fragmented pieces, but both were still moving, unpinned, competing for power in her—Mervion's—body.

Hassan scrambled to his feet, puzzled.

"I'm Mervion—in Gaultry's body." Mervion held out her hand. Martin, somewhat sheepishly in Gaultry's opinion, helped her up, bewilderment writ large on his handsome face.

"Mervion." Gaultry scrambled up and took her sister in her arms. "I thought you were going to die." It felt strange to hug her own body Mervion shared her discomfort. They released each other rather more quickly than they would otherwise have done.

"This is stupid, Gaultry," said Martin. He seemed genuinely alarmed.

Gaultry glared at him. "Tell me another one that I need to know. It's not as easy as you'd think."

Mervion interposed her body placatingly between them. "You must understand, Sir—"

"Call him Martin, Mervion," Gaultry said. "He doesn't stand on ceremony. Lucky for you we got rid of the geas before this happened," she told him meanly.

"Goddess curse the geas!" Martin snapped. "The pair of you can't stay this way!"

"You must understand, Martin. Gaultry has just risked her life." Mervion at her most soothing. "I don't think either of us have the strength to fix things just at the moment. You mustn't scold her."

Martin had the grace to look mildly embarrassed, though he recovered soon enough. "My apologies, Lady—may I call you Mervion? It was a shock to see a stranger looking out from your sister's eyes. I was unprepared for such courtesy."

Gaultry glared at him. The last thing she wanted to watch him do was charm her sister. Especially while her sister was in her body! She watched as Martin took Mervion's hand—Gaultry's hand!— and kissed the fingers. Then his gray eyes went suddenly solemn. "I had a message for you from your father," he said. "My own blindness prevented me from fulfilling it. Your father cast a geas for your protection. It seems I passed this loving message to Gaultry only."

"I can remember a little of how the Chancellor spoke against you," Mervion said, her face going dark. "He was angry when the first reports came of Gaultry's escape. I can only thank you for fighting so bravely for my sister's protection."

Martin smiled his wolf's smile. "Heiratikus exaggerated my role, I'm sure. There were many of us working to help you."

"Why don't you go explain to Prince Benet that his Chancellor is dead so there's no one left to be scandalized by his marriage?" Gaultry couldn't watch the two of them together a moment longer. "I'm sure you'll do it far better than I could."

Martin blessed her with his most vibrant smile. "I see your confidence in me has greatly improved."

"You might also have them send someone along to the cells below the new palace to free Mariette."

His expression grew serious. "I'll see what I can do." He slipped away to the side of the throne and called for the Prince's attention.

"A charmer."

Gaultry looked sharply at Mervion, and realized that she was being teased. Successfully.

"You don't know the half of it." Gaultry felt so very tired. After all she had been through, it would have been so nice just to have sat in her own body on the edge of the dais and had a moment of quiet. "Gods, Mervion. This isn't much fun." The Glamour-being was broken in her, but neither piece had found a place to rest.

Mervion came to Gaultry and squeezed her sister's — her own — hand. Even that didn't feel right.

Gaultry, suddenly overcome by the noise and confusion, was embarrassed to discover that her eyes had filled with tears. "It hurts, Mervion, having this unpinned Glamour in me. Worse than a physical pain."

Mervion looked at the throne, where Martin was conferring with the Prince. "Perhaps," she said, turning to Hassan, "perhaps we can take Gaultry somewhere while this all sorts itself out."

"We can take her to Duchess Melaudiere's suite. It's not far," Hassan said.

"When they get Mariette out she'll need Melaudiere's rooms, I'm sure," Gaultry said faintly, though the thought of a quiet place to rest herself was suddenly infinitely appealing.

Hassan smiled. "The Duchess's suite will accommodate everyone."

"Let's go then. If we each take one of Gaultry's arms, we can help her walk there." Typically, Mervion was back in charge. Gaultry was grateful to be able to cede control. It was true that she had Mervion's body, but it couldn't be said that the Glamour-creature she was sharing it with was sure it was going to be an experience she'd remember with joy or fondness.

▼

chapter 25

Gaultry had nightmares. The moment her conscious mind sought rest, the combined strength of the Glamour-magic surged to strength and made her sleep miserable. With Gaultry's soul-being trapped yet unanchored in Mervion's body, the creature could not reintegrate itself from the fragments into which Gaultry's psychic attack had torn it. Yet despite its weakness, it retained enough self-motivating will to prevent her own soul-being from settling, or even from finding a moment's peace.

"Ready to wake, child?" The voice was mellow, a little sly, and rich with the Great Twins' magic—a familiar voice. Gaultry sluggishly rose to consciousness, trying to remember. "Time to wake, Gaultry, time to wake." It was Dervla, Tielmark's High Priestess.

"You didn't come to the wedding," Gaultry said, opening her eyes.

"I was there." Dervla's pale eyes bore into Gaultry's. "Any closer, and I might have been the one to chose Tielmark's new Princess.

"I didn't see you," Gaultry said. "Not before, not after."

Gaultry lurched to a sitting position. For a moment she thought everything was back to normal, but then she saw her body standing across the room and knew things were just as they had been the night before. Well, almost just as they had been.

"Thanks for taking me for a bath, Mervion." Mervion-in-Gaultry's-body had tied Gaultry's hair back with blue and white ribbons, and dressed her in a neatly cut blue and white tunic and trim royal blue leggings—clothes her elegant sister would normally not have chosen to wear. "I hope you've recovered better from last night's battle than I."

"You've been asleep for two days, Gaultry."

"Two days?"

"You went into a trance. It took three of the Great Twins' priestesses to break it."

Gaultry looked at Dervla. The woman's thick dark hair, flecked with gray, had fallen down from the green wire laces that had held it in a pile up on her head. The Priestess looked tired and drawn—older than when Gaultry had last seen her. She gave Gaultry a tired smile and took her hand. "The Great Twins wanted to help you, so once again my power is yours, Gaultry Blas."

"Your power saved my life in Haute-Tielmark," Gaultry said. "Maybe meditating would have been the better way to Glamour-power."

"Don't be a fool, Gaultry. You've done well. Better than any of us imagined. Waking you up was the least we could do. Now—if you're ready—we'll perform the final piece of the spell."

"I'm ready." Gaultry stumbled up out of bed, and almost fell onto the floor. Her legs could barely support her own weight. Steadying herself against the bed, she teetered for a moment before regaining her equilibrium. Mervion gave her a troubled look, and reached to smooth the hair back from her face. "I'm all right," Gaultry told her, ducking out of reach. "Let's just get this done with." It was amazing how unpleasant she found it to have Mervion in control of her body—let alone finding herself possessing her sister's.

Returning to the Keyhole Chamber to perform the spell felt eerie. Though Heiratikus's belongings had been cleaned away and his corpse removed, it was hard not to remember the room as it had been, and hard not to look closely at the floor where his body had lain after she had killed him. The altar had been cleansed. There was no sign of the blackened circle that had consumed Issachar.

Dervla had called four pairs of Elianté and Emiera's priestesses, and a partner for herself. Mervion and Gaultry were to make up a sixth pair, in a circle of twelve around the altar.

"Twelve for the Great Twelve," Dervla said.

Even with a whole cohort of the goddesses' priestesses in attendance, the separation of spirits and Glamour-magics into the proper bodies would not be a simple task. Mervion and Gaultry stood at opposite sides of the circle, staring into each other's faces across the altar.

"The first part of the casting will separate the Glamour-souls back into your respective bodies," Dervla said. "It's an ancient spell. We know it will work. Returning each of your own souls to its own body will come after." The High Priestess's confidence was justified. Dervla read the spell off a withered slab of black bark that she laid on the altar. There was a weird short-circuited merry-go-round through all the bodies in the circle, an unpleasantly long dance, before the Glamour-spirits were properly settled. Dervla sealed the errant spirits back within each twin with a burst of power that had left everyone in the circle shaking and uneasy.

That left Mervion and Gaultry staring across the altar at each other, uncomfortably aware that they were still stuck in each other's bodies, and not feeling either sisterly or happy about the exchange.

"Now, Mervion," Dervla said, "you and Gaultry will have to forge the next step together. You must use all your magic — Gaultry, you must reach out, as in a spirit-taking. Mervion, you must use all your sympathy powers to draw your sister to you. Remember, you will have the whole circle to draw on for strength."

Dervla moved confidently back to her place in the circle. Her gathered priestesses, looking nervous, began to sing, calling the Great Twins to witness the spell.

Gaultry was sure that meant Dervla wasn't sure if the spell would work. She stared at Mervion as she tried to ready herself for the casting. After so much confusion, it was hard to trust the spells. Her sister, diligent and attentive, had already pushed aside whatever doubts or fears she might have harbored, and begun her casting. Her gentle touch, her warmth, reached across the circle of singers, across the cold stone of the altar, to brush her younger sister with spectral fingers. Then, suddenly, Gaultry was flooded with confidence— Mervion was filling her with confidence, soothing her younger sister's fears and worries, pouring encouragement on her, wanting her to succeed.

Gaultry had never realized that her sister's ability to fill her with confidence was a spell.

With her sister backing her strength, the casting of her own spell should have been easy, but something in Gaultry had hardened during the adventures of the past two weeks. She could not let go, did not want to let go. Did not like the press of her sister's encouragement. An unbearable pressure beat on the young huntress, projected by all the members of the circle, demanding she give up her self.

"Let go, Gaultry! Let go!" Dervla snapped, imperious and angry, calling the names of the women who had hold of Gaultry's hands on either side. "Make her let go!"

"Leave me alone!" Gaultry cried, furious with the priestess for having distracted her. "Let me do it my way!"

Something let go. The spell came out in a glad rush, forging a channel out to Mervion, across the altar, a channel so strong and potent, it was almost visible to the naked eye. Her soul-being rushed gladly to follow it; Mervion's came rushing from the opposite direction to meet her. Gaultry had a giddy sense of floating, up in the air over the altar, of Mervion's soul, a wispy specter, passing her—and then she was back in her own body, looking out of her own eyes. Mervion smiled happily at her, as she stood across the room, clenching the hands of the priestesses to either side of her.

Sweat drenched Gaultry's body. The tidy suit Mervion had dressed her in that morning was wet to the point of dripping.

What a relief to be done with it, to have done it.

The last of the magic sputtered and dropped. Gaultry loosed the hands of the priestesses at her own sides, and darted across the room, grabbing Mervion in a long hug, the hug they had not felt comfortable taking when things had been wrong. Then she took Mervion's hands, stood back, and looked her over critically. There were dark circles under Mervion's eyes. Her hair hung scrappily out of the hasty braid Gaultry had tied it in before coming up to the Keyhole

Chamber. "You took much better care of my body than I of yours," Gaultry said. "What was I doing for those two days I was under?"

Mervion smiled wanly. "Well, you weren't eating, and I don't think the doubled Glamour let you have much rest."

They exchanged another long hug. Gaultry could feel her sister's heart hammering in her chest; she was sure Mervion could feel hers. It felt good. The final relief.

She shouldn't have held up the spell with her stubbornness. She gave Mervion a shy look, wondering if her sister understood the unpleasant surprise she had given the young huntress when she'd cast the sympathy spell.

Behind them, the priestesses who had formed the circle chattered and congratulated themselves on the casting's success. Dervla, looking more tired than ever, came forward to clasp Gaultry's hand.

"That was well done, Mervion—and Gaultry." Her eyes were a little cool as they passed over the huntress twin. Dervla wasn't a woman who liked being shouted at.

Gaultry nodded. "We needed your help."

"That's true. I thought for a moment you weren't going to let go." Dervla's pale eyes scanned her, speculative.

"Where is the Duchess?" Gaultry asked, changing the subject. "I half expected her to be here to help."

Dervla sniffed. "These are matters for the Great Twins, Gaultry, not for the Great Fish."

Gaultry gave the priestess a level look, but managed to bite back an angry answer. "And Mariette?" That was an easier question.

"She's somewhere about," Mervion answered. "She took a shift by your bed on the first night."

"She's well?"

"A court doctor fixed her up. She's taken a fancy to that chipped tooth. She refused to have it pulled."

Gaultry smiled at the thought of Mariette arguing with some court doctor about her tooth.

"So that's that then."

"Not quite." Dervla looked at Mervion and they both frowned. "There's the question of the honors due a certain young woman."

"And the matter of the Duke of Arleon wanting to reward one of his subjects for service to the Crown," Mervion added.

The Duke of Arleon was her father's patron.

"I don't know about Arleon," Gaultry said, feeling shy. "I could slip back to Paddleways and let them decide what they'd like to do without me."

Dervla laughed unpleasantly. "Not unless you want to cause old Tamsanne the bother of a court-load of visitors. The Prince has arranged rooms for the pair of you here at court."

Gaultry's heart had been hammering in her chest, but her sense of its location in her own body had left her feeling empowered and strong. Now she could sense the feeling slipping from her, to be replaced by a feeling of dread somewhere in the pit of her stomach. Mervion, catching her sister's expression, laughed.

"Goddess, Gaultry, what are you worrying about? Emiera's life, after what you've faced these last weeks you should be grateful for some pampering."

Gaultry shot her a hunted look. Mervion laughed again. Dervla, tidying up her herbs from the altar, joined her.

Gaultry herself didn't see what was so funny.

Later, in the privacy of her new chambers, Gaultry felt herself becoming somewhat more resigned to the fuss. She and Mervion had been given a suite of rooms that consisted of a modest bedroom and workroom and a somewhat grander salon with long windows that led out onto a marble terrace. The view encompassed a small deer park. A gracious double staircase led down from the terrace into the park. Gaultry had intended, once in the privacy of these chambers, to convince Mervion that she should talk to people about allowing her to go home to Arleon Forest, but the lush green of the deer park—and the deer themselves—had been such a distraction that she'd barely noticed when Mervion had made her excuses and left her alone to settle in. Although the little park was nested within the castle walls, it was a private place, a little wild and neglected with spring growth. The only other rooms that looked out onto the

small park were the Prince's summer quarters—and those of the
Lord Chancellor. There being no Chancellor at present, Gaultry
had the park to herself.

It was delightful. She visited the watering pool and walked
among the graceful leggy creatures, then—though she had a moment of doubt before she did it—she took from the rangiest doe and
had a run under the trees. The young huntress had done so much
forced running in the past weeks that she'd almost forgotten the
sheer joy of running for pleasure. A buck and another doe raced with
her—Gaultry lost the race, but not by a disgraceful margin.

"Are you enjoying yourself?"

Martin was waiting on the terrace when she returned from her
run.

"Who let you in?"

"Mervion, on her way out."

"She might have warned me."

"You weren't here to warn. How are the deer?"

"They're fine." Gaultry flushed.

The young huntress was suddenly conscious of grass stains on her
knees, of bark and brambles in her hair. It hadn't taken her long to
soil the clean clothes Mervion had secured for her. Martin, neatly
dressed in Melaudiere's green and gray livery, was almost offensively
immaculate by contrast.

"How's Mariette?" Gaultry asked, trying to find a neutral subject.

"She's fine. She'll be here soon—she wants to wish you well."

"They've given me these rooms," Gaultry said. "I think the Princess at least wants me to stay for a time." She stared round at the
pleasant furnishings, the worst of them far beyond what she was used
to.

"There's much unfinished business here at the Prince of Tielmark's court," Martin said. "Some of it even your own."

They shared a smile, and Gaultry reached out to offer her hand
to him.

"There are some matters that need untangling," she agreed. His
words to her before they'd parted at the Bissanty border.

A bell rang within her chambers, and the doors were thrust open.

"Gaultry!" It was Mariette, jaunty as ever, her blue eyes sparkling, her mass of black curls tumbling down over her shoulders. "I hear you're staying!"

Gaultry grinned. "Of course I'm staying," she said. "I've only just arrived."

About the Author

Katya Reimann recently returned from a six-year sojourn in Oxford, England, where she was co-founding member of the Kamikaze Punt Club. When she wasn't messing about in boats, she was completing a D. Phil. in eighteenth-century literature at Oxford University. Her dissertation focused on "maritime criminality," (which is the academic way of saying that she wrote about pirates).

She worked for two summers as a stencil-cutter for a monument company (which is the euphemistic way of saying she lettered tombstones). Her stonework experience has since involved her in more artistic projects, most recently as an artist's assistant for large-scale stone sculptures in Holyoke, Massachusetts, and also in Radnor, Pennsylvania, and Richmond, Virginia.

Wind from a Foreign Sky is her first novel. Katya lives in Cambridge, Massachusetts, where she is working on the sequel to *Wind*.